The Gynesaurs

To Liz
your support is as bra!
welcome as a good
Here's your prescription
Rx take the Gynesaurs
with wine until finished
Cheers & thanks
Pat.

The Gynesaurs

What happens between the stirrups, stays between the stirrups.

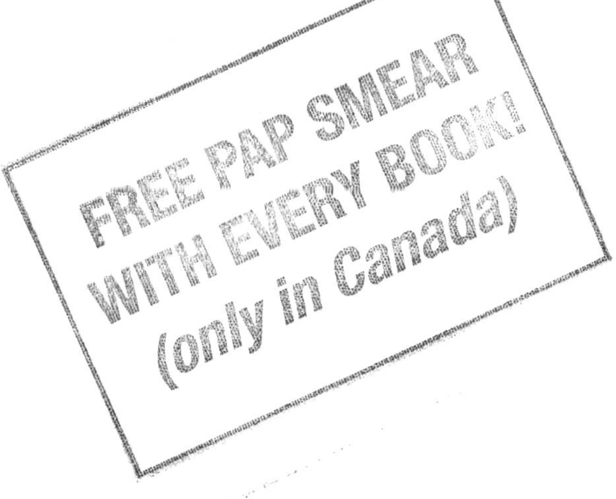
FREE PAP SMEAR
WITH EVERY BOOK!
(only in Canada)

P. H. Oliver

patoliver@hotmail.com

This is a work of fiction. All the characters organizations and events portrayed in this novel are either products of the author's imagination or are used fictitiously.

ISBN: 1548830755
ISBN 13: 9781548830755
Library of Congress Control Number: 2017911039
CreateSpace Independent Publishing Platform
North Charleston, South Carolina

DEDICATION

To all women,
but two specifically,
Mildred Ifold Oliver and Christine Oliver,
You still live here.

ACKNOWLEDGEMENTS

FIRST AND FOREMOST, MY GREATEST thanks to Joe Dell'Aquila, stalwart, loyal and clever - who in another life must have been a Border Collie.

To Evan Dell'Aquila (you know that you've done a good job when you turn to your child for advice).

To Gillian Oliver, a great surgeon and an even better sister.

To Maria Serafin – don't ever change.

To Alicia Sevigny (editor), a great surgeon of another kind.

To my readers for their interest, time and valued opinion: Evan Dell'Aquila, Erica Dell'Aquila, Jessica Dell'Aquila, Pamela Knight, Ellen Novack, Christine Oliver, Gillian Oliver, Mildred Oliver, Lea Porter, Maria Serafin, Jill Summerhayes and Sharon Meredith Williams.

To The Rights Factory Writers: for their early input and encouragement, and to Sam Hiyate for calling me a sesquipedalian – even if he didn't use that exact word.

To The Frayed Knots for always giving me an ear, a good word and a glass of wine.

TABLE OF CONTENTS

CAST OF CHARACTERS

Anthea Brock - An Obstetrician/Gynecologist, born in Canada when her parents Ralph and Sian Brock relocated there for five years, but raised mainly in London, England and Wales. Upon divorcing her husband, Ian, she returned to Canada to set up a new medical practice. Confirmed Best Auntie to other people's children and dogs.

Molly McGilvery - Dr. Anthea Brock's nurse. Widowed with three young children, Orlagh, Callum and Fiona. Caretaker of her Down's Syndrome adult brother, Angus. Main aspiration: to be a siren/sexpot in sensible shoes.

Carolina Stiletto (Car-o-leen-a) - Dr. Anthea Brock's secretary. Daughter of Carmelo and Lucia Stiletto. Her father was a murdered Mafia member. She is a lover of books, booze, men and trouble - in that order.

Glynda Wicksteed - Dr. Anthea Brock's secretary. Abandoned by husband "Art The Bastard", and left penniless to live with his mother, Edna Wicksteed. When Glynda finds her voice, she lets it do the talking.

Honourary Gynesaurs

Sandra Carr - Fossilized Pharmaceutical Rep. and ex-delivery room nurse who knows the ropes and where the bodies are buried.

Dr. Clive Gentile - Semi-retired OB/GYN., who assists in surgeries. Married and still desperately in love with his wife, Audrey. Long time family friend and mentor of Anthea. Calypso music lover.

Gavin McCafferty - male medical student trying to prove that he's more than just a pretty face and become part of the pack - any pack.

Georgia Saxon - The teenage granddaughter of "Tyrannosaurs Rex Saxon", being of prime biological, reproductive age is more of a Velociraptor than a GYNESAUR, but doesn't let that stop her from nipping at their heels.

"Tyrannosaurus" - Rex Saxon - Chief of the Ob/Gyn department. Revered for his surgical skills, feared for his social skills. Pretends not to be aware of his nickname, but likes it.

Family:

Art The Bastard – Glynda's estranged husband – legitimate by birth, bastard by character.

Ralph and Sian Brock (nee Gryffydd) - Anthea and Gryff Brock's parents.

Gryff and Hilary Brock - Anthea's brother and his wife. They have three young children, Lewis, Cordy, and Edwyn.

Auntie Ceri - Anthea's maternal Aunt, sister of Sian Brock, mother of Huw and Alyn. She runs interference while interfering.

Ian Ifold - Anthea's ex husband whom she met in medical school in England. Twice married, twice divorced – all Anthea's fault.

Angus McGilvery – Nurse Molly's younger brother, who has Down's Syndrome. Rat fancier and door to door sales enthusiast.

Edna Wicksteed – Glynda's mother-in-law, Art the Bastard's mother, and surprisingly enthusiastic Presbyterian.

Friends and Co-Workers:

Elizabeth Bellamy - very flexible dance instructor.

Bob The Nurse - ex-College U.S. football star, now a delivery room nurse, still capable of a great catch.

Bernice - Dr. Rex Saxon's secretary and permanent office fixture.

Jack Flynte - Anthea's neighbour and owner of Scarlett the Irish Setter. Lover of thoroughbreds.

Roger Mead - widower of Sheila, friend of Angus and Molly McGilvery, rat and Molly fancier.

Rita the O.R. Clerk - part-time musician in a Blue Grass Band

Melinda Thackery - Gynecological patient and wife of the Hospital CEO, Daniel Thackery. Daughter in Law of Tristan and Sybil Thackery. Posh as shit.

Gerald Walker - Supreme Court Judge and supreme philanderer. Husband of Terra.

Merddyn Meredith - old friend of Ralph and Sian. Retired architect and active eccentric.

Four Legged Friends:

Spock - Anthea's misunderstood Bull Terrier.

Twiggy - Anthea's Rescue Greyhound.

Lovey (Beloved) - Molly's ancient mut.

Scarlett - Jack Flynte's slutty dog.

Locations:

Ty Bleu - Anthea's country house in Canada (Ty (rhymes with "pee") – Welsh for house, Bleu – French for Blue).

The Cwtch (rhymes with "butch") - The Gryffydd/Brock family's seaside retreat in Wales. "Cwtch" is a Welsh term for snuggle or hug.

SECTION ONE

HOMECARE STUDIES: LEVEL 1

"Sometimes happiness is as simple as finding something that you thought you'd lost."

Dad

Anthea

A DRY PAW PUSHED INTO Anthea's face and rested beneath her nose so that she woke to the musty smell of the outdoors. Spock, a one-year old Bull terrier snored loudly beside her and Twiggy the Greyhound's silky back warmed the parts of Anthea left exposed by Spock's nightly nesting ritual. Most of the sheets had gathered around him and he lay in the centre, penis exposed, drooling onto the freshly laundered sheets.

A shaft of light found its way past the blackout shades and promised a bright morning. Anthea stretched and thought about what she needed to accomplish today - staying busy would keep the sadness at bay. She'd have to drive in to town to stock up on some food, get her snow tires removed, pay some bills and *Oh shit,* she thought, *what I'm going to do for the hospital fund raiser?* She'd skillfully avoided being involved for the last few years by keeping a low profile. But last year, she'd made the mistake of saying to Dr. Saxon that it was a "crashing bore" and he'd seized on that comment in a most unpleasant manner and said that she would have the opportunity to liven it up next year when she was the Chair. Typically, it consisted of a black-tie dinner, in an upscale environment, a few dry speeches on how essential the money was to get this or that necessary machine/ service/ addition followed by a silent auction where everyone was expected to buy someone's cousin's original painting/sculpture/pottery or restaurant voucher for more than it was worth. Attendance was abysmal last year despite being propped up by the coercive power of Saxon himself. He simply threatened to actually put effort into the task of making their working days more miserable than he makes them by just being himself. *Good personal insight on his behalf.*

I can do this, she convinced herself as she peed into the toilet bowl. *I am a good organizer; I just have to be creative. I'll go for a long walk with the dogs this morning and I'll think of something really unique to make people want to attend.*

Looking back at her from the bathroom mirror was a woman of thirty-nine, who in a shabby bathrobe and a shower cap on her streaked blonde hair looked like a tired, forty-nine-year-old, who had the pale, dead-eyed stare of a well-used street walker. The dependable company of a good Shiraz the night before had left her face puffy and the bright blue of her eyes was confined to two small dots surrounded by black circles of slovenly mascara. As she wiped it away, she appreciated that the strong bones underneath her face had kept most of it from sliding into her collar; that the long shaft of a slightly hooked, aquiline nose had become less of a burden over the years as she had embraced what she called 'The Margaret Atwood School of Intelligent Beauty'. Still, she couldn't resist putting her hands on the side of her face and stretching the skin upward to see her younger self grin knowingly back at her. "If I trusted doctors, I'd get a facelift," she said to her reflection, but then, acknowledged her conflicted posture on the matter. There was something about having a story on a face that intrigued her, though perhaps not the one about the well-used street-walker.

She tried to shake off the few remaining cobwebs of sleep by swilling her face in the sink and brushing her teeth with a keen vigour. The toothbrush grazed the back of her throat and she found herself retching into the bowl. Her stomach curled inward and a wash of vomit spilled out, the red tinge of last night's wine colouring it. Her stomach had been protesting lately, undoubtedly another sign that she wasn't rebounding like she used to. Taking deep breaths and wiping the last of it from her lips, she reached for the foundation cream then hesitated. "To hell with it, it's a weekend. No war paint needed."

Pulling her stretch jeans over her hips she credited them as possibly the best gynecological invention ever – they weren't the crotch cleavers of yesteryear. She grabbed the old Irish cable knit sweater her mother had made her, inhaled its oily scent and enjoyed the feel of its familiar caress. Once she put on her wellies, it would be like being a kid again. These clothes were her freedom fighters: freedom from tight skirts, lady shoes and useless accessories. She could sit anywhere, any way, anytime and she and these clothes would look the better for it. She laughed at her own hypocrisy when, without thinking, she applied a glossy, red lipstick to her thin lips. *Lipstick is not an accessory. When evolution catches up, all women will be born with it in their right hand. You can look like an old potato, but once you apply red lipstick, you look like an old potato, with red lipstick, who feels fabulous!*

The dogs bolted out the open door, peeing immediately on the dewy grass. The mist clung to the earth like a lover's breath and slender fingers of light sifted through its veils. She took a hot mug of tea onto the porch, wrapping her cold hands around its belly. The morning was kind for the season; bits of green nudging the last, stubborn patches of snow into the past. She lifted her face to the warmth of the eager sun and let her mind settle for a minute on the face it ushered from her subconscious - *Ian*. There were deep creases in his forehead where two crescents made the trunk of what she had called his, 'tree of knowledge', giving him the piercing stare of a man constantly entertaining the great mysteries of the universe. In their med school days, he had said it was simply because he didn't understand the question. He was sure that, that deeply quizzical look he had perfected had got him through more tough tutorials when he had had neither adequate sleep nor preparation. He fooled the Profs into believing his brain was actively processing information when in fact, it was sitting like a deflated pig bladder in his cranium after a night of debauchery with his rugby mates. She had pushed that face away so often lately; the scaffolds of his cheekbones, severe, until an astonishingly frivolous smile erupted from beneath them.

Anthea found herself chuckling as she remembered what he had told her after the fiasco of their first meeting in anatomy lab. She had scolded him for the prank he pulled on her and called him 'a complete turd'.

"Indeed," he said, tracing a circle around his face with his finger, "and to further that metaphor, I guarantee this face will keep floating up in your dreams like a reluctant turd in a toilet, forever!"

"Shit, shit, shit," she said aloud as she acknowledged that he was right. She hadn't moved on after the divorce. She would never be able to forget Ian . . . especially after what happened in the crematorium in Wales a few weeks ago when he had shown up, ragged with grief over her mother's death. The two had become so close over the years that when he and Anthea divorced, Sian had said it was like an amputation. Anthea knew they had kept in touch.

Twiggy's bark from the bush beyond the yard pulled Anthea back to the present as she walked through a feathery patch of wild ferns, letting the light touch of their heads tickle her fingers. She felt a selfish gratitude that her mother had gone suddenly. That she didn't have to see the slow decline; each organ shutting down, cell by conquered cell. Sian's heart had tired of the chemo and had seized her without notice, in the local library. She collapsed in the Mystery aisle, perhaps aware that fate was going to pull off an even greater surprise ending to her own story. The phone call buckled Anthea's knees but a long goodbye would have buckled her soul. "Poor Dad," she groaned. At that moment, she resolved that she wouldn't shorten this visit with him, no matter how difficult it would be to get another three weeks' coverage after suddenly taking a week off to fly back when her mother died. She'd call in every favour.

Twiggy persisted and Anthea scolded herself for not paying attention when she noticed that Spock was nowhere in sight. She called repeatedly and pushed into the bush to see if he had caught a trail in there. "Fuck," she said. *I should have kept him on his leash. There's too much pup still in him to ignore his impulses - huh! What's my excuse?*

Anthea thought back to that recent encounter with Ian - his lips pressed onto hers, his tongue searching with the same stealth of his hands; that mad stupidity they had allowed, not far from her mother's newly rendered ashes, *in the backroom of the goddamn cremation centre! How the hell do I rationalize that? We just felt so sorry for each other? No, I am an idiot. I've fucked everything up. Fucked us both up all over again. He's remarried for Christ's sake! I'm an idiot AND a home wrecker!* Still, thinking of it made her shiver with an odd mixture of delight and shame.

Twiggy started off over the hill ahead and darted back as if to encourage Anthea to follow. As they scrambled through the tall grass, she heard an agitated voice. "Off, off – stop it you stupid thing. Get off her!"

Anthea reached the summit and was shocked to see a bit of excitement she would never have anticipated. Spock had mounted an Irish setter and was wilfully engaged in his first meaningless sexual encounter. The owner of the setter, stood with his arms flailing more vigorously than Spock's hips, trying to stop the romance. He shouted to Anthea in a pitch, elevated and thinned by his hysteria. "Is that your fucking dog?"

"Yes," Anthea replied, "it is my '*fucking* dog'." A giggle betrayed her appreciation of the ridiculous situation; he however, was less inclined to humour.

"Get that thing off my dog," he screeched. "She's in heat and I don't want her breeding with that monster. I'm not going to touch it. It'll probably take my arm off."

Anthea stopped laughing, as she realized that this wasn't helping and heaved at Spock's dynamic haunches. Both his resistance and persistence underscored the fact that bull terriers are, pound for pound, the strongest dog breed and mentally incapable of giving up. He didn't . . . until he was quite finished.

"I'm so sorry," Anthea said, another treacherous snicker following. The more she looked at the man's resolute face the larger the impulse grew. The more she looked at Spock's self-satisfied pant, the louder she laughed, eventually erupting into a full blown, bent over display of complete and helpless hysterics.

Beneath the grey shawl of the approaching dusk, Anthea drove past the front of the Victorian hospital building. A mess of scaffolding looked as if it was propping the poor, tired thing up, like the corset of a crumpled dowager who'd been left in the corner of a vibrant party. Anthea identified with her.

The drive home became quiet as the car was enveloped by the yawning countryside and she turned the steering wheel to hug the corners of the winding road, enjoying the rare curvature of its spine. In Canada, she missed the attention seeking behaviour of the British roads as they roiled and twisted, but then, missed the quiet cooperation of the disciplined Canadian roads when driving the clogged arteries of Britain. She smiled; such was the plight of living a trans-Atlantic existence: being plagued by the remembrance of one when encountering the other. Most of all, she missed her Mam and Dad together: the familiar banter, one teasing the other over small excesses or oversights, the subtle stroke of a shoulder, a naughty pat of the backside, the inevitable lean of one into the other like two old headstones in a graveyard, declaring eternity.

Eternity. How she wanted to believe that there was one. *That Mam would be waiting at the gates to greet them all and give them name tags and a glass of wine – a set of wings maybe . . . or a pitch fork . . . I'll feel better once I see Dad again. His voice sounded more vital on the phone than it had been for weeks. It was as if, in talking about the plans for Mam's interment ceremony, he had resurrected her. He spoke as if she were beside the phone, nudging and whispering her suggestions, as usual.*

The bent figure of her father in his misery came into Anthea's mind. The desolate face of Ian followed it. Seeing Ian again had unsettled Anthea; unravelled the neat knots she had tied so firmly years before. If leaving him the first time was the wrong thing to do, leaving him this time was right. She felt sure of that now, with three thousand miles between them. She found her cheek wet and groaned at her self-indulgence.

The headlights swept past the trees, lined up like sentries along the driveway leading to her sanctuary, 'Ty Bleu' - 'Blue House', named so by the former owners in acknowledgment of their Welsh/French Canadian heritage. Spock and Twiggy were raising a welcome from behind the side door of the farmhouse.

She grabbed her briefcase and purse from the back of the car and trotted to the house. Before the door was fully open, a rush of wet chops licked Anthea's salty cheeks and she wiped them once again, for the best of reasons.

The dogs bounded in front of Anthea, Twiggy, easily outrunning the pup, Spock, to retrieve the ball. She reached into her pocket to find the dog treat packet empty and acknowledged that the training session for Spock would have to come later. Nothing could be accomplished without them. At just under seven months, Spock had only managed to master some basic commands - breathe, eat, sleep. Even when the ball was thrown right at him, more often than not, it would bounce off his nose and the ever-watchful, agile Twiggy would catch the ricochet and bring it to Anthea's feet. If Twiggy was water, Spock was gravel: his ungainly trot, evident when he realized running for something he couldn't eat was so unnecessary.

Anthea's mind wandered back again to Ian and when they first met in the anatomy lab. She remembered the smell of formaldehyde guiding her as she wound her way through the groaning corridors of the old medical building. Alfred, the clerk, would smile up at her from his desk, as she leaned over to sign in. She noted that he was probably a nice-looking man in his day and it was a shame that he didn't wear his false teeth more often.

"Getting some extra practise, Miss?' he said.

"Yes Alfred. We've got a test coming up on Monday and I need to look at some arms."

"Well, you go on in, Miss, there are a couple of other characters in there, so you won't be alone. Good luck on the test. You'll make a beautiful doctor. I only ever had the ugly ones."

"Aww, thanks Alfred. Perhaps I'll be lucky enough to do your prostate exam one day."

The old man let out a loud guffaw. "That would be my pleasure, Miss. I've willed my body to the medical school and I'd feel cheated if I weren't alive at the time of your examination."

"Good to know, Alfred."

Anthea put her hair back in a pony-tail, pulled up her sleeves, put her lab coat on and pulled at the heavy door leading into the lab. The cadavers peered out from behind their plastic bags with a collection of bored expressions, like you see at some cocktail parties.

She nodded to the two figures looking up from between a female cadaver's legs across the room. One did a double take and then granted her a beautiful smile followed by a chivalrous nod. As she glided past to enter the back room where the Limb Box, a massive wooden chest of preserved arms and legs were kept, she could hear them arguing over the location of the ischiocavernosum and bulbocavernosus muscles of the female perineum. She couldn't resist doing what she knew would get a reaction. "The ischiocavernosum muscles are above and to the side of the clitoris and the bulbocavernosus muscles are below it."

The two men stared back at her, transfixed and seemingly none-the-wiser, so she added, "Now don't tell me you need help finding the clitoris – puh!"

The less attractive of the two spoke up, "I had to show him – twice."

His lab partner put his hands on his hips and feigned being wounded by the remark. “Rowan, I told you, it’s hard being a 23-year-old virgin. It’s nothing that practice won’t cure.”

“Ian, some of us just have natural talent. You need to watch a few more times . . . I’m sorry,” he said to Anthea. “I’m just babysitting him for the day.”

With that, he came forward offering a gloved hand to Anthea. “I’m Rowan Clyde, ignore my friend, Ian, here, he’s a cretin as well as a virgin.”

“Hmmm,” Anthea said, passing on the hand-shake and indicating she didn’t have her gloves on yet. “At 23, maybe they’re one and the same . . . but, he is a very cute cretin.”

“Perhaps, but he’s completely untrainable. I’ve been here for hours and we’ve made no progress.”

Ian pushed Rowan aside with a flourish. “Tell that to your girlfriend,” he said, looking deep into Anthea’s eyes. “He’s got a girlfriend and she’s a mad cow. She’ll slaughter you both if you so much as look at him, so it’s me you should go after.” He made a courtly bow. “Ian Ifold, at your service, Ma’am.”

“Hmm, what kind of gentleman are you to call his girlfriend a mad cow?”

“Oh! It’s alright, she’s my sister. Now, will you come for a drink with me tonight?”

Anthea let a smile escape. “Thank you for the chivalrous invitation, but I’m afraid I can’t tonight, I’m swotting for a lab test.”

“Tomorrow, then, or the next day, or the one after that?” he persisted.

“No thanks - don’t need the distraction.”

She turned quickly and put on her gloves. She went into the back room and raised the heavy lid to the enormous Limb Box, letting it rest on her back as she reached deep into it for an arm. There were fifteen or twenty of them in there, all entwined as rigid hands grasped the wrist, ankle or upper arm of another. She pulled on the shoulder of one and shook it to release it, but the leverage wasn’t there. Reaching further in, her toes left the floor and she hung over the box, in a mighty struggle with the body parts. Ian came up behind and tipped her into the box, closing the lid. "Now then, I won't let you out until you agree to go for a drink with me," he said.

Anthea squatted in the dark stink of the box, hardly believing what twisted and misguided idea this idiot had imagined would charm her in to a drink. She resolved not to say a word, but to remain quiet. She felt above her head for the lip of the lid and held it down. "Asshole," she whispered.

Ian leaned on the box, looking at his nails. "I'm ready anytime you are. Say you'll go out with me, just once. Don't make your mind up about me right away."

Anthea shook her head wanting to tell him in no uncertain terms that her mind was quite made up and to open the fucking box. But she remained quiet, a plan forming in her vindictive mind.

She heard Rowan's voice. "What the fuck are you doing, you psycho? Let the girl out, she probably fainted in there, Jesus!"

Anthea felt the lid lift but she held it firmly closed with all her strength. Ian's voice rose to a slightly higher pitch. "It was just a joke, man. I thought it was funny."

"It's jammed shut now, you wanker! You've got an unconscious girl in there and we can't get her out. We'd better call the old man."

"Oh Jesus, Jesus," Ian said, dissolving into a state of panic. "I didn't mean this to happen."

Anthea seized this moment to grab a grizzly wrist in each of her hands and push her back against the lid as hard as she could so that it hit the back wall with a mighty bang. She jumped up, hair wild; teeth exposed, screeching like a banshee. The two men let out a chorus of girlish screams as Rowan ran out of the room, vaulting over Ian, who had either slipped or collapsed in fright – he, himself, was not sure.

"Go to Hell, you motherfuckers!" Alfred said, running into the lab, cricket bat in hand, ready to do battle with the living . . . or the dead.

CLINICAL STUDIES: LEVEL I

CAROLINA STARED HER DOWN FROM behind the counter of Dr. Anthea Brock's Obstetrics and Gynecology office. She sensed this woman was no amateur in these matters and was used to getting her way; used to dropping her name like a thunderbolt upon mortals who dared hold her gaze. *Time for a slight rearrangement of this bitch's universe,* thought Carolina, *but use your inside voice first.*

"I'm very sorry Mrs. Thackery; Dr. Brock is tending to an emergency. We're running behind already and we can't be sure exactly when she'll be here."

"That's Mzzz. Thackery," the woman spat. "My appointment was for eleven, why didn't you call me to tell me she'd be late? I have to be at a very, very, important meeting at noon."

Carolina had caught the drop and ascent of Ms. Thackery's eyelids as she assessed her challenger. She had not missed the dismissive sniff that followed, as the woman judged her to be the spawn of an underclass. It might have been the plunge of Carolina's leopard print dress, her plate-sized, hoop earrings, the hot coral, stiletto heels that flashed from beneath the desk, or the nest of black hair that grew like a tumour above her forehead, but unintimidated, Carolina used the bat of her own false eyelashes to do the same.

"Well, Mzzzz. Thackery, we didn't plan this inconvenience; we just haven't found a way to predict emergencies in time to reschedule people in *advance* of them. I think that's why they're called emergencies – and this isn't a spa, so scheduling only an hour for a gynecological appointment was perhaps a little short-sighted - even if we were on time, you wouldn't have made it to your very, very important appointment. Do you want to reschedule?"

"No! I do not want to reschedule. I want my appointment at the time I made an appointment. And, who are you – Carolina," she said, peering at the nameplate on the desk, "to be lecturing me on my timing? I don't think you know who I am."

"It's pronounced 'Car-o-leen-a', I'm a person not a state and while I don't know who you are, I do know what you are . . . Mr. Thackery's wife?"

"Yes, Mrs. Daniel Thackery, the C.E.O. of the hospital and he is a good friend of Dr. Saxon, Chief of the Ob/Gyn department. This won't go well for you. I've never been spoken to like this by a - *a clerk*. I shall report your afontery to Dr. Brock when I see her."

"Effrontery," Carolina said.

"What?" the woman said, hesitating.

Carolina spoke slowly, enunciating her syllables. "The word is effrontery. No one has 'afontery'. It doesn't exist."

Melinda was processing this information when Glynda ran over to the front desk, knowing diplomacy was not Carolina's strong point. "Er, Carolina, you go have your lunch," she chimed. "I can take over now, thanks."

Carolina took a long breath in, which pushed her abundant breasts out of her black, push-up bra like a pout, and cast them further into the steady sight lines of Mrs. Daniel Thackery. The silence served to emphasize the rustling of magazine pages as they were turned, unconsciously, by the four other patients in the waiting room who were watching the stand-off.

"It's OK, I'm not hungry," Carolina said.

"You just said that you could eat a horse. Go ahead. I'll handle this," Glynda offered, a smile pinned onto her face.

"Eat a horse? I could easily devour an old dragon," Carolina sneered, under her breath, "but I'll restrain myself."

Glynda lifted Carolina's elbow and tried to wedge her own slim hips between Carolina and the desk. She felt resistance and pushed more forcefully against it, eventually succeeding.

"Ms. Thackery, you probably remember me, Glynda Wicksteed, from the symphony fundraiser? We always appreciate your support so much. Now, why don't we just reschedule you for an early morning appointment? Those have a better chance of running on time."

Glynda felt a pinch on her buttocks, but suppressed a reaction. She flicked her hand behind her attempting to stop Carolina's increasingly painful assault.

"Next time, perhaps. It's nice to deal with a server who understands my needs, Linda."

"It's, Glynda."

"Of course, Glenda."

An untidy figure appeared at the doorway and in a slow growl asked, "Who parked in my spot? The one very clearly marked 'Dr. Anthea Brock'? I've been driving around for twenty minutes trying to find a parking space. Who owns a silver Jag?

Ms. Thackery's splendid, spotless, wrinkle-free face peeked over the collar of her white, Italian, leather coat as she came as close to genuflection as one could without being in a church.

"Oh! Dr. Brock, I must apologize. I must not have seen the sign.'

"You mean the very large, red one I had specially made for Dr. Brock so people wouldn't miss it?" Carolina said helpfully, as she peeked around Glynda's stubborn hips.

"I - I'll move it right away."

"I'm afraid you won't be able to, I parked behind it and I'll move it after I've seen the patients who've been waiting soooo long for me."

A small quiver crossed Ms. Thackery's lips just before Carolina saw them pulled like curtains to expose her preternaturally white teeth.

"I'll just make a quick phone call," Ms. Thackery said as she turned away and dialed her masseus.

"Take your time," Carolina said flicking her pen against the desk pad. "All these nice ladies are before you."

Anthea went to the nursing station and let her eyes glance down the appointment roster. A heavy sigh escaped as she flipped the four pages of names. Carolina glided away from the front desk to rest her chin on Anthea's shoulder and hiss into her ear. "It's worse than it looks. We've got the medical student starting this afternoon too."

"Shiiit!" Anthea said. "Let's hope she's not another idiot like the last one. Some people are born pathologists - shouldn't be working with live tissue. Is there *any* good news?"

"Yep, it's Friday; another long, lonely weekend!" Carolina sighed.

Molly, Anthea's nurse, peered around the door of Examination Room Three, rubbing her hands with sanitizer. "We can't seem to beat this waiting list down, no matter how long we work."

Anthea shook her head in defeat, looking at a new pile of referrals. Going to Britain for three weeks would just put them further behind, but not going wasn't an option. "What's the 'pearl necklace' here for?

Molly leaned over to view the day's list. "Mzzz. Thackery? She's the hospital CEO's wife and you don't want to know."

Anthea's eyes narrowed. "Oh, her. . . and she's the menopause, isn't she?

"You're a genius, Dr. Brock."

" Yes, but I am *not* God - *she* is, apparently. I tell ya, all the hormone therapy in the world couldn't fix her personality; she needs a friggin' Proctologist to get her head out of her ass.

Let me start with a nice patient."

Molly handed Anthea a thick chart. "Proud Mary, coming right up."

"Hello, Mary," Anthea said, her face softening as she grasped the ancient lady's hand. She let her left-hand stroke the pale, thin skin gently, noting signs of dehydration. Mary tried to rise from her chair and lost her balance. The multiple, paper drapes that she had secured around her pelvis dropped away and her withered pelvis was exposed. Anthea caught her in time and placed her back on the chair, amongst the untidy papers, like a bird toppled from its nest.

"I'm here for my oil and lube job," Mary said, "couldn't get up on the table this time, damn it!"

A draught lifted the smell of alcohol to Anthea's nose. "Don't worry, Mary, I'll help you up in a minute when we're ready to change your pessary."

Anthea pulled the chair over and sat eye level to Mary. The palest of blue eyes looked out over cut-glass cheekbones. She'd lost more weight in the last couple of months.

"Mary, have you been drinking this morning? I can smell alcohol on your breath."

"Oh, I do have my brandy in the morning, just to get me going, like. It gives me a little pick me up, you know."

"How much do you have? You're still driving yourself aren't you?"

"Oh, just a smidgen, doctor, not a lot, and I don't drink anymore until bedtime."

" How much do you drink at bedtime?"

"A few more smidgens then, but I don't have to go anywhere then and it helps me sleep."

Mary's speech was not impaired, her eyes were bright and she walked confidently over to the gyne bed when asked. "I'm not a drunk, doctor. I do drink responsibly, promise."

"I understand, but, you weigh nothing. I don't want to see any more weight loss. Make sure that you eat. It would take very little alcohol to effect you adversely. Also, alcohol affects the bladder; it'll make your incontinence worse - makes the pessary less effective. I'd rather you didn't drink first thing in the morning, certainly not if you're going to drive. It wouldn't take much convincing for them to remove your license at your age. "

"I've had a smidgen in the morning all my life, just like my Granny McFinney did. It's like breakfast cereal to us."

"All the same, Mary, not a good idea. Stop the smidgens or take a cab."

Mary's lips pursed as she allowed her legs to be lifted into the stirrups. "No drink, no sex, how's a girl to have any fun?"

"There's no reason you can't have sex."

"My husband's dead 20 years."

"Mary, I don't like you drinking on your own but sex on your own is recommended. I can give you some information if you'd like."

Mary pondered this. "Well, maybe a smidgen."

Anthea paused as she put her hand on the exam room door. It had to be done.

"Mzzz. Thackery, sorry to keep you waiting, but as you see we're a very busy office. Babies are the bosses around here," she said cheerfully, but firmly.

Melinda Thackery rose from her chair in a plume of perfume, her toothy brigade standing on ceremony. "But of course, Dr. Brock, no need to apologize for that Carolina woman; good staff are hard to find. You know, I once found a dirty toilet brush in my Hermes bag after I caught my ex-cleaning lady stealing the best clothes from the donations bag. Really unprofessional, I thought."

"Hmmm," Anthea said. Then, taking an audible breath in, she continued. "Well, more to the point, Carolina, my secretary, has been with me for years, and while she has been described as 'exuberant', most people enjoy her and find her extremely helpful."

Anthea explained that she viewed her practice as a team effort and therefore couldn't guarantee that Melinda would not encounter Carolina or indeed a delay due to a delivery again. She offered to transfer her care to another doctor or to continue with this visit if she wished.

"But, I want you as my gynecologist," protested Ms. Thackery, "Dr. Saxon himself recommended you. I don't settle for second best in anything, certainly not my health."

Ms. Thackery recognized the resolve in the doctor's eyes. She knew she had to change her tactics and retreat. She lowered her voice to a conspiratorial whisper as she crinkled her pert nose.

"Of course, I'll buy this 'Caro-leena'- if that's how you say it, *something nice* and we'll be fine. I get the female doctor I want and she gets . . . *something nice.*"

Anthea cocked her head, trying to follow the twisted logic but quickly assessed it as a waste of time. She sat down and opened the chart. "So, I see you're experiencing classic menopausal symptoms - moody, temperamental, irritable. Any hot flashes, night sweats, insomnia, decreased libido or vaginal dryness?"

"Everything! Though, some of the herbal remedies seemed to help?"

Anthea turned the intake sheet to the medications section and saw a lengthy list of herbal extracts. "I want you to stop all these, right away. I'll send you for some blood tests and we'll discuss whether you're interested in any Hormone Replacement Therapy."

Ms. Thackery flinched at the suggestion. "Oh, I don't want any hormones in my body."

"Well, it's the lack of them that are causing the symptoms. According to your history, you're a good candidate for them - no contraindications, very low associated risk."

"But I'd rather have *natural* therapy, not drugs."

"Consider this; at the very least, we know exactly what's in these prescription preparations. I know nothing about this list of *natural* products you've probably paid a fortune for which clearly haven't worked or I assume you wouldn't be here."

"I just don't trust the big drug companies," Ms. Thackery said with a shrug.

"But you trust the unregulated, spurious claims of a product sold by a part-time high school arts student?"

Ms. Thackery sighed and crossed her long legs. "I've never heard it put quite that way."

Aware that she might have seemed too abrupt, Anthea tried to moderate her tone.

"Your choice, of course, but I trust you came here for the knowledge and advice of my discipline which I will give you in detail. Ultimately, menopause won't kill you. You don't have to do anything at all, if you don't want to."

Anthea reached for a clutch of pamphlets, wrote out a blood requisition, and rose from her chair as a signal that the appointment was over. Ms. Thackery looked startled. "What, no pap smear or something?"

"You had one with your G.P. just a few months ago - normal - no need to repeat it. You can book your follow up at the front desk. We'll see you then, alright?"

Just as Anthea took the first step out of the room, a deep, throaty groan made her look back. Ms. Thackery had thrown her silky head into her hands and was trying desperately to suppress the convulsion of sobs that wracked her thin frame.

There was genuine heartbreak in Melinda Thackery's voice as she scolded herself for what she saw as a breach of character. Anthea touched Melinda's shoulder. "Melinda, I know you are a strong woman and don't like to show vulnerability, but you *are* in a doctor's office. What is it that has upset you so much?"

"My husband's cheating on me and I'm sure he's given me something."

"I see." Anthea said, "We can fix that. Have you confronted him yet?"

Melinda shuddered, drawing her coat tighter to her chest. "No, I haven't. Thing is, I'm not sure I want to. Her voice thickened again. "I love him so much. I don't know how I'd leave the bastard."

Carolina thumbed through the charts impatiently. She paused at the L's, pulled one out and let it drop to the floor with a noisy clap. Her orange fingernails strummed through the T's and pulled two others, allowing them to drop thunderously to join the others. Glynda shuffled over.

"What seems to be the problem, Carolina?"

"It's that kid, what's her name - Saxon's granddaughter?"

"Georgia? Isn't she a darling!"

"Yes, that one. Tell her that if she doesn't learn her fucking alphabet, I'll crush her darling little texting thumbs in the filing cabinet. It's chaos since she came. I can't find any of the charts."

"Well, she's just starting, give her a chance," Glynda pleaded.

"All you ask of a filing clerk, is that they know approximately what order the letters of the alphabet occur. Carolina's eyes widened. "Am I really asking too much?"

Carolina's eyes lifted when she heard someone clear their throat at the front desk. She pushed Glynda out of her path, a wide smile decorating her face. She sucked in her stomach as she leaned her long frame over the front desk to address the young man in greens and a backpack.

"Can I be of any help to you?" The words floating on her breath.

"Hi, I'm Gavin, Gavin McCafferty."

Carolina's Medusa green eyes probed Gavin McCafferty, freezing him momentarily.

"Er, I'm Dr. Brock's new medical student?"

"You're a man."

Gavin twitched uncomfortably, his jaw releasing from the spell just a little. "Yes, yes, I am."

Carolina's orange mouth parted and if a forked tongue had flicked from it, Gavin would not have been surprised. She curled a painted talon as a signal to come hither.

Carolina led Gavin to the lunch room. "There's a fridge for your lunches. There's a microwave and toaster oven for hot stuff." She turned and gave Gavin the once over. "Speaking of 'hot stuff", let me introduce *you* to the others. I'll be right back."

Gavin smiled shyly at Carolina. He was used to the way women acted around him. He had long decided to take his cousin's advice and deal with it with a sense of humour and accept it as payback for all the years women had been treated the same way by men. He didn't regard it as a curse, because he was well aware of the halo effect of symmetrical features. It was an evolutionary advantage and he should accept it as such. However, all his life he had found it to be a complication that got in the way of his desire to be received as a serious man of science and not the lead in a TV medical drama.

He was putting his lunch in the fridge when Carolina walked back into the staffroom with two other women behind her. Looking at them, there couldn't have been three more different looking specimens if you had selected for contrast. Carolina was simply frightening – like some flamboyant, wilderness creature that proclaimed its territory by making itself seem larger than its true dimensions. She was built on a different scale than the average woman, with legs that began directly at her waist and seemed never ending. Her broad shoulders supported breasts that filled the entire space that her upper torso claimed for itself. The strong bones of her face left inordinate distance between her features allowing the definition of each of them to be appreciated independently of each other. Behind her, was an older woman, who had the proportions of a prima ballerina, her long neck, aquiline nose and discretely shadowed eyes, aloof and swan-like.

"This is Glynda Wicksteed, the other secretary," Carolina said, "and that's Molly, Dr. Brock's nurse." She pointed to the third, shorter woman, who looked like she had climbed down from a Ruben's painting, having no angles anywhere about her. Her hair was an unruly mop of fiery curls clasped into a large clip atop a face almost devoid of pigment. In a period drama, she would have been the milkmaid.

Carolina raised her index finger and wagged it at Gavin. "And I'm Carolina Stiletto, yes, Stiletto, like the knife, so don't ever piss me off."

"Oh, don't listen to this old windbag," Molly said with a laugh. "Her bark is worse than her bite. Mind you when she does bite, she's like one of those bull terriers - her jaw locks and she leaves with a pound of flesh."

Glynda deserted the pack with a graceful movement toward Gavin. The frilled cuff of her blouse caught the air and with a ripple of silk she shook his hand warmly. "Yes dear, just ignore Carolina - such an uncouth slattern. Welcome to Dr. Brock's practise. She's in with a patient and I'll introduce you to her as soon as she comes out. Carolina, you'd better go back to the desk. I'll orient young Gavin."

Carolina's face dropped sharply. She looked at Molly and mouthed, "Is she fucking kidding?"

Molly grabbed Carolina's arm and pulled her out of the room. "Now, now, *Signora*, there'll be plenty of time for you to torment him - to the desk with you!"

"But, he's mine. I saw him first. And that's *Signorina* by the way. I'm a reformed virgin."

"Really?" Molly said, "You're old enough to be the Blessed Virgin Mary herself. Leave the boy alone."

The door to Exam Room Three opened and Anthea stepped out. She took Melinda Thackery's chart over to Carolina and spoke in low tones. "Cut this one some slack, Carolina, you two actually have a lot in common. Did I just say that? Well, you'll see when you do the dictation. Be nice." Carolina opened the chart and read the clinical notes.

"Dr. Brock," Molly said, "this is Gavin McCafferty, our medical student."

"OK, Gavin. We're running behind today, so I'll just throw you into the deep end. Go and assess the obstetrical patient in Room Two, she's pretty uncomplicated. Molly'll get you the chart."

"Oh, but . . .," Molly protested.

"Room Two, Molly." Anthea batted back.

Molly took the chart from the desk and handed it to Gavin, looking steadily into his eyes, saying, "This is a test - courage, my love."

Gavin read the chart, sighed deeply, put a brilliant smile on his face and entered Exam Room Two to assess Mrs. El Sayed, who whipped her black burqa over her face with a shriek and stood like a sinister apparition before him.

Melinda Thackery came out of the exam room with a fresh coat of lipstick, just as Carolina came from the lunch room, steaming coffee in hand. Melinda dropped her gaze sideways, turning her shoulder away as she hung her Chanel purse from it, knowing her eyes were still red and swollen. She had never been able to cry prettily. Carolina touched her arm, feeling the softness of the leather. She lifted the full, steaming cup of coffee to Melinda's face and said, "Coffee?"

Molly and Anthea leaned opposite each other, chins resting upon their hands listening to protests rumbling from Room Two.

"You're evil," Molly said.

Anthea responded nonchalantly. "The boy has to learn. It's not all easy stuff like organic chemistry and surgical techniques."

A male voice erupted above the others. "No, no, no male doctors. Get out!" and Exam Room Two spat a shaken Gavin McCafferty out like shit from a donkey.

"Mr. El Sayed wants to see you Dr. Brock. He won't let me near his wife."

Anthea looked into Gavin's deep-set eyes. "It says in the Koran that a male can only touch a female if it is medically necessary or to put out the flames if she is on fire. So, unless Mrs. El Sayed spontaneously combusts, Gavin, what would you suggest we do?"

Gavin's face froze, ambivalence seeping like sea water into his glacial expression.

Fifteen minutes later, Anthea emerged from the room and strode purposefully toward the lunch room. "I need food and a vodka." She saw Gavin's double take from the corner of her eye. "Only kidding, I may just have the vodka."

She waved to him to follow her and opened the lunch room door to find Carolina and Melinda Thackery, face to face, draped over the lunch table, misty eyed and hands clasped in what could only be a most unholy alliance. Anthea excused herself and waited until she saw Carolina escort the troubled Ms. Thackery out of the clinic with uncommon attentiveness.

At the lunch table, Glynda offered up a floral, china teapot to Gavin. It was an old Royal Albert Country Roses pattern she had been given years ago. She had several others at home that she liked better, so she brought this one to work, in an attempt to banish the nasty habit her co-workers had of putting a bag in a mug, adding water, microwaving it until it had sludge floating on the top and calling that a cup of tea.

Anthea noticed Carolina's absence and Molly explained that she was moving Anthea's car for her new best friend Melinda. The thought of common enemies making strange bedfellows crossed Anthea's mind. "My guess is that they've probably been exchanging, 'men are assholes' stories – we've all got 'em. Sorry, Gavin, you may hear a lot of man bashing around here. Don't take it personally. Carolina has christened us, 'The Gynesaurs' – a bunch of bitter old hags – way past our reproductive prime, destined to die alone and be eaten by our cats. It's a very loose association. You don't *have* to be a woman - it's more a state of mind. Mostly, you have to whine and complain about the sorrowful state of your life and resent the hell out of anyone else who actually has one."

Carolina swept into the lunchroom not missing a beat, "If anyone is having a good time, you have to run them down and pick out small-minded criticisms of them – like a Tyrannosaurus picking out the eyes of a creature it ran down and savaged. See? It's a very healthy approach to accepting your own pathetic existence."

Gavin smiled and opened his sandwich container. "No problem. I'll just keep my head down and my mouth full."

"That's one of my favourite positions too!" Carolina volunteered from the doorway.

Glynda splattered tea onto her crisp, white blouse. "Really, Carolina, it's a shame that you are always compelled be so crude."

"Yes, all those charm school lessons, come to nothing!" Molly said feigning regret.

Carolina looked at Glynda. "If I haven't been able to corrupt *you* after all these years of being around me, I'm sure he'll survive a few months without too much damage."

Molly pondered a question, "I really hope I'm past my 'reproductive prime, not that I'll ever get a chance to test it!"

"Don't worry it's, like, 14 or something," Carolina said. "Jump up and down, and if your ovaries rattle like maracas, like Glynda's do, you know you're finished with all that nonsense."

Glynda pursed her lips, unwilling to give Carolina the point.

Gavin took up the question. "Isn't a woman's reproductive prime in her twenties?"

Anthea chuckled. "Pretty much and after 35 it plummets into maraca territory! Gavin, your may as well know now, that any preconceived ideas you have about the delicacy of women's conversation will be shattered when you're here. We feminists didn't burn our bras just so we could run through Elysium with our breasts flapping in the wind, you know. We did it so that we could scratch the balls we grew to get there, without apology."

"Yes, I must say I've scratched a few in my time." Carolina said.

"Where the hell's Elysium? Why is that familiar?" Molly asked, thinking perhaps she'd seen the sign on the way through Mennonite country.

"It's not hell, it's heaven!" Carolina pointed out. "It's where the Roman heroes would go when they die."

Carolina looked directly at Glynda. "Oh, if you like reading about the Romans, read about Caligula. Now there's a twisted son of a bitch - prostituted his sisters, killed off the rest of his family, and made his horse a priest - my kinda man. You'd love the movie too, Glynda, I'll lend it to you."

Carolina knew her classics as Glynda's follow up google searches always confirmed. This didn't surprise anyone anymore. Glynda changed the subject quickly by asking Gavin how his first morning went.

"Well, I sure hit the floor running."

"Running from Mr. El Sayed, you mean," Molly said, breaking into a laugh with the memory of his bewildered face.

"Ya, that caught me off guard. I don't know who was more shocked, me or Mrs. El Sayed."

Anthea shrugged. "People have to realize that they can't demand 'Designer Doctors' unless they're willing to pay for it. A doctor is a doctor – their gender is irrelevant. OHIP isn't perfect but it's a gift Canadians give their citizens and I believe it makes our society better than those that don't have it . . . and that's my sermon for today. Amen."

Gavin pledged to try to be efficient and not hold them up too much.

"Don't worry. She won't let you," Molly reassured. "You just try not to waste a minute, because one minute multiplied by sixty patients and you're an hour behind already."

"Got it," Gavin said, swallowing another fast bite, and trying to avoid looking directly across the table where Carolina sat licking her lips after each bite of pasta, like a Venus Fly trap.

Anthea suggested they all say a little bit about themselves for Gavin's benefit.

Gavin began, "I am single – no distractions from school. Raised in a small mining town in Northern Ontario which none of you have ever been to or heard of or will ever want to go to. I'm an only child and am the first one in my family to go to university."

"Bravo, Gavin. Do you find older women attractive?" Carolina asked.

Molly grabbed her empty lunch bag and put it over Carolina's head. "Just pretend she's not here. She's impossible."

Carolina sat as still as before and added, "Blindfold's work for me – kinky, but inspiring." Glynda clasped her hand to her mouth, suppressing a smile.

Anthea reached over and tapped Gavin's hand. "If you want to sue for harassment, I'll back you up."

Carolina whipped off the bag. "OK, OK, I'll back off. Just don't leave me alone with him. I have my desires. I'm not a dried up old gourd like Glynda," she said, shimmying in her seat while singing, 'La Cuceracha'.

Glynda tutted, a look of resignation over taking her face.

"No one's spared with Carolina," Anthea said.

"I'm an equal opportunity purveyor of hyperbolic aspersion," Carolina agreed.

"Are you?" Molly said. "That sounds impressive! Is it?"

"Yes," Carolina explained. "Those are some of my best words."

Molly lifted her hands to the others. "And here's me thinkin' she was just another crazy bitch."

Carolina feigned insult. "A crazy bitch who uses big words!" Then with a mischievious grin, she added, "A Sesquipedalian Bitch."

Anthea held up her hands, as if to quell the masses. She motioned for Molly to speak next.

"Oh!" Molly said, "Molly McGilvery, I'm the boring one. I was raised right here in Kitchener. I'm a widow, with three kids and a brother who lives with me." She sat up, pursed her lips and tugged at her smock. "Yes, I'm the only Gynesaur who made damn good use of her 'reproductive prime'. You'll probably meet my brother, Angus, at some point. He has Downs. Dr. Brock hires him for a few hours a week to stock the rooms and do little odd jobs. He loves it here. He feels important."

"He's more reliable than Saxon's granddaughter, I'll tell you that," Carolina noted. "He's a doll."

"Oh, he likes Carolina," Molly said, turning to Gavin. "He calls her his girlfriend."

"Hey, Angus and me - we look after each other," Carolina said with both thumbs up.

"Dr. Saxon is the Department Head here," Anthea pointed out. "His granddaughter, Georgia, is doing a high-school co-op placement here. She's, ummmm, chirpy, talkative and well, a little distracted. Saxon cornered me. I owed him a favour. You'll meet him. You'll meet her . . . interesting genetic hybrid there."

"What do you mean?" Gavin asked, interested.

"Oh, don't let me influence you. You'll see," Anthea said.

Gavin observed the knowing glances that passed between the women. His blue gaze came to settle upon Glynda.

"Me? Oh, I'm just me," scoffed Glynda, batting her hands like a cat covering its droppings in a litter box. "Surely, you don't want to know about me?"

"OK, then, my turn," Carolina said quickly.

Glynda continued talking over Carolina loudly, in her adult voice. Carolina placed her chin on her hand and let her eyes glaze over.

"Glynda Wicksteed. I am a sixth-generation citizen of Kitchener – on both sides of my family. We are descended from one of the first Mennonite settlers in the area and have many streets named after various family members. Mummy and Daddy were part of the Modern Mennonite movement and I was raised in what most would consider a privileged existence but hard work was still emphasized as important. I really don't need to work but I do because I think it's important to do something useful and I am fulfilled on a daily basis helping people with joy in my heart. I was married briefly and if I'm truthful, the only good thing my husband left me with was a personal relationship with Jesus - oh, and his mother – not Jesus's mother of course, my husband's mother – Edna."

"Well, that's a story for another day," Anthea said. "My story's quick. Born in Canada, British parents, returned to Britain as a kid, came back to Canada without my ex-husband, Ian, because I'm off British men. No children, two dogs, three cats. Over to you, Carolina, the short, P.G. thirteen version, please."

"Who me?" she fluttered her eyelashes, resurrecting Glynda's princess posture. "I am the daughter of an ex-Mafia man who was found hanging from a bridge with his hands and feet bound. Was it an accident you ask? Well, possibly. I'm quite sure he didn't intend for it to happen."

Gavin let out a burst of laughter, soon to realize, he laughed alone.

The hospital corridors looked like the inside of a child's fort; beige cardboard boxes hurriedly taped together to form avenues in which to navigate your way. Once you went into them, eventually, you would be released into a brightly lit settlement of desks with very busy inhabitants wielding clipboards, which seemed to need constant attention. Men with tool belts walked the halls like gunslingers, eyes narrowed beneath their hardhats, stopping occasionally to stare at something no one else saw. Measuring tapes crossed like swords and elicited much hushed discussion. Anthea led Gavin through the labyrinth toward the O.R. listening to the agony his faux-pas had cost him.

"Get over it, Gav, I assure you, Carolina has already. She shocks people intentionally."

Gavin swept his floppy, blonde hair back from his face and smacked his forehead with his palm. "Yes, but I feel awful. That's a terrible thing she suffered – her father was offed and I treated it like a joke. I thought it *was* a joke!"

"You think she didn't know that? I can't say she didn't have a dramatic history, she did, but I swear, Carolina wouldn't be happy if there wasn't something theatrical to define her. You apologized. Let it go and start thinking about the tragedy of bladder repairs. We have Mrs. Kinsky next and hers is hanging outside her body, right beside her uterus."

A loud voice rose from around the corner. "I don't give a damn what your research says; that piece of equipment is a piece of junk and get it out of my O.R. We don't have money to invest in something that doesn't live up to its promise. The deal's off."

"Ahhh," Anthea said, raising her hand to her ear. "That's the delicate call of the indigenous species . . . Tyrannosaurus Rex - Dr. Rex Saxon – I know - sounds like a soap opera name, doesn't it? Keep your head down, or he will bite it off and spit out bone splinters like darts."

Gavin looked around nervously. "Boy, he's angry at someone."

"He's angry at everyone; all the time, about everything. Now, stand aside - watch me charm him."

A tsunami of green came around the corner, rushing through the doors, filling the corridors with a noisy storm of complaint.

"Lovely to see you Dr. Saxon, you're looking particularly animated today."

"Fuck off, Brock. I don't need the sarcasm, thank you very much."

"Just trying to keep the workplace civil, as you had reminded me to do at our last staff meeting."

A low roar rumbled from his chest as he trampled his way past, stopping only to sniff the air momentarily, step backwards and dip his massive paws into a box of chocolates that lay open on the desk. He stuffed a handful into his mouth and chewed loudly on his forage. Through a thick, gurgle of chocolate caramels came the order, "I also reminded you that it's your turn to head the Hospital Fund Raiser, since you had so much to say about the last one. Can't wait to hear your big plans for it." He loped away into the distance and all eyes rediscovered the fascination of their clipboards.

HOMECARE STUDIES: LEVEL 11

Carolina

"COME RIGHT THROUGH," SAID THE voice from the intercom. Carolina encouraged her Camry through the iron gates hoping that it wasn't going to act up again. She emerged from its shell, securing the door by banging it with her formidable buttocks. She leaned there for a moment and took in the stately home. *French Colonial*, she thought. *Some people've got it all.*

Her shoes clacked noisily as she walked to the house, pausing to rub her hands against the deep rose of the polished doors. She was startled when they swung open. Melinda's face looked surprised but pleased to see her.

Carolina surveyed the opulently carved table in the centre of a marble hallway with a staggering bouquet of flowers that were a long way away from the carnations she kept in her own hallway.

"What a dump, Melinda!"

"Yes, isn't it? You should see our place in Palm Beach. I can hold my head up there."

Melinda Thackery threw her head back in a gesture worthy of Marilyn herself and Carolina wondered how those kinds of women got that one piece of hair to bounce back into place just above the left eyebrow. *No wonder I hated her*, thought Carolina. *She'd better have an even shittier story now than the one she had before, or I'll just go back to hating her.*

"Well, I said I'd come, and I'm here," Carolina said, flipping her hands out in an extravagant pose.

Melinda folded her lips over those remarkable teeth. "I know. I really appreciate you taking a chance on me. I don't know, something I do just turns people off. It's nice that you gave me a second chance when I really needed it. It just shows you who you can meet at the gynecologists."

Carolina couldn't have imagined where they would have rubbed shoulders otherwise.

Melinda floated into the conservatory at the rear of the house and offered Carolina a glass of wine. Voluptuous plant life posed throughout the winding pathway that led to a plush yellow couch. Carolina sank into it and raised her face to the sun pouring through the white lattice work above. "Is this considered outside?" she asked as she was handed a glass wine.

"That's a strange question," Melinda said. "What do you mean?'

"I'd love a cigarette. Can I smoke here?'

Melinda looked over her shoulder, as if she was being watched. "Not really, but if you've got one, I'll have one too."

"You smoke?"

"No. The answer, if you're ever asked, is, 'No.'"

Carolina appreciated the red velvet liquid as she spun it and watched it cling to the throat of the glass. "Good legs," she said.

"Thanks. I work out," Miranda responded, crossing them as she lit her cigarette.

"I was talking about . . . never mind," Carolina said as she let the deep berry flavours drift into her nostrils before it surrounded her tongue. She swilled it through her cheeks and swallowed gratefully. Before she knew it, she was telling Melinda about her father. "You know, my father didn't know much, but he made a great wine. He'd spend a lot of time in the cantina – cold cellar you'd call it, clucking over his 'damigianas' – they're big, glass jugs that you keep wine in, like a neurotic chicken over her eggs. He took such time with me - made me sample the grapes and taste the wine as it matured. The smell of grapes brings his face back to me as if he were standing with us."

Melinda sensed that Carolina was enjoying one of life's bittersweet moments. "Is he dead now?" she asked gently.

"A coupla times over, I'm afraid."

"How did he die?"

A shadow crossed Carolina's face and Melinda thought she saw the shine of tears. "Oh, I've really done it now, haven't I? I'm sorry Carolina, you don't have to tell me. But, if you're in the mood to talk, hell, I'm in the mood to listen. Misery loves company, as they say. You've seen me at my worst. You can't be a bigger mess than I am right now."

Carolina smiled back at her, willing her composure to return. "Ya know, maybe after a couple more of these, bella."

The soothing heat of the water in the hot tub felt like a lover's tongue lapping at the goose bumps forming on Carolina's breasts. The night air breathed upon her face; cold whispers chastising her for a naughty performance as she drank, naked from a large bottle of wine, in an outdoor hot tub looking out at miles of expensive real estate. The moon's full face hung around her and Melinda like a third person anxious to be included in the gossip. In the distance the keening of coyotes, worrying over their own melodramas drifted to them. Melinda's head hung sideways on her shoulders, bobbing every now and again, the water extinguishing her cigarette. Carolina spoke, allowing herself the rare indulgence of envy. "I tell ya, this is the fuckin' life, this is. I could get use to this. What's a girl have to do to marry into all this shit?"

"Well, y'know, when me and Daniel first met, he had nuthin'," Melinda said, the alcohol robbing her of her polished speech and uncovering the lazy patterns she grew up with. "Oh, he was good lookin' and all, but he didn't have shit. I put him through biz school, workin' shitty jobs. Nobody gave us nothin'. We had to make it for ourselves – an' we did – made some shrewd investments that paid off big. He doesn't need to work, I'm sure he only took the job at the hospital cuz I just wasn't enough for him."

Carolina frowned and held up her index finger as she collected her next sentence. "Y'know, some people need to work – for a sense of accomplishment. Shopping and tennis and having lunch with other people who shop and play tennis and lunch just isn't enough for some idiots. They want to do something useful – no offense."

Melinda looked wounded. "That's not all I do. There's bookin' holidays too."

Carolina nodded, and took a loud gulp of her wine. "Now, there's a truckload of fuckin' misery. How *do* you manage?" Her mind bounced to another thought. "Though being a big shot at the hospital would give a guy great access to a shitload of women to fuck. Hard not to cheat when you're surrounded by a smorgasbord of adoring women all liftin' up their tits while they're reviewing protocol."

Melinda stared out of her static face, imagining the possible scenarios. Carolina reached over and smacked her forearm playfully. "Hey, sorry, didn't mean to spell it out for you. Here, you need a little more anaesthetic, girl. I can see you're hurtin' bad."

"Yep, that's me. I'm bad, nutt'n but bad," Melinda said taking a deep swig of her wine.

"Shit, give a girl a drink and all that pretty talk falls away an' ya start talkin' like a yokel."

"Hell yea! I am a yokel, always was."

"A yokel in Prada," Carolina observed.

"Capital of Czechoslovakia, right? I got a purse from there."

The two naked women were dancing on the back lawn to Leonard Cohen's 'Closing Time', seemingly inured to the coolness of the evening breeze. Perhaps it was the wine. They gyrated, with cigarettes in their mouths, raising their somewhat tubular breasts to the moon by cupping them in their one free hand while waving a bottle of exquisite Barolo in the other. This was the scene that Daniel Thackery walked into.

"Melinda. What the fuck . . .?"

Melinda lurched from her arabesque and slipped, hard onto her buttocks. Her face became flinty and twisted. "What the fuck am I doin'? What the fuck are you doin' here? I thought you were with whatever little bitch you're havin' it on with!"

Carolina wobbled up to him and pointed her finger into his chest. "Seems like you are not welcome here anymore, buddy, so fuck off – it's what you do anyway, right?"

Daniel looked at Carolina, trying to ignore the lavish pelt of pubic hair she sported between her legs. "Who are you?" he asked Carolina. "Melinda, are you a lesbian now . . . and a smoker?"

Carolina pointed her finger between his eyes. "No, asshole, we're just having a nice time without you. You gave her an S.T.D! Don't worry; we gave her a prescription for you too, so your dick doesn't fall off."

Daniel turned his face from Carolina's finger, a look somewhere between puzzlement and devastation sweeping over it. He batted the finger away with enough force to spin the unstable Carolina almost 360 degrees, and asked Melinda, "You have an S.T.D? How? I've never been unfaithful to you."

Melinda stood unsteadily, looking aside and down. She chewed at her lip, trying to organize a lie. Carolina rolled like a Ninja, reassembling her errant body parts to come to a stand. Then, with a precision that belied her sodden state, she lunged at Daniel. "Ya right!" Her right fist connected with his jaw and he flew sideways, on to the damp grass, looking like a crumpled suit.

Melinda shrieked and scrambled to his side. "Oh, my God, Carolina, what the hell? . . . Daniel, Daniel talk to me darlin'."

Carolina's silhouette swayed in the moonlight. "Darlin' my ass? He had it comin' to him. He's lucky the wine's so good or I'd a hit him with the damn bottle."

"Are you crazy?" Melinda shrieked. "I don't want to hurt him, for God's sake. What's wrong with you?"

Melinda held Daniel's head and kissed his cheek as she tried to provoke a response. His eyes opened slightly and he groaned pitifully.

"But he cheated on you!" Carolina reminded her. "Besides, he'll be alright; he's just got a glass jaw, the sissy."

Melinda looked up at Carolina, her mascara forming two dirty pathways down her cheeks. "No, no, I *thought* he was cheating on me. . . I always kinda think he's cheating on me. Why wouldn't he cheat on me? So . . . so . . . OK, maybe I tried to make him jealous and . . . ," She looked down, like a shy schoolgirl, "and . . . OK, I hooked up with my masseuse – just the once! I . . . I didn't want to admit what I'd done at the doctor's office. I . . . was ashamed, so I said I'd got it from you, Daniel. Oh! Daniel honey, I'm so sorry. I don't deserve you."

She wailed into the night air and attempted to help the disoriented Daniel to his feet. He pulled his arm away roughly, looking small and defeated. Melinda motioned to Carolina. "You'd better go, Carolina. I know this is all my fault – always is. I'll try to stop him from laying charges."

The logistics of the situation filtered slowly through Carolina's sluggish brain. "Yea, soooo, are we still buds?"

Molly

Molly looked through the meat isle of the grocery store, but after a quick glance at her watch, decided to pick up a roast chicken from the deli instead. She threw it into the cart beside the Joe Louis and the makings for tomorrow's lunches and raced to the check out, glancing at her watch as she pushed the cart. She could see another woman's determined face as she picked up her pace to reach the empty checkout before Molly. The woman's cart was loaded, heavy with multiples of the same product, but this tiny woman summoned the strength of a shot putter and swept into the alley a second before Molly.

Seeing an opportunity at the express desk, Molly decided to take a chance at processing a few extra items beyond the posted eight item limit.

A pensioner walked up behind her holding up a single brick of butter, so Molly waved her through sheepishly and began to unload quickly. A teenager came forward with a can of pop and Molly gave him the same courtesy. Three more carts lined up with two or three items a piece. Molly apologized as she reloaded her cart and stood behind the last person. No one likes a cheater and Molly could feel her face burn with regret at her flagrant misdemeanour. In minutes, the line lengthened and overcome with remorse, she stepped back into the next check out where The Gloating Hoarder licked her thumbs and offered up her coupons to the clerk, one by one.

"How are you today?" came the chirpy welcome from the young girl behind the till.

"Surviving," was Molly's flat reply.

The total came to forty-eight dollars, fifty-three cents, and Molly's anxiety at using her debit card was well-founded when it was declined. The clerk raised her thin eyebrows and offered to try it again. Molly opened her wallet to pay with cash but saw nothing but change. "Shit."

The clerk fidgeted uncomfortably.

At the end of the counter, The Hoarder packed the last of her haul into her shopping cart, taking what Molly thought was a sadistic interest in her plight.

Molly handed eleven dollars to the girl. "I'll take the chicken and the potatoes. Put the rest back," Molly said with a sigh.

The clerk offered to keep them aside, but Molly declined, knowing she would not be back for them.

A hand came from behind Molly's back, offering two twenty-dollar bills.

"Let me get this for ya, hon. I've been in that position and Lord Tunderin' Jesus, it's a piss off, ain't it?"

Molly turned and looked into the small, close set eyes of The Hoarder.

"I just won at the Bingo and I want to play it forward, as they say, right?" the woman said, thrusting money into Molly's hand, then squeezing it shut.

"Oh, thank you so much. I'll get it back to you, promise. Give me your address," Molly insisted, grateful for the kindness.

"No, no, that's not the deal, hon. Let me do this. I'll get more outta it than youse."

Molly, felt her heart swell, "Really?"

"That's for fockin' sure, hon. Pay the lady."

Rose St. was a collection of war time bungalows lined up tidily along a crescent that was a haven for street hockey. Molly could make out Angus's bulky figure tending the goal while Callum and his friends fired the ball into the net. She pulled up along the side of the road and lowered her window. "Callum! I told ya before, make sure Angus puts a mask on. I don't want him to lose another tooth."

"Aww Mum, it's OK. He says it doesn't hurt."

"Callum McGilvery, do I have to beat the stupid out of you? Why don't you try being the goalie and see how you feel about it?"

"But, he's a grown man, Mum, he's tough and he's having fun."

Angus rocked back and forth like a boat on water, taunting the kids who came forward to score. 'Ya got nuthin', punk, ya got nuthin'."

It was a fair game. He stopped most of them, albeit from the younger players. The older boys had perfected *the deek*, taking advantage of Angus's slow reaction time. Just then the ball ricocheted off the post and hit Angus in the side of the head.

"Callum, do I have to get out of this car and kick yer arse or what?"

"Alright, alright, Big Red, settle down. I'll make him wear it."

Molly gave a brisk nod. "And it's Mum to you, you little wanker."

"What's a wanker?" Angus asked.

"It's what you do when Mum's not looking," Callum whispered to Angus as he attached the face mask to Angus's large head.

The house was throbbing with loud music and she could hear Orlagh and Fiona in the basement. Molly shouted down over the din for the girls to set the table. She took the bags into the kitchen and smiled when she saw the place settings already arranged, and the dishwasher emptied. Five-year-old Fiona broke the magic by pointing out that Callum hadn't taken the garbage out – "again."

Molly promised to have a talk with Callum and told Fiona to call them in from outside. She had to get Orlagh to gymnastics practice by seven. As she nipped at the heels of each child in an attempt to herd them to their various destinations on time, Molly was shocked when Orlagh announced that she didn't want to go to gymnastics. After gentle prodding Orlagh confessed that it was because her floor routines were nowhere near as good as her competitors who were able to pay for a professional choreographer. Molly desperately cooed out all the appropriate motherly encouragements, knowing that the cost of going that route was beyond her means.

"Ah well, you just do your best and I'm sure it'll all be fine. You're very graceful, so you'll outshine them all, sweetie."

"I'm looking at all the dance shows to try to get some cool moves."

"Well, that's resourceful. Good for you. You'll be proud that you're doing it yourself."

"Yea, well, the judges don't award points for that. Maybe if I'm good enough, I can get into the higher group. Their coach makes great routines."

"Just keep working hard, then, you never know."

Molly thought that she might be able to pick up a few weekend shifts at the hospital to off-set that cost, but a choreographer wasn't in the cards. She sighed, acknowledging that nothing extra was in the cards these days. "Did everyone do their paper routes?"

"Yep, this morning and after school."

"Did anyone give Lovey her medicine?"

At the sound of her name the old dog scrambled from her bed and tottered towards them, her diminished frame threatening to collapse beneath her, as indeed it did.

"Up a daisy, Beloved," Orlagh said, as she lifted the dog like a precious thing.

Molly smiled and pulled on Orlagh's silky braid. "Ah, you're good kids. Tell Angus I've got a Joe Louis for him."

A wretched mourn came from Angus's bedroom. Molly dropped the dish-cloth and ran upstairs to find Angus bent over, rocking back and forth; deep sobs shaking his stocky frame. Fiona stood beside him, her white hand, small against Angus's broad back. Her freckled nose was red and wet with tears, her curls shivering with the tremors that she tried, bravely, to subdue. Molly raised Angus's shoulders and saw the rigid body of Thor, his pet rat, cradled in his hands.

"Did I kill him?" Angus asked plaintively.

Thor had not been well these last few days. He coughed and shook. The vet had said to Molly that he had probably caught Angus's recent cold and it had become a secondary respiratory infection –pneumonia. "Who knew that rats could catch diseases from humans?" Molly had remarked at the time. Intravenous antibiotics had seemed to perk him up enough to bring him home, but ultimately, Thor succumbed.

"It wasn't your fault, Angus," Callum said from the doorway.

"No effort was spared," Fiona said, quoting her mother's pledge a few days earlier.

"That's right," Molly said, holding Angus's large, wet head close to her breast. "It happens."

"It's not fair, but it happens. He'll be with Dad now. Dad always wanted a rat."

"We'll give him a great funeral, Angus," Fiona promised. "I'll dress up all fancy, with flowers and we'll sing beautiful rat songs for him."

"Do you know any?" Angus asked, looking hopefully into her eyes. She hesitated and wiped her nose on her t-shirt, "Oh yes, I know lots of them. I'll only sing my favourites."

The solemn procession was lined up in front of the walk-out kitchen window waiting for Fiona, who was busy preparing a surprise. Angus held a shoebox in his large hands and stood immobile, head down, eyes swollen from the bitter sting of his grief.

Fiona came rushing down stairs with a sparkly wooden box in her hands offering it up to Angus. “This is for Thor,” she said, “Callum took his key chain collection out of it and gave it to me to decorate so that Thor would have a beautiful coffin.”

Molly felt her throat thicken. It was the box Cieran’s aftershave came in. The one she gave him the Christmas before he died. Callum had seen its potential for one his many collections and Molly had no doubt that he would have given some consideration to parting with it.

“Look,” Fiona whispered, her hands slowly pulling back the sliding lid. “Callum pasted his silk hanky inside. Isn’t it beautiful?”

It was the blue kerchief Molly had bought Callum to go with his Confirmation suit, now recruited for a higher purpose. Molly ran her fingers over the soft material. “Thor will be comfy in there.”

“Let’s show it to Thor, Angus,” Fiona said, her shoulders lifting with excitement.

Angus turned the box this way and that, so the glittering colours of the stars, suns and rainbows could be appreciated from all angles. “I know, for sure, that Thor liked sparkly things, cuz he ate some tinsel last Christmas.”

When he saw the inside, he turned and gathered Callum and Fiona into his arms. “Make one like this for me when I die,” he said.

“Yea,” Fiona promised, “but much bigger!”

Molly reached into a nearby grocery bag and produced a small pot of miniature daffodils. “Orlagh bought these for Thor’s grave. She was sorry she couldn’t be here because of practice but she says she’ll pray for his soul.”

Molly also pulled out a picture frame with a very flattering photograph of Thor in it. He was standing tall, his mouth was wide open and the extraordinary delicacy of his tiny, pink hands could not be missed.

Angus placed the rigid body of Thor into his casket with a last good bye. Molly took over when it came to closing it, as she anticipated some problem sliding the lid over Thor's ample abdomen. This she managed with unexpected ease and some relief. The solemn procession wound out the doorway and into the garden, where Callum had dug a hole large enough to fit a Labrador retriever.

The casket was lowered into the cavern and all had agreed that Fiona would begin the eulogy. This she did, with a relish that was almost disturbing in its detail. She reassured Angus that this rat had not done anything bad in his life. He hadn't ever bit Batman, the cat when the cat tried to eat him. Molly rolled her eyes remembering the times they had come home to find Batman draped over poor Thor's cage, willing him to move from a strategic center point that his paw could not reach. Fiona went on to explain that Thor was not involved in the Black Plague she had heard about from her teacher when she had wanted to bring Thor in for Pet Day at school. He was also a good listener and eater. She continued to commend him for almost never peeing on her when she held him, which she appreciated because it smelled bad. She began a song for him that she had seemingly made up as she went along and after several verses, some very familiar, Molly gently asked her to wind it up, which she did, reluctantly, as there were several more verses, but she ended with, "and he had the best teeth in the house!"

After that, there was very little more to say about Thor, that hadn't been said or sang. Angus rose from his squat beside the grave to speak and after two deep breaths and three failed attempts, found himself too overcome to say anything more than, ". . . my best friend."

Glynda

Glynda browsed the racks at Ginny's Boutique, stopping now and then to feel the crisp fabric of the new spring lines. *Finally, some bold colours to herald the cruise wear season. I could use a few new skirts to show off my legs,* she thought. *They're the one thing I don't have to work too hard to maintain,* and at that thought, she sucked in her stomach. *Shopping is always a good motivator to get to the gym straight from work. It curbs my appetite and stops me from reaching for that bag of chips when Edna starts on about something someone hadn't done for her correctly. No one can do anything right for Edna anyway.* Glynda recalled her mother-in-law pushing at the pretty beads she had bought her for her birthday, *rearranging them around that skinny, turkey neck of hers as if her touch would transform them into something she could appreciate.* Edna had bent closer to the mirror, turning her head this way and that and then stood back and pronounced, "They look a little cheap, I think."

Glynda feigned a smile and reassured her, "I don't think so, I'd wear them."

"Well, yes, I think they would suit you better, dear. You have them."

Glynda had felt her hands tingle. She wanted to reach out and pull the necklace tightly around Edna's throat until they made her eyes as round and red as the beads themselves. *Perhaps it's dementia*, she thought, although, a nagging doubt crept in when she acknowledged that Edna was like this years before. She remembered what Art had told her when she had asked him if his mother had made any comments when he introduced her as the girl he was going to marry. Edna had said, "That girl with the silly name, seemed very clean, if nothing else." Art, in his own way, tried to comfort Glynda by saying that Edna never said anything good about anyone, except her dead husband, Horace. Art also said that he believed that his father died early because Edna had slowly sucked the will to live right out of him. He described him as, "a man who had stopped struggling years ago and eventually became a dried up, fragile collection of grey flakes hanging on the sticky threads that was left of their marriage." That poetic image was in the note Art had written before he left the two women in his life forever to "turn Gay" as Edna put it. He had also siphoned a fortune from their joint estate and left Glynda largely dependent on Edna's good will – something Glynda never spoke of to anyone and something Edna never stopped pointing out. Glynda took comfort in believing the misery she endured from that woman would secure her a very gilded place beside The Saviour in the afterlife. Edna would be several floors below her smelling of sulphur.

The movie theatre was almost empty and so finding a seat to suit Edna's myriad criteria wouldn't be as difficult as last week. Glynda pointed to the middle of the fourth row up. Edna scowled and shook her head so forcefully that a splash of coffee spilled from the coffee cup onto her coat. "See what you've made me do? No, that's far too close." Edna's eyes scanned the theatre like a missile launcher.

Glynda pointed a few rows from the back and began her way to that row. She looked behind her to see Edna shuffling down the only row with a family of six already seated. A muffled squeal came from one of them as Edna's heel found a vulnerable foot. With a blatantly insincere, "pardon", Edna eventually placed herself and her large hat in front of a couple sitting in the row behind. Glynda could see the man behind raise his hands to his wife mystified why this woman had sat directly in front of them when she was surrounded by empty seats. Glynda walked around to the other side of the theatre so that there would be no need to disturb the family again and crouched low in her seat, beside Edna. The man behind them groaned again and with a curt, "excuse me", tugged his coat from behind Edna's back and moved several seats to their left for an unobstructed view. Edna cast him an imperious look, and pronounced to Glynda in a loud whisper, "How rude!"

This movie selection was not a success. There could be no doubt of Edna's displeasure as they left the cinema. "What are they thinking making a modern movie in black and white, with no talking in it? What nonsense is that? Artist, my foot, how can you call it art when it has no colour in it at all?"

"But it won the Oscar for best picture," Glynda offered feeling helpless.

"Puh! If I can find that pimply faced creature they call the manager here, I'm going to ask for our money back. When I go to the cinema, I pay for colour and sound and I expect to get it. Did you know it was silent, Glynda?"

"Well, yes. I guess I should have warned you, I forgot. But, you didn't like all the sex in The Bridesmaids last week, so I thought this would be a safe choice. I liked it. I thought it was sweet and entertaining."

"I can't say the dog didn't have talent, but really, otherwise it was a complete waste of money. Don't tell the manager you knew that it was silent. We can say they should have made that clear before we bought our tickets."

Glynda felt a spasm of panic. "No, no, we don't have time for that. I've made reservations at the restaurant for seven and we have to get there . . . what with traffic and all. It was my choice. I'll pay for it."

Edna sniffed and for once, shut her mouth tightly. This isn't the way to The Red Lobster," she said peevishly.

"I know," Glynda said, "I've got a surprise for you. We're going somewhere different tonight. I've made reservations at a new restaurant that's opened up called 'Cin Cin'. It's Italian. Flavio, a friend of mine from the choir is a part owner of it and I've heard good things about it. He's also part owner in The Mill, but you always say that's too expensive. It would be really nice to go somewhere different."

Glynda could see that scowl creep over Edna's face and that growl that rumbled into her voice whenever she didn't get her way, but this time Glynda was determined not to let her win; not this time. Glynda stood her ground.

"But, we always go for lobster and I like the crab cakes. You don't know what they've got at this other place. 'Chin Chin?' It sounds Chinese to me not Italian, and you know I only like one type of Chinese food. Italian – has too much garlic anyway. I get my reflux. I really think it would be better to go to a nice Canadian place." Edna's head did the turtle manoeuvre. It retracted into her collar and her chin disappeared into the multiple folds in her neck. Glynda resolved to ignore Edna's displeasure.

The parking lot was full. Edna pointed out that there was always parking at Red Lobster. Glynda countered that a full parking lot was a sign of a good restaurant and saw parking across the road. Edna said she didn't feel up to the walk. Glynda said she'd drop her off at the door, and as she pulled up to the curb she felt an overwhelming urge to push the old horror out of the car. "I'll be right back. Wait right there."

Glynda parked quickly and ran across the road to the restaurant. She opened its front door, expecting to find Edna waiting for her. She wasn't there. The young man at the desk smiled a beautiful Mediterranean smile and asked if she had reservations.

"Why, yes, under Wickseeed. In fact, my mother in law may be seated already. I dropped her off first," Glynda said, straining her eyes in the low light of the crowded restaurant, then thinking that Edna might be in the washroom.

Glynda sat uneasily at the table, sipping the water, the waiter had poured. She kept a keen eye on the washroom door near the entrance. Looking over her shoulder she caught sight of Flavio, who was serenading an enraptured young couple with his violin. He bowed his head discretely to acknowledge Glynda, following that with a sly wink.

Nervous that perhaps Edna had had one of her 'turns', Glynda decided to check if she was in the washroom. She looked under each of the occupied stalls for Edna's fat ankles, but did not find them. Curious, she went outside to the front of the restaurant to see if Edna might be there. A woman from the store beside Cin Cin's approached her and asked, with concern, "Is your name Linda?"

"No, Glynda. Are you looking for me?"

"Yes, that's it, Glynda. Your mother wandered in our store and is a little disoriented, I think. She told us that you'd taken off and left her."

"She did, did she? Well no, I just dropped her off because she didn't want to walk from the parking lot," Glynda said, irritation obvious in her voice.

"Oh, I understand . . . when they get that age. . ."

"Yes - but no, she's fine, nothing wrong with our Edna that a gun couldn't fix."

The smile fell off the woman's face. "We have to have patience with the elderly, you know, my own mother gets confused easily."

Glynda heard the judgement in the woman's voice and nodded, following her into the neighbouring store. Two other women were beside what they later called, 'the dear old thing', one rubbing Edna's frail, veiny hand.

"Edna," Glynda said, "what brought you in here? This is a fancy underwear store. Surely you're not ready to trade in your huge white briefs for frilly red knickers?"

Edna sent a sweet smile Glynda's way. "Oh no, dear, I got lost again. You shouldn't have left me in a strange place."

"Ahhh, yes, because you are incompetent," Glynda said, smiling back at her through tightly drawn lips. "I forgot - just like you do when things don't go your way."

The other women looked at each other, then back to Edna, uncomfortable and uncertain what to do. Glynda lifted Edna's arm firmly and said, "Thank the nice ladies for looking after you, *Mom*."

Back at the restaurant, she plonked Edna into the chair. "Well, too bad we started out on a bad foot," she said, staring squarely into Edna's small pale eyes. "I'm sure nothing more will go wrong. We are going to have a good time here tonight, aren't we?"

"Why, of course dear, whyever not?" Edna said, opening the large menu in front of her face as if she were closing a curtain.

The waiter took their orders and returned with a red wine for Glynda, followed by calamari, salad and a gnocchi entre. Edna had water and a bread stick, having found nothing on the menu to her taste. The ebullient chef came out from the kitchen and expressed his dismay that Edna had not eaten. He offered repeatedly to make her anything she wished, "anyting!" Edna shook her head firmly and sensing that she was not to be won over, his face communicated an apology and he retreated to the kitchen.

Flavio, swept over from another table, playing an opulent Neapolitan love song, while flirting innocently with Glynda. He knelt beside her and held her blushing gaze, while Edna wrung the neck off another bread stick. He raised himself gracefully and swung over to Edna just as the song reached a startling crescendo; his nimble fingers more than a match for it. Edna's head jerked to stare into his eyes like a chicken spying an insect and announced loudly, "I believe I may have soiled myself."

CLINICAL STUDIES: LEVEL II

AFTER A MORNING SPENT IN surgery with Anthea and her Assist, Dr. Gentile, Gavin wondered if he would ever claim the confidence that transforms those deft surgical manoeuvres into the seemingly casual gestures the two surgeons performed as they discussed recent Oscar moments. They had seemed to be part of the same organism; a four tentacled sea-creature governed by one brain. Instruments and suction pipes engaged in a synchrony that never needed the bark of a choreographer. Now and again Dr. Brock would interrupt the Oscar patter to draw Gavin's attention to a potential trouble spot; a rogue artery that needed discipline, while Dr. Gentile's lyrical bass would continue seamlessly. "Indeed, that Miss Jolie could use a few more pounds on her distressingly thin leg – oh! There's a bleeder - no problem, boss, I've got it."

"Glad I taught you so well, Dr. Gentile," she told the old man, watching his eyes crease until the deep-set black of them could no longer be seen. They had the familiarity of a long-married couple; confident in the other's support, content that no teasing comments would be misinterpreted as insult.

"I was once Dr. Gentile's student, Gavin, when I was training in England. He got me this job," Anthea said.

"I hate to think how long ago," Dr. Gentile ventured, the lilt of his voice aligning pleasantly with the Calypso music playing in the background. "I'm pretty sure I had my hair back then. Oh, I was a handsome devil in those days – like you Gavin." he remarked.

"You still are, Clive," Anthea said. "If you weren't so devoted to that wife of yours all the women would be throwing themselves at you."

"Ah yes, my bride, Audrey. I was lucky in love. At the first kiss, I was lost to other women."

"Don't want to hear about it Clive – remember, the only suction I get these days is in the O.R. – clamp right here, please." Blood spangled through the tissue as she made another incision

By the end of a long morning, the nervous sifting of so much information that seemed to be treacherous at the very time you needed it had eroded Gavin's confidence; so many subtleties that could turn a red herring into a missed diagnosis. The third flight of stairs tested Gavin's tired legs but, as he made his way to the Doctor's lounge, it was his mind that needed rest the most. Nevertheless, he skipped Anthea's offer of a quick cafeteria stop and opened his notes for the upcoming clinic, reviewing the clinical features of AIS along with the hormone profile and genetic karyotyping necessary for firm diagnosis.

Androgen Insensitivity Syndrome (AIS) is when a person who is genetically male (has one X and one Y chromosome) is resistant to male hormones called androgens. As a result, the person has some or all of the physical characteristics of a woman, despite having the genetic makeup of a man. The condition is divided into two main categories:

- *Complete AIS*
- *Incomplete AIS*

Complete androgen insensitivity (1:20,000 births) prevents the development of the penis and other male body parts. The child born appears to be a girl. Often not diagnosed until late puberty, they have no uterus, no axillary and pubic hair and cannot menstruate or achieve pregnancy. Their sensitivity to female hormones allows breast development. Testes may be found in the pelvis or other unusual part of the body and may be removed to prevent the possibility of malignancy.

Incomplete AIS patients may have both male and female physical characteristics to a greater or lesser degree. The vagina may be incomplete with partial closing of the outer labia; there may be a micro-penis and testes in the abdomen or other unusual part of the body.

He re-read the treatment protocol and possible physical and psycho-social complications of this fascinating condition. He remembered hearing that there was speculation that Wallis Simpson, the Duchess of Windsor had A.I.S., but knew little more than that. Dr. Brock had advised him to freshen up on it as she had a family of girls stricken with the disorder coming to see her for follow-up appointments in this afternoon's clinic.

Gavin found the obstetrical cases easier to manage than the vast spectrum of gynecological problems that were often laden with minefields of controversy. The complexities were over-whelming, as few were amenable to simple treatment options. Occasionally, the beauty of a cure by surgery presented itself – a hysterectomy for endometrial cancer or prolapse of the uterus, but more often than not, management of symptoms became a delicate balance of pros vs. cons; gains and losses measured, negotiated and agreed upon between practitioner and patient. There was the rub. Patients, as Dr. Brock had declared, were "either highly informed or highly miss-informed with nonsense taken and/or misapplied from talk shows, the internet or dubious health practitioners;' both had their challenges.

The afternoon clinic began with the quiet purr of computer keys tapping, syncopated with the regular flushing of toilets, as the obstetrical patients lined up to produce their routine urine samples. Molly came out and grabbed one basket of urine samples, taking the collection to test for protein and glucose.

Glynda saw Dr. Saxon's grand-daughter arrive and trot, pony tail bobbing, into the lunch room. She finished explaining the finer points of producing a perfect urine sample to the new patient and bolted into the lunch room. "Hello Georgia, how was your weekend?"

The teenager blinked to reveal glittery purple eye shadow decorating the upper orbits of her eyes; they were almost as shiny as the rhinestone rings that pierced the nasal septum, and her eyebrow. Her black hair sported random tufts of red and purple.

"Great," Georgia said. "I saw some porn at my boyfriend's house - pretty weird stuff, I don't know if I'm into that."

Glynda gasped.

"She's yanking your chain, Glynda," Carolina said as she breezed past and gave Georgia a high five. "But, before we get too chummy, my little porn star, you have *got* to be more careful with the filing. You do know your alphabet, don't you? Now, I know X is your favourite letter – especially when there's three of them, but, sadly, you've got to pay attention to the other ones too. Plus, you can't change their order. N should *always* come after M. This is *not* where you can express your creativity."

Georgia cocked her head, as if this was news to her. Glynda folded her arms and shot Carolina a look that let her know she was interfering. She spoke in a silky tone. "Georgia dear, you've just got to concentrate a little bit more. Maybe don't put that thing on your head when you work".

"It's called 'an iPod'," Georgia said, hands indicating quotation marks. "How will I hear my music without it?"

Carolina shook her head and leaned into her. "You don't, Sunshine. You do the job right or you'll be what's called, 'Fired'. By the way - love the eye shadow." And with that, Carolina flicked her hair with her hand, as she'd seen Georgia do so many times and strode off with a pronounced bounce in her step, pony tail swinging.

Georgia blew a large, pink bubble with her gum, popped it and said, "I'm not sure if I like her or not." Glynda nodded and attempted an awkward high five in agreement.

Shortly thereafter, Gavin and Anthea arrived and Anthea dashed to the washroom to wretch into the toilet bowl. This stomach upset was puzzling. *If I didn't have an IUD I'd think I was pregnant. That yogurt – lactose intolerance maybe?*

"All rooms fully loaded," Molly announced, and thrust a new OB chart into Gavin's hand.

Anthea looked through the day sheet and reminded Molly that The Patterson girls were coming first thing in the afternoon. "There are three sisters," she said to Gavin, "two with known A.I.S. and the youngest one has to be given more detail about the condition today. The older girls are just here for a check-up, so, Molly, when they arrive, put the parents in with the little one."

"Three, in one family?" Gavin asked, quickly reviewing the statistics in his mind.

"Yep, that beats the odds, alright. You probably won't see such a thing again. But, you have intelligent parents and kids in this case and you'll be surprised how well they're coping with it. They're successful, well-adjusted kids. I'll review it with you before you see them."

Georgia came out of the washroom and visibly staggered when she set eyes on Gavin.

"Oh Gavin," Anthea said, "this is Georgia, our high school co-op student. Georgia, this is Gavin our Med. student."

"Hi Georgia," Gavin said, "I guess we're both New Kids On The Block – eh – do you know them?"

"She was a fetus, Gavin," Anthea said. "Welcome to the old farts club."

"Georgia's green eyes sparkled as she looked up through the thick, black circles surrounding them. Her jaw slackened and her pretty mouth curled up at the ends to invoke a rather disturbing, predatory look for a fifteen-year-old.

"Ya, whoever," she said. "Maybe you can tell me more about them later."

Anthea, looked at Georgia, then looked directly at Gavin and mouthed, "Jailbait."

The back door to the clinic opened and banged shut. Carolina watched Angus, Molly's brother, shuffle sadly past toward the station they had set up for him to do his job. Glynda had posted his name on an authoritative looking plaque above his cubicle and ensured that he had his own stapler and hole punch, clearly identified with his name on it. Throughout the week they would all deposit work suitable for him to do during his bi-weekly visits. He would do these simple tasks with rigorous attention to the details whether it was putting stamps on envelopes or feeding the shredder. Having been told how sensitive patient information must be treated, he valued the title of 'The Shredator' that Carolina had bestowed on him. She had also made an equally authoritative looking plaque with this title on it and mounted it beside the one Glynda had made.

Beyond all this, Angus's favourite task by far, was refilling the gel squirt bottles, used with the doptone that assessed the fetal heart. He would place the soft plastic, three-litre container under his arm and squeeze the blue gel out of it, into the smaller containers. Air accumulations within the large container would inevitably erupt in a series of obnoxious sounds, which gurgled like vented body gas. These erratic farts could be heard throughout the office, in accompaniment to Angus's own paroxysms of laughter as each and every one made their presence known. Today, Carolina doubted that even that eagerly anticipated job would initiate joy in him, having heard about the tragic death of Thor. She gave Georgia money to go and buy Angus a sympathy card from them all,

"OMG, who died?" Georgia asked.

"A small but important friend of the family."

"A dwarf?"

Gavin restrained his response this time; for fear that it might be true. He did not want to insult Molly as he had Carolina previously. He just had a hard time knowing when these people were serious or not.

"No Georgia," Molly said, "it was a rat; Thor, Angus's pet rat." She crossed herself with reverence and Georgia followed suit.

"Are you Catholic Georgia?" Glynda asked.

"No, I just thought it looked cool."

Georgia's round eyes squinted as her head dropped sideways. "Awww, that's awful. Poor guy, but where am I going to find a dead pet rat card?"

The three Pattison girls were at the front desk with their parents, their epicene beauty, seen as a collective was striking to behold. They were slim, with the taut look of the elite athletes they were. The two older girls had faces that looked like they had been carved out of marble and the wide set blue eyes hung between glorious cheekbones and a strong brow. Brit was a pale blonde and Zoe had chosen to dye her hair a dark, glossy brown which only served to accentuate her startling eyes even more. The youngest, eight-year-old Carly, darker toned, looked nervous, her exotic brown eyes darting to various points of focus in the office.

Glynda took their health cards and welcomed them back. Brit and Zoe took Carly over to the baby photo corner where she giggled when she saw the large glittery sign that Glynda had made saying, 'Our Graduates'. It was like looking at a garden of flowers; some had the full blossomed look, with eyes and cheeks like a petal burst; others had the pinched promise of a bud not yet ready for the sunlight.

Anthea called Gavin into her office to review the girls' file, noting the estrogen dosages the older girls had been on to maintain their feminine physical characteristics. She explained that, seventeen-year-old Brit and fifteen-year-old Zoe had Incomplete AIS and had very similar presentations. The girls had testes in the abdomen removed as infants to prevent the risk of them becoming cancerous and the older two were using a dilator to try to expand the vaginal vault so that they could accommodate intercourse in the future. The youngest, Carly, was born with a micropenis – ambiguous genitalia. At just eight years old, she didn't understand the complexities of her condition and was asking her mother when she would get her period. The parents wanted this discussed in greater detail today with a view to reassuring the girls of their gender identity, which at present was firmly feminine.

Gavin was transfixed. "How do you reassure them?"

Anthea warmed to the subject. "I heard one expert on the issue use the most brilliant logic to help patients deal with this condition. He said that, the fact that these patients are by definition, insensitive to male hormones, they are in many ways more female than a 'normal' woman who has that sensitivity and is therefore influenced by both testosterone and estrogen. I liked that simplicity, but ultimately, like all of us, the brain will decide whether we are male, female, or a subtle blend of both or neither and that makes the whole issue a delicate conundrum."

Anthea noted the creases deepen in Gavin's forehead. "It's not to late to switch to pathology," she said, as she handed him the chart.

They entered the exam room where Carly sat with her legs swinging, sucking on a lollipop, very interested in discussing why she looked different 'down there'.

Anthea felt that Carly accepted her diagnosis well, the knowledge that her two sisters shared the problem seemed to normalize the situation. As they made their follow up appointments, a call came from the delivery room. Mrs. Capo was in mild labour and wanted her epidural before her face turned ugly and Mrs. Cheng was crowning with barely a change in expression. The good doctor abandoned the clinic immediately and Molly was left to explain the wait to the room full of women waiting. Molly had perfected her patter about 'babies being the bosses' and asked them all to 'please bare down' with them.

There was a weak acknowledgement of Molly's attempt at humour. Most often there was a good-natured acceptance of the fact that only a certain amount of planning could be imposed upon the world of obstetrics and gynecology; that they might be the cause of the next inconvenience.

The delivery room was humming and Anthea and Gavin were greeted by Cora, the Charge Nurse who yapped at her like a terrier. "Mrs. Cheng, Room 3 - precipitous delivery, quick, quick or you'll miss it."

They reached the delivery room in time to see a black thatch of hair open the bulging perineum. Anthea cued Bob The Nurse, who was prepared to do the catch if necessary and took over the duty just in time. The baby slithered out into the doctor's firm grasp and proceeded to loudly scold the adults for not being punctual.

"We've got one with a handle," Anthea announced. "It's a boy."

The shrieks of surprise informed everyone that the couple hadn't known the gender beforehand.

"Oh-oh!" Anthea said sharply. "Somebody catch him!"

Gavin responded and lunged toward Anthea, thinking she was about to drop the baby.

"Not him, – him!" Anthea said as she cocked her head upward, indicating Mr. Cheng, who was far paler than his original colour and was about to fall backward, in a faint. Gavin moved quickly, but Bob The Nurse, a six foot four, former University of Arkansas varsity line backer, arrived first to deftly pick Mr. Cheng up and cradle him very much like his son was being cradled by the doctor.

"Got it!" he said and Bob The Nurse carried his 'baby' out of the delivery room, so that they wouldn't have to step over him.

Anthea giggled. "Aren't we lucky to have scooped the only male delivery nurse in the province but also one who happens to be able to catch anything?"

Bob The Nurse looked over his shoulder and winked. "Glad to be of service, little lady!"

"That's 'Doctor Little Lady to you, cowboy," Anthea corrected. "Gavin, you can deliver the placenta. You may have to do a little massage to get it out first."

Gavin welcomed the opportunity to be fully in charge of something, having had even Mr. Cheng's welfare taken away from him. He attempted to coax the afterbirth from the uterus, but it proved harder to evict than either the baby or Mr. Cheng. Finally, he could see it descending the vaginal passage and asked Mrs. Cheng to push one more time. Her strong pelvic muscles thrust the placenta out in short order and the wobbly thing eluded Gavin's conscientious grasp. It landed on the floor with the sad thud of a water balloon.

"Got it!" said ever present Bob, who whisked it way as if running for a touchdown.

A dejected Gavin followed Anthea out of the delivery room. Anthea felt his disappointment and tried to console him. "Hey, don't sweat it. It's not like you dropped the baby."

Just then, the door opened again and Bob The Nurse came out with what looked like the newborn swaddled in his arms. He placed it, ceremoniously, in the astonished Gavin's arm saying, "Congratulations! It's a placenta!"

"Smile," Cora said, as Gavin looked up from the veined, quivering mass, in time for her to take a photograph in celebration of his first, if somewhat clumsy, delivery.

Down the hall, Mrs. Capo was holding a mirror up to her face and applying fresh lipstick. Upon seeing the doctor, she gave a nervous laugh and put it away. Anthea picked up her chart. "So, you're only a fingertip dilated, and your contractions are 30 minutes apart – probably a little early for an epidural. You should probably go home and wait until things get a bit more active.

"Doctor, I'm in pain. I don't react well to pain. I told you, I wanted a c-section, but ya wouldn't let me. Gimme the shot now, please."

"Mrs. Cappo, prudence would dictate that we wait until your labour is a little more established and a c-section is only done, if necessary."

"Who the hell's Prudence? If that's the snotty nurse who told me to go home before, I'm not going anywhere. I don't want to have my baby in the damn car. Massimo, say something, here!"

Massimo, her husband, fished a large almond out of his mouth, completely void of its chocolate covering and deposited it in a box full of equally denuded nuts by the bedside. He shrugged, shook his head and performed a series of mysterious gestures with his hands. Small, percussive squeaks came out of his mouth which was drawn apart like the neck of a balloon. Everyone waited politely for Massimo to formulate a sentence and when the wait became slightly embarrassing, Anthea repeated her request more firmly.

Mrs. Capo frowned, "What if I have the baby in the toilet like my friend did?"

"Then we'll call it John, or Lou – sorry, one of my favourites. Besides, you're a first timer – very unlikely that you'll go that fast."

Massimo let off a loud guffaw that startled everyone. "Lou, I like that."

The negotiations continued and Mrs. Cappo put her five-inch stilettos back on her swollen feet, against medical advice and said she'd be back later to see if her 'service' had opened.

When they left, Bob The Nurse held out the box of almonds that Massimo Capo had sucked bone-white with a smirk. Anthea waved her hand with a smile, declining his kind offer. She tried to banish the thought of the half-processed almonds from her mind, astonished to find that such a minor assault to the senses caused her stomach to turn.

As she picked up the phone a hearty thump on her back made her drop forward momentarily. The unmistakable boom of Dr. Saxon's voice followed directly. "Brock, ya've got me on the ninth and I told ya that's the one day I couldn't do."

She turned and looked up into his large, florid face which was looming over her like a predatory animal. His bull neck folded into his colossal shoulders, rivers of sweat finding their way from his forehead, disappearing into his O.R. greens. "Ya gotta change it. I've got a championship hockey tournament to play in, so fix it."

Anthea stared straight into where his pupils should be - a guess, because his eyes were overtaken by red pillows of skin. They reminded her of the slits in a Second World War bunker. His thick, white hair, longer than one would expect for a man of his era, gave the bunkers a snow-capped, Alpine flavour. "Dr. Saxon," she said, "you're unhappy with the call schedule again? Did you email me the On-Call Request Form?"

"I don't do that shit. I left a note in your box. Did ya check it?"

Anthea opened her mouth to insist that she did, but thought better of it lest she find a crumpled strip of paper stuck to the back of the box like his last submission. "Was it on the proper form that I gave you and not a ratty little scrap like last time?"

"It was on paper. I wrote on paper."

Anthea knew the argument was pointless and she had to get back to the clinic. Gavin stood, uncomfortably beside her, trying not to attract Saxon's attention. Saxon's paw reached around him and grabbed a handful of the white almonds from the box on the desk. He threw them quickly into his mouth and crushed them, his jowls quivering with each assault.

"Good nuts," he said, a renegade piece escaping his mouth and landing on Gavin's neck.

Anthea took a deep breath to combat another wave of nausea and said, "I'll see to it."

Back at the office Anthea frowned when she saw the name Hilda Kroeger. She explained to Gavin that Hilda was just two weeks post hysterectomy and was reporting significant bleeding. Molly's notes indicated no obvious signs of infection or pain which was reassuring, but Anthea remembered this hardy, no nonsense, eighty-five-year-old German woman and had an inkling of what might be occurring. She entered the exam room, followed by Gavin.

"Mrs. Kroeger, you told Molly that you're fine with the medical student examining you?" Mrs. Kroeger responded in heavily accented English. "Indeed, Doktor. Vee all haf to learn to do our job vell, ya? Body parts are body parts. Vee get on wis it, ya?"

Anthea smiled and introduced Gavin to Mrs. Kroeger. He summoned his most professional demeanour as he lifted the drape covering her legs. "Nice to meet you, Mrs. Kroeger."

"Call me Hilda, meine liebe. Unt don't be shy."

"Now, I hear you've been having some bleeding the last few days. Exactly how much – spotting - like a period or soaking a pad?"

Hilda reached for a plastic bag she had laid beside her and pulled out a few bloody pads, waving them like the small flags people flap when the Queen's doing a Royal Walkabout. She had studiously kept them to illustrate the amount of bleeding she'd had over the last two days. "Before zat I had a beeg gush, unt soaked shroo mien oontervear, but now it iss much bettah. I vasn't going to bozzer you, but mein daughta, she made me. Vat a fuss."

"Well your daughter is right. A large amount of bleeding at this stage should be followed up. What were you doing at the time? Were you walking around a lot?"

Hilda looked puzzled. "Ya, off course! I can't clean out za cow shed lying in mein bed, can I?"

Anthea nodded, her suspicions confirmed. "Hilda, you've been a bad patient! I did tell you that you would have to take it easy for six to eight weeks – no heavy lifting."

"Ya, I only sweep unt lift a few vegetable crates, - zat iss all."

Anthea was skeptical. "What was in them?"

"Potatoes."

"Potatoes?" Anthea repeated. "Hilda, they don't make women like you anymore, but, promise me that you'll get some help for the next little while. You can't be doing so much or you won't heal well. There doesn't seem to be any infection. This bleeding is probably from strain."

"But zey were only smoll potatoes!"

Anthea shook her head.

"Heavy bleeding is never 'small potatoes', Hilda."

Only Gavin appreciated the pun.

"OK, OK, Doktor, I vil get Volfie, my husband, to do moa."

"How old is Wolfie?"

"He iss ninety-von.

The last patient made a follow up appointment and the day's wrap-up began.

"Some patients just make your day," Anthea said as she recalled the woman's husband who had asked what their return policy was for ugly babies.

"What did you say?" Gavin asked.

"I said it was a strictly no return policy, because we only deliver beautiful babies, and that's exactly what I'd told his mother when she tried to make a return."

Gavin smiled. "Boy, I can see that I have to get some snappy answers in my arsenal. That was the same guy who asked me if I knew whether Dr. Brock would allow them to film the delivery because he wanted a sequel to the conception."

"And what did you say?" Molly asked.

Gavin paused and shrugged, looking disappointed in himself. "I said I'd ask Dr. Brock! – OK, I'm a loser!"

Molly winced as she carried the bucket of used speculums to the sink. Arching her aching back, she said, "Guess who was up until midnight last night trying to help make up a gymnastics floor routine? My daughter, Orlagh, is in gymnastics," Molly explained to those who wouldn't know. "She's trying to get into the upper group and to do that she has to place in the top three All-Around scores at a qualifying meet. Imagine, *me* in the basement, in *tights,* trying to come up with some *moves!* The only good moves I've ever had in my life were bowel movements – my dancing career began and ended when I ruptured a bursa doing 'The Bump'."

Carolina put her finger on her lip and looked up. "Hang on, I'm still working on the image of you pinging around your basement in tights . . ." Carolina put her finger to her head and struck a thoughtful pose. "Yea . . . it's not pretty – how'd it go?"

Molly's face gave them the answer.

"And there's another reason I'm glad I don't have kids," Carolina noted.

"Oh, believe me," Molly said, "They grow on you."

"Yea, like mold . . . with snot."

Anthea understood. "I wish I could help, but there's a reason I'm a surgeon and not a dancer. My ballet teacher asked my mother not to bring me back. She said my mouth was much more active than my feet. But, guess what? I've enrolled in ballroom dancing lessons to find a new teacher to torture. I've got my first class tonight."

Georgia, very carefully, filed the discarded charts back into the filing cabinets, trying to suppress any creative energy. She took a minute to find Molly scrubbing the red gore off some scary looking instruments. Georgia put her hand up to her mouth and gagged loudly. Molly looked sideways at her and asked her if she was planning to help clean up the mess or make another one.

"Soooo, gross," Georgia whispered as she gagged again. "Ummm, yea, Molly, can we talk somewhere else, where there's no insides hanging off anything?"

Molly loaded the autoclave with instruments and turned the knob to begin its cycle. She took off the lab coat and gloves and turned to Georgia, "Yes, my dear. What can I do for you? Condoms? Lube? Pregnancy test?"

Georgia gave a wry grin. "All three, please!"

Molly gave no sign of doubt.

"Kidding!" Georgia chirped. "It's more about what *I* could do for *you*."

"Explain," Molly said.

"Well, I heard about you trying to make a floor routine for your daughter, and I can help you with that. I was a National Level gymnast and I *loved* doing choreography - AND I had some great moves in my routines that I could teach Orlagh."

Molly's eyes widened as she comprehended what Georgia had offered. "Really?"

"Really! I'd be glad to help. It'd be fun - AND, don't worry, I was *really* good."

"Really? *Really* good?" Molly repeated, her face full of hope and appreciation. "You'd do that for us? I could pay you something."

"Nope, not necessary. I'm doing this for my soul."

"You're worried about your soul?"

"Yep, I'm not sure, but I think I may be spoiled. So, I'm going to do something for nothing and I'd much rather do choreography than work with ugly people at the food bank."

Privy to her noble purpose, Molly decided to accept this gracious offer for the good of Georgia's soul.

Carolina put the patient results into a file folder and carried them into Anthea's office. She hesitated to leave, waiting for Anthea to finish narrating the dictation she was working on. Anthea paused and looked to Carolina.

Carolina scratched her head, seeming, at an uncharacteristic loss for words. Anthea waited for them. "Ummm," Carolina began, "Just an off the cuff question. Can you catch an STD by being in a hot tub with someone who has one?"

Anthea's face didn't betray the curiosity that the question had caused. "Well, I would say no; there are chemicals in the water and you'd need pretty close physical contact for contamination."

"Even if you didn't have a bathing suit on?"

"Again, you'd have to have intimate physical contact." Anthea repeated very slowly. She was determined not to ask why, resolving to let Carolina tell her the details on her own volition.

"OK, thanks," came the reply as Carolina bounced out of the room.

Best to leave it like that, thought Anthea as she opened the results file to see Melinda Thackery's positive gonorrhoea status.

HOMECARE STUDIES: LEVEL 111

Anthea

THE PILE OF CHARTS WAS slowly whittled down to the point where Anthea could see over them. It was 6:30p.m. and she had just enough time to stop for a sub before her ballroom dancing class. A wave of childish anxiety came over her as she anticipated her first day. *What if I'm the worst in the class? What if they've all taken classes before and I'm the one the instructor always has to stand beside to go over the moves again and I still don't get them? What if I trip?* She pulled out the dance shoes she'd bought and looked at the height of the heel.

The dance studio was in a tired-looking strip mall right next to a dollar store. She was tempted to go in for a quick look for all those must-have things that you don't know you need, and end up spending a lot more than a dollar. *What happened to your chip bag before you found the plastic clips to close an opened bag? Just how many spatulas should a kitchen have?* These are the questions that haunt a dollar store addict. So, she slipped in and spent sixty dollars on ridding her mind of having to find the right top for the Tupperware for at least another few months, when they would all mysteriously disappear to wherever the other sock goes.

Having thus stalled her entrance again, she willed herself to open the door of the dance studio. A woman of impossibly perfect proportions lit up the dim hallway with a wide smile as she glided to sit behind the desk. Elizabeth Belamy could have been anywhere between fifty and seventy as

Anthea surmised that she was probably an older woman who had a good surgeon or a younger woman who looked her appropriate age.

"Hello," Anthea said, "this is a beginner's class isn't it? I want to make sure that there's nowhere lower you can put me."

"Oh, my dear, I have coached the most uncoordinated of people and I tell you what, they always get better - never worse!"

"Comforting," Anthea said, as she walked through to the cloak room and began putting her dance shoes on. On the other side of the panel she could hear a man's voice talking to a classmate. "I tell you, it really pissed me off. I'll have to wait another season to breed her now. You know how haughty and aloof Brits sound, even when they're apologizing. You *know* they don't really mean it when they say they're '*owfully* sorre, *reeeaaly* I em. It's owll reeeaaly rother funne, isn't it?' and make you look like the jerk without the sense of humour."

A cold chill ran through Anthea's spine. *It's him. It's the dog fucking guy: the fucking dog guy. Shit. Shit. Shit. And what the hell's he talking about? He doesn't have a sense of humour – the jerk!* She felt the fight or flight impulse overtake her; flight seemed appropriate. A warm hand grabbed hers and pulled her into the studio. Elizabeth wound her through a turn and set her into the middle of the floor. "Let's all form a circle and introduce ourselves."

The others came forward and Anthea waited for the moment of recognition from The Jerk. He came to stand beside her where she smelled his very pleasant aftershave, noting that he had great shoulders and a profile worthy of a Roman coin. He gave a shy glance in her direction with a nod and a suggestion of a smile – no hint of recognition. It dawned on her that at that first, unfortunate meeting, she had sunglasses on and a sweatshirt with a hood pulled over her hair -rather a good disguise if that was what she was intending. She returned his smile and was about to speak when she stopped herself. When she began to speak again, she put on her best Canadian accent.

Looking directly at Anthea, Elizabeth Belamy asked that each of the class members say why they wanted to dance. Anthea collected herself. "My name is Anthea Brock and I am *not* a dancer." She then tried a quick deflection, "and who are you?" pointing to 'The Jerk' who stood next to her. Elizabeth cut in before he had a chance to begin. "Strange, I could have sworn you had a British accent when you first came in."

"Oh no, I'm a canoe-carrying, Mountie lovin', maple syrup sippin', Tim Horton's drinkin' Canadian eh?" She found herself saluting as she said this and cringed when everyone responded with forced laughter at her little pantomime. She could smell the wet paint from the little corner she had put herself into. *Idiot.*

"Well, after all of that, you've managed not to tell us anything about yourself, Anthea. Go on, give us something," Elizabeth said.

Anthea made it a policy not to introduce herself as a gynecologist in a social situation because she knew she would spend rest of it giving advice on vaginal itching – and that's just the men. She recalled being loudly questioned when lined up at the meat counter by a woman who wanted to document her haemorrhagic bleeding episodes. The fact that this woman held ticket number three and Anthea, number nine, prolonged the exchange, since after being served, the woman came to stand in line beside her holding a bloody roast in her hand like a dismembered body part – which, in reflection, it was. The woman was of Russian extraction and spoke as if she were trying be heard in Moscow without the benefit of technology,

"Doktor, I have massive blooding . . . big chonks come from my pee pee, beeg as thees rrrost." She held the bloody thing up to Anthea's nose, shaking it for added effect. "I so estonish, I want fall down. Toilet bloddy – like big sacrifice, all over – rrreally, rrreally – beeg mess."

Anthea noticed the middle-aged man who had been waiting behind The Russian, had began to turn an unpleasant colour. He had been watching the meat clerk slap a large, trembling, calf liver he had ordered onto the scales in front of him. He waved his hand weakly and turned away, walking quickly toward the exit.

No, unless someone recognized Anthea, the pride of waving her title around had long worn off. So, she said, "I'm a health professional, who wants to try doing something dangerous – scrap-booking was full so I signed up for dancing."

At the end of the class, Anthea was pleased with herself. She had managed not to arouse any suspicion in the increasingly attractive Jack and not to savage the fine bones in Elizabeth's pretty feet when she partnered with her. She thought she might be evaluated somewhere near the top of the class in terms of aptitude, beaten handily by a gloriously beautiful, young couple who were in a class of their own, gliding around like a Disney finale, her neck curved over her shoulder and her back arched, in that uncomfortable pose you see professionals do. Anthea realized that years of being bent over a patient in surgery had rounded her shoulders and just standing with them straight was enough to think about at this point.

Elizabeth praised everyone's efforts and even offered one sulking wife a morsel of hope by saying that at least her husband had moved more than he would have if he had been home on the couch. Ecstatic with this praise, he put his arms up in triumph and suggested they go for beer and chicken wings.

Anthea could feel her legs tingling with the warmth of exertion and the surprise that there had been any was reassuring. She guessed that new muscles had been recruited into the task of trying not to crush Elizabeth's little cat paws. Even if the social prospects were poor, at least she'd get some exercise and learn a new skill.

As she collected her belongings from the cloak room she answered a call from her travel agent confirming her flight plans. This resurrected the cosy thought of being back at The Cwtch.

The Cwtch was a sprawling stone farmhouse that clung to the shoreline of Rhosilli Bay in the Gower Peninsula of Wales. Sian Gryffydd, Anthea's mother, had grown up in that home, named by her grandfather. Like most Welsh homes, grand or humble, it was elevated beyond stone and mortar and its unique personality acknowledged by a christening. Her great-grandfather had aptly referred to it as his 'Cwtch', using the Welsh word for cuddle or 'place to cuddle'. Just saying, "The Cwtch", summoned in Anthea a sense of belonging, a sense of being where she was meant to be and returning to its fold never failed to bring her peace. There was nowhere she could feel closer to her mother than there.

She let a ripple of sadness be nudged away by imagining the faces of her brother, Gryff's three kids. Edwyn, was just six months old when she last saw him. She let herself recall the delight she felt inhaling his sweet breath as he made a wet assault to suck on her nose. He was like a chubby Lamprey eel seeking a victim. His seven-year-old brother, Lewis, mostly a rambunctious terror, showed great restraint and interest in Edwyn as his personal possession. Four-year-old, Cordy, or 'Cordy Cordelia Gryffydd Brock' as she liked to be called, without concession to the amount of effort it took to address her, had less affection for the usurper. She called Edwyn, 'The Bad Baby' and she would secretly pinch him when she thought no one was watching. Then, batting her cool, saucer eyes at any curious adult, she would shrug and announce, "He cries a lot."

The gut wrench Anthea felt now, when she talked or even thought of those kids disturbed her. She had never felt it before her mother died, but suddenly they had become more precious, more necessary. She couldn't deny a new vacillation occupying her mind - some sort of insidious panic tied to that irritating drip of hormones spilling into her veins. *Perhaps the certainty that it is destined to go silent is praying on my mind. Was this grief? Mortality? Or, heaven help me – loneliness, gnawing at my resolve to remain childless?* Until recently, she had never acknowledged a lonely day in her life. There had just been days without the distraction of pleasing anyone else.

"You look far away. What's on your mind?" Elizabeth had her wrap around her shoulders and keys in her hand. Anthea apologized for keeping her and left the building.

The evening was kind for spring; the chill of the day before having been sucked out of it, leaving a fresh promise of redemption from winter's catacomb. Anthea took a deep breath and bit down on her bottom lip to suppress a tremble. She wasn't cold. She put her head down and opened the car door as she waved goodbye to Elizabeth from the empty parking lot.

As she sat in the driver's seat listening to Leonard Cohen groan his plaintive ode to a famous blue raincoat, she could feel her chest tighten trying to restrain an emotional impulse. She gave into it, throwing her head back, closing her eyes and opening up her throat, full throttle, to sing along. The dashboard began to blur into dribbles of red and white light.

A loud knock on the car window interrupted Anthea's melancholy duet, startling her into another full throttle release of her favourite word. Jack's face was pressed against her window. He was pointing and shouting but couldn't be heard over Leonard. She let the window down to hear him say that she had a flat tire on the passenger side of the car.

"Oh fuck! Thanks," Anthea said, "thanks a lot, Jack. I've got a spare in the back." She got out of the car and opened the trunk.

"Do you know how to change a tire?" he asked, seemingly astonished at the prospect.

"It's the first thing my dad taught me - wouldn't let me take driving lessons until I could change one in my sleep."

"Oh, good, do you mind if I watch? I don't know how to do it myself but maybe I can help."

Anthea grabbed the storm bag and emergency medical kit from the trunk along with an embarrassing number of empty wine bottles. She lifted the panel and cursed again when she saw that the spare was not there. She'd forgotten to put it back. This was another good reason for missing the men in her life. Her father and Ian always took care of things like that. Neither of them would have ever let that happen. She'd been in a rush and left it in the garage, planning to do it, but never following through.

"I'll have to call C.A.A.," she said, mildly embarrassed that she had led Jack to believe she was so competent. When he offered to drive her home, her fatigue won out. She knew he lived close by and she could get the car towed and deal with it tomorrow.

They pulled up to the outbuilding on her property and she thanked him but dismissed the thought of inviting him in for coffee. It was late and she had an early start in the morning. He lived next door and there would be better opportunities to socialize. She opened the house door and realized that she had left her tote bag in his car. She quickly trotted back down the path to find Jack pinned up against his Land Rover, his back arched and head turned over his right shoulder, in perfect ballroom posture trying to avoid Spock jumping like a wild thing up to his face.

Anthea pulled Spock off him apologetically.

"Yea, I get it now," he said. "You're the crazy British woman and that's the little bastard who knocked up my Scarlet!"

Carolina

Nothing in the small bungalow had been updated since 1975, but everything shined like new. The surfaces were cleaned with a toothbrush so that the joints did not collect dust or oils that might betray their age. The toaster was taken out each morning from its original box, used gently, shined and then replaced in that box, under the counter. Every small appliance got the same treatment and with a few disappointing exceptions, they were still perfectly functional. One sturdy wooden drawer below the orange melamine counter opened to reveal sub-divided compartments that separated pencils, note pads, tape, sharpeners garbage ties, coupons, scissors and multiple other useful tools - grouped, stacked and labelled so that no common rifling would be necessary to find what was needed. This was the part of Carolina's brain that did not allow the chaos of the other parts to wander in.

Tonight, she had planned to make lasagna with the home-grown tomato sauce she had retrieved from the cantina in the basement. She put a clean table cloth on the dining room table so that the fresh pasta could be laid to dry on it, and then brought out the eggs, and flour in preparation to mix the dough. Lastly, she put on the Neapolitan CD her mother had brought from Italy and filled a large glass of red wine to the brim. She dug her hands into the soft, white belly of the dough, massaging it until the birth of what her mother called, "La Bambina".

The vision of Lucia as a young mother playfully folding the thick, cylindrical mass into a tea towel and placing it in young Carolina's eager arms came to her mind. Carolina would carry it around the kitchen, singing to it, rocking it, patting its bottom as if trying to calm a crying child. Later, they would coax it into long, thin ribbons fit for the "neck of a beautiful

Signorina" and these would eventually be layered with the rich blood of the tomato sauce, the flexible tendons of mozzarella cheese and lightly seasoned meat to create their masterpiece.

Carolina cut one piece to keep for herself and wrapped up the rest of it to take into work, as the phone rang. Carolina answered it flatly.

"Carolina? It's Melinda."

Surprise filtered into Carolina's voice. "Melinda? How's it goin', girlfriend?"

"What the hell's on your radio?"

"That's a Neapolitan love song about lust, infidelity, rage and revenge. Just a sec, I'll turn it down."

"Huh, does it mention my name in it? They're playin' my song."

Carolina made a face. "No, it can't be; it doesn't mention gonorrhea."

"Hilarious."

"You did give your husband the prescription Dr. Brock gave you for him, didn't you? Wouldn't want that poor guy to be blind as well as have a broken jaw."

"Does gonorrhea make you blind?"

"No, relax, just kidding. That's syphilis."

". . . which I don't have, right?"

"Right."

"You're positive?"

"Yes, I'm positive that you're negative for syphilis."

"Shit," Melinda smirked, "blindness might be a blessing. At least then Daniel couldn't see how bad he looks. He's still drinking through a straw. You've got a hell of a right hook."

"Yes, I know, it's not the first time I've used it."

"Well, I thought you'd like to know, he's not going to press charges. I took care of that."

"Good, because I've already got an assault charge pending –it wouldn't look good to have another one so soon." Carolina anticipated Melinda's interest and smothered it before it had chance to blossom. "Don't ask."

Melinda took the advice. Carolina reached for her cigarettes and refocused on the subject at hand. "The guy's a fuckin' saint, Melinda."

This wasn't anything Melinda didn't know, but hearing it from Carolina lit it up like a neon sign. Her voice trembled. "He's moved out - until his head clears, is what he said."

"I won't preach, but what are you gonna do?"

"I've got a bit of a plan."

"Don't you have any better friends than me? If I'd have known you were such a loser, I wouldn't have hung out with you."

"Yea, but you're the loyal type."

"Yep, I've never let a week-long relationship get spoiled by gonorrhea before, why start now? Come on over. I've got lasagna for you."

The large, water glasses that served as wine glasses in Carolina's home sat on the kitchen table. Beside them, a bowl of home-made nuts and bolts, lovingly made by Glynda and presented to the office staff with great ceremony, would serve to curb her appetite as she waited for Melinda to arrive. Carolina turned the toasted shreddie around with her fingers. *No fucking competition for my lasagna.* After two or three minutes of waiting, she decided to count Melinda as late and re-filled her glass to the brim.

The door bell rang as Carolina feasted on a pretzel stick and opened the door. Melinda was loaded down with brown paper bags that made a clinking sound. *Bells calling the faithful,* thought Carolina as she welcomed Melinda with a kiss on both cheeks.

"I was just going to drop some stuff off at the dry cleaner and that word 'dry' made me pick up the phone and see if you were home. The girl needs some company," Melinda said.

"I'm with ya there, honey. I feel like shit too."

"What's with you? You've got the perfect life."

"Oh yea, welcome to Happy Land." Carolina poured what was left of the wine and gave it to Melinda. "Cheers."

Melinda waved her hand. "Wow, I haven't even got my coat off yet."

"What? You can't take your coat off with a drink in your hand? What are you, an amateur?"

"Well, if you're gonna insult me. You'd better keep my hands busy, so I can't hit ya. On second thoughts, I don't think my right hook can compete with yours - keep the drinks comin' baby."

Carolina felt an uncomfortable but mercifully infrequent feeling of remorse descend upon her. "How is Daniel anyway? Ya know, the guys got a glass jaw."

"He's stopped using the straw now, so that's good. But he's not willing to move back in until I promise to go to therapy again."

"Well, what d'ya call this?" Carolina said chinking her glass against Melinda's.

Melinda sighed, "I was never right for him. He should have married, Cindy, the girl his parents wanted him to marry. She's boring, but after me, he might enjoy that."

Melinda took a deep drink and looked around the small, orange kitchen. She felt at home here. Sitting on the plastic of the aluminum chair took her back to the one she'd sat in as a child; to the kitchen where she told her father she'd been accepted to nursing college. She was the first of her family to apply to a post high-school institution. She remembered the change in his face at that moment, the one she realized was pride. She also remembered his flat acceptance that it had all been too good to be true when she later told him she was dropping out to support Daniel through his schooling. Daniel's parents had cut him off when he had announced his intentions to marry her. They had warmed up briefly when the prospect of children arose, but after successive miscarriages ended any hope, they renewed their subversive campaign against her.

"He's with them now," Melinda said. "We were supposed to go to a fund raiser tonight, so he took them instead. They're at The Fairmont right now. That old bitch of a mother of his is probably chewing his food and spitting it into his mouth as we speak."

Carolina patted her hand while refilling their glasses. "Here, have a nut . . . or a . . . a bolt? Or whatever the fuck you call the other shit that's in there."

"What were your parents like, Carolina? Did you come from a happy home?" Melinda asked.

Carolina's eyes looked up, as if into the past, her head swayed side to side, taking the measure of the situation. "Yea, in a really fucked up kinda way."

"Is there any other kind?" Melinda said, sincerely.

"My Mom, Lucia, was a sweet little Italian lady, who could ignore shit even if she was sitting in it. She adored my father, and he adored her. She was a seamstress, a tailor really. She'd make my dad suits that made him look like the '*Bella Figura'* he wanted to be seen as."

Melinda's puzzlement prompted Carolina to elaborate. She explained that *Una Bella Figura,* is an Italian expression for casting the proper image, of beauty, style, taste and behaviour. The Italian consciousness of how they dress, the quality of the fabric, the details, even when they don't have money, you present yourself with the one good outfit you own with a certain standard of care. "Like my style. It's all about the details."

Melinda choked on her wine, coughing until her face turned the same colour as it. Carolina slapped her back attentively. "Slow down there, you old wino. Do you want a funnel?"

Melinda shook her head and stared into Carolina's face looking for some evidence of sarcasm, but found none, so she said nothing.

Carolina warmed to the subject. "My mother always said that my father was a 'business man', but there was no business that I could figure out. He kept unusual hours, never talked about his work and I never met anyone he worked with. That is until he was found hanging from a bridge with his hands tied behind his back. At his funeral, I met all kinds of hard faced men who kissed our cheeks with tears in their eyes and called his death a terrible accident. Did they think I wasn't going to find out the truth? That I didn't read papers? But always, to my mother, my father was, "*Una Bella Figura*" – go figure."

"Did you love him?"

"More than anything. He was the gentlest crook I ever knew. He made me feel like I was the most precious thing in the world. He'd tell me how smart I was. He'd buy – or shoplift – books for me - built a little library for me. He'd pick up my favourites and ask me to tell him about it. I'd tell him to read it – I'm not sure, but he might have been illiterate – in English anyway." Carolina's face softened. "I loved him so much."

"Have you ever been married?"

"Naaa, I've never found a man like my father – criminal activity aside."

"Maybe, you haven't let a good man love you."

"I just think I bring out the worst in them."

Melinda contemplated this. "I don't seem to need anyone to bring out the worst in me. It's just what I do. Daniel is a good man, *too* good for me. My shrink says I fear abandonment, so I provoke it as a test. Does that sound familiar?"

"You mean, maybe it's us not them?"

"I heard someone say once that the greatest gift is not being loved, it's being able to love," Melinda said wistfully.

"Hmmm, that's heavy shit. Who said that, your therapist?"

"No, Daniel."

"Sooooo, maybe it *is* us?"

The two women considered this momentarily and a low, gutsy laugh rose to smother some uncomfortable truth. Their heads, heavily marinated by now, fell together across the table.

"Naaah!

Melinda sank back into the chair and bathed herself in the details of the kitchen. "I love this room. I feel good here."

"You've got a thing about man-made textiles?

"I guess. It's honest in a fake sort of way."

"Like you!" Carolina said, allowing a smile to crawl across the harsh angles of her face.

This comment startled Melinda as it sank into her consciousness like a pebble shattering a smooth surface, droplets of truth thrust up into the air to be examined in the daylight.

Carolina let it be. "Yep, nothin' in this house has been touched since the seventies. I've thought about updating, but no point really – maybe when I find my father's 'stash' that my mother was always looking for. He called it my 'university fund'. My mother's plan for me was a rich husband."

"He left some money?"

"So my mother said. She was convinced that before he was killed, he hid some in the house here. Her guess is that he was probably killed over the short fall."

"Wow, so have you looked?"

Carolina remembered her mother combing every nook and cranny, seeing her small, busy hands pretending to clean, but searching, examining every joint, every crack, every unexplained mound in the garden. "She never found a thing. I think she didn't want to believe that he left us with nothing. Sad isn't it? She needed to believe that he loved us enough to risk doing that. That's her mythology."

"Wouldn't he have told your mother where it was, if he'd hidden money here?"

"Maybe he was afraid they'd come after her. Who knows? There probably wasn't any. Anyway, what's this plan of yours?"

Melinda stared into Carolina's misty, black-rimmed eyes as an idea formed in her mind,

"Carolina, do you trust me?"

"Why do I need to?"

"Because we're going on an adventure, but you have to trust me and don't give me any bullshit."

"Once again, why would I need to?"

"I'm going to be Henry Higgins and you're going to be my Liza Dolittle!"

"Pygmalion and Galatea?"

Melinda cocked her head, a moment of confusion settled on her face. "OK, I'll bite. What the fuck's that?"

Carolina launched into the Greek myth about a sculptor called Pygmalion who turns his creation into a real woman called Galatea and pointed out that Eliza in My Fair Lady was an adaptation of this.

"I like the name Liza better, Galatea sounds like a fuckin' yogurt brand."

"I think it's a beautiful name. I like those ancient names like Aglaia, Euphrosyne and Thalia, don't you?"

"My God, they sound like diseases – I've got euphrosyne of the bowels and I can't leave the toilet."

"Melinda! Euphrosyne is one of The Gratiae - the Three Graces, Aphrodite's attendants. They represent charm, beauty and creativity – not a bowel condition!"

"Well, aren't you the mystery? Ya know, sometimes I wonder where you come from. How do you know all this crap?"

"I read."

"So do I – OK, mostly magazines, but haven't stumbled over those gals so far. What are you reading?"

Carolina shrugged and looked away, knowing that Melinda didn't really want to know.

"OK, *Miss Piggy-malion*, or whatever the fuck her name was," Melinda said, "Here's my plan. We're gonna crash the fund raiser."

Melinda rushed out to the car and brought in three gowns she'd brought with her. She held each one of them under Carolina's chin, evaluating them for fit and colour. "You're gonna be gorgeous when I'm done with you and there are a lot of rich, single men for you to prey on. Besides, I'm not going to let my mother-in-law talk about me behind my back, without looking me in the face."

"That's a Yogism"

"A what?"

"A Yogism – a malapropism where the last part of the phrase contradicts the first part. Yogi Berra, the baseball coach was famous for them."

Melinda sighed, "I know you're gonna, so please explain in agonizing detail."

Carolina smirked. "It's physically impossible for your mother-in-law to talk about you behind your back, while looking you in the face – see?"

Melinda raised an eyebrow. "It isn't if she's two faced"

"Well done."

The cigarette smoke curled into Carolina's eyes, making her squint as she grabbed the strapless, red, sequined number that she was instantly attracted to. Melinda winced and held up a long, deep purple gown. "I was thinking of this one. It's a bit more . . . elegant and . . . generous. You're a little bigger than I am."

"Nope, this is my dress. It's definitely me."

Carolina writhed into its heavy bodice, the pleasant waft of Melinda's perfume still clinging to its fabric. The skirt had some give to it as she pulled it over her hips, thanks to an inset of gathered silk on one side that offered a playful glimpse of the thigh when she moved. "Sexy" she said as she twirled in front of the mirror. The dress obediently lifted outward with the turn and came dutifully back into a tight silhouette when she stopped.

Carolina's breasts were thrust up, not far from her chin, as Melinda strained to close the back of the dress. "It's a bit short . . . and tight, don't you think?"

Carolina reached into the bra cups to rearrange her breasts, resulting in an even more precarious mammillary landscape. "Perfect," she sighed

Melinda realised that things were not going according to plan, and insisted that the purple dress would be a better fit.

"It's boring, you wear it," Carolina said turning side to side, pulling some things up and other things down. "I don't need to breath."

"No, I'll wear the black one – it's cocktail length like yours is."

Sensing defeat, Melinda clutched at straws. "Here, it has a nice jacket that goes with it. You might be cold."

Melinda did win a few battles, having washed Carolina's face free of the heavy black liner and bubble gum pink eye shadow, she worked quickly, softening the highly-arched brows and the sharp nose with a pallet of soft browns and ivory. She left the voluptuous lips free of colour and allowed them to catch the light with a pale lip gloss and twisted the dry, black hair into a discrete chignon at the base of the neck. Pleased with her handiwork, she allowed Carolina to see the result. "There, your face looks like it belongs one of those famous Italian paintings, where the woman is coming out of a shell."

Furrows invaded Carolina's brow. "Botticelli's Birth of Venus? What the hell, Melinda? I look ill. I look like beige wall paper. Besides, I'm more into Matisse's Fauvism movement." She reached for the red lipstick.

"I have no idea what you're talking about and I'm not going to ask in case you tell me, but you did say you'd trust me, so please, back away from the red lipstick! I'm telling you, this look is classy, understated. Believe me, with that rack no one will mistake you for wall paper. Remember, Oprah said, 'less is more.'"

"Coco Chanel."

"What?"

"Coco Chanel said that, not Oprah," Carolina insisted.

"Nope, you're wrong on this one. I saw the episode."

Grumbling, Carolina slipped her feet into what she called her 'Scarpe di Putana' or 'slut shoes' - six inch, strappy red stilettos and rose like a tower before Melinda. "Let's do this!" she said excitedly, as she slipped a bottle of Grappa into her evening bag.

Melinda finished back-combing the front her own hair and pinned it into a gentle bouffant crest above her forehead. Little needed to be done to her face as she never left the house without a perfect make up application.

Melinda held out the jacket hopefully, and an unusually cooperative Carolina put it on because it was so sparkly. Watching her walk out of the house and into the waiting limo, Melinda thought her Eliza Doolittle was certain to turn heads at The Fairmont, but for all the right reasons.

The limo pulled up to the front of the hotel and a uniformed doorman reached to open the car door. Carolina released her long legs into a wide straddle to get onto the red carpet eliciting a startled response from the doorman which she enjoyed witnessing immensely. *This is the life,* she thought. She reached over and kissed him on the moustache. "That's your tip, handsome," she said provocatively.

Melinda exited as quickly as possible and thrust a twenty into the man's hand while pulling Carolina forward into the foyer. "Stop blowing him kisses!" Melinda scolded. "Remember, this is a classy do."

Melinda flagged the Concierge by name and whispered in his ear. He nodded as if his head were on a spring and said he'd look after everything. He walked off purposefully and returned in a few minutes beseeching the two women to follow him into the ballroom. Melinda waved him away when she spotted her target. "So sorry to be late, Daniel," she said, as if waving a white flag.

Daniel's chin would have dropped into his soup if his jaw was not still partly wired shut. Carolina thought she saw a soft smile cross his face as he encountered Melinda, but it was soon shut away when the discomfort of both his injury and the circumstance registered upon him. "My God, Melinda," he said, "I didn't exshpect you tonight. Pleash, shit down, shit down."

The imperious matriarch sitting beside Daniel turned her head abruptly towards him, eyes flashing like an emergency beacon. The grey-haired gentleman beside her, his father, could only blurt out, "Daniel?" and place a hand on his wife's diamond encrusted bracelet seeking to quell her outrage. The two, acutely aware that many curious eyes must have followed these statuesque women across the room, were a model of restraint as they relinquished their own impulses to the custody of their son.

Melinda let loose her most dazzling smile, which the elder Mrs. Thackery resisted with a fierce narrowing of her eyes and mouth. Daniel's face seemed conflicted between hope and hopelessness. His kind eyes tried to hold Melinda's in some silent entreaty, but she willed them away, avoiding his gaze like a beaten dog. She only felt her power return when she stared into the hollow orbits of her mother in law. All of this was lost on the old man who, in his great distraction, had soup drooling down his chin; his attention transfixed on the arresting proportions of Carolina's bosom. She had removed her demure jacket with the skill of a stripper and stood holding it in the air beside him.

"Shall I sit beside you, Mr. Thackery?" Carolina cooed.

"Oh, pardon my manners!" Melinda said slyly. "Sybil and Tristan, allow me to introduce Carolina Stiletto, a good friend of mine . . . eh and of course, Carolina, you've met my husband, Daniel."

Daniel smiled that strange, insincere smile of a man whose jaw had been wired shut upon being re-introduced to the person who was responsible for its wiring. "Yesh, yesh, Carolina I remember, though I would have hardly recognised you. You look sho different tonight."

"Yes," Carolina said, "this time I have clothes on."

"I beg your pardon?" said Sybil, not knowing how to look more disapproving than she had been previously.

"Yesh, Mother, permit me to eshplain," Daniel said uncomfortably. "Lash time I shaw Carolina she was in our hot tub, you shee. Carolina'sh a . . . a good friend of oursh, a good, good, good, friend, ishn't she Melinda?" Daniel cast an imploring look at the two women, begging their cooperation. He had already begun to sweat.

Sybil looked at Tristan, nudging him so hard that he gasped agreement. Tristan, however, made a remarkable recovery, letting his gaze settle once again, to closely monitor Carolina's breathing pattern.

"Melinda," Sybil said dryly, "I thought you were going to be away for a few weeks at that "spa" you go to for your 'refreshment'. Did you stay because of Daniel's accident?"

Daniel spoke before she could, "- me falling of my bishycle like that – when I hit gravel. I was sho shorry to shpoil your plansh, with my . . . 'acshident', honey."

Melinda's face softened. She looked down onto her plate then up into his eyes. Her voice turned to gossamer. "You have no idea how sorry I am that you were hurt, Daniel."

"Me too," Carolina echoed, wincing.

Daniel's lips thinned and Melinda thought she saw tears welling in his eyes, but it was hard to tell because both were still a bit red and swollen from 'his bishycle acshident'.

Luther Vandross's voice covered the room like velvet and Melinda mouthed the words of the song quietly, to herself. She felt herself begin to yield to its sentimental message and she swayed gently side to side. Then, aware of Sybil's critical eye, she steeled herself, anticipating the wag of Sybil's skeletal finger and its power to pierce any emotion that threatened to pollute her carefully guarded social landscape and cause a scene.

"Letsh dansh." Daniel's hand was on Melinda's shoulder.

"Why don't you eat your veal, for goodness sake?" Sybil commanded.

"Not hungry," Daniel said as he swept Melinda into his arms and held her as if some other force was trying to rip her away from him. Her feet barely touched the floor as they made a dramatic getaway to the other end of the hall.

"Also, it's not liquid," Carolina observed.

Sybil's head twitched like a pigeon at a senior's picnic. She looked back and forth at Carolina and Tristan and spat his name out so forcefully that he jumped as if she'd put a cardiac paddle on his chest. "Trrristan! Look, it's the Walkers. Call them over here. I want to be sure we get an invitation to their summer party." She turned to Carolina, "The Right Honourable Gerald Walker. He's a Supreme Court judge, you know. Very learned man – and she's from the Montgomery family. You don't want to miss the do they throw every summer. It's a stunningly beautiful affair."

Carolina filled her face with what looked like fascination. "What was it like last year?"

"Oh, we didn't go, we were out of town," Sybil said distractedly.

"And the year before?"

Sybil bit her lip. "We had a family wedding, I think – couldn't go."

"Shame," Carolina said with a pout on her face.

"The shame was, that we've never been invited to the damn thing," Tristan confessed.

Sybil chose to ignore this and was standing up waving her arms to catch to The Walker's attention. When they moved further away, she trotted across the room and dragged them to the table, glowing with the effort, as if she'd bagged a Sasquatch.

Upon seeing Carolina, Gerald Walker purred, "I'm very sure we haven't met, perhaps we should."

Gerald Walker was a sleek man. His greying hair curled back from his temples like the wings on Mercury. His silver-grey tuxedo jacket gave off a subdued lustre that complimented his senatorial aspect. Deep set eyes betrayed a hint of the same steely colour as they locked into Carolina's own. He slid into the seat beside her with the fluid grace of a magician who left his audience staring at the empty space he had occupied a moment ago, only to reappear elsewhere.

His wife, Terra, a perky, blonde with disturbingly inflated lips, was caught in Sybil's ghastly grip and squeaked like a small woodland creature resigned to its fate. She was pulled down and consumed by Sybil's looming shadow. Terra's head darted side to side occasionally, trying to see where her husband's hands were.

Carolina allowed a slight curl of her lips to invite Gerald's attention. "I'm Carolina Stilleto – yes, like the shoe." She crossed her legs slowly, her skirt slipping away to reveal her thigh through the diaphanous silk inset. She raised her arched foot to let the red stiletto heel rest perilously close to the bulge on the right side of his inseam.

Terra stretched her neck around Sybil's head only to be met by Tristan's florid face. "Boo!" he said with a giggle, happy to have his wife's attention diverted from his drinking.

"Now, Terra, how are the plans for the summer going? Any plans? Anything you're planning?" Sybil bleated, completely engaged in a pursuit of her own.

"Wasn't stiletto originally a small, thin, knife?" Gerald said, reaching his hand beneath the table and resting the tip of his middle finger on Carolina's ankle.

"Stiletto – well, that sounds dangerous, Carolina. Are you dangerous?" Terra said, her high-pitched, staccato voice trilling with a nervous vibrato; her large dolly eyes peeking over Sybil's shoulder.

Gerald licked his lips, letting his finger explore Carolina's calf and said quietly, "I hope so."

"I hope so too!" Tristan said, having leaned into Carolina's shoulder, grazing it with his moustache.

Carolina emptied her wine glass and turned to Gerald. "Walker . . . know what I heard about the name Walker? You'll find this fascinating."

"I couldn't be more fascinated than I already am."

Carolina smirked. "Let me try." She let her foot fall to the floor. "The Walkers were what they used to call the poor assholes who had to walk up to their chins in tubs of horse and human urine to set the dyes for the old Indigo trade. That's what your ancestors did for a living - one of them at least."

Terra's face hardened. That was one more thing she didn't like about this woman who was after the man she had stolen from another woman.

"Surely not!" Sybil Thackery cried, snatching Terra's hand in hers as if to protect her from a terrible assault. "That sounds like nonsense to me. No! Surely the Walkers were the men who beat the bushes for bird hunting and such. It's a grand old name and I think, Miss Stiletto, that you are mistaken."

Gerald let a slow smile take over his face as he kept Carolina in his sights. "Hell, no better reason to be pissed off than that! – explains a lot about my family."

"Don't mention it. Glad to be of service," Carolina said, looking sidelong into Gerald's eyes. She reached across the table for her purse allowing her breasts to spill forward, threatening to land on Tristan's veal scaloppini and glided from the table towards the Ladies Room.

All the eyes at the table watched her walk away from them, the roll of her hips, fluid beneath the spangles of her dress as they caught the light. It was as if a posse of paparazzi had found their prey.

Carolina squatted over the toilet. She wiped herself carefully and took a long swig of the grappa she carried in her purse. She overheard the giggle of two women entering the bathroom in mid-conversation.

"They're dancing now, but I have it on good information that things are not going well. My mother is a good friend of a good friend of Sybil. I don't think it would take much to get his attention – she's a wreck and he's gorgeous. You should go for it, Cindy. "

"Well, I lost Daniel once, I don't want to lose him again. Maybe he sees what a mistake he's made now."

"What have you got to lose?"

The heavy wooden doors of the cubicles closed and Carolina could hear their watery duet begin as the streams of urine hit the water below. She washed her hands quickly, then sprayed herself with one of the perfume selections on the counter. *Not bad,* she thought and popped it into her purse.

She reviewed her reflection in the mirror and judging it to be in need of renovation, she applied a thick coat of glittering blue eye shadow, redrew the faded lines around her eyes with an upward curl at the corners, which she thought made her look Egyptian, added strong brush strokes of blush to sharpen the contours of her cheekbones and topped it all off with "Riot Red" lipstick which overreached the borders of her lips to make them look even fuller. Finally, she freed her hair from the chignon and fiercely back-combed it into a dome-shaped helmet worthy of Bellona, the Roman Goddess of War.

She noted the faces of the two women who were talking as they emerged from the toilet stalls, so that she could point those bitches out to Melinda.

"Why not, I'm free," continued the plain, red headed one, who Carolina assumed to be Daniel's old flame, 'Cindy'. She turned to the petite woman and bent her knees so that their faces were level. She lifted the woman's freckled chin with her index finger and said, "It's good that your free, honey, because, take it from me, no one would pay for this. Leave Daniel the hell alone or I'll flatten what's left of that bad nose job."

The two men rose deferentially as Carolina returned to the table. Sybil and Terra released a noticeable startle at the sight of her much-enhanced make-over. They glanced at each other, knowingly and released a smirk of disapproval. This was all lost on Tristan and Gerald whose faces lit up like schoolboys ogling a centrefold, as they competed to pull a chair out for her. Carolina downed her wine with a toss of her head and felt the confidence of a puppet master overtake her. "Let's do shots."

She placed the grappa on the table and poured a hefty shot into the empty wine glasses. She held the bottle up to Sybil and Terra in a manner that asked if they wanted to partake. They demurred and cast a censorious look at their husbands. The shots were downed before it could be registered and a refill followed quickly.

"Trrristan!" His name came out of the back of Sybil's constricted throat. Her face boiled with rage as he discharged the second and then the third round.

Tristan rose unsteadily to his feet and tried to look as masterful as was possible, given that he was swaying like a granny at a sing along. He picked up a French loaf from the bread basket and waved it menacingly in front of Sybil. "Here, Ssssybil. Why don't you practise on this, so that something other than my name can come in your mouth for once, you staggeringly tedious old shrew." With that endearing declaration, he grabbed Carolina's hand and said, "Let's dance, sweetheart."

Carolina pulled Gerald along with them and the three took over the middle of the dance floor.

Sometimes it's as if the Great Director in the Sky is watching in the wings, orchestrating a musical score for humanity. But, as Tristan, Gerald and Carolina danced together to the pulsating rhythm of 'Freak Out'- that is exactly what Sybil did in response to Tristan's unfortunate outburst. She strode out on the dance floor and attempted to pry away Carolina's leg, which was clamped firmly on Tristan's normally arthritic hip. It had found its way there, so that Carolina could perform her signature move that involved her arching backward until her hair swept the floor to the beat of the music. Due to Sybil's interference, everything became unhinged and the whole circus act toppled to the floor, Gerald amongst them, as Carolina was holding on to his tie at the time. Fortunately, both the men's fall was broken by the inside of Carolina's fleshy thighs thus protecting them from serious cranial injury, if not from serious social embarrassment. It all ended rather artistically, with an arresting tableau for the onlookers. On the way down, the skirt of Carolina's beautiful, beaded dress flared out like rose petals, as did her legs, to reveal what became obvious to everyone. She was not wearing panties.

Molly

Angus clutched the sympathy card he had received from his co-workers at the office. He put it in the middle of the mantel piece beside the small pot of Forget Me Nots that Georgia had thoughtfully bought to go with it. Molly promised that they'd plant them on Thor's grave.

Angus nodded as he adjusted both the card and the flower pot several times before he felt that they had been shown to their best advantage. Molly watched him, his stooped posture still telegraphing his anguish. She suggested that he take his walk before supper, fresh air a remedy for everything. The nod came again and Molly's heart seized with helplessness. Any other time Angus would have chattered on about every detail of his day at the office. Carolina, his self-professed girlfriend would figure large in the anecdotes. He called her his 'Sparkly Girl', and she would encourage his gentle flirtation.

Angus loped up the street, head down, hands in his coat pockets. Mrs. Porter, a neighbour he had known since birth, hollered a jovial, "Hello Angus," and he returned a weak, "Hello, Mrs. Porter" without looking up and gracing her with his usual smile.

"Something wrong, Angus?" she called as he passed.

"My friend died," he muttered.

Mrs. Porter's hand flew to her mouth and before she had time to ask who, Angus had disappeared around the corner. He walked past the school and past the Dairy Bar where he was a regular customer. He gave no thought to the penny candy he usually purchased there; where Mr. Gupta, the proprietor, had the patience to help a picky customer like Angus agonize over which, of the multitudes of small candies were to be included in the bag for a dollar. Today was not a day for making such serious choices and besides, Angus had no appetite for even the most tantalizing treat.

Angus stopped at the graveyard, its old monuments standing like guardians to the village as the setting sun cast them against its canvas. A main road wound its way through the middle of it, making the graveyard more a part of the village landscape than separate from it. It had no sinister dimensions for Angus; it was just where the dead people were living.

He made his way down a grassy incline to sit on his favourite seat. As he approached, he heard a sound from behind the large maple tree that shaded it. It was a deep, strangled moaning, wet with tears. His face collapsed into a frown as he tip toed to the tree and peered around its broad trunk. He looked down on a crumpled figure, whose balding pate, roasted red by the sun, was surrounded by a messy mass of greying hair. The man's shoulders shook as his tears fell onto the dusty ground beneath him. Angus watched them and felt his own tears push their way out of him to drown his own eyes. No amount of exertion could stop a long, keening whine escape from Angus's chest, to join the sad dirge from the stranger below him.

The man was startled, but suppressed his reaction when he looked up into the agonized face above. Their eyes locked and words could not have transmitted desolation with more clarity than that wretched duet. The man reached his hand up to Angus and brought him down to sit beside him where they wept hand in hand.

"I'm Roger. What's your story, buddy?" the man said to Angus. He released his hand to pass it under his nose with a sniff. Angus riffled through his pocket and produced a wad of neatly folded tissues he put there every morning on Molly's orders.

"Thanks . . . thanks," Roger muttered, as he gave his nose a mighty blow. They both wiped their leaking eyes in unison.

"I'm Angus Nolan McGilvery . I'm twenty-nine years old and I live at number 6 Rose Street."

Roger smiled. "I'm Roger, Roger Mead and I'm fifty years old and I live at number 82 Oak Street. Nice to meet you, Angus. Why are *you* crying?"

Angus choked again and coughed out his answer in a thin voice. "My best friend died and I miss his tiny little teeth."

Roger tried not to react. "My best friend died too and I miss holding her tiny little hand."

Angus jumped with excitement. "Thor had tiny little hands too!"

Roger knew this was an earnest response and gathered his face into a serious expression of concern. "What exactly was Thor?"

Angus returned Roger's sober look and held his emotion in check. "Thor was my rat. The only rat I ever loved and he had tiny little teeth – like me – see?" Angus lifted his upper lip to display a row of what were, indeed, tiny white teeth with one gap just off the centre of the row.

"Love is hard," Roger said.

"Did you ever love a rat?" Angus asked.

"Ah, yes. Yes, I believe I did. I had pet rats when I was a boy. It started out as two and ended up ten. I found good homes for all of them though, so don't worry about that."

Angus managed a smile. "Good. You knew I'd be worried about that. I like that about you, Roger."

"Well, that makes me feel better than I've felt all day, Angus. I like you too."

"Who died?"

"You mean who was *I* crying over?"

Angus nodded and clasped Roger's hand hard again as if, by doing so, he could stop the new tears he saw shining in Roger's eyes.

Roger pointed to the grave stone in front of them, as he summoned his voice. “Sheila, my wife. She’s there – died of pneumonia.”

Angus drew in a breath and threw his arms around Roger as they both gave into a new wave of sadness. “So, did Thor!”

“To share a hiding place, physical or psychological, is as intimate as love,” muttered Roger, more to himself than to his new friend.

Angus had heard him and tried to interpret what had been said, sensing it important. “What does that mean?”

Roger smiled weakly. “Sheila told me that. She read it in Fugitive Pieces - one of her favourite books. I think it means Angus, that you and I have a lot in common.”

Angus nodded and squinted at the gravestone before him.

“Would Sheila have liked Thor? A lot of people don’t like rats.”

“I know she would have. She loved creatures, all creatures. She thought spiders were beautiful. We weren’t allowed to kill them in our house. We had to name them. She’d pick them up and carefully take them out to the garage - mainly because I was scared of them. She had a big heart.”

Angus looked up at Roger, his face sad with the weight of a new memory. “Thor had big balls.”

“So, did my Sheila,” Roger added with a smile.

Glynda

The weekends seemed long for Glynda. She found herself constantly looking for reasons to avoid Edna. There was only so much gardening to do even in the spring. She’d already read the Giller prize list and was looking for another good book. She’d spend a long time in the bath, waxing everything she could reach. She’d give herself a facial or do her exercise regimen, trying to beat her rebellious stomach into submission. At least tonight, there was choir practise and she looked forward to wrapping herself up in a glorious shawl of music.

Each time she attended she would hope that this might be the time that Lorna, the Choir Mistress, would give her a chance to sing a solo part.

So many of the other members had hinted that she could carry one, but somehow, Lorna always managed to claim the part for herself, given that she 'had sung at Roy Thomson Hall and all' which sounded impressive enough to quell anyone else's ambition. But, Eva, a woman whose harsh face was made up of a series of straight lines, told Glynda recently that, Lorna was nine at the time and it was actually as part of a trio, which was part of a choir, which was part of a festival; so, not quite living up to the impression given.

Lorna was a tall, terrifying woman, who wore swirling capes, colourful scarves and loud perfume. Her speaking voice had authority and her singing voice had volume, but it tended to warble and didn't have the range and clarity that Glynda could muster if she had a confident moment. Eva stood next to her in the choir and would look with admiration at her when she hit a particularly difficult note with apparent ease. It was nice to be noticed in that small way.

The local concert was fast approaching and last Monday, Lorna had handed out the intended program. Glynda looked down the list of songs expectantly, but did not see her name beside any selection. *Oh well,* she thought. *What does it matter as long as I get to sing.*

Eva's hand shot up. "Lorna, may I suggest that Glynda take one of your four solos? I think we'd all like to hear her sing one." She turned to the rest of the choir for support. "What do you say?"

Glynda drew in a sharp breath and put her hands up in protest as one by one her peers clapped in response.

"I'm not sure Glynda is ready for that yet, Eva," Lorna said, "much as I'd like to see her push herself out of her comfort zone. All in good time, but perhaps not yet."

Eva was not to be batted aside. "Oh, I know you're the Choir Mistress and all, but I think everyone agrees that her time has come."

Another strong ovation sprang from the group.

Lorna, cocked her head to the side and pursed her fuchsia lips. "Of course, we'll do it. Next year." She picked up her baton. "Now, let's not waste any more precious time, one, two, three and . . ."

The pianist started the introduction to, 'Like a Bridge Over Troubled Water', punishing the keys with her enthusiasm. Only Glynda began the song, fading out as soon as she noticed no one else was. Eva and Lorna stared each other down.

Lorna's right eye started twitching noticeably. "Yes, well, perhaps this would be a good song for you to start with, Glynda."

Glynda drove home, elated that she would finally have a chance to sing a solo. She tried to find some balance between her exuberance and the apprehension she knew performing in front of an audience would cause her. Her stomach had already launched its surly complaint and she loosened the waistband of her fitted skirt for comfort. She reached for another Tums and chewed it quickly. *I'm going to do this,* she thought. *I can do this. Why can't I just enjoy the opportunity, for once? I've waited long enough for it.*

She walked through her door and went directly to the kitchen. Maybe a bit of food would help quell the anxiety in her stomach. She opened the fridge to see what she might make for dinner – *nothing gaseous*, she thought, *something plain.*

She sighed and realized that she had better check if Edna wanted something. Hopefully, she would have made herself something earlier and Glynda wouldn't have to count her fussy preferences into the decision. She restrained the urge to shout out to Edna, as more than once she had been scolded for doing so. 'What are we carnival barkers?' So, she went to see if Edna was in the main floor bedroom, which she had taken over to avoid the stairs.

Glynda knocked gently at the door. She knocked again with more force and still heard no answer. Putting her ear to the door, she could hear the TV so, she knocked again loudly.

Maybe she's dead, thought Glynda and a guilty sense of relief crept over her. She immediately chastised herself for such an unchristian thought, wiping the relish from her mind while asking Jesus for forgiveness . . . and strength. The vision of Edna, dead in her chair had brought fresh, but forbidden pleasure. She opened the door, bracing herself for whatever she might find behind it.

Edna was propped up in her floral wing chair tossing a chicken ball from Lucky Star Chinese into her gaping mouth. "Oh, there you are," Edna said through the mouthful. "Got tired of waiting for you to come home and make dinner, so I ordered out."

Glynda reminded her, "It's Monday, you know I have choir practice Mondays, so we eat late."

"I'd starve if I waited until you thought of feeding me. It's ten past eight."

Glynda's stomach lurched again. Edna wasn't incapable of getting her own food. "Maybe it's time to think about getting a care-giver in during the days, when I'm working." *That should shut her up,* Glynda said to herself.

"You'd like that, wouldn't you? Why don't you just sign me into a home and let me rot? You think you'd get all of this for yourself, don't you? Well, my son's going to get everything, not you."

The bile rose in Glynda's diaphragm.

"And where is this saintly son of yours? Even God doesn't know, because when he took most of your money and all of mine, he must have gone to Hell – and the joke is, it's probably a better Hell than the one I'm living in."

Edna turned her head away from Glynda and stared out into the tulips, their bright, bobbing heads wet from a steady drizzle of spring rain. "I didn't order any Chinese for you."

CLINICAL STUDIES: LEVEL 111

ANOTHER MONDAY MORNING PUSHED EVERYONE out of their beds like a precipitous delivery. They were ripped from the soothing warmth of the blankets only to be met with the harsh slap of a workday routine. Gripping the small comfort of a coffee mug, Molly and Carolina stepped out of their cars into the parking lot, and with a nod of greeting, one followed the other up the stairway to the office.

Glynda sat stiffly at the reception desk, watching the phone, willing it to ring in the new week. She was as crisp as the freshly ironed sheets of the bed she'd gladly left behind as soon as the first bird sang its matins song. That morning, after a cool, Spartan shower, she had skillfully wound her hair into a tortoiseshell clip and slid into the grey shirt dress that she had laid out the night before, beside the pearl earrings and necklace. She made a splendid cup of tea in the Colglough Ivy patterned teapot that made her welcome the mornings even more. After mixing two bowls of oatmeal, she put one on a tray along with a steaming cup of tea and took it up to Edna's bedroom. She knocked gently and left it on the floor, not having the stomach to let Edna's sour visage steal the sweetness from the day before it had even ripened.

Out on the flagstone patio she savoured the first sip from the thin, bone china teacup and looked upward. The blue of her woolen sweater matched the pale skin of the sky which was laced, here and there, with delicate pink bracelets of cloud. This moment could never disappoint.

She welcomed the work week; its dependable return for her vigorous investment, whether it be from well-deserved fatigue, the satisfaction of a grateful patient, the vibrant office chatter or the predictable chaos that made the clock's sovereignty shrink.

This week there were two choir practices, in an effort to prepare for the concert. She squeezed herself with pleasure at the thought of finally winning a solo. In her mind the grand swell of Verdi's lament to the endurance of suffering, Va Pensiero, rose up as a fitting score to the morning panorama. She could see, hear, taste, smell and feel God's presence, and if that was all she had, then that was all she needed to make her life complete. This was him speaking to her. "Don't forget my haemorrhoid cream this time, Glynda," Edna said, standing at the doorway in her pin curls and flannel nightgown. "You forgot to bring it home from the clinic on Friday and I don't want to have to pay for it. It's not covered by the drug plan and I don't want the one that is, because it doesn't have the little spray nozzle on it. I don't like to use my fingers." With that, she shut the door firmly and left Glynda staring at the garden gargoyle.

Sitting at the clinic desk drinking a second cup of tea, Glynda made a mental note to ask Anthea if she could take a sample of the new haemorrhoid cream home to her mother-in-law. This thought was interrupted by a delivery man dropping off a package. After signing it she took it to the lunch room, guessing it was for Molly, who had just poured herself a strong, dark coffee. Glynda gave a cursory look at Carolina who was sitting at the table with her head down on her arms. This was not an unusual posture for Carolina on Monday mornings.

Gavin took a book out of his satchel and began refreshing his memory on the Human Papilloma Virus, as he knew several patients from the Colposcopy clinic would be returning for their results this morning. He saw the anxiety the condition provoked in them.

> *"HPV: There are many types of this common virus, 30% of which are sexually transmitted. Type 16 and 18 pose a high risk of cervical cancer and Type 6 and 11 can cause the most common STD, genital warts in both men and women . . ."*

"I think this is the package you've been waiting for, Molly," Glynda said, handing it to her.

"Oh, my dilators, finally," Molly said as she broke the seal and opened the box to examine the contents. She took out a pink, phallic object and waved it as she spoke. "Shit, this isn't a medium, this must be a large. Look at the size of it! How are my vaginismus ladies expected to dilate their vaginas with something the size of *this*?" She reached into the box again and produced another much smaller sample. "Look, this is the smaller one and they are supposed to go from this little one right onto this humongous thing? I don't think so – they've screwed up again."

Gavin looked up with interest. "Is vaginismus the only application you use them for, Molly?"

"Well, let me make it clear, Gavin, I don't use them personally - after three kids a strong gust of wind gets me whistling while I walk, but to answer your question, we use them for women, primarily virginal women with spasm or vaginal agenesis – like the Patterson girls, who need to stretch the vaginal passage, but also for some post-surgery patients or for elderly women with atrophic vaginas. Anyway, this is way too big of a jump for most – they're not labelled, but this has to be a large not a medium – what do you think?"

Glynda turned to tidy the table napkins and Gavin considered the question academically. "I'm not sure I can make an objective answer to that question. I haven't done the appropriate research."

"Well, I have," Carolina said, lifting her head from her arms, "and that's actually pretty damn small if you ask me."

Glynda left the room quickly, sure that she'd heard the first patient arrive at the front desk as Gavin leafed quickly through the pages of his medical pocket reference.

Vaginismus: The result of a sudden reflex of the pubococcygeus muscle, causing any form of vaginal penetration to be painful or impossible. Incremental dilation of the vagina can prove helpful.

Vaginal Agenesis: in this congenital disorder of the reproductive system, one in 5-7000 females is born with an absent or incomplete vaginal canal and\or uterus. Because the outer genitalia appear normal, VA is often not diagnosed until late puberty when the patient has not begun menses.

Vaginal Atrophy (Atrophic Vaginitis), occurs often but not always, after menopause when estrogen is depleated. The vaginal tissues become thin and irritated making penetration painful and difficult.

"Good Morning, Sunshine," Anthea said, putting on her lab coat, "still cramming?" She threw down a chart. "Here's one for you. The results are positive and she'll need a laser vapourization. Room One."

"OK," Gavin sighed, "here goes."

Molly was just stepping out of Room One and Gavin watched as she tried to insist that the patient take some money.

"Please take it," Molly said to the woman, who held her hands up in a gesture of protest. "You helped me out of a tight spot and I'm glad I have the chance to give it back to you. Oh, here's the medical student now, Dr. Brock will be in later."

"Aw Geez," came the gravelly response from the thin, wiry woman speaking to Molly. "It weren't nuttin, hon. Funny that we sees each other agin' when I've gots a problem wid me muk now, don't cha think? An' tanks for givin' me this 'un, he's not a bad bit nice."

Gavin felt himself colour. He wondered when he'd get over his discomfort with flirtatious women. They did it on purpose, he supposed, to try to get that very response from a male in a female environment. One day, he'd be able to come up with a cool and charming response and not act like a fourteen-year-old schoolboy.

"Hello Brenda, I'm Gavin. You may remember me from the Colposcopy Clinic, I was assisting Dr. Brock."

"Shore, shore, I never forget a pretty face, darlin'. Youse got 'em results for me? I've been wondrin' about what's what an' me nerves is rubbed right raw. See, I never heard of a Clupos . .. Coplos . . . whatever the bejuzus you call that ting yer put up me mukker." Brenda began to undo her pants, whipping them off along with her underwear, Gavin hesitated. "Umm . . . mukker?"

She jumped onto the gyne bed and lifted her feet into the air, pointing emphatically between her legs. "You know, me down belows there. Me muk we calls it at home."

Gavin tried to stop the rush of blood that again flooded his face, but failed as he reached for Brenda's clothing. "Yes . . . the colposcope, it's like a microscope that magnifies the cervix so we can see abnormal cells - but you don't have to get changed today, I just have to give you the results, please, you can get dressed and sit on the chair."

Just then, a knock came on the door. "It's Dr. Brock, may I come in?"

Brenda jumped off the bed and opened the door, standing naked from the waist down. "Here's me, finally naked with a good lookin' young man and he tells me to put my knickers back on."

"Sorry Brenda," Anthea said laughing. "Look, we'll come back in when you're dressed."

"No, don't be fussing. I'll put mesel' to rights in a minute."

She looked at Gavin while Brenda struggled with her pants. "So, have you gone over the results yet?"

"Ummm, no," Gavin admitted, "I haven't had a chance yet."

"Well, OK, you go ahead, and I'll be here if you need me."

Gavin gulped and waited until Brenda was sitting comfortably. Gavin explained that the pathology showed abnormal cells and went over the details of laser vapourization treatment.

Brenda blinked and her forehead creased. "Ya don't say. Do I have The Cancer, Gav.?"

"No, not at all. It's true that in some instances, if left untreated, H.P.V., in some circumstances, can cause cervical cancer, but if treated and monitored that should never happen."

"So, I gots The H.I.V.?"

"Oh no, Brenda, H.*P*.V.– very different than H.*I*.V.."

"Now, how'd I ketch sumin' like that, then? I always put paper on the toilet seats."

Gavin nodded, "It's not from toilet seats, Brenda, but it is a sexually transmitted disease."

Brenda stared into his eyes, puzzled.

"It's from having unprotected sex," Gavin said. That's how you catch it."

"But I'm not a dirty girl, Doctor Brock, I don't sleep around, honest. I did have sex with me boyfriend once or twice – just to give him a little taste of the goods y'know, but I told him he couldn't have it anymore 'till he married me. I told him I wasn't a dirty girl and even after those times I took a toothbrush and I scrubs me down belows till it shined. I didn't want to get pregnant, y'know."

Gavin looked at Anthea hoping for help. She didn't throw a life jacket.

Gavin flipped the chart to recheck Brenda's age. "You're fifty-one, Brenda, not likely you'll get pregnant now - and you know, you can't prevent transmission . . . or pregnancy with a . . . toothbrush, right? I would advise against you doing that, you could get nasty abrasions too."

"Lord Tunderin' Jesus, I don't want to ketch them as well. But I likes me mok to be clean and tidy, Gav., not all mops and brooms. I'm not a dirty girl."

"I'm sure that you're not . . .em . . . dirty, but in the future, just clean the area with a mild soap and water. We'll take care of the virus."

"Are you sure I can't scrub the buggers out?"

"No, no Brenda. Leave that to us, and you'll be fine, promise."

Brenda pursed her lips and clutching the information package Gavin gave her, winked at him. "No, tanks for everytin', Gav. I trust ya an' I trust your girlfriend, Dr. Brock too."

"May I ask a question, Brenda?" Anthea said. "Did your boyfriend and you get married, after all?"

"Hell no, the bastard trew me over for a dirty girl who gave all the byes sex without marryin'. An' look what he gave me for nuttin', I tell ya."

Anthea squeezed Brenda's hand. "I'm sorry that didn't work out, Brenda. You're better off without him, I'm sure."

Gavin touched Brenda's upper arm in a gesture of solidarity.

As they exited the room, Molly's worried face headed them off as they reached for the next chart. "Hold on, we just got a call from ultrasound. It's about Sharon White's babe – fetal demise."

Anthea opened the chart Molly had handed her and noted that the patient was thirty-two weeks gestation. The ultrasound was on its way indicating a placental abruption. "Damn. Does the patient suspect? Any bleeding?"

"Just a little "show" yesterday, nothing more. She didn't go to triage because she had a pre-booked ultrasound this morning . . . she has no idea. Room Three."

"Why would she? Shit, shit, shit. Poor girl."

Anthea reviewed the chart with Gavin, noting that it showed good growth, good fetal heartrate and movement. "No damn reason to suspect anything. This is a tough one. You'd better stay here."

When Anthea eventually exited Room Three, muffled sobs could be heard from within.

"Molly, bring Sharon a cup of hot tea, please. She's calling her husband. He doesn't work far away. Let me know when he's here. Thanks."

Molly's hand touched Anthea's forearm, gesturing towards the next exam room. Mrs. Walsh, had been informed the week before, that her baby had a harelip. Anthea had spent a great deal of time to reassure her that these days it was easily fixed and that the baby was perfectly formed otherwise. She was here requesting an abortion.

Anthea rolled her eyes in disbelief. "Are you kidding?"

"I wish."

She turned to Gavin, "This was an Assisted Reproduction pregnancy, too. It was tough to get her pregnant – and now *this*? What can I say? The irony is too much. I'm not losing two babies in one day. Listen, I'm pro choice, but let's make sure she understands the situation."

Lunch came late that morning, and the afternoon patients were already beginning to arrive.

They all sat around the lunch table as Anthea came out of the Room One followed by two bereft figures holding one another as if a chasm loomed beneath them, as indeed there was.

Glynda took their arms and told them she would call them with the details when she could get the induction of labour organized. She asked if there was someone she could call who could drive them home. Sharon's husband wiped his eyes with a shaking hand and said it wasn't far, and that he'd be alright.

Anthea sat down at the table as if dissolving into the chair. Carolina pushed a plate of lasagna towards her. "Here, ya still gotta eat."

"Thanks, it sure beats the powdered soup I brought today."

Carolina handed a plate to Gavin.

Did you make this on the weekend, Carolina?" Glynda asked.

"No," she replied, "I was too busy making trouble on the weekend. I made this one during the week, but sometimes when I can't sleep I get up and make it then freeze it. It relaxes me."

Molly giggled. "You can't sleep at night and you think, 'I should get up and make lasagna noodles?'"

"Sure, do you think I'd bother to get up to make a powdered soup? No offence, Anthea."

"None taken," Anthea said savouring the first burst of flavour from the tomato sauce and the delicate ribbons of pasta, thin as skin. "Forgive me, but I wish you many sleepless nights!"

Anthea waved Georgia into the lunchroom when she saw her come through the back door.

Glynda squirmed in her seat as if uncomfortable. "Just a very little piece for me, Carolina, my clothes are getting tight." She tugged at the waist band of her pencil skirt and after a bite, she put down her fork and reached for her purse.

"Ya don't like my pasta, Glynda? I admit, it's not bits and bites – or a bolts and bits or whatever you call it. But, I do my best." Carolina said.

"Nuts and bolts. No, it's not that at all. Your lasagna is the best thing about you, Carolina."

A groan came from the rest of them.

"Ya know, I agree with her. It probably is my best feature, with the possible exception of my long nipples."

A shriek of laughter rose out of Molly while Gavin spluttered bits of his lasagna into the surrounding field of fire, one particularly large piece landing on the breast of Glynda's pristine grey dress. Horrified, he picked at the errant piece and flung it into the garbage. He began strenuously rubbing her breast with a wet napkin, begging to pay for the dry cleaning.

Carolina picked up a large piece of her lasagna and held it a small distance from her own breast. "Shit, Glynda gets to insult me *and* have Gavin rub her tits – maybe I should roll around in my lasagna to get a little male attention!"

Gavin realized what he was doing and stood, swerving side to side, not sure what he could say or do to make this situation more tolerable for poor Glynda. Glynda popped two Advil in her mouth and swallowed a gulp of her tea.

"Boy, I'm giving you a headache, already, Glynda?" Carolina said.

"No, Carolina, you usually affect me a little lower than that."

"OK," Carolina said looking suitably put out, "any more of that and I'll resort to physical torture. I've got one or two pounds on you."

Glynda managed a smile. "Yes, they're a little lower down too."

Carolina affected a pounce from her seat, making a show of throttling Glynda. Glynda jumped from her seat and the sudden movement made her yelp in a paroxysm of pain. She held her abdomen, bending over with the attack. No one believed it was anything but genuine, and they all sprang to her side with concern.

Anthea went into diagnostic mode as Molly and Carolina helped Glynda to her seat. "Where precisely does it hurt? Any fever, nausea, bleeding?"

Glynda willed her face to drop its mantle of agony, but the pain thrust itself at her again. She struggled to answer the question and free herself from being the centre of attention. She tried to stand up but quickly crumbled back to the seat, holding the right side of her pelvis. Sweat poured from her pale forehead.

Anthea told Carolina to call Dr. Gentile since he was the gyne on call for the ER today.

Glynda nodded, unable to suppress a low moan as another wave of pain shook her.

Later that afternoon, Anthea vacillated as to whether to let Gavin attend the next patient. She decided against it when Molly tipped her off that the young woman was obviously overwhelmed with anxiety over her complaint. The presence of a good-looking male medical student would not help the situation. Shelly Smythe wanted a labial reduction.

The young girl had the dimensions and face of a model and her flaxen hair swung in a silky arc as she reached into her tote for a magazine. She wet her middle finger with her tongue and flipped quickly through the pages until she found what she was looking for. She held it up to Anthea and pointed to a picture of a playmate straddled to expose a pink, vulva stripped of all pubic hair beyond the smallest oblong patch above it. "I want a pretty one like this."

Anthea resurrected her ever-more popular speech about how normal human anatomy varies widely between individuals. That the condition in no way effects her reproductive ability and is considered a cosmetic procedure and that therefore government medical plans would not cover the cost of it.

After an examination, she said softly to the troubled girl, "Believe me, I'm quite sure that I have seen many more vaginas than you will ever see, and yours is well within the limits of normal. It's just not like that one. Are you sure you want undergo a painful surgery that might still not guarantee an exact replica of what you see as ideal?"

"I feel ugly," she responded, looking down into her yellow handbag, a tremble beginning to inhabit her Paris Pout. "I don't want a boy to see it when it looks like that."

"That's just one part of you, Shelly. You're not disfigured or abnormal. I'm sure a boy will love you for what you are - for looking like a real woman not an airbrushed playmate with genitals more like someone who hasn't passed puberty. These magazines are making unobtainable images that are barely human. Have you thought of it in that way?"

"No. I haven't talked to anyone about it. It's too embarrassing. My friends say I'm perfect but they don't know that I'm not." She dabbed at her cheek with a ragged tissue.

Anthea sighed and passed Shelly a box of tissues. Anthea asked the young woman to give it a second thought and if after that, she wished to proceed, they'd book the surgery. Shelly wiped her eyes again, worried that her makeup was running and gave a weak nod of agreement.

As Anthea closed the door to the exam room she acknowledged her own vanity and how each woman has to struggle to draw an ever-shifting accord with her body that hopefully stopped somewhere short of tyranny. She was plucked away from that thought by Gavin waving the next chart at her. She walked over to him. "What is it?"

"Ummm, primary infertility - well not really infertility yet, because they haven't really tried to get pregnant."

"So, why are they here?"

Gavin tried to put the problem succinctly. The couple were both 38 and had decided initially not to have kids, but now were second guessing and wondering what the risks of a pregnancy at their age would be.

Molly stopped to whisper loudly in Gavin's ear, "The risk of pregnancy is *kids!*"

In the exam room Anthea and Gavin listened to Angela and Rob Fisk explain their dilemma.

"Well Rob travels a lot for work and so do I," Angela began. "Between us both, we're hardly home more than two weeks a month and sometimes not at the same time."

"Yes," agreed Rob, "and when we are home we have a lot of catching up to do with our friends and activities – you see we're both tri-athletes and we have to make training time a priority. We try to put in a two-hour workout a day. So, we've heard about all of this . . . this ovulation monitoring and that, well, how are you going to get time to do that Angel baby?'

"Yes, it's all so precise and demanding, it would sort of take over our lives, wouldn't it?"

Anthea nodded, "Well, you're right, it would. And there's no point in doing it unless you commit to it – the same kind of commitment you give to your jobs or your triathlons. It can be expensive and time consuming – like children! There's no getting away from it – ask your parents."

Angela and Rob took a long look at each other. Angela rolled her dark eyes. "Sounds like a shit-load of trouble to me, lover."

"Yeh, you'd probably have to give up your hot yoga too and you just paid for another session. What d'ya think, Angel baby?"

Angela pulled her hair behind her shoulders, thinking about how much she loved the hot yoga, "Yaaaaa," she said, "that's a tough one."

Gavin sat with his hands clasped between his knees looking back and forth at each one, unsure where this might lead them. Anthea felt that she'd walked into a Saturday Night Live skit. She stood up and handed the lab work and Assisted Reproduction information package to them. The two sat there, still mulling over the pros and cons of a change in lifestyle. Angela's forehead squeezed out a wrinkle. "It's a much bigger commitment than I thought, honey. It's kinda gonna wreck everything."

"You know," Anthea said, filling in a long silence, "I don't have children myself, but I do have two dogs, and not to trivialize the matter, but even looking after dogs was a big adjustment for me. I shudder to think what a baby would do."

Minutes passed as one muttered softly into the gaze of the other. Anthea stared beyond them at the chart depicting fetal growth. She felt the colour drain from her face as sweat broke from her forehead. She reached to flick on the fan beside her and willed herself to take slow deep breaths.

"Yea, babe," said Rob, patting Angela on the head, "maybe we should get a dog first and see how that works out for us – a small dog, like one that we can carry around and makes small poops."

Angela pulled more vigorously on her hair. "Yea, or even a gerbil or something to start off with. Great! We've reached a decision!"

As the happy couple trotted out, thanking her for her expertise, Anthea waved weakly, shut the door quickly and vomited into the sink.

At the end of the day, Anthea, Carolina, Molly and Georgia walked across the street to the hospital to visit Glynda. In the dusky light of the early evening, a cool wind rose from the street and tugged at the light coats that the sunny morning had coaxed them into wearing. Winter was reluctant to release its grip and while the bald patches of sidewalk were navigable, dirty snow dunes still lounged at the side of the roads.

As they walked past the pharmacy, Anthea broke away telling them she'd catch up in a minute. She looked over to the counter and saw that Weird Peter was behind it – the biggest gossip in the hospital and possibly still holding a torch for Anthea. He saw her and asked loudly what he could get for her today.

"Oh, a nice big box of anti-flatulants, Peter, thank you," she shouted back from the entrance.

He reached over the counter and pointed to the aisle beside her. "These, I can personally recommend," he said, "excellent product – or lack thereof." His pointy shoulders shook with delight, in admiration of his own wit.

Anthea smiled and held up a pack of gum, "Just kidding, actually."

She artfully escaped Peter's tender mercies and found the others stopped in their tracks by the looming green front of Dr. Saxon's belly. "Well, if it isn't my little pudding!" he bellowed, arms outstretched, as if he were quoting Shakespeare on a Stratford stage.

"I'm great, peaches, how are you?" Anthea answered.

"Cute Brock, but don't pout when I tell you it's my little Georgie Porgy pudding and pie I'm happy to see," he said, as he took his granddaughter into his hairy arms and lifted her off the floor, crushing her upturned nose into his barrel chest enough to explain why it went that way.

"Are you whipping Dr. Brock's office into shape for her?" he said into her spiky head of hair "Maybe she'll have the call schedule out on time now."

Anthea winced and smiled showing both sets of teeth like a cornered dog.

Carolina risked stroking one of Georgia's quills, taking care to linger on Saxon's forearm after the fact. She captured his gaze and cooed, "This little doll is directly under my supervision, Dr. Saxon, and I look forward to giving her a constructive and rewarding work experience." She let loose a wide smile which was in stark contrast with the one still pasted on Anthea's face.

Saxon lifted his head like a bull noticing a toreador's cape for the first time. His small eyes, like blue pinholes, poked out of the white clouds of his wind-blown eyebrows as they examined Carolina. "Well, a good mark would be very helpful to her average, wouldn't it Pudding? She has big plans."

"She'd make a wonderful librarian, Dr. Saxon," Carolina said, "such attention to detail." He released his granddaughter, his large hand rubbing the side of her face. "You keep up the good work, sweetie." His smile fled back into the deep crevasses that imprisoned it. "Brock, see to it that I get that schedule and we need to meet about the fundraiser soon, too. I've told everyone that you have big plans for it, so it better be damn good." With that, he retreated into the corridor, swaying like a ship in angry water.

Carolina tilted her head as she watched him leave. "Such a lovely man. Do you have a grandmother, Georgia?"

Georgia's face dropped. "She's dead."

"Pity," Carolina said.

Anthea passed between the two letting the corners of her mouth whisper a surreptitious warning into Carolina's ear. "Back off, Granny. Don't even think about it."

Glynda felt her hand being rubbed gently and lifted her heavy eyelids to see four concerned faces hovering above her. Molly asked how she was feeling, rearranging the bed covers to make them perfect.

"I don't know. I'm not in pain, but I can't remember what exactly Dr. Gentile told me when I first woke up – something about tension?"

"Torsion perhaps?" Anthea said, "when a growth gets big enough to topple the ovary?"

Glynda nodded. "That's what caused the sudden pain . . . no pain now, I feel great!"

Carolina took Glynda's other hand. "I know - it's the drugs. That's how I feel every night."

"Ha, didn't know what I was missing. An altered state has got its merits." Glynda said.

"Now, what do they call a Christian who falls into sin, Glynda?" Carolina asked, tapping Glynda's hand.

Molly batted the answer at Carolina. "A Catholic."

Their laughter was interrupted by a cough from the doorway. Edna stood there looking small and worried. She held a plastic container in her hand. "May I come in?"

They all looked at Glynda who beckoned to Edna and introduced her to the others. After some small talk, they left Glynda with Edna, but not before Glynda told Anthea that she had given Dr. Gentile full permission to share any information with her.

Edna approached the bedside and opened up the plastic container. The comforting smell of chicken soup escaped into the room. "I made this myself for you, Glynda – as soon as I heard what happened. Would you like some now?"

Glynda raised herself onto one elbow and felt her stomach rumble in reaction to the stimulus of the soup. She looked into the eyes of the old woman and thought they were puffy and red – more vulnerable than she had ever known them. Glynda whispered a thanks and Edna pulled a spoon from her bag. "Do you want me to feed you? It might be hard for you to sit up."

Glynda struggled to a sitting position and Edna was there propping up the pillows for her. She took the first sip of the warm liquid and let it run down her throat. It soothed the dryness that remained from the tracheal tube and she could not help a murmur of pleasure escape from her mouth. "This is great, Edna. I didn't know you could cook like this."

Edna brought her face forward and Glynda thought she might kiss her cheek. "I've become lazy. You've taken such good care of me. It's time I took care of you. You're all I have."

The stupor of the anaesthetic seemed to fall away from her as Glynda realized the novelty of this situation. *I probably haven't woken up from the surgery yet. This can't be real – Edna, a nice little old lady who makes chicken soup? Oh God, I've died and I'm either in my heaven or Edna's hell.*

A hand tugged her sleeve from behind and Anthea turned to meet Dr. Gentile's thin, creased face. It was solemn and the blessing of his beautiful smile did not cast itself upon her, as was its custom. A chill shot through her as she quickly surmised the most likely reason he had made a point of catching her.

Dr. Gentile sighed and thrust his hands in his pockets. "I did a frozen section and it's a carcinoma. I did a hyst, as she had consented to, took the ovaries and I guess we'll know the staging when we get the final path. I'll try to get her a consult at a Tertiary Centre immediately for chemo and such."

Anthea's stomach clenched and she felt dizzy and nauseous again. She looked for a place to sit and felt Clive's strength at her arm. She noted how flimsy a professional demeanor is when the patient is someone you know well. It falls away like onion skin; the cracking of it muting the voice delivering the news, distancing it, as if they were calling from another room. Since her mother's death, it took so little to let that grim shadow drape itself over her shoulders. It suppressed every breath, invaded every conversation; snuffed the joy out of the smallest of daily pleasures. It could revisit her without invitation or warning and gnaw at her resolve to remain objective. Its dark fingers would pick open sores on her skin, oozing fresh insult.

Clive's voice fell to something short of a whisper. "I'm going to tell her now. She's lucid enough."

Anthea clasped her hands and brought them to her face.

"Breathe, Anthea, gather yourself, my dear," Clive said. "Remember, even if it is the worst case, a lot depends upon the staging of the disease. We owe it to Glynda to be optimistic at this stage."

Anthea knew that she had to be there to deliver the news to Glynda and walked to the room trying to push the dread back into the hole it had crawled out of. The sad spectre of a brave face, ravished by cancer broke the surface of Anthea's mind. That cheeky sparkle that had always flashed from her mother's eyes was replaced by a hopeless apology for the heartbreak she saw in Anthea's own. Sian Brock had never had time or patience for self-pity. She said it was an ungrateful condition. Her body had carried out millions of complicated tasks for her benefit on a daily basis for seventy years, tirelessly scouring, repairing, sifting, arranging and rearranging to keep things in working order; recruiting from its well-planned reserves to fight battles she had never even been aware of. It had allowed her a life that had shined like polished stone, smoothed and warmed by the touch of people who had loved her from birth to death. How can she blame it now when the task had finally become too much; when the last cell in the last system that supported this good fortune was overwhelmed, fighting to the bitter end? Not such a tragedy she had said, more of a triumph.

Anthea leaned against the mass of the stone feature wall they were passing and felt her frame get smaller. She felt the cool surface warm under her touch and allowed her fingers to grip the ridges that rose in waves from it. Clive's furrowed forehead met her own as his hand squeezed her shoulder. "You don't seem well. You don't have to come, you know," he said, the round, melodic tones of his Caribbean origins wrapping around her fears like a soft blanket, plucked from in front of a hearth on a winter's night. "You're thinking of your mother, aren't you?"

She nodded and let an unconscious smile escape. "You remember how much she loved her own eccentricities and made a point of teasing people with them. She claimed to be an Atheist but told us that she believed, like the ancient Celts, that stones held the souls of ancestors. The inconsistency of her theories never bothered eccentrics and that's why she became one. It meant you couldn't win an argument with her."

"Well, facts can be very inconvenient," Clive added, with a smile.

"True enough, but I've just convinced myself that I felt her presence in that stone there."

She looked into his kind face, carved and weathered like a rock cliff; steady and unshakable now, as he had been during other bleak moments that had clutched at her happiness. Anthea wiped a stray tear from her cheek, and willed her voice to be strong. "Clive, if you weren't so desperately in love with your wife, I would steal you away from her."

The deep lines that appeared either side of his wide, engaging smile must have weakened the moral resolve of so many women he encountered. "Yes," he said, "love is a curse - one that I am happily enslaved to. But even at seventy-one, I never tire of hearing such things from a lovely young lady with an Oedipus complex. It will give me much needed romantic energy this evening and Audrey will have only you to thank."

Anthea waved a finger. "You tell her I'm after you."

"I've told her that for years, my dear. I don't want her to become complacent."

He took her arm in his and they continued to Glynda's room. Anthea peered around the door way to see that Glynda had company. She saw the back of a well-dressed man, his thick mane of silver hair curling down toward the collar of his blazer as he arranged an impressive bouquet of yellow roses at her bedside. Glynda's face was alight with joy, as she swept her hair self-consciously behind her ears, suddenly aware that she had no makeup on. "Flavio! What a surprise. How on earth did you know I was in hospital?"

Flavio gestured emphatically and spoke with a strong Italian accent. "Eh, I joost saw you Modder-Low at da restaurante earlier today an' she tell me. She say, maybe you like a leettle beet of company – so I come! I hope is OK – yes?"

Anthea put her hand on Clive's chest. "Wait . . . let's wait. You're on call tonight? We can come back when you have a minute. This could be the best of medicines."

It was a few minutes after five and Clive had gone into a delivery. With any luck, it would be uncomplicated and they could call back in to see Glynda after. He came into the lounge about forty-five minutes later and said he was ready to talk to Glynda. Her stomach lurched and she wished that she had eaten something while she had a chance, it might have settled it a bit.

Glynda was sitting up in bed, reading what looked like a bible. She had put her make up on and her blonde hair was brushed, falling softly behind her ears to rest on her thin shoulders. Anthea realized that she'd never seen her with her hair in anything but under the strict command of a bun and she now saw how truly lovely her face was. Glynda beamed at the two of them, closing her book. "Well, two of my favourite people. Tell me, how are you? Then you can tell me how I am."

Clive, ever the professional, sent her an easy, confident smile. He clasped her hands in his own and said, "I am fine, and look at you, I can hardly believe that you just came out of a major surgery."

Her eyes looked squarely into his, and she returned his good will. She pointed upward, "I have another powerful ally besides you two."

"I believe you do," Clive said. "This is your strength."

Anthea's face must have betrayed her anxiety and Glynda said, "From the look on your face, Anthea, I'm going to need all the strength I can get. It's not good is it?"

Anthea made an effort to speak, but Clive held up his hands. "Glynda, my dear, we cannot make any pronouncements yet, as you know. But, the tumour did look suspicious to me. So, I did what's called a frozen section, there and then, and it confirmed a carcinoma – a cancer. So, because of that, I did a complete hysterectomy, ovaries and all, and sent it off to pathology. It is a process called 'staging' that is important. It will tell us the specific type and stage the cancer is in. Let's wait and see what that tells us, and we'll go from there. People do win these battles, my dear."

Glynda reached for Anthea's hand, still smiling bravely. Anthea scolded herself into doing the same, but feared speaking.

"You're right, Dr. Gentile," Glynda said, "and whatever the outcome, I can deal with it. I've always put my faith in God and I accept that he knows what path he wants my life to take."

Anthea nodded, in a firm, resolute agreement, she only wished she felt. She willed her voice to be as unshakeable as her gesture. "Yep, between us and God, we've got ya covered, Glynda, and we're not ready to hand you over to him without a fight."

Glynda showed no sign that the gravity of the news had imposed upon her. "I've already had two blessings today, you know. Edna has been very nice to me, she brought me home-made soup, and Flavio, a friend of mine brought me this beautiful bouquet."

Anthea curled her fingers around one of the roses. "The flowers are a blessing, Glynda, Edna's a damn miracle!"

Glynda laughed out loud and her eyes shone just a little. "Where there's one, there could be another."

HOMECARE STUDIES: LEVEL 1V

Anthea

ANTHEA PULLED OVER BESIDE A pharmacy, checking her calendar for the third time. She aligned the ovulation dates on the pregnancy wheel to the date of her mother's cremation, and estimated that she could be no more than nine weeks pregnant, if that last light period wasn't one. *Really? Really? I'm going to be the one per cent of women who gets pregnant on an IUD AND, one of those idiots who didn't insist on a condom? No way, no way,* she thought. *Maybe I'll be lucky and just die of syphilis.*

She turned the car back on and put on her indicator. "Fuck" she said, clenching her teeth as hard as she clenched the steering wheel. She turned the ignition off again to go into the pharmacy.

The pregnancy test sat in the passenger seat, willing Anthea to pick it up – *It's like one of those quiet, sneaky babies who look directly into your soul and find it wanting. If you ignore it, you're deeply flawed, and if you don't, you end up holding it far longer than you want, while it puts its wet finger up your nose. People think their babies are far cuter than they are.*

As the busy streets gave way to the country roads, Anthea pulled the car over, grabbed the pregnancy test and quickly peed onto the stick while crouching behind the open car door. A car full of evil, curious children drove passed slowly and Anthea could see them waving frantically as they pointed and hooted like wild monkeys. *It's a conspiracy the little parasites are all in on it together.*

Ralph's plangent tones were soothing to Anthea. Despite calling him every week and checking with her brother, Gryff to see how he felt their dad was doing, she worried constantly about how he was coping without their mother. She knew that he would put on a brave front for her with every phone call. Only the occasional silences while he grasped at his composure, betrayed that grief was still a daily agony.

"Oh, it's you, Anthea, love," he said. "You sound just like your mother."

"Oh Dad, I'm sorry. I wish it was she calling you."

"Don't you fret, lovely girl. I'm alright. You just put one foot in front of the other and get on with things. Your mother wouldn't tolerate us doing anything else. Remember how she'd scold us? She'd say, 'Life is for the living, Ralph, don't you be burying yourself with me.' I tell myself that every day. It's like she's here beside me, smacking me in the head."

Anthea relished the memory of her mother's playful 'love taps'.

"I can't wait to see you, love," Ralph said, his voice travelling the vast distance to nestle into her ear. "I can't believe that in only *ten sleeps*, you'll be at The Cwtch with us again."

Memories blossomed in her mind of when they would escape London and follow their noses, like homing pigeons, to the Welsh coast. The old, white cottage or *bwthyn* squatted stubbornly atop ragged cliffs, holding its ground against the torment of the sea. Four generations of the Gryffydd family had lived their lives within its thick stone walls. The carbon in their breath, the vibrations of their voices, the secrets of their dreams had seeped into those walls to form its formidable exoskeleton, holding their vulnerability to the outside world at bay. When they turned off the curve in the road, down the narrow, winding driveway that breached the sanctum, any assaults that clung to them fell away. Worries, like parasites bewitched, released their mandibles and dropped into the leafy walls of the passage. Two gryphons, Gelert and Gideon, loomed atop the entrance to the inner yard, ready to pounce on anyone who came with intent to be productive.

He went on to tell her that her mother's sister, Auntie Ceri was insisting on picking Anthea up at the airport and coming to stay at "The Cwtch" with Gryff and the kids. He added, "God help us all."

Anthea looked at the photograph of Gryff's kids on her mantelpiece. She imagined a small, white silhouette of a child beside the other children – a place saver. *It's the ghost of that bundle of differentiated cells trying to grow inside me; fighting as hard to survive as that last living cell did in Mam - before its tiny little mitochondria sighed its last breath and was snuffed out.*

Anthea shuddered and thrust herself back into the conversation by reminding Ralph how helpful her aunt had been to them during the last months of her mother's life. He had to be nice to her.

"Oh, you can get use to a bad smell if you're around it long enough. She's just so damn bossy. No wonder she can't hang onto a man for very long."

"Speaking as another bossy, independent woman, who can't hang on to a man, I feel I have to defend her."

"Don't be silly, there's no comparison – you're pretty."

Anthea knew there was no point in trying to resolve the old rivalry that he and Auntie Ceri had enjoyed for years. It was Auntie Ceri who had introduced her mother to Ralph when he and Ceri were in law school together. Her mother would take no sides, in fact, she would more likely add fuel to the fire, openly pointing out the weaker parts of the one's character to the other and enjoy watching them bicker over it. She found them entertaining; both firm in their stubborn, self-righteous convictions as they competed for her favour. She gave it to neither.

Putting down the phone, the goodbye was sweeter now, knowing that she would be able to put her arms around her father's shoulders in ten sleeps. But, this agreeable feeling only lasted as long as it took her to realize what she had to get done before leaving. *Hopefully, Carolina would come to look after Spock, Twiggy and the cats. Clive's covering the clinic, I'll have a quick meeting about the Fund Raiser to get Saxon off my back and . . . get an abortion.*

The panic took hold of her. Her eyes stared into the photograph again, features beginning to organize themselves in the ghostly face. *A baby? Ian's baby. A baby born with an IUD sticking out of it's nostril! Ian can never know. He'd want to keep it, regardless of our promise to act like the 'hot crematorium sex' had never happened. He was going to work on his marriage and I was going to work on my life . . . all I've really worked on is destroying four lives. It's great being a heartless bitch.*

Statistics echoed through her mind like bingo numbers as she sifted through her closet and threw a few items into the open suitcase in the corner of the room. 50% *chance of miscarriage with an IUD pregnancy - 25% chance if the IUD was removed in early pregnancy, 4 times the risk of infection and second trimester loss, increased rate of ectopic pregnancy . . . I've got to book an appointment . . . Anthea, deal with this! If I order my own blood test and ultra sound Carolina will see the results – maybe I'll call Clive tomorrow – do them through his office - no, I'll just go to Toronto - how am I going to get two days off? Fuck! Ok, I'll do it in Britain – less explaining to do. I'll just say I have to see a friend in London for a few days. There's time.*

All she needed to be sure of, was that it wasn't an ectopic pregnancy. All she really needed right now, was to get to an ultra sound machine – *easy!*

The need to check something off the list was irritating her and there was no time like the present to solve this issue with Jack Flynte. She did regret telling him to, "fuck off and get a sense of humour", instead of apologizing. He had given her a lift home, after all, and she should have been more ameliorative. *But really,* she told herself, *anyone who cares that much about proper breeding in anything alive is probably not someone I'd get along with anyway.* Then, when he told her that she should shovel the filth out of her dirty mouth to make room for a thank you, well, before she knew it, she'd told the 'delicate little prick to go back to his tramp of a dog.' *People are as sensitive about their animals as about their children, and I should have known better than to stoop that low.* But it got him. He just spluttered something incomprehensible and slammed the car door, not noticing a document folder slide out into the dirt. She found it on the driveway on the weekend. It was his divorce papers: *no surprise there.*

She could have mailed them, but decided that she probably should make an attempt at an apology. *He lives next door and that would always make things awkward and he was a single man who, while he was a little geeky, also didn't qualify as a Troll. Also, it would be good for Carolina to have a neighbour she could call when she came to look after the dogs if she needed to. At the very least, I'll suggest that we should try to get on as neighbours- if only to make one part of my life less complicated. I'll hand deliver the folder.*

She had a very good bottle of wine in the cupboard and she'd take it over in an hour or so. By then he should have returned from the dance class she had successfully avoided.

Through the window, a light spray of rain caught the orange glow of the outside lamp of Jack's house and made it look like a candle holding back the darkness. First, she would just take the dogs for a pee on the leash and go over the rise and see if his car had returned yet. If it was there, she'd take the dogs home and walk around to the front of his house, like a polite neighbour would do. She pulled up the hood of her black raincoat, put on her wellies and resolved to make a new friend.

Twiggy and Spock tugged on their leashes, anticipating freedom, but she held them as she climbed the incline beside her property for a look at Jack's driveway. She could just make out his black SUV parked in front of his house. She felt a flutter of nerves rise in her stomach as she rehearsed what she might say when he opened his door to her; *something congenial and contrite.*

She turned to make her way back to the house and her foot found a loose stone that rolled beneath her boot, taking her balance from her. She put her hand down to break the fall and in doing so, gave Spock the opportunity to bolt away from her. She watched him bounce over the horizon towards Jack's back walk-out window and stare through it, tail wagging, panting with excitement. Twiggy licked a spot of mud off Anthea's face like a worried parent with an old tissue full of spit.

"Christ," she muttered looking at her mud-covered hands, knowing her bottom probably looked the same. "Spock, come!" she called in an undertone that tried to register authority, but was not likely to be heard by anyone but him. Spock looked back at her, his tongue flapping with each quick breath, his small, beady eyes acknowledging her own but not comprehending what it was, *exactly,* she was asking of him. Could she be more *specific*, please?

"Come! Come you fucking asshole dog!" she yelled. Spock sniffed the air and then licked his crotch, returning within a few licks to stare again into the window.

Anthea squinted in the dusk, and couldn't see any signs of movement in the room that Spock was surveying. Maybe he's somewhere in the rest of the house, she hoped, and quickly ran down the embankment to get Spock. She had just grabbed his leash, when a muffled series of yelps came from beyond the glass in the corner of the room. Anthea peered through the glass door. A half naked blonde woman was straddling a man in an armchair, rutting with some athleticism. The woman tossed her head back into a substantial arch while her breasts slid back and forth on her chest. This is how she saw the two shadowy figures of Anthea and Spock at the window. The woman sprang back and attempted to cover herself with a nearby pillow as Jack ran angrily to the window, bits of him bobbing before he thought to subdue them with his left hand. His right was reaching for a lethal kitchen mop. Anthea turned to run up the hill, shouting, "I'm sorry, I didn't see anything," which, if she'd thought about it, implied that she did.

Jack held up the mop and shook it at her, keeping his other hand where it should be. "It's you again. What kind of sick weirdo are you, peeking through my windows? You crazy bitch!"

Anthea scrambled as best she could, fighting against Spock's overwhelming strength and enthusiasm to see his girlfriend, Scarlet, the Irish Setter. "No, no," she protested, "I was just chasing Spock - really. He got away from me . . . I'm not a . . . a weirdo, honest, I'm a gynecologist. . . shit, no . . . please apologize to Elizabeth, for me too. Tell her I won't be back to dance class."

Anthea gave the leash a mighty heave and pulled the still reluctant Spock by the collar. "I'm going to cut those fucking balls of yours off tomorrow!"

Jack looked down at his own handful and held on to them more affectionately as he yanked the blinds across the window, cursing his nosy, nutbar neighbour.

Back at the house, under a warm blanket, Anthea lamented yet another lost romantic opportunity. Now that Jack knew she was 'The Fucking Dog Lady', and oh yes, having seen Elizabeth Belamy ride him like a rodeo clown, she had lost her enthusiasm for it. *Although, I should return his divorce papers. Maybe when he's done with Elastic Elizabeth, I could stop swearing and . . . after the . . . after things are taken care of, Jack and I could live happily ever after; just we two and the dogs. Doesn't that sound fucking likely? No, I'll just throw them on his porch in a drive-by delivery.*

Carolina

The foyer of Aurora Lodge was bathed in late afternoon sunshine. It entered tall windows that stretched two stories high above the nodding, white cotton heads of the ancient women, sitting in a quiet circle of floral wing chairs. Their upper bodies were curled into question marks as they each failed to resist the pull of a pleasant nap. Their crumpled pastel figures were dappled by the play of light darting through the sway of evergreens lined up outside like a chorus of showgirls kicking up their skirts.

As the front door opened, the wind sent a breathy song, spilling momentarily, into the circle of elders, nudging one or two of them back from sleep. One curious face twisted into disapproval as Carolina waved a greeting, her twelve colourful bracelets jostling noisily. Another let a broad smile loose with a comment about how she wished she could wear those sorts of shoes again. A third, a tiny sliver of pink, stood in her path and ordered her out of her house.

Carolina stood her ground. "Sorry, Mrs. Foster, I have to see my mother."

Mrs. Foster's face softened. "Does she live in my house?"

"Yes, Mrs. Foster, just down the hall there."

"Well, I don't know what all these people are doing in my living room. Tell her to get the hell out too."

"Will do, Mrs. Foster, will do," Carolina promised, as the nasty piece of gristle that was left of the old lady shuffled away, muttering other complaints.

The cleaning carts were being wheeled passed as Carolina navigated the meandering hallways, holding her breath against the occasional waft of human waste.

One of the staff nurses hailed from further down the hall and told her that her mother had been rummaging through the room again, unwilling to leave it. Perhaps Carolina could coax her to go for a walk.

Carolina gave a cursory knock on the door beside the photo of Lucia Stiletto. It was one of Carolina's favourite pictures of her mother. The angle and flattering light did its magic and you could see the younger woman's face rise out of its current landscape. The wide set, hooded eyes, dark and capricious; the defiance, always lurking just below the curl of her smile that had once carried her into her husband's arms against her father's thundering disapproval; the inconstancy that many who knew her now, put down to Alzheimer's but that Carolina knew was not. She peered in to see her mother standing in her nightgown rifling through the contents of a dresser drawer.

She embraced the old woman from behind, "Come stai, Mamma?"

Her mother made the smallest of acknowledgements that she had been touched, looking suspiciously at Carolina then resuming her inspection. Carolina ran her fingers through the thin, grey wisps of hair, pulling it back from her lined face and twirling it around her fingers.

"Mamma," she said, and continued in the Barletano dialect her mother insisted she use when addressing her, "why are you still in your nightgown? It doesn't look good this late in the day. Here, let me get you dressed and do your hair and we'll go out for a walk. It's windy, but it's a beautiful day today."

Again, her mother released her gaze from the drawer and set it on Carolina without any response. Carolina went to the closet and chose a red jersey dress that would be easy to slip over her mother's head. She began to sing a traditional folk song that was a favourite when growing up, as this usually spawned her mother's cooperation. She was able to remove the nightgown and negotiate the flaccid skin of her once proud breasts into a loose bra. She raised the stiff arms and pulled the dress down, checking first that the diaper below it was dry. Without making her stand, she let the skirt of the dress gather around the old woman on the chair, while she slipped off the black house slippers and carefully pulled knee high stockings up each calf. It was when the red shoes with sparkly bows were properly placed on the delicate bones of her feet that her mother muttered a faint, "Grazzie, bella."

Gathering the white gauze that her mother's hair had become, Carolina remembered the weight of the shimmering mane she would play with when as a child, she ordered her mother to be a customer in her hairdressing salon. It would be brushed and braided and rolled into various exotic sculptures with numerous barrettes and flowers thrust into its folds. Now, she arranged it skillfully into a thin bun to cover the pink bald spots that had leached through her scalp. She touched a faint line of perfume either side of her mother's neck and inhaled its familiar scent.

Carolina held a coat behind Lucia and attempted to guide one arm through the sleeve, but there came an abrupt, "Not yet . . . after." It was then Carolina realized that Lucia Stiletto wanted to show herself off a little as she promenaded the hallways to the exit. She drifted through the foyer, like an exotic scarlet flower in a garden of daisies. *Like mother, like daughter,* noted Carolina.

There was no other conversation from Lucia during the half hour walk around the grounds despite Carolina's constant parade of questions about spring flowers or recent dinner menus. She brought Lucia to the dining hall and after a gentle kiss on each cheek let an attendant take her arm and guide her to her seat. Flora was a large, Jamaican woman with a smile that could not fail to elicit one in return, "Oh, it's you Lucia!" Flora said, "for a moment I thought Sophia Loren had come to dinner with us."

Carolina glanced at her watch and thought she might make the business office before it closed. She reached into her purse and pulled out the notice that she had received from the retirement home, reporting that the monthly payment was past due for the third time. She'd better talk fast again and reassure them that she'd do better in the future. Despite her promise to Lucia not to sell the house, maybe it was time to consider it. Her mother was now getting to the state that she wouldn't miss it any more – she may not even miss Carolina anymore.

This question weighed on her mind as she drove home. It was only knocked out of her thoughts when she remembered that she had Melinda's dress in the dry cleaner bag in the back of the car. She pulled to the side of the road, found her cell phone and dialed Melinda's number. She could return the dress and maybe have a quick visit.

There was a pause from the other end of the phone, slightly longer than was comfortable. "Eh, well . . . it's close to dinner time and . . . well Daniel will be home soon, so maybe another time – OK? I don't need that dress anyway, in fact – just keep it. Don't worry about returning it."

Carolina felt the distance in Melinda's voice - an aggravation that hadn't been there before. "Look, I won't stay long. I just thought it'd be good to see you. I've had a shitty day."

Umm, sorry, Carolina it's just not a good idea for us to . . . really . . . keep the dress. It's a Dior."

The flat tones said what Melinda was avoiding with words and Carolina didn't like to be taken for a fool. She bit her lip. "Melinda, you got my messages, didn't you, but hoped I'd just go away like a bad smell if you distanced yourself. If you don't want to hang around me anymore that's fine - I get it, but spare me the run around and the fucking Good Will donation."

Carolina slapped the phone down and gripped the steering wheel. She drove to the gates of Melinda's home and saw that they were closed. She grabbed the dry-cleaning bag from the back of the car and hung it on the curl of the iron gate, pressed the intercom and drove off.

At home, she kicked off her shoes, released her hair from its constraints, put on her satin robe and went into the small study at the back of her house. She poured a long glass of Shiraz and collapsed into her chair to the melancholy strains of Leonard Cohen's Joan of Arc, a present from Anthea last Christmas.

As she sank into drunken despondency she let her gaze wander through the room, reaping comfort from the titles of great literature, philosophy and history that went from floor to ceiling. *Homer, Dickens, Proust, Russian shit like Dostoyevsky, Tolstoy and Solzhenitsyn and of course, everything Ol'Wil ever did.* She considered re-reading one of his comedies to lighten her mood. Despite her cynical nature, she liked when things ended with a wedding.

Her phone rang and she ignored it. A reluctant glance at the display showed the name Gerald Walker. *Gerald Walker – that smarmy bastard at the fund raiser – great.* She surmised that her life wasn't substantial enough to be a tragedy, it was probably more like a dark comedy and the joke was on her. *Fuck!*

Molly

After making elaborate arrangements with Georgia to help with Orlagh's floor routine, Molly left for home and pulled up to the untidy front yard of her split-level bungalow. She suddenly saw it objectively. It was still light enough to see that the paint on the front porch was peeling, part of the driveway had sunk and needed filling and the lawn looked like it had one of the fascinating skin diseases she had seen on some patients. Stubborn tufts of spiky grass staked their claim amongst vast scabs of pebbles and dirt. *It's like a man with a bad comb-over,* thought Molly. Molly's lawn had grubs, so it was really a comb over with lice in it. Not attractive and all the neighbours were afraid of catching it.

She sighed and then thought of Glynda. *Poor Glynda.* She shook any negative thoughts from her mind and considered the immediate problem. *What I'm going to put on the table for dinner. I really should cook something that doesn't come out of a box tonight.* She tried to think what takeout food didn't come that way.

Molly opened the front door and saw Lovey struggle up from her mat and come waddling over, head down in a posture that showed undying adoration. Her wet nose brushed Molly's cheek as she stooped to give her old dog a hug that left no doubt that the devotion was reciprocated.

Fiona ran out from the living room bestowing another wet kiss on Molly's cheek. "Hi Momma, you smell like Lovey! Callum gave me some yogurt, cuz I was hungry."

"That's good," Molly said, wiping the residue from her cheek. "What's he doing?"

"He's in the office on the computer. He said he's doing his research."

"Research again, is it?" Molly said, remembering the sort of research that she had had meant to put parental controls on a few weeks ago.

She opened the office door and saw Callum hit a computer key quickly. "Callum, I swear to God, if you're on those porno sites again I'll have your arse in a sling. Let me see the history."

"Relax Big Red! It's not that, honest, I was just on Facebook with my friend – and it wasn't a child molester either."

"Really, how do you know that? They pose as kids, you know."

"Hang on, I'll ask him if he's doing that."

"And did you take Lovey for a walk today?

Callum turned to his mother, shaking his head. "Mom, she won't walk anymore. We get half way up the street and she lies down and won't get back up. I have to carry her all the way back home."

Molly nodded, acknowledging this new development. "OK, thanks for trying. Where's Angus? He should be home by now."

She heard the front door open and a loud, "I'm home," fill the hallway.

"Shut the door, Mom, so that I can get back on the porn sites, please," Callum said. Molly clipped the back of his head and went to greet Angus. She took his coat from his shoulders and they wandered into the kitchen where they both stared at the open fridge for some time, each wrestling with a quandary of their own. "So, Angus, how was your day at the centre? Anything new?"

"Oh yes, I met my new friend – not at the centre but at the graveyard."

"At the graveyard? What on earth took you there?"

"I like going there to visit the dead people – so does he. We sit and talk about stuff there."

"Talk? At the graveyard? About what? What do you talk about?"

"Mostly Sheila, who lives there now."

"Who's Sheila? Angus, who's this new friend of yours? Is he a kid?"

"It's Roger. He's fifty. He's great. We hold hands and hug a lot."

Molly swung around from the frying pan. "Oh, Dear God in heaven! You do what?" She caught herself and lowered her voice trying to restrain her panic. Just then the door bell rang and Angus swept to the door. Molly followed him, irritated by the interruption by, what would probably be someone trying to sell them something. Angus almost always bought anything he could if you didn't catch him - chocolate, Christmas cards, a new water purifier.

Molly rounded the corner in time to see Angus throwing himself at a compactly built older man whose flat cap flew off his head with the hearty embrace.

"Roger Mead!" Angus chimed. "Roger, Roger, Roger, I'm so glad to see you! Hey everybody, it's my friend Roger Mead!

Roger smiled a wide smile, reaching one hand out to Molly and holding out Angus's knapsack in the other. "You forgot it at the graveyard, buddy. Thought ya might need it."

Molly quickly made an assessment of this Roger character who liked to 'talk' to a young man who was clearly mentally challenged. It was always a struggle for her to give Angus some minor freedoms within his own community, balanced against the cold, cynical voice at the back of her mind that saw the potential for someone with sinister intentions. Life can't be lived like that, she rationalized but this instance roused the Tiger Mother within her; it sat back onto its haunches ready to pounce.

Roger had a pleasant face, rounded by the few extra pounds he carried but the features were well defined. His nose was large but formed a worthy centerpiece for the cheekbones that rose up beside it. It rambled in a curved path down his face, swerving from one side to the other telling a tale of past injury. His eyes were like small hazelnuts partially buried by a negligent squirrel in the furrows of his orbital cavity. His hair had been lifted straight up over the crown of his balding head by the momentum of the hat that had been knocked onto the step beside him. Seeing it, Molly was reminded of the state of the lawn she had fretted over earlier. Backlit by the wan light of the evening, his hair haloed his face and his crooked smile had the charm of a wayward angel. *Just the kind of face a psychopath needs to be successful.*

Molly took the back pack giving Roger a sharp, "Thank you." She reached for the open door and as she began to swing it shut, Angus pulled Roger inside and said, "Roger, Roger, come in. I want to show you my bedroom. You'll love it."

Roger put his hands up and looked directly at Molly, sensing her unease. He explained that they had both been at the graveyard where Sheila his late wife was buried. He caught a sly attack of emotion at those, still foreign words, and swallowed quickly. "Angus was grieving Thor and we found that we had enough common ground to share tears and even a few chuckles. I hope you don't mind me imposing here today, but I do have something I wanted to thank him for and the back pack had his address on it."

Molly noticed Angus's excitement at seeing his visitor. He had drawn his hands up and clasped them to his chest, almost shaking with delight.

She softened and chastised herself for being so abrupt – in manner and in thought and invited Roger in for a cup of tea.

"Angus," Molly said, "are you glad that you have a friend calling on you?"

Angus said nothing. He squeezed his face into a tight grin, burying his head deeply into his powerful shoulders.

"Relax Angus," Molly said putting her hands each side of his face. She introduced herself and let them both follow her into the kitchen. Roger giggled as he sat at the old wooden kitchen table and pulled out his cell phone. "I think Angus did something very thoughtful for me today. Let me show you . . ."

Roger held up the phone to the two anxious viewers. "That's Sheila's grave and that," he pointed a thick, unmanicured finger to a small patch of Forget Me Knots beside the white headstone, "that's Thor."

Angus released the tension he had wound up inside him and like a massive Jack in the Box, sprung up in the air, arms wide and flailing. "Surprise!"

Molly's hand flew to her mouth. Roger let out a hearty gust of laughter and when it stopped his hand blotted his eyes. "That was the best surprise I've ever had, Angus, thank you."

"Yea," said Angus a wide, small toothed grin filling his face like a neat row of corn kernels with only one missing. "Now they won't be lonely cuz they have each other."

Molly bit her lip and spoke softly, "Roger, would you like to stay to dinner? I was just going to order Chinese food."

"Well," Roger said, looking at the pamphlet Molly held up, "I'd never think of ordering Chinese food from McGregor's Chinese food, that would be like ordering pizza from Wong's Pizza."

Angus began to giggle, his broad shoulders shuddering with glee.

"Angus," Molly said, "what's so funny?"

Angus drew a deep breath and tried to speak, but another fit of laughter overcame him, so much so that he bent over and crossed his legs, still helpless to form a sentence.

By now, Molly had been infected by Angus's predicament, which gave Roger the licence to join in – no more aware of what the joke was than she.

"Angus, don't pee yourself, go to the washroom." Callum said, having come to see what was going on in the kitchen. Fiona clasped her hand to her mouth overjoyed to hear anything that involved a reference to bathroom activities.

Angus, waving his free hand emphatically, while clasping his crotch with the other, finally stammered out, "There's . . . there's nothing 'wong' with that!"

A loud chorus of whooping and groaning erupted from his audience but he found himself unable to accept the accolades and he scuttled off to the nearby bathroom. A loud, and very long stream of urine hit the bowl with an accompaniment of deep sighs and moans of relief.

Molly held her hands up to Roger and said, "Welcome to our fine dining establishment."

Roger sent her a wide smile across the kitchen table. "Dinner *and* first-class entertainment. It's been a long time since I've had such a belly laugh." He paused and swallowed, his face became serious for a moment. "I think I'd forgotten how . . . thanks." He coughed and willed himself back from a slippery slope. He excused himself and soon came back into the kitchen raising a bottle of white wine in one hand and a bottle of red in the other. With a sideward glance at Angus and with much gravity in his deep voice, he asked Molly, "Would you like a white one . . . or a *wong* one?"

Angus threw himself back in his chair with such appreciation for Roger's quip that he would have toppled, if Roger's strong arm had not caught it.

"Thanks, Roger Mead," Angus said, and looking at the rest of his family, added, "Don't I pick great friends?"

Roger filled the glasses and said, "I propose a toast to Thor and Sheila who are probably cuddling in heaven right now."

Time passed quickly and Molly was surprised that it was time for her to pick Orlagh up at the gym. Roger reached for his coat and was helping Molly on with hers when Angus came around the corner and thrust himself on Roger, slapping his back, unaware of his strength. "Roger, come again and we'll play darts, I'm really good, I get most of them in."

Molly rolled her eyes. "Yep, in your thighs, in the wall - some of them even on the dart board!"

Roger walked out with Molly and opened her car door. He smiled shyly and with a quick nod walked toward his own car. Just as quickly he spun around to reopen Molly's car door. "Molly . . . am I . . . and if I'm not . . . could I . . . could I . . .?"

"What?" Molly said, interested.

"Could I drop around to see Angus . . . and . . . all of you, again some time?"

Molly smiled. "Sure," she said brightly and then, again looking him straight in the eye, muttered, "Damn."

"Damn?" Roger said, hesitating at his car door.

"Oh, nothing. Just thinking of something else."

"What, what were you thinking of?"

"Oh, my . . . lawn, damn lawn, such a mess. I have to take more care of it."

Roger came back to her car window and glanced at the grass. "I could help you with that. I'm good with lawns. How about I pick up some stuff and come over sometime to treat it? I'll treat you too. This time, I'll bring some food – we can finish off that wine . . . er, if you want. If I'm not too . . . um . . . not in the way."

"Great," Molly said. "It's a date, then."

"A date? Not that kind of a date probably – I'm too . . . way too old for you, sorry kid! But, that's not what you meant, of course."

"No . . . I mean . . . yes . . . I meant, you're not . . . too old, at all . . ." Molly said, unable to sustain her strong focus on him.

"Hell, you look so young."

Molly squeezed his hands, appreciating the sincerity of the compliment and suddenly bothered by the stray curl dangling in her eye. "Angus told me how old you are and besides, don't worry, he and the kids are aging me fast. I'll catch up to you soon."

Glynda

The night staff had all settled into their desks, welcoming the break from the routine chaos of the Labour and Delivery Unit and Anthea saw the opportunity to slip into one of the empty rooms where a portable ultrasound machine sat like an unexpected gift. "I'm just going for a quick nap in Room 12," she told the desk clerk. She closed the door, drew the bed curtains and quickly rolled the machine into position. It glowed like an oracle, its soft hum gearing up for duty as she tilted the screen toward the bed. She rifled through the cart for a plastic sheath to put on the wand and took off her greens pants and underwear. She climbed onto the bed, holding the gel bottle in one hand and an impressive looking vaginal wand in the other. Flexibility can be useful in these situations.

And there it was. She was no Radiologist but had seen enough to know a yolk sac when she saw one. The IUD sat in place as redundant as Christmas decorations in July. She moved the wand to try to see if she could pick up a heartbeat yet. If her dates were correct, and she was just over six weeks, it might be possible. *Expected Date of Confinement – Hallowe'en – The Goddess is a comedian!* But, footsteps outside the door made her retract the wand quickly, shut off the ultra sound and pretend to be asleep. The door opened a crack and she heard whispers from a nurse looking for the ultra sound machine. Anthea grunted from underneath the sheets when the intruder cursed and grabbed gloves from the dispenser to dispose of the messy sheath.

"Jeeeez, I wish people would clean up their own mess." In the darkness of the room, Anthea wished that that was the only mess she was responsible for.

Glynda smiled and spoke of God's wisdom. Her face was clear of emotion, erased by the days of praying she had done. She looked up at Anthea and said, "Don't take this too hard, Anthea. This is where us 'fanatics' have the upper hand on you Atheists. There's got to be some advantage to all that worry about the hereafter; you see, when you find yourself in the neighbourhood, stopping to rest there seems a pleasant thought . . . funny . . ."

Anthea waited for her to continue, and when she didn't, asked, "Funny?"

Glynda took a long breath, a shudder coming from deep in her chest. "You'll appreciate this, Anthea. One good thing, is that I'm not leaving any children behind. At one time, that was all I wanted. Now, it turns out to be a weird blessing."

Anthea couldn't look at her. All words escaped her and when Glynda reached for her hand she clung to it tightly.

"Now," said Glynda brightly, clapping her hands as if she were about to announce a toast, "I'm going to ask you to do something difficult. I'm not going to tell anyone the real prognosis. I'll do the chemo, but I'll say it's just a precaution and the outlook look is positive. I don't want all sad eyes and pats on the hand. I'll tell them I'm one of the lucky ones."

"There's always an outside chance of remission. It's not as good as a lC classification, but it's not a Stage Three either. Depending on how you respond to treatment, a remission can happen and give you much better prognosis than the statistics might dictate," Anthea said.

"Yes, and that would come under the heading of miracles."

"I've seen it happen, Glynda. I have."

"And you've always said you didn't believe in them. Mind you, I counted it as a miracle when you hired me after Art left me with nothing - not even very good typing skills: I believe they happen all the time."

As Anthea waited for elevator, the doors opened and Clive stepped out of it. Upon seeing Anthea's face he turned back into the elevator, putting his arm around her shoulder without saying a word. Just before the doors closed Anthea said to him, "That woman's never had a bit of good luck."

CLINICAL STUDIES: LEVEL 1V

BOB THE NURSE CALLED OVER from the delivery room to let Anthea's office know that Dr. Brock would be a little delayed as she'd just gone into a twin delivery. Georgia let Molly know immediately that, "Dr. Bob had just called to tell them that Anthea would be longer than the normal thirty to forty-five minutes because it was twins and not a simpleton."

"I think you mean 'singleton', Georgia, honey," Molly said.

"No," insisted Georgia, "I'm pretty sure he said simpleton."

"Right, gotcha," Molly said with a pointed finger. "Gavin and I better start the clinic off. It's the last one before Dr. Brock leaves and it's a long one. Carolina, will you let the patients know we'll be a little behind schedule, and that we have a simpleton on our hands, please?"

Carolina winked and directed Georgia to the fax machine where she had a pile of referral appointments to send back to the family doctors. Georgia sighed when she saw the amount and asked if she could do something more important than faxing, filing or restocking rooms.

Carolina looked over her shoulder as she handed an OHIP card back to one of the patients with a smile. "Can you do a pap test?"

Georgia cast her big brown eyes to the ceiling and twisted her shiny mouth. "Eewww, no, I mean one of your jobs. One with no icky bits!"

"You're a natural, Georgia, the medical world is waiting for you to follow in your grandfather's footsteps."

Molly was setting a new patient up in a room and Gavin called the next patient.

"Tiffany?" he called into the waiting room. A slim young man rose from his seat and walked toward Gavin. Gavin smiled and asked, "Is your girlfriend or wife in the washroom?"

The young man walked passed Gavin and said, "Nope, that's me."

A couple of the women in the waiting room glanced up at the exchange and then just as quickly turned back to their magazines.

Carolina clenched her teeth, regretting that she hadn't headed that off at the pass. She left the desk and saw that Molly had not been available to apprise Gavin beforehand. Carolina put a warm hand around Tiffany's shoulder and steered him into the exam room.

"The doctor will be with you in a minute, Troy, just have a seat."

Gavin stood in the hall apologetically, the chart now open to the information he should have made himself aware of before he called the 'post op' patient. Tiffany was a female to male Transgender patient, who was not yet able to officially change his name to match his masculine appearance. Carolina pointed out that the name they wished to be called was in brackets beside their original name. "Shit," Gavin said quietly to Carolina, "I'm an idiot."

"You learn, Gav. Go in and talk to him. Troy's a great kid. He'll understand."

Gavin nodded, scolding himself for his naivety and sloppiness. *Always read the chart thoroughly before calling the patient.* Troy had just had a hysterectomy and bilateral salpo-oophorectomy. This was usually the last stop in the transition from female to male, after having the breasts removed and taking a long course of testosterone shots and therapy.

Gavin opened the door and gave Troy a look that showed his disappointment in himself. "I'm sorry, Troy. Will you forgive my stupidity?"

Troy waved a hand and gave Gavin a generous smile. "Hey Doc, don't worry about it. I'm so happy to be here, I can't be mad at anyone anymore."

"I can imagine how it must be to finally look like who you feel you are, Troy. Congratulations."

"Thanks, Doc. Thanks. Is Dr. Brock away today?"

"She's just finishing a delivery. I'm her medical student, Gavin. If you'd rather I didn't examine you first, that's OK."

"Heck, no, I just brought her a little gift, that's all. But you can examine me. You need the practice."

When Gavin came out of the exam room, he was relieved to see Anthea there. He immediately confessed his mistake but reassured her that the patient was not upset and in fact allowed an examination that showed everything to be well-healed. Anthea, went in to see Troy, satisfied that he could start normal activity. "How are your parents doing with this now?" she asked.

Troy winced; a sadness invaded his handsome face. "My father doesn't talk about it and my mother says she's fine with it, but I know she still cries every day."

The little smudge Anthea had seen on the ultrasound screen days before came into her mind. It raised a fishy little head, gave a sleepy, pitiful look and seemed to ask for reassurance.

She swept it away as quickly as it had come.

Anthea put a hand on Troy's sunken shoulder. "They'll be alright, you know. I'm not a parent . . .," the word 'yet' almost slid out of her mouth, "and never will be . . . but I was told once by a brilliant one after my divorce, that 'a parent is only as happy as their saddest child'. After all is said and done, the only thing that a parent truly wants for a child, is for them to be happy. This is new and lonely territory; one rite of passage they've never navigated. They don't know how to prepare you for it and they're afraid for you. They already know how brave you are, but show them how happy you are."

Troy smiled and presented a small box, wrapped in rainbow paper.

Anthea protested the necessity of gifts, but unwrapped it and held up a silver pendant for a closer look. "It's beautiful. Is it a Celtic Knot?" she asked, looking at it more closely.

"They call it a, 'Let Love Out' sign," said Troy. "It's a heart and an infinity sign."

Anthea was touched by such a thoughtful gesture.

"Dr. Brock, I know that you just delivered a baby, but you know, you've kind of given me a rebirth too, a second chance at life – as Troy.

"Everything alright?" Gavin asked Anthea as she emerged from the exam room. He thought he detected a shine in her eyes that might have accounted for her brusque attention to the chart. He was concerned that he had done something to hurt someone who needed allies.

Gavin fiddled with his papers until Anthea spoke. "No problem, Gav. - all good."

Anthea had noticed some mild cramping today but nothing more. To have this decision taken out of her hands with one big period would be a relief. It surprised her how much the thought of actively ending the pregnancy was bothering her. *Stop dithering. Be practical.*

Anthea pushed her own papers around the counter. She thought of Troy's honest gaze burrowing into her own, as if conducting an unconscious interrogation. *Does he feel less loved or more loved by his parents? Have they let him down more than he could ever have let them down and will the answer to that ever be fully explored or admitted? Is the kind of love that answers those questions instinct, learned or simply absent? What if you didn't measure up?*

She felt herself scrape these questions back into a little casket in her mind; the one she would relegate her baby – Ian's baby, into. *Problem solved.*

Anthea commanded herself out of this mindset. "Let's talk about the next patient. Gavin, this is a rare opportunity for you to have exposure to complete didelphys. This lady's a riot. Tracey's had three kids, two from one uterus and one from the other. More often the second reproductive system is rudimentary, but as you can see from the ultrasound, she has two ovaries, two well formed uteruses and in fact two vaginas – within one vulva. She's here for a tubal ligation."

As Gavin began the pelvic examination, Tracey said to Anthea, "Doc, make sure that you don't miss any extra of those tubes you're tying. I probably look like a weird sea creature in there. In fact, put them in a jar for me and I'll give them to my asshole husband. He always sings, 'More Than A Woman' to me and I assure him that I am twice the woman he deserved." Tracey made a drumming motion, "Pahrum – pah! Maybe I'll make a key chain out of them for him."

Anthea allowed a welcome laugh and noted to herself how lately she was moved from a near tearful state to joy, or indeed the reverse. She resolved to be more objective. Tracey kept up this banter the whole time Gavin was examining her, so his embarrassment evaporated and he was able to identify the salient anatomy. This was a clinical experience that few students would ever encounter.

The next patient did not wish Gavin to be present. Afraxo was a young Somalian woman who had been circumcised in the most brutal way possible. Her whole outer anatomy had been cut away then crudely sewn up to ensure virginity. Scar and keloid tissue had accumulated to such a degree that it was causing obstruction to proper urination and to some extent, menstruation. Anthea had told him that she suspected hematometra - menstrual blood backing up into the uterine cavity.

Afraxo's husband, Khaalid, an educated man who was actively campaigning to eradicate this mutilation in his country, brought her to Canada and hoped that her suffering would be minimized. He explained that she had almost constant infections and pain and hoped that her fertility had not been compromised as she wished more than anything to have children. "What would life be without them?" he asked.

Quieter, cheaper, easier and they'll probably grow up to disappoint you, or worse – you them.

Afraxo's sugery was one that Anthea had wanted to schedule before she left for Britain, and a cancellation had made it possible to put her in the following day. However, she needed to explain that Dr. Gentile, would be managing her practice in her absence. Hopefully, there would be no complications before Afraxo returned for her post-op in six weeks, but if so, she would have to be prepared to see a male physician. Anthea could see Afraxo look to her husband for his answer to this problem. Khaalid touched his wife's hand and spoke softly to her in their language and her anxiety was eased by his soothing manner.

"Of course, Doctor," Khaalid, said, "we are grateful for this opportunity and we will be sure to see him immediately, if we need to. Don't worry."

Anthea knew that Khaalid was reassuring her that he would not let the fact that there was a male doctor delay their reaction to any infection or concern. He wanted Anthea's trust that he was an honest and enlightened man and that his wife's well-being would not be compromised by such a situation.

As she left the room, the teenage girl who was seeking a labial reduction to achieve an imposed standard of perfection came to Anthea's mind.

Lunch was provided by Sandra Carr, a veteran drug rep who had been peddling birth control pills seemingly since they were invented. She was not typical of the bright-eyed beauties who usually came to the office, but the girl with her was. Chloe Elliot was everything Sandra wasn't, and never had been. Chloe was a slender, impeccably groomed, recent business school graduate with a confident, affable manner. Sandra was an ex-delivery room nurse who had a certificate from a college course back in the days when that was possible. She hadn't just seen the trenches, she had dug them. Her weathered face was too unorganized to be considered attractive, symmetry seeming to have completely deserted her, and her teeth hadn't been disciplined by braces, but she could win you over with her dry observations of the absurdity of life.

"G'mornin' Dr. Brock, I brought this 'new kid' with me today because I'm retiring and she's taking over my territory." Her voice had the resonance of a gravel truck, betraying her pack a day habit.

Chloe stepped forward to shake Anthea's hand as if she were one of the Von Trap kids being introduced to the new nanny. Anthea was taken by surprise. "Are they making you retire, Sandra? Cuz you're one we're gonna miss."

"Oh no, they couldn't do that - I've got too much to bribe 'em with. I'm old and I don't want to die at my desk. I want death by exhaustion from a young lover like my husband had." She looked over Anthea's shoulder and saw Gavin standing behind her. She swung her arm up and pointed an arthritic finger at him. "He'll do."

"Sorry, we're not renting him out, Sandra," Anthea said, "We're going to lock him up in a storage closet and bring him out now and again just to look at him."

Gavin shrugged. "I'm just an old woman's plaything."

Anthea shot him a withering look. "A well-preserved old woman, you mean," she nodded her head in his direction, "and thank God he's got a sense of humour or we'd be up for sexual harassment."

"It's funny," Sandra said, "In my younger days I had to endure sexual harassment on the job; now, I'd pay for it."

Chloe stood between them, her large eyes leaping from one to the other looking like she was at a tennis match. They may have settled slightly longer on Gavin and this wasn't lost on Sandra. "Do you have a girlfriend, Gavin? If you don't fancy Chloe, here, I'm still free."

Chloe's pretty hand flew to her forehead. This was unlike any of the other client introductions she had experienced and she found herself entirely unprepared. She giggled nervously.

Gavin kept a completely deadpan face, determined not to be flummoxed. These women had given him access to a new brand of humour, and he enjoyed it. "Well, let me just call my girlfriend and break up with her, and we're on, Chloe."

Chloe's mouth opened and closed like a goldfish. She finally rallied and squeaked out a rapid, "OK, do it quick, before you change your mind."

Sandra gave Chloe a hearty slap on her thin back, which sent her a step forward. "Atta girl."

Anthea's head swung toward Gavin, then back to Molly who had just come into the lunch room to eat. Molly's face reflected the same stunned expression as Anthea's. Almost in unison, the two of them spoke to Gavin, "You have a girlfriend?"

Carolina and Georgia joined them and they all sat around the lunch table looking forward to the fine lunch Sandra had brought them.

"OK, so who's the girl you've been cheating on me with, Gavin?" Carolina said, wanting to get all the details out of him.

Gavin gave them the shy routine and looked down at his pasta. "Well, not really – more a, 'person of interest' - a girl I met the other night."

Chloe wagged her finger. "You're cheating on me already? You son of a . . . gun."

Sandra looked over at Chloe like a proud mother as the others pretended to console her. "Hey, and I had you down as a lightweight - you'll be OK, kid."

Anthea raised her pop can and the rest of them followed. "Hear, hear! Welcome to The Gynesaurs, Chloe."

Chloe raised her own pop can and let it meet the others with a tinny clang. "Oh! I've heard of that exclusive club. Will I be a Prospect, like in a biker gang?"

Carolina didn't miss a beat. "Yea, we give out pads instead of patches, bitch!" Then, warming to the thought, "I can see them now, they'll be triangle Poise pads – with a pissed-off dinosaur on them. We can stick them on our purses."

"Ok, why triangles?" Molly asked, knowing there'd be a cryptic reason behind Carolina's choice.

"Since you ask, the triangle pointing upward is an ancient symbol for women or female deities – it represents the uterus."

"Oh yes," Anthea said nodding, "that's right, remember The Davinci Code? The downward triangle represents the male penis."

Molly kept her pop can raised, a flush of colour rising in her cheeks. "Well, speaking of penises, I have some news too. I'm seeing a nice, older man. His name is Roger."

A murmur rose up into a chorus of good will. They had seen Molly and her family reel from the sudden death of her husband, Cieran, four years ago. To see a shine on her face now, made them all smile.

Anthea perked up. "Oh, I'm going to Britain in a few days to see a man – the only one who ever really loved me, warts and all – my dad. I certainly haven't had any luck with any other men lately. All I've done is fight with them – like my idiot neighbour."

"Me too," Carolina said. "I'm beginning to think it's my fault or something."

"No, ladies," Sandra said. "If we let them think we think it's our fault, we'll miss that wonderful look of bewilderment that comes over them when we explain that it *is* their fault."

Gavin put his hand up. "I'm bewildered."

"Adorable," Sandra growled.

Georgia perked up and stared at Gavin's profile. "I've been seeing boys since I was ten – don't tell my grandfather. Besides, the boys my age are immature. I like older men – ones with a driver's licence and a car and a job and no pimples."

"Phew," Gavin said, "tall order, Georgia. I still get pimples."

Georgia nodded. "They're probably *beautiful* ones."

"Yes," he agreed. "Yes they are."

Molly grabbed Georgia's hand. "Oh, we didn't tell you guys. You should see what Georgia's done with Orlagh's routine. Well, I haven't seen it yet, Orlagh won't let me. She wants it to be a surprise this Saturday at the meet."

Georgia hugged herself, clearly excited at the prospect.

"Alright then," Anthea said, "now I know who to come to for help if I need any dancing in the hospital talent show I'm gonna put on. I quit my dance class - don't ask why, like everything else in my life it's too complicated and embarrassing to explain."

"My grandfather was a ballroom dancer, you know?" Georgia volunteered.

"Whaaaat?" Anthea said, spitting out her coffee. "Wait," she held her hand up to her forehead, "no, no I can't envision it. Saxon, a dancer?"

Georgia's face remained very serious. "Yep, and a good one too. He won all sorts of awards with my Granny when they were young. That's before he got fat. Don't tell him I said that."

A devious plan began to hatch in Anthea's mind, interrupted when Sandra looked at her watch. "Chloe, you've hardly eaten anything. We have to go. Eat up quickly."

Chloe put her hands on her annoyingly flat stomach. "Oh no, I shouldn't eat anymore. After all, who can eat everything they want to?"

The other women all looked down at their empty plates.

The afternoon was full of more predictable cases, and Gavin was kept busy. He was learning fast and Anthea felt good about his clinical skills. She tracked his management of patients and found him prudent, reliable and gaining the confidence he would need to bring his academic skills to the table and allow his instincts some latitude. That's what separated the good from the great.

When Georgia passed by with some supplies, Anthea called her aside. Georgia had refused her offer to surreptitiously pay her for helping Molly's daughter. "You're a good kid, Georgia."

Georgia couldn't suppress a petulant tone. "Why does everybody sound so surprised when they say that?"

"It's the nose, lip, eyebrow and belly ring. Oh, and the tattoo."

"Tattoos," Georgia added. "Don't tell my grandfather."

"Your secrets are safe with me – but, there is something you can do in exchange for my silence."

Georgia's eyes widened. "Anything you want. He'd be so mad if he knew where I put one."

Anthea dragged her hand across Georgia's face, made a kissing sound and said, "Take a seat, I've got a brilliant idea for the Fund Raiser."

As she locked up the office that night, Anthea noticed a new photograph pinned onto the "Our Graduates" section of newborn babies. It showed Troy jumping in mid-air, arms stretched out, fingers fanned into two victory signs.

HOMECARE STUDIES: LEVEL V

Molly

THE FEW DRESSES IN MOLLY'S closet were out of date. Even then, they probably wouldn't fit, because she sensed, *I've put on a little bit of weight over the last . . . OK, few years, and OK, more than a little bit of weight.* She told herself that she still had the figure of a goddess, it just happened to be one of those ancient fertility goddesses they find in archeological digs.

Roger had invited her out to The Mill restaurant, somewhere Molly had driven past, admired for its stone edifice but never expected to see the inside of. *This was a real date,* she thought and would have had a spring in her step, had her ankles not been so swollen and sore from a long day on her feet.

She reached for the black dress that she remembered was a jersey knit and was very comfortable, indeed roomy the last time she'd worn it . . . to Cieran's funeral. She couldn't remember whether it was easier to put it over her head or to step into it, it was a matter of where the weight had gone most, her breasts or her bottom. *Safe to say it would be my ass.* So, she attempted to thread herself through it, arms first. There was some resistance at the bust line, but the spongy tissue there was co-operative enough to get it to her waist. A mighty heave over the hips and it was on. She looked in the full-length mirror. *It fits like a glove – a surgical glove.*

"Damn, damn, shit, shit, frick! I can't wear this. There'd be more room in a condom."

Callum banged on the door, a mischievous grin on his face. "Condom, do you need a condom, Mom?"

"Callum, that's enough of your smartass comments. Get Orlagh for me."

Orlagh came into the bedroom with gentle smile on her face which quickly changed to an unpleasant reaction to the dress. "Whooo, just a little tight, Mom. Try something else."

Molly, sank beneath the task. "I don't have anything else. This is it. Everything else I have is casual. And look at my hair. I look like a Brillo pad."

Orlagh put her hand to her chin. She rummaged in Molly's closet and brought out a long, silky red cardigan. Then Orlagh reached for a red belt and after piercing one more hole in it, it fit on Molly's waist. It took fifteen pounds off her silhouette and covered the bits of her under the arms and on the backside, that looked like a distressed sausage.

Orlagh dragged her mother into the bathroom and twisted her hair into a loose up do, leaving a few curly tendrils here and there. She ordered her mother to sit on the toilet and let her apply more makeup than Molly had ever had on her face. Her initial reaction was to wash her face, but when coaxed into some skillful blending, the effect was more pleasing to Molly. In fact, she felt beautiful. A few cheap sparkly accessories she'd bought at the January sales, thinking she would never have a chance to wear, made her look Oscar-worthy.

"Have a great time, Mom," Orlagh said, kissing her mother's creamy skin. "I'll look after everything here."

Molly mouthed a silent thanks to her daughter then thought of something she hadn't asked,

"Are you all, alright with this – with me dating – dating Roger?"

"Oh Mom, he's great, we like him and just remember how understanding I'm being when I bring home an older man."

Molly reached out and smacked her daughter's pert backside just as the doorbell rang.

Orlagh ran down the stairs, trying to race Angus, Callum and Fiona to open the door. Even Lovey hoisted herself from her bed to walk slowly to the door.

Roger put his hands out wide when he saw the five faces greet him behind the door. "Wow, what a welcome party." He had a bouquet of flowers in one hand and chocolates in the other.

"Her curfew is ten," Callum said firmly.

"How come I wasn't invited?" Angus asked.

Orlagh invited him in and they sat around the kitchen table waiting, looking back and forth at each other. Lovey had her head in Roger's crotch, hoping that there was food coming. Roger didn't disappoint her, reaching into his pocket for a dog treat.

"That's why I like you," Angus said. "But I'd like you more if you invited me to come too."

Molly stood on top of the stairs and felt her stomach lurch with what she hoped was excitement, not anxiety. The kids seemed to like Roger, but she regretted their involvement. This could all go terribly wrong and it would have been better that they weren't part of it. This was her first and only date since Cieran died and she didn't know if she was ready to enter the world again. It was easier, in many ways to keep it at a distance, perhaps until the kids grew up. By then, she'd be too old to care about men. A lot of the elderly widows she had spoken to said they preferred a good book and a gin and tonic to looking after another man. They had a point. There was the toll taken by nursing a dying husband for two years while keeping the kids from seeing the worst of it; his agony, his truculent turns, his anger at not seeing his children's future, which leached out in ragged rants. Then, after Cieran's death, trying to rebuild each little life on a daily basis was like trying to put a delicate piece of porcelain back together one shard at a time, struggling with its ever-changing pattern; hoping to see one eventually emerge and call it normal. "Here goes," Molly said tugging at the back of the dress. "Here goes."

Carolina

It was hard for Carolina to see Glynda lying in the hospital, looking so vulnerable. It put her off her game. Since she was first hired at the office, the two had sparred amicably, each knowing what was fair game to tease the other about. They were polar opposites in almost every way, but there was a certain bent in their humour that found common ground. After some initial rivalries were overcome, where they may as well have peed on what they felt they did best, the territories became delineated and the daily office practices became seamless. There were never any volcanic rows and Anthea marvelled that two such diverse people could sustain such a good working relationship. Their two private lives rarely intersected, except when it was a work social, such as Christmas celebration or when Anthea would treat them all to theatre tickets as a perk.

But now, walking back to her car after the hospital visit, Carolina felt an unease that she couldn't explain. First of all, she had resolved not to curb her acerbic demeanor when visiting, because she knew that Glynda would not thank her for it. So, she put her head around the corner of the room and saying, "Don't feel guilty for putting your feet up, I'm having no trouble doing your job as well as mine – even had time to give myself a pedicure in the downtime."

Glynda gave a wry smile and countered. "If you didn't bring flowers and chocolates, don't bother staying."

"I brought better than that, I brought you some magazines and root beer – your favourite."

The two bantered, with Glynda playing down the seriousness of her condition and Carolina inferring she was a hypochondriac – basically by calling her one outright. It was an enjoyable exchange, though neither laughed at the others jokes – that was a tacit agreement from the very beginning. But still, Carolina felt a sense of doom. *Perhaps it was what everyone felt when someone you know well gets a bad diagnosis. Your own life, which you think is circling the toilet bowl, suddenly seemed likely to crawl out of it. Tottering along the rim seems more agreeable than before. No, it wasn't just that.* But as to what it was, she couldn't say.

As she drove home, the vision of Glynda gasping at the porn Carolina had put between the cover of People Magazine and of her trying to explain the smell of real beer from the root beer bottle, brightened her up.

Carolina ate her supper, and pondered the weekend stretching out in front of her. She was looking forward to going to Orlagh's meet tomorrow, more to support Molly than to support her daughter. This was a real bright spot for the kid, but even more so for Molly, who felt the pressure of single parenthood. No one in the office could identify with the constant and unrelenting attention needed to hold everything together for the children after the chaos of grief had seized them. Orlagh had grown up quickly, becoming her mother's collaborator and Molly wanted this opportunity for Orlagh to excel in something purely her own; she was prepared to do anything to support it. *The least I could do,* thought Carolina, *is show up and stop Molly from screeching at the sidelines, as per Orlagh's strict orders.*

Carolina took a quick look at the TV guide, then at the movie channel, then at the pay per view and just as quickly turned them off. Her phone sounded and she saw another text from Gerald, 'Just tell me to stop and I will.' She began an answer but decided against it. Instead, she went into her library, sank into the red wing chair and drank in the beauty of her bookshelves; the gloriously decorated spines of old classics. She let her fingertips caress the skin of one of the antique poetry books she'd discovered, each one like found treasure. Her mind surveyed the ordeals within them: the sadness, the deceit, the fury, the passions, the charity, the triumphs, the outsiders - Humanity. She poured a glass of merlot and opened Paradise Lost.

Anthea

The coffees were too hot for her hands, so Anthea had to put them down frequently on her way to Dr. Saxon's office. She had a packet of chocolate almonds under her armpit and was concerned that they'd melt if she didn't retrieve them soon. *Why, am I doing this for that cantankerous old asshole? There are so many other important things I have to do before I leave and here I am responding to his summons like a fucking indentured servant to discuss something I haven't even had a chance to consider. Somehow, he brings it out in people. His presence, his manner, his old-school sense of entitlement works like a spell on everyone who enters his orbit. He's like fucking Jupiter: the god and the planet. His gravitational mass draws smaller matter into his orbit. We all spin around him like little moons and rings of gas; sycophants to his needs and moods. Maybe the coffee and almonds will sweeten the old asshole's disposition.*

She entered his secretary's office and welcomed the opportunity to put the coffees on her desk.

"Oh thanks, Dr. Brock, you're a life saver," Bernice said. "You remembered I take it black,"

Anthea graciously handed her own coffee to Bernice.

As far as anyone knew, Bernice had been hatched not born. She was so old, no one had been here longer than she had, including Dr. Saxon. The deep creases in her face looked like the back of a beige cotton skirt someone had sat on for a very long, hot bus ride. The skin above her eyelids crossed the orbits of her eye sockets diagonally like the billow created by curtain ropes. One felt an impulse to draw them back to let more daylight in. This accounted for her habit of tilting her head backward when talking to you and literally looking down her nose at you. It was impossible to take offense at her haughty attitude when you realized the reason for it.

Somehow Bernice, whose age could be anywhere from seventy-five to a hundred and twenty, had defied the mandatory retirement age of the hospital to continue her iron-fisted grip on the administration of the department. There was no policy or person involved in that sphere, for which she could not recount agonizing details that you had no need of knowing. Getting away from her before she recited all of them was the difficulty.

"He's in there but is on the phone to Rita the O.R. clerk, you know, she's the one who always wears the 'live strong' bracelets, led the 10k walk last year to raise awareness for cancer? She's got streaked blonde hair and a crooked tooth, with a slight overbite? Well, I was talking to her about some other ideas I had for raising money, but maybe you're the one I should mention it to. Rita is in a bluegrass band with Bob The Nurse – you know him – Arkansas Bob? – anyway, they're very popular and maybe we could get them . . ."

"Hold that thought, Bernice," Anthea said, "I may get back to you on that – look, he's off the phone and I've only got a few minutes – I'll just go on in, if you don't mind."

Anthea gave a cursory knock and heard a grunt from behind the door. Saxon did not look up from the papers he was reading. "Oh, it's you Brock, sit down,"

Anthea looked at the two chairs in front of her; both had piles of folders on them as well as his coat and briefcase. "Ummm, I brought you a coffee and some chocolate almonds, Dr. Saxon, your favourite," Anthea said, as she struggled to make room for them on his desk.

"Yes, I see. You shouldn't have done that – on a diet - just sit down, will you?"

He tapped a pad of paper with his pen. "Enough small talk, what are you going to do about the fall fundraiser? I hear you're leaving in a couple of days for three weeks – three weeks? That's a very long holiday, isn't it? How did you manage coverage?"

"Clive Gentile is very kindly taking over for me. It's all arranged, and not really anything you have to be concerned with."

"Well, it's up to Clive to say whether he can handle that sort of load at his age, but I'm concerned about the fundraiser, because I'm in charge of making sure it happens and that means you're in charge of making sure it happens. You had all sorts of suggestions for us last year. Have you put them into place yet – before you abandon us for three weeks?"

Anthea bit her lip. She didn't like his inference that she had criticized his efforts last year and not done anything about it, even though the truth was, she had criticized his efforts last year and not done anything about it.

"I'm on it. I already have a great idea. I'm going to have a fabulous dinner and silent auction followed by a staff talent show which will have a panel of celebrity judges to pick the three finalists and then the crowd will decide the winner . . . we'll call it . . . em . . . 'The Best of Medicine!' Yes! That's brilliant! How's that?"

"That's all contingent on you knowing any celebrities and anyone with any talent. Besides, who's going to be stupid enough to make a public spectacle of themselves in front of their peers? It will be a debacle. Look, considering the state that you're in at the moment . . ."

Anthea pounced, giving a reflexive response that she regretted immediately. "State? What state? I'm in no particular 'state' that you need be concerned with."

Saxon finished his thought calmly. "I know that you're grieving your mother – lovely woman by all accounts . . ."

"I beg to differ – not about my mother, of course, she was indeed a lovely . . . lovely woman, but I think people will actually be motivated to come and attend because it won't be like one long anaesthetic like last year; boring old drones making very long speeches out of very short topics. I wanted to drown myself in my soup bowl. I've seen more vitality in a coma ward."

If Saxon's face could become more sour than normal, it might have been at that moment.

"What I was going to say, was that I'll relieve you of your obligation and I'll make someone else do it. We don't need a three-ring circus with song and dance routines and such nonsense – you're making it more complicated than it needs to be. Fund raisers are meant to be boring."

It dawned on Anthea that Saxon was actually trying to be nice. It didn't suit him - or her at that moment. She didn't want sympathy or exigencies made for her and carrying her idea forward would keep her mind off all the other shit that was haunting her. Working harder was her remedy for almost any problem. She was a workhorse, a Clydesdale, built to pull the heavy loads that scare away the lightweights. In this way, she liked to align herself with the Old Guard, like Saxon and Clive, who believed the Churchillian mantra that it's not what you can do, but it's what you can do when you are tired that counts.

She lowered her voice and allowed a smile to float in Saxon's direction. "Thanks, Dr. Saxon, I do appreciate your offer, but I will persevere and I promise you, you'll be surprised – very surprised by how well this will come off. People – including your granddaughter have given me some great suggestions that I'm going to follow up on."

"Well, you can't save people from themselves. Can't say I'm not intrigued. You have a lot of work to do and so many celebrities to canvass in such a short time. Oh, and if you need to dump your student on someone, I'll take him on, if that helps."

As she muttered the beginning of a faint thank you, he barked, "Don't let me keep you now."

The meeting was, evidently, over. Anthea rose and stood looking at the top of Saxon's thatch of grey hair. Her hand reached surreptitiously to the desk and grabbed the chocolate almonds. She turned slowly and began to walk out.

"Shut the door," Saxon said, "and leave the almonds."

They landed inches from his face.

Bernice, busy with a phone call, waved her hand to Anthea as she walked by. Most people left Saxon's office quickly.

"Yes, Rita," Bernice said into the phone. "I am *so* excited. I'll be booking the cruise next July for my sixtieth birthday.

Anthea was grateful, though surprised, that Saxon had volunteered to help cover her, and relieve Clive of the added responsibility of a student, conceding that he was not such a sour old bastard after all. Gavin would get some good O.R. experience assisting a fine surgeon like Dr. Saxon, who was unparalleled in his skill.

Still, she had to prepare Gavin for a trial by ordeal if not for the joy of Saxon's company. There was something about him that rattled even the most confident of people. He spoke in short, terse sentences, rarely looking directly at the recipient, except when they did something he judged inept or provocative, and then he would turn them to stone with a prolonged and silent stare that chilled the room. She knew that all the preparation in the world would not go that far in alleviating the dread of Gavin's first real encounter with Tyrranosaurs Rex.

When it happened, it involved a patient with a particularly difficult case of endometriosis that had invaded her bowels so deeply that the possibility of releasing the colon without damage was slim. The procedure would be done through the use of a laparoscope, which required the surgeons to manipulate their instruments while watching the procedure by way of a screen. Even Saxon, with all his experience had expressed concern over the outcome of this surgery. He had emphasised that it was their job to try to maximize the young woman's potential for fertility, without compromising bowel or bladder function or indeed death by sepsis if a minute assault on the integrity of the bowel went unnoticed and feces leaked into the peritoneum. In releasing the tissue, it would be like separating two delicate pieces of paper glued together by the disease.

Gavin thought his heart would beat out of his chest with the worry of inflicting damage on this young woman who longed for pregnancy. Saxon's laboured breathing was interspersed with curt directives as to where he wanted assistance as he slowly and steadily he released the ovary from a cocoon of adhesions. It was as if some bizarre spider had colonized the pelvis of this girl, sucking away her fertility and leaving her body wracked with pain. These thoughts and Saxon's presence loomed over Gavin as he tried to maneuver the instruments exactly where they would be needed. It was hard to know if the sweat on Gavin's forehead came from the heat of the theatre or the anxiety of the task.

When it was finished and the patient stabilized, he got a cursory nod from Saxon, who grunted and then left the room. It was the last patient of the day, and Gavin felt an exhaustion he had not felt when doing surgery with Anthea. He also felt abandoned; left without any sense of whether he had met Saxon's standards. He emptied his water bottle into his body, parched from sweating since eight that morning. His neck and shoulders ached and his hands felt tight as he made his way to the doctor's lounge.

Bob The Nurse approached Gavin in the hallway and gave him a high-five.

"What's that for?" Gavin asked.

Bob The Nurse narrowed his eyes and nodded, then began to explain in his slack-jaw Arkansas way, "Just talked to Saxon and he said, and I quote, 'The kid's got good hands'. Comment like that from him –why that's like puttin' a crown on your head."

Gavin took this in with relief. "Huh, he didn't say anything to me."

"Nope, and he won't. But, ya musta impressed him, so enjoy the moment. Let me ask ya somthin'. I got a theory. How are you at video games?"

"Pretty damn good – spent a lot of time alone in my room with them as a kid. Why, you want to play sometime? I'll beat your sorry ass."

Bob The Nurse smiled and slapped Gavin on the back. "Thought so. Nothin' prepares ya for doin' laparoscopic surgery like gunnin' them games, boy – 'gratulations."

Molly

The Old Mill Restaurant's location on the edge of a gorge made sitting by the window, a much sought after booking, especially at night when the warm amber of the lights made it all the more enchanting. The plush seating and whispering of water rushing to the bottom of the gorge made the spot as soothing as a womb. Molly felt breathless as the Maître d' bestowed a genteel bow upon her and drifted through the restaurant guiding her to her table. This must be what beautiful women feel like every day thought Molly; it feels like everyone is admiring me as I pass by.

When the waiter left to fetch the wine, Roger leaned over and whispered to her, "Did you see everyone admiring you as you walked by? I did."

Molly squeezed herself, unable to hide her joy at his comment.

"You are a smooth one, Roger Mead. You sure know how to make a woman blush!"

"And you sure know how to make a sad man feel happy. You know, it's as if I just stepped into sunshine. That stone I had in my chest has rolled away, and I have Angus to thank for it, and of course, Thor."

Molly wanted that to be true; *Beautiful Angus.* She was so use to the unwelcome admiration that came her way when people found out he was her brother, whom she'd taken into her home when her parents began to fail. Dare she even hope now, that, when the story of their meeting was recounted, if she and Roger continued, Angus would be the hero of it – with, of course due posthumous credit to Thor? *Slow down Molly girl*, she cautioned herself.

The waiter returned and filled their glasses. They each helped each other decide what they would have as appetizer and when it arrived they, instinctively, halved their portions and transferred it to the other's plate.

"Oh," Molly said with a giggle, "Look at us. We're both the type of people who love to dote on someone aren't we?"

Roger felt his throat clutch and reached for his wine glass. He paused and looked away at the cascade of water beside them then looked back at Molly, the wide smile returning to his face.

"Yes, we're definitely doters. You know, I thought I'd grow old with Sheila. We'd joke that it would get easier to put a smile on each other's face when we were ancient– we'd just have to reach into the glass and put our teeth in." He caught himself and touched her hand, "Oh, forgive me, Molly this is *our* night out. I have to learn to leave the past behind."

Molly rubbed the rough skin of his hand. "Roger, we can't leave the past behind, I think it might be what binds us at this moment. Just going out with someone is 'moving on' for me. To tell you the truth, as silly as it may sound, being here with you, there's a part of me that feels like I'm cheating on my husband."

Roger reached for Molly's other hand and held both up to his mouth. "I'm glad to hear you say that, because I can't tell you how much courage it took to ask you out. I've not done this before either. Sheila . . . Sheila was everything to me. I never looked at another woman . . . until you."

Molly could see the waiter hovering in the corner, their entrées balanced on his tray ready for serving. He had not wanted to disturb a tender moment. Molly looked him in the eye and waved him over.

The waiter, a mature man, perhaps in his sixties spoke with an accent of some European strain. "I no like to interropt romance - even for da best food, Signora."

"Not much gets between me and food, honey," Molly said, patting her stomach. "Don't worry about it."

The waiter cocked his head. "I tink da gentleman would no agree, Signora, de attensione of a bella donna is a much more – desirable - eet ees food for de soul!"

"These damn Italians know exactly what to say, don't they?" Roger said. He turned to the waiter. "Now, tell me what my next line should be, I'm trying to impress this lady."

The waiter shrugged. "Perhaps, a toast to good impressions - eh?"

The two were slow to finish their meal, the conversation meandering from childhood memories to how Roger intended to make this stolen time up to Angus with hockey tickets if it was OK with Molly.

The bottle of wine emptied easily as did the burden of their mutual losses. Molly spoke of Cieran, her husband who'd come into the family when her father was becoming quite infirm. He had won Angus's affection and became a surrogate father to him. "When Cieran died, his death crippled us all," Molly said, "but for Angus it was even more devastating. He chooses his people and within the same year he'd lost my dad and my husband. Angus has got such a sweet disposition, but for a while he was so angry at the world, I thought he'd never be himself again. So . . . so . . . please don't take offense, but don't let him get too attached to you . . . we . . . he, couldn't take another loss so soon."

Roger wanted to reassure her that he did not intend to take this responsibility lightly. "I know me seeing you complicates things but . . . I don't know how to put this . . . I'm not normally an impulsive person. I don't usually act on intuition, or gut instincts or romantic notions - hell, I'm an engineer! I like formulas and structure and certainties, but . . . I don't know, Molly, Sheila's death has changed me. All the certainties I had have been taken away and buried with her. I wanted to crawl into that box with her because it seemed easier than going on without her . . ." His eyes brimmed and a tear began to navigate its way down the creases of his face. He caught it with the back of his hand but another followed. Molly's finger swept that one away.

"I know, I know, Roger. Look, we both need to take one slow, step at a time, eh?" Her voice shook. "It's all still so raw, isn't it? All it takes is a couple of glasses of wine and what we thought was securely put away, tumbles out again. But how good is it that we both had what everyone in any book, movie or song is seeking. We may never get that again, and maybe we shouldn't expect it, but let's see what else is out there for us. We have to be brave."

Roger clasped her hands again. "What I wanted to say, was that when I first saw your face, I felt something I didn't think I'd ever feel again. It hadn't even crossed my mind to ask anyone out and I certainly didn't intend to when I came to your house. When I heard myself asking you out, I decided that my gut guided me to love once before and maybe it will once again . . . shit, am I scaring you? You hardly know me. I'm coming on too strong, aren't I?" He took a deep breath that shook his chest. "Before I blow it, let me put it this way. Can we take those small steps you were talking about *together* and see where they go?"

Molly nodded and blessed him with a smile that showed him he hadn't blown it at all. "Small steps," she agreed, letting her wine glass kiss his.

The waiter walked purposefully from the kitchen and upon seeing the two, hands clasped and tear stained, diverted his glance from their table and found a reason to go back into the kitchen. Molly noticed his head peering through the small kitchen window, then retreating behind it, not wanting to interrupt another delicate moment. Molly's quiet sobs turned into a rush of laughter as she saw that the restaurant had emptied and that they were probably keeping the staff. She made a gesture to call the waiter over.

"You like him because he was flirting with you."

"Hey, he made my night calling me beautiful! That's worth a good tip all by itself."

"Well, what do I get if I call you beautiful?"

"Stick around and see." She winked.

The waiter flew to the table and assured them they needn't rush. Molly thanked him and asked his name.

"No problemo, Signora. My name ees Flavio, and eet 'as been my pleasure."

Carolina

Poor Satan, thought Carolina. She had always sympathized with the ambitious torment that caused him to declare, 'Better to reign in Hell, than serve in Heav'n.' Thoughts above his station brought about his fall from heaven into the 'unhappy mansion' he spoke of, making him the ultimate fallen angel. *Piss God off - you're going straight to hell.* That, she concluded, was her father's fatal flaw too. Carmelo Stiletto had pissed off the local Mob Boss and got thrown into the 'unhappy mansion' head first too.

Carolina tried to remember what her mother had told her about the events surrounding her father's death before it became impossible to tell whether the turbulence of Lucia's mind had addled it. She wanted to hold on to the version that fit with the man she remembered: A man who was adored by family, friends and neighbours alike; as someone who you could count on for help. Once, a woman in the grocery store introduced herself, held Carolina's hand tightly in her own, and told her how Carmelo had sat night after night with her dying husband, helping her wash his wasted body. When he left her house, she said that she'd found a roll of cash in the bedside drawer, which she was certain had been put there by Carolina's father.

Lucia, had said that he was a brutal fighter, physically and mentally unwilling to give up on life, until it gave up on him. That was what brought him to the attention of the underworld, where they saw a use for such character. "But he only beat up the bad men," she would insist.*Not likely*, thought Carolina. *But, at some point, he turned his mind to taking what he thought he was rightfully owed; of claiming a piece of heaven for himself. . . for me. Ultimately, Papa was struck down with the kind of biblical fury unleashed on the rebel Satan.*

There were rumours that not all the money lost in the deal was recovered. By then, Lucia was in such a state of mental agitation, that Carolina had come home many a day to find walls and floors ripped up; patches in the garden dug up and every nook and cranny, inside and out, obsessively investigated. To this day, a disoriented Lucia still riffled through her room at the nursing home, looking for the money she was certain Carmelo had left for her to find. Every visit was filled with either a distant stare or a manic plea to help her find the lost cache. Carolina raised her eyes to gaze around the room again. If it ever existed, it couldn't have been overlooked by Lucia in her years of plundering their small home.

The phone rang and Carolina checked that it wasn't Gerald attempting to reach her again. If it was, she had decided to tell him that as hard as it might be for him to believe, she wasn't interested in a sleazy liaison with him. Thankfully, she didn't have to break his tacky little scrotum of a heart; it was Anthea,

"Hello Carolina, what are you up to?"

Carolina looked down at Paradise Lost and thought, *who'd believe me anyway?* "I'm reading People Magazine."

"Oh, you like that one. So, I stopped in to see Glynda earlier and she told me you'd brought her a pile of trashy reading material."

"Oh yes, what did she tell you about it?

"Nothing really, except that she actually hadn't had chance to read it yet because she'd let her mother-in-law Edna take it home to read first."

"Crap," Carolina said.

"Why, what's the problem with that?"

"Nothing, nothing, I'm sure Edna will find it . . . interesting."

"Why do I get the feeling there's something you're not telling me?"

"Because there's something I'm not telling you – and I'll let Glynda fill you in on that – never mind, why did you call anyway? Is there something you haven't told me?"

Anthea paused to search Carolina's words for signs that she may have guessed about the pregnancy. She quickly surveyed her own behaviour the last few days to see if she'd betrayed herself in any way. Carolina could sniff out insincerity in anyone like a bloodhound tracks a fox.

Anthea felt the urge to confess her secret. She felt the need for someone to scold her for delaying a trip to the abortion clinic, but the cramping was continuing and against all logic, she hoped it wouldn't be necessary. Carolina would use her best rhetoric to shake some sense into her by saying something like 'Stop being a pussy and get the fucking thing done. You'll make a terrible mother.' She'd clear the office schedule and send her packing.

"Carolina, I'm . . . I'm . . .

"Yea, yea, you're totally grateful that I'm going to look after your babies when you go to Britain."

"No . . . it's not that . . . it's . . . speaking of babies . . ."

"It's that you want me to make sure I don't overbook the Obstetrics clinic for Dr. Gentile . . . I KNOW already. You've told me all this. Move on!"

"Move on, indeed," Anthea said, her courage sucked out of her.

"Look, I'll do you a big favour and stay at your beautiful country retreat with Spock and Twiggy two of my favourite buddies."

"I'll stock up the fridge and the bar."

"Great, two of my other favourite buddies, see you then.

Molly

The walk along the riverbank was pleasant. The clamouring of the waterfall made them raise their voices to be heard. A kind wind teased Molly's hair, tugging at the russet tendrils and releasing them to spring back to place for just a moment. Roger offered his arm and she took it gratefully, concerned that the uneasy relationship she had with her high-heels would end badly. She admired those women who regarded high-heels as allies in their daily quest; who shopped and posed and descended staircases in them, then pirouetted to settle on a chair and cross their legs, unconscious of how miraculously they had performed. No, even her wide-width Naturalizers didn't contain that kind of magic: they were full of latent treachery, so she hung onto Roger like a desperate ex-girlfriend.

Roger liked the way Molly clung to his arm. It had been a long time since he'd felt his strength appreciated in that way. His gaze kept drifting to her profile and he thought he saw a couple of men let their eyes linger on her as they passed. He gave into an impulse that had stalked him throughout the evening and he turned her shoulders to him and planted a firm kiss on her open mouth. She pulled away, and his heart sank. Her eyes were wide and flashed with something he wasn't sure he could interpret. He looked down, like a child caught stealing a cookie and decided not to go for a second, with perhaps, more tongue involvement. This thought had hardly settled into his brain, when Molly pulled his face toward her own and involved her own tongue in his mouth with some expertise.

"We can't go back to my house," she whispered into his bad ear. "The kids are there; can we go to yours?"

It was Roger's turn to pull away as he quickly inspected her words for any misinterpretation on his part. *You probably got it wrong, Rog, you're half deaf in that ear.* But to Molly he said a collection of grunts and partly formed words that made him sound like he had a profound stutter. He was looking for any of the following words, 'yes, you bet, no problem, let's go' or perhaps, 'Hallelujah!' Instead, he asked her to repeat the question. Before she had the chance to even pretend that she hadn't said what she had said, Molly's phone rang. It was Callum.

Molly grinned uneasily as she opened her cell phone. Callum was reporting that Orlagh might be ill but didn't want to spoil Molly's night out. He could hear her groaning and flushing the toilet a lot. She was shaking and sweating, worried about her meet tomorrow.

"Has she got her period?" Molly asked.

"Mom, we don't share these things."

Molly shrugged as she put away her phone. "Sorry, Roger, duty calls."

She turned and began to walk briskly in the direction of the car, her ankle turning over. Roger caught up and looped his arm in hers, telling her that a broken ankle wouldn't help the situation.

During the short drive to the house, neither spoke of Molly's possible offer of generous sex or indeed, Molly's generous offer of possible sex. Roger played the conversation over in his mind and began to wonder if he had heard her incorrectly. *Better play it safe, Rog.*

Molly sprang from the car as they pulled into her driveway. Roger called to her, uncertain of whether he should follow. She turned back, realizing that she should thank him before dismissing him. "Thanks for everything, Roger. Good night." She ran off up the front stairs of the house threatening to drop a shoe like Cinderella herself.

Glynda

Edna had been busy. Glynda's office friends were coming to visit her today and she had made an apple pie that morning so that they would have an alternative to the lemon loaf she had made yesterday. It had been years since she had worn an apron, and she had chosen the one with the heart shaped bodice with red frills all around it. Wearing it had taken her back to the nineteen fifties; a time when everything in her life felt organized and under her control.

She'd been a young mother then, attending to her beautiful son, Art, who had not yet begun to show signs of his pathology. Looking back, she remembered him lying and cheating, just like any other kid his age, but luckily, he was charming enough to deflect any fallout onto someone else. That was always his downfall, she concluded; he was easily led into trouble by a tempting opportunity to do the wrong thing.

She knew that he adored her, but nevertheless, she was glad that she'd been canny enough not to trust him with the bulk of her fortune. She sensed his weakness for the next shiny thing, and looking back, some of his male friends were very shiny. In this respect, Glynda had not been his usual type, and that, at the time, offered Edna some hope that he was willing to settle for a plain and ordinary life with a wife who could have provided that so well. *She would have been perfect if she wasn't barren. You can't blame a man for losing interest and falling in with a bad crowd when he has that to cope with. I should have tried harder to get him over his gay phase. Now, I have to rise to the occasion, once again, and take care of his wife in her hour of need.*

Edna had been quite shocked when, that woman Molly and her daughter, with the ugly name, turned up the day before Glynda got out of the hospital with a load of homemade frozen meals and even more surprised when they rolled up their sleeves and started to clean the house. *All this fuss over Glynda?* She didn't suppose they'd do that again. One thing she could say about Glynda is that she had always kept the house spotless and it, no doubt, would have bothered her to see the state it was in when they had arrived to clean it. So, all she had to do now, was wait hand and foot on Glynda, who, in fairness, tried to do as much as she could for herself and so, wasn't too demanding. But, truth be told, this was only the first week of her recovery and after that, chemo would probably begin to drain her energy even more. Edna made a note to herself to address this issue.

Upon their arrival, Edna led the guests into the parlour where Glynda sat in the yellow chintz chair, with her feet up. Before her illness, none of them had ever seen Glynda's home. They had never been encouraged or invited to drop in. As they had walked up the pathway that led to the grand Victorian, red brick home, they were met by two powerful turrets that straddled the stalwart black doors sitting above a wide stone staircase. This was braced by ornamental walls that curved from the top into a curlicue at the bottom, and it was not hard to imagine, well-dressed Victorian ladies sipping afternoon tea on the white veranda when weather permitted. It was not a mansion, but certainly a presence on a street full of gracious homes. There were signs that it had not been as well attended to as others that had been updated and restored to perfection. Nevertheless, they could not help cooing with admiration when they approached.

"Your colleagues are here, Glynda. Don't worry, I will go and make the tea and get the dessert I made for you," Edna said loud enough so that everyone heard.

Anthea placed a colourful bouquet of flowers into Glynda's arms and gave her cautious squeeze so she would not crush either.

"Hey, Glynda," Carolina said when she saw the magazines Molly had brought for Glynda, "did you ever read the magazines I brought you in the hospital?"

Glynda frowned. "No, I didn't come to think of it. I should ask Edna if she's finished with them. I saw her carrying one around the other day. I'm sure she'll get them to me when she's done with them. Now, tell me, was Orlagh well enough to compete?"

Molly grinned and reached into her purse, the sound of metal clanging as she proudly held up five medals. In the other hand, she held up a video of the meet for Glynda who, like the others had seldom missed the opportunity see Orlagh perform. Glynda lept at the medals and put them around her own neck, excited at the prospect of watching the video later. She gave them all a serene smile. "Thank you, all of you, I've never been so well looked after. You've all been so thoughtful I . . ."

Edna came clattering into the room pushing a noisy tea trolley stacked with bone china tea cups and her baking perched on a three-tiered, silver cake tray that threatened to throw itself off to avoid shaken cake syndrome. Molly rushed up to steady the thing, lifting the cart onto the carpet in front of the sitting area. They all lauded the old woman's efforts and their praise was noticeably well received as she raised the teapot and began to serve the hot tea.

"So," Glynda said, as she accepted her cup, "are any of you going to the Church concert tonight? Anthea, you bought several tickets? Four, I think."

The women all cast their eyes to Anthea who looked mystified. "I bought tickets?"

"Yes," Glynda assured. "You said you'd give them to the staff. That was so nice of you, because we're trying to raise money for the African orphanage I told you about."

Anthea looked to the rest of them who studied the pattern on their cups. "Oh, yes," she said, "the orphans."

Glynda looked uncomfortable. "Oh, you forgot. It's OK, obviously, I can't go and sing there now and you did say at the time that was why you wanted to go. So, don't worry, give them back to me. I'll look after it."

Anthea reacted quickly. "Oh, no Glynda, of course I'll go. I can finish packing later. And, I know Carolina isn't busy tonight, so I'm sure she'll come along, right Carolina?" Anthea ignored the daggers that flew at her from Carolina's direction. Molly, sympathetic to Anthea's plight, volunteered to attend as well.

Gavin winced. "Sorry ladies, but I do have a prior engagement – with my text books. I'm with Saxon again tomorrow and I want to know my stuff or he'll eviscerate *me* instead of the patients"

Anthea swallowed her cake quickly. "It won't matter – he'll eviscerate you anyway – then he'll throw your entrails on the floor and predict your future in medicine like they did in the old days – it's never good news – especially if it's *your* entrails."

"Haruspices," Carolina said.

"Huh?" Molly said, her mouth dropping open as she looked squarely at Carolina.

"Haruspices – that's what the Ancient Greeks called the seers who were trained to divine the future from intestines."

"WHERE, do you get this from?" Molly declared, hands open and looking skyward.

"One thing I've always noticed about you, Carolina," Glynda said, "I never liked your taste in clothing, but I've always *loved* your taste in reading. You really are a font of exquisite knowledge – there, I've said it. Now, don't expect any more compliments from me!"

Carolina blushed, but no one could tell because of the fake tan she'd applied several days earlier. "I do like to read good books, but just to make you all feel better, I watch Jerry Springer reruns."

"Your life is a Jerry Springer rerun," Molly said.

"I wish that weren't true. Now, let's figure out tonight."

Glynda stirred her tea. "It'll be a good concert, I'm sure. There are some wonderful singers in the choir. The Choir Mistress, Lorna Devine has a really beautiful voice. And, I'll repay you for the extra ticket.

Edna's thin neck stretched up beyond her white collar. "Well, if you ladies don't mind, maybe I'll go with you."

Glynda's eyes flashed with concern. Edna was never good company even when she was trying to be.

"Great," Molly said, unconsciously patting the old lady on her dowager's hump, feeling the spinal processes which poked out like those of a decrepit old dragon.

The church was a large, modern structure cluttered with war-like apexes that looked like a collection of spears aimed skyward. At the back of the building was a cylindrical tower that housed the concert hall. They entered the foyer and were greeted warmly with nods and smiles from the busy congregation. Nearby, soft drinks and desserts were on sale and Anthea brought a selection to their table.

"Hmm," Molly said, "I thought it would be like a concert hall set up. It's more like a cabaret."

Edna stiffened. "They have funny goings on in this church. Nothing is what you expect it to be. I'm a Presbyterian and things are done properly there."

Carolina muttered to Anthea, "No 'goings on'? We have nothing to fear but Presbyterians."

"I beg your pardon, I didn't catch that," Edna said, her neck stretching up again as if she were about to gobble.

"I said, nothing like the good old Presbyterians," Carolina said loudly.

"They founded this country. Basically, carved it out of the stone," declared Edna.

"Right after the Jesuits," Molly said, sure of her history here.

"Well, those damn Catholics can't keep their nose out of anything, can they?" Edna lectured, warming to the subject. "If there's money to be made, they make it their business."

Molly knew that she had been put in her place and that place was to agree with Edna. Her sense of humour saved her from any offense and she simply answered, "Well, where do you suppose the term, 'The sun never sets on the British Empire', comes from?"

Edna looked sympathetically at Molly, as if she were a child confused by the ways of the world. "Why, my dear, because in those days, everyone wanted to be British. In India, they're still more British than the British are. They have better tea than you can grow in England."

Everyone looked away, for fear of laughing outright. There was unspoken acknowledgement of her age, stupidity and delicate temperament. The same restraint that Glynda had demonstrated over the years when discussing her mother-in-law settled over the group. Anthea guessed that it was more likely that Glynda had done so, to make her situation seem more agreeable than it was, rather than out of respect for this crusty old bag of nonsense.

Glynda never complained about anything; never solicited people's sympathies or confidence. She was adept at always maintaining a reserve that kept everyone at a pleasant distance. The cancer diagnosis must have been an inconvenient intrusion into that distant existence, what with people showing up with food and help, for which she had shown a generous tolerance, but was surely uncomfortable with.

Lorna, the Choir Mistress strode onto the stage with some majesty. Her speaking voice was deep and mellow; her body, tall and commanding. She wore a long, black dress with a colourful duster jacket, reminiscent of the 1920's flapper coats. Its royal purples and ambers caught the light as her arms moved the fringes of the sleeves. Her full, red lips enunciated each letter of her words of welcome and the effect was entrancing.

The choir filed on in a uniform of black skirts and white tops. Soon, their throats opened up and the hall pulsed with a strident rendition of,

'Mine Eyes Have Seen The Glory Of The Coming Of The Lord'. Lorna seemed to reach down inside each member of the choir to pull their voices from their chest and release it into the air. A wave of applause followed and died down when Lorna began her series of solos. Her velvet contralto wove its way through the hall and into the appreciative ears of those listening.

Carolina had been disappointed that there was no alcohol at the event, but had anticipated such a possibility and so had brought a large mickey with her. The fact that she was not driving made it possible for her to lace her drinks liberally without the concern of sharing with the drivers. This gave Carolina no reason not to surreptitiously season Edna's drink as well; her reason being that it might soften up the old nightmare.

It seemed to be working well and when Carolina leaned over to ask Edna if she had enjoyed the magazines she had given Glynda. She turned and whispered into Carolina's ear, "I haven't sheen sho mush dick shince I wash a Can Can girl in Dawshon Shity." She swayed backward, almost falling off her chair, then swung in to correct herself with a squawk, "Oh, I meant Daw-son Cit –ty not Shitty!"

Molly and Anthea had turned their chairs toward the stage and so were not able to appreciate the altered state of Edna Wicksteed. But, Carolina felt that she had unleashed someone who had been imprisoned within Edna's brittle exterior for too long. She poured more gin from her mickey into Edna's fruit punch.

The intermission came far too soon and Carolina almost carried Edna to the toilets as she was "feeling a tad dizzy". The fact that she weighed no more than a hundred pounds helped Carolina drag her to the cubicle. She didn't want to endure the disapproval of the other two, if they found out that she had been responsible for getting an 83-year-old senior, pissed. She propped Edna back in a chair that had arms on it, which would help keep her erect.

A pasty man with a bad comb-over took to the mic. Merle Fringle's hair was dyed a far younger shade than his face would have merited and there was not one good angle on his body. Even his elbows were upholstered for maximum comfort, and his green sweater vest was stretched open between each successive button by his substantial belly. He had a voice that reminded Carolina of a TV personality – but exactly who, she couldn't indentify immediately – *Oh yes, it's Ernie from the Muppets.*

He wanted to share a story with all the newcomers to the church tonight and he cast his eyes in the direction of Carolina's table. He said he had previously led a wayward life, cheating repeatedly on his wife. He said that someone meeting him now, a good citizen of the church, might find that hard to believe. Carolina leaned over to Edna and said under her breath, "Fuck yea, he's such a babe." To which Edna let out a loud and somewhat inappropriate torrent of laughter.

Molly looked over her shoulder and smiled. "Having a good time, Edna?"

Edna reached for her glass and said, "I like the punssh."

Merle announced that as a sinner, he had explored every unspeakable act and then he proceeded to speak about them. How he'd stolen from his previous church to buy illegal drugs and to pay for unnatural sex with demons sent from Satan himself. *Poor Satan always gets bad press,* Carolina noted.

Then Merle began pacing the stage, arms flailing and his feet stomping on the, "tail of that infernal demon who pokes me with his clawed finger, yey, day and night, night and day."

Anthea and Molly looked back at Carolina, disturbed at the direction Merle was taking with his welcome.

"And, YOU!" he pointed at their table. "YOU will find eternal damnation too, unless you let JEE-SUS into your life - YEY! Into your HEART! Hallelujah - into your SOUL!" He banged on the podium and executed a surprisingly agile jump into the air to emphasize his point. "SOMETHING brought you to us today. SOMETHING'S missing in your life and you, my friends can find it HERE! Have a personal relationship with our Lord JEE-SUS and he will deliver you into his arms. Hallelujah! Praise the Lord."

It suddenly became obvious, when everyone else in the hall, had risen to their feet, closed their eyes and began swaying their arms above their heads, that they were the only non-members of the congregation there. Edna was swaying too, but that was just because she was trying not to fall off her chair.

By now, Merle had gone into a seizure of rapture that had his flesh shaking like Beyonce as he and his acolytes beseeched JEE-SUS to save their new friends.

Anthea, Molly and Carolina gave each other a grim look and quickly walked out of the side door muttering that they had come for a concert not a conversion. Molly turned to ask where Edna was.

"Shit, I forgot her." Carolina said.

Molly shrugged. "Maybe she wants to stay, tell her we'll wait for her in the car, she can come when she's ready."

Carolina squinted and said, "Mmmmm, I don't think she could if she wanted to."

"What do you mean?" Anthea said.

"Well, you know, she's . . . frail, and . . . and . . . drunk."

Carolina left Anthea and Molly puzzled by this remark and soon came out of the hall carrying Edna under one arm, like a cheap blow-up doll.

Edna was shouting back at the congregation. "I SAID I AM A GODDAMN PRESBYTARIAN!"

SECTION TWO

FOREIGN AFFAIRS

THE RED SUV PULLED UP at the departures level of the airport. As much as Carolina loved Spock, the dog had breath that could sicken a sewer rat and so she reached for the cigarette she kept in her coat pocket for such times as these when quitting smoking seemed like a bad idea. Her head pounded and even the thought of water was too disturbing, despite Anthea's insistence that it would help.

"What do you know, you're only a doctor," Carolina snapped. "Can you get your bags out yourself?"

"No problem, I packed light," Anthea said, as she pulled two oversize luggage bags from the back of the van. "Thanks for looking after the kids," she said, as she kissed Twiggy and Spock goodbye. "Be good for Auntie Carolina!" Spock turned a few circles and proceeded to poop on the car blanket.

"Just go. Just go," Carolina said, gagging.

Anthea waved and hurried into the terminal. Carolina grabbed the blanket and threw it into a nearby trash can.

Anthea saw this from the entrance and yelled, "That's a Burberry!"

Carolina shrugged, "It's a shitty one. Here, do you want it?"

Anthea knew she was beaten and continued on her way.

After crawling through the various lineups, she had to pay extra for her overweight baggage which was a result of being so rushed when packing that she exercised no discretion in what clothing she should take. Worse, was trying to find that one illusive pair of shoes that would do for a fashionable party, hiking in the mountains, and sloshing around at the seaside. She made a note to invent them at some future date.

~

Heathrow hummed with the mixed murmurs of excitement and exhaustion. *There's that look,* thought Anthea, *which overtakes the faces of people waiting in airports. After a while, that expectant light in the eye, so eager to engage life's next challenge, is replaced by a vacant stare of resignation, akin to that of a primitive people, whose gods have turned against them -and that's just the staff.*

Anthea spotted her first suitcase as it took its joyride down the carousel and she managed to pull it off before it went for another turn. She didn't recognize her second bag because it had been wrapped in cellophane so completely that the bold pattern was obliterated. It looked like a terrifying sci-fi chrysalis that might, at any moment, spawn a slimy arachnid; the kind that springs forward and sucks your innards through its uncoiled proboscis. Anthea wrestled it off the ramp as it passed. The small mercy was that it still had its wheels.

She made her way to the exit and began her search for Auntie Ceri. She heard a, tinny, 'Yoo- hoo,' coming from a crowd to her left and searched the faces. A hat that looked like a rotting bowl of fruit caught her eye and she knew, without examining the features, that it was Auntie Ceri.

Auntie Ceri yelped when their eyes met as she barrelled through the crowd like a scrappy Jack Russell, not paying any heed to various body parts that were in her path. She embraced Anthea, smothering her with red kisses and bold perfume.

Ceri was a small woman, like all the Gryffydd line. No one thought of them as small though, because their large heads and imperious ways made everyone else feel less significant when in their presence.

"Hello, my darling girl!" Auntie Ceri said, rocking Anthea side to side in vigorous clutch. She held her niece's face between her gloved hands and sighed, "It's like looking at Sian herself. Oh, I'm so glad you're here. How could you leave me with no girls to spoil, only your brother and my rotten boys who never call their mother."

"Well, you do have little Cordy."

"Your brother keeps her away from me, I'm sure of it. I hardly get to see her once a week – makes the frivolous excuse that she has to go to school."

"That's just unacceptable. We'll soon put a stop to that," Anthea said wrapping her arm around her aunt as they each wheeled the suitcases to the parking lot.

"Fancy luggage," Ceri said.

"Thanks," Anthea said loading the mummified remains of her suitcase into the boot of the car.

Driving out of the airport Anthea couldn't stifle a joyful exclamation when she saw the tulips and daffodils bobbing their pretty heads to the beat of a playful wind. They looked like a class of adolescents plugged into their ipods, grooving to a beat that was unheard by observers. "It's a real treat to see flowers in full bloom, truly a promise of kinder days to come."

Ceri thought her niece looked pale and worn out and put it down to too much work and too much sadness. "We could all use some kinder days, that's for sure."

"How's Dad been doing by your estimation? He always tries to sound positive and on the mend when I call. He doesn't want me to worry about him, but I do."

"He's made of tough stuff, your Dad, but those two were devoted to each other. You can tell he's lost. Even his voice has changed. Hearing him speak now is like hearing someone talk when they've just been singing." Ceri reached over and squeezed Anthea's hand. "I want to prepare you; he's lost a lot of weight and he looks wretched. That's the truth of it. I think having his kids and grandkids around him will be a tonic - put the bounce back in his step – put some life back into him."

Anthea couldn't speak. She folded her lips inward to stop them from trembling. *Kids and grandkids . . . they have such power? I'll never know. I'll never know.* She took a deep breath and pulled the words from the back of her throat. They came forward, thick with emotion. "I hope so .

. . being back will be good for me too . . . but I don't know if I can keep it together for him."

Anthea looked over at her Aunt, biologically the closest genetic entity to her dead mother. There were so many similarities that had gone unnoticed when her mother was alive, that now sprang into aspect. The lift of the cheekbones, the turn of the small, snub nose, the suggestion of a cleft chin, but most startling and at the same time, reassuring, was the voice. Anthea could close her eyes and hear her mother's lyrical tones wash through her ears like the ebb and flow of an untroubled sea. *Babies hear and recognize their mother's voice in utero.*

"Maybe you shouldn't try, love. There's good medicine in tears."

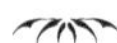

Auntie Ceri drove with the attitude of a gun slinger. She would squint her eyes and stare the other drivers down, daring them to challenge her domination of the road. If the Mini Minor had had limbs of its own, it would have been idling at a busy intersection with a wide straddle and arms poised, ready to shoot. Ceri would order other drivers around with confusing hand signals that flapped like panicked birds. All this, while launching a constant stream of swearwords at those who didn't do her bidding. This would be peppered into her speech, so that a normal and even pleasant conversation would bracket her traffic directives. Anthea soon learned that it took some careful editing to filter what was meant for her passenger and what was meant for the "idiot mother fuckers" who shouldn't have a licence.

Just before reaching the M4 highway, Ceri discovered that she had made a wrong turn and pulled into a parking lot to turn around. She had slowed to a crawl as she surveyed the area for such an opportunity, which frustrated the easily frustrated driver behind her. The man, in a large truck, followed her into the parking lot and was blocking her exit. She responded with a wave of her hand in an effort to draw his attention to her inability to move ahead. Stubbornly, he remained in front of her, clearly intending to give her some of her own medicine. At this point, her sign language became more specific and she gave him the two fingers with both hands. Not satisfied that he had understood, she rolled down her window and told him directly to, "Get the fuck out of the way".

The man unleashed his bulky six-foot four frame from the truck and walked over to Ceri's car window. Anthea now became a little alarmed and advised her Aunt not to roll down the window again. Ceri rolled down the window and squinted up at the man. "Are you trying to be funny sunshine, or are you really such a fucking asshole?" The man leaned into the window, no doubt intending to intimidate her.

"Now Mother, you need to do two things, clean up your dirty mouth and give up your licence."

Ceri reached for her phone and held it up to his ear. "Why don't you say that to the police operator I have on the phone here, I'm feeling very afraid of what you might do to a dying senior citizen and her doctor." She then spoke into the phone herself reading off his licence plate, slowly and deliberately.

The man balked and backed off slowly. "Alright, alright, I'm going. Steady now . . . I'm going." He jumped into his truck and drove off. As he passed, Ceri shouted out the window, "And I'm not your fucking mother, she's probably home fucking a goat, hoping she'll get a smarter kid this time."

Anthea covered her face and sank down in her seat. Her lame attempts to calm her Aunt had been completely ignored and she was relieved that the British driving population was rarely armed. This could have been a blood bath. Ceri, turned to Anthea with a broad smile on her face, and said, "Can't let the bastards win, darling. Now, which way was I supposed to turn again?"

After a couple of hours drive along the M4, the landscape began to rise to meet them and Anthea pronounced aloud place names on the map she found in the door of the car. They took on the descriptive Welsh patterns that described the ancient reason for the place name, Llanrumney, Llantrisant, Llanelli – Churches named after various saints. Abergevenny,

Abercraf or Abertawe were all places on or near the mouth of various rivers and then, her lips tackled some of the more bewildering names, such as Rhyd-cymmerau Bechfa, Machynlleth, Cwmtwrch, Ystradgynlais, or her personal favourite, Llechryd. "Well, aren't you clever?" Ceri said, genuinely impressed. "Perfectly enunciated! I'm surprised you remember any Welsh, at all."

Her mother had made a great effort to familiarize her with these magical names and Anthea had been enchanted enough to learn how to pronounce the sibilant 'll' and the guttural 'ch'. On their frequent journeys into Wales, she and her brother Gryff, would have contests to see who pronounced the names more correctly.

She would always pull the one he never mastered out of the bag when a chocolate bar was at stake, Llanfairpwllgyngyllgogerychwyrnd robwllllantysiliogogogoch. She would trump him further by being able to translate it – Saint Mary's Church in the Hollow of the White Hazel near the Rapid Whirlpool and the Church of Saint Tysilio with a Red Cave – for a second chocolate bar. She would eat them slowly in front of him. This was the only means she had of punishing him for the times he would tease her into a frantic state by hanging Clementine, her favourite doll, by the neck from some inaccessible place.

She soon learned to only eat her winnings in front of him when her parents were nearby, for fear that he would snatch them and gobble them up like some predatory animal. She genuinely enjoyed seeing his mouth water as she rolled her eyes and moaned in over-acted ecstasy, promising him that she would leave him a bit at the end; then proffering a brown, watery, sliver perched on the tip of her index finger. His lips would disappear and he would whisper to her that when she was sleeping he would snap that finger off, but she would put her face right up to his nose and tell him that, it was just his heartbreak talking. If she had any steel in her, Gryff had placed it there.

Soon she saw The Sleeping Giant in the distance, which was a mountain that, when viewed from a particular angle took on the astonishingly accurate profile of a man lying down in the distance. It was always a part of their journey down to Rhossili and it provided a cue that they were near their destination. Her father would pull over to the side of the road just outside of Caer Lan in Glamorgan, and no matter what the weather, they would get out of the car and pay homage to The Giant with a grand bow. As a child, The Sleeping Giant both intrigued and terrified her. Would he one day rise up from underneath his green shroud and turn his sleepy gaze to her own? Just in case, she would bow quickly and clammer into the car.

The daylight was fading as they saw the warm glow of the farmhouse spill from the windows into the dusk. When she opened her car door, Anthea paused to smell the cool, wet air and let her ears fill with the deep, regular breathing of the sea. She couldn't see it, but she sensed it move beside her like a massive, primeval reptile.

Ralph Brock came running out of the doorway to greet his daughter. Anthea saw a gaunt, frail, old man, with clothes hanging from his slight frame like spent candle wax. His teeth looked too big for his face which was deeply lined and grey in colour. Perhaps it was the poor light that made him look so weary, even with the added animation of his delight in seeing her.

In her heels, she was taller than he and as his face burrowed into her neck she thought she felt a shudder come from his chest. He coughed to cover the impulse to weep and when they drew apart they both laughed aloud and wiped the moisture from each other's cheek. "None of that nonsense, sweetheart. I won't have us blubbering like a couple of old ladies."

"Oy!" Ceri said, "I resent that stereotype. And don't worry about my sciatica as I do all the heavy lifting around here." She made a performance of dragging Anthea's broken suitcase out of the car. "Look at the fancy luggage they have in Canada. It's got more plastic than one of my knickers."

Ralph put his hands on his hips and surveyed Ceri, still struggling with the luggage. "That is one damaged old bag, for certain. And the suitcase doesn't look good either." As frail as he looked, Ralph managed to dodge the handbag that would have hit him on the side of the head.

"Oh, you two are at it already," Anthea said. "What am I going to do without Mam here to officiate?" A small, but serious silence took over for a second, and Anthea saw her father reorganize his face into a smile.

Ceri filled the void. "Are any of the others here yet?"

Ralph told them that Gryff and the kids would be arriving the next day.

"Good," Ceri said, "Once those little banshees of Gryff's come, it'll be a three-ring circus around here. No peace and quiet and I'll have to hide my chocolate."

"Ceridwen Gryffydd," Ralph said, using the long form of her name, "you're the one that gets them so riled up that they are foaming at the mouth." He turned to look at Anthea. "Then she declares, 'Adult Time!' and goes off to bed with a bottle."

Anthea shrugged, glad to see that some things never change.

Anthea felt a sense of relief to have Auntie Ceri here. She felt that some of the responsibility of navigating this bittersweet visit would be lifted from her shoulders. Auntie Ceri wouldn't let anyone feel sorry for themselves for long; that was a Gryffydd trait that both sisters had embodied and one that Anthea tried to emulate. It was deemed useless, it simply got in the way of one's progress; better to cut it off than drag it around like an unattractive rudimentary appendage.

Since her sister's death, Ceri had made it her business to watch her charges carefully, not missing the smallest nuance of distress without assuming a protective posture – like 'the crouch', Gelert their border collie, would do when the kids ran separate ways.

Ceri had retired from her successful law career and had the time to make her presence available to the herd she now shepherded alone. How much easier must it have been for her when her sister was in the other corner of the field, gently coaxing the flock to where the two had agreed they should be. The almost daily phone calls had served to pass the information needed, to interfere where they thought they should. When the two were in the same room, the collaboration was mostly done through a series of mysterious eye movements – The Gryffydd Glare, the family had named it. When it rested upon you, you were compelled to trot into place and ditch the 'Black Sheep' routine. That was not to say that independent thinking was discouraged, quite the opposite – validated by the fact that the two sisters rarely agreed on any political or academic theory – even if they happened to – which always came as a deep disappointment to both. But, where family was concerned, it was something you were always part of, no matter how misguided your opinion amidst a host of opinionated people, you had to show up and share it.

The Cwtch hadn't changed. The red floral, overstuffed couch and chairs squatted like sumo wrestlers, claiming their territory, unapologetic for their appearance. A fierce fire cackled in the stone fireplace as the cat slept on beside it, and unlike the dog, claimed disinterest in the excitement of a new arrival. Anthea stopped at the door and let the scene curl around her, reclaiming her as its own.

Ralph and Ceri looked at each other, glad to have the farthest stray back in the fold. Ralph clapped his hands together, rubbing them with delight. "Right then, let's have a nice cuppa tea and a bowl of cawl I made yesterday. You hungry my darling?"

"No, I'd rather just go straight to the wine, if you please." Ceri said.

"I wasn't talking to you, old woman. I was talking to the pretty one."

"Well then, you furuncled old troll, see if I share the fifteen-year-old single malt that I brought, with *you*," Ceri warned.

Anthea disappeared into the chair beside the fire and said, "Carry on, you two, carry on."

A warm hand stroked the hair back from her forehead and Anthea heard the gentle voice of her father. "Come on lovely girl, better go to bed now."

She had kept her eyes open long enough to enjoy the bowl of traditional lamb stew her father had made, but by the time he and Ceri got into the scotch, she had slipped under a blanket of fatigue and was asleep. The fire was still roaring, and the two seniors showed no signs of giving the evening up.

"I want you to get a good rest tonight. I have a surprise for you in the morning," Ralph said.

"A surprise? What is it?" Anthea asked.

"Well it wouldn't be much of surprise if I told you now, would it? You've always been the impatient one when it came to presents. Remember that year when you secretly opened your presents and then tried to wrap them back up again? No one was fooled but we all pretended we were and watched you give the performance of your life."

Anthea gave him a sideways look. "Yes, how could I forget, when you've played it over and over on video? Besides, I was a mere child then."

"You were fourteen, I believe," corrected her father.

Anthea gave her father and her Aunt a hug. Ceri, whispered in her ear. "I have a little surprise for you too. We'll talk about it tomorrow." Too tired to anticipate what all these 'little surprises' could be, Anthea shuffled off to the billowy nest of down that made up her childhood bed.

The morning breeze lifted the veils of the bedroom curtains, and left its cool breath on Anthea's face. She inhaled its scent, mixed with that of the freshly washed, crisp linen. She looked at her wristwatch to see that it was five fifteen in the morning. One anxious bird was raising the morning alarm, and that urgent song, floating atop the moaning sea, coaxed a smile from her sleepy face. This time, it wasn't one of those relaxation tapes she would listen to when attempting to find her misplaced 'chi'. It was real and it was waiting for her just outside her window. She had slept the sleep of the dead and relished the thought of going outside with a hot cup of strong Glengettie tea.

She dressed quickly, then ran to the bathroom for a satisfying pee, followed by a quick vomit.

Down in the kitchen, she looked out the window as she filled the kettle and stuffed a left over Welsh cake into her mouth. She could just make out the stone garden wall and the flash and rumble of mountain ponies running past it. Maybe later she could entice them back with an apple or carrot.

"Put another couple of bags in the pot, there's a good girl," said her father's rustic morning voice. She turned to see him putting his old Aaron knit sweater on. "This will be a good time to show you my surprise,"

"This early? Boy, you *are* excited about it."

"Indeed I am. And so will you be when you see it. Let's have our tea and then we'll be off. Dress warmly."

"Dress warmly? Where are you planning to go at this hour? The sun's not even up."

"That will be the beauty of it. You'll see."

Another hoarse voice came from the staircase. "Do not go without me. I'll be down in minute. I'll have a cup of tea and a paracetamol, please," Ceri demanded.

Anthea was intrigued that Auntie Ceri would get up this early with a hangover.

Ralph put his hat and scarf on and held a duffle coat up for Anthea. "I hope you like it. – Gryff and Ceri's boys helped me with it too, fair play."

Anthea, handed a cup of tea to Ceri, who held her head and said, "Can somebody shoot that bloody bird. I don't do 'chirpy' in the morning, so please, nobody do anything enthusiastic."

"Too late." Ralph said, handing them each a torch.

The three set off through the light mist, the dew making their muddy wellies shine again.

"I heard you retching in the bathroom this morning," Ceri said under her breath to Anthea. "I didn't see you drink anything – you're losing your imunity."

They rounded a small copse of trees leading into the pasture just as the first rays of the sun reached over to illuminate it. Anthea stopped in her tracks when she set her eyes on the meadow. In its centre was a large stone circle. Twelve large standing stones stood upright, like some mystical squadron, their tips disappearing into the low hanging mist. They might have been planted there by some extravagant god eager to claim the meadow for himself or more likely, thought Anthea, *her-self.*

"It's for Mam, isn't it?" Anthea said without looking away from the spectacle before her.

"Yes," Ralph said, surveying her face for her approval.

Anthea recited aloud, "Not as showy as Stonehenge - something more modest in scale, but still . . ." Ralph and Ceri helped her finish the quote, "well, you know, showy."

That was what her mother had requested, in jest, whenever she was discussing how she would like to be "disposed of" in the future. It was a family joke which was repeated like a chorus by everyone when she would begin the sentence, "Well, when I die, I don't want any fuss at all. Nothing elaborate or overdone, you understand. I just want to be roasted like a potato crisp and put under the altar of a pagan stone circle – not as showy as Stonehenge, something more modest in scale, but still . . . well, you know, *showy*."

Anthea walked up to the outer stone, stroking it like the live thing she imagined it to be. It was a good couple of feet taller than she was and wider than her arms could circle. She leaned her face to its shoulder and kissed its mottled blue coat. White starbursts of quartz blazed from within it as if they had been harnessed from the heavens by an exacting jeweler. She touched each stone as she walked slowly around the perimeter of the circle until she came to the two that had a lintel perched on top. She looked back at her father. "Is Mam here?"

"Not yet," he answered, "but we'll put her there soon – at the interment."

Anthea scanned the stone circle, the mist now lifting like a curtain, allowing her to see a hushed audience of trees beyond, seemingly awaiting her response as much as Ralph and Ceri.

"Oh Dad, Auntie Ceri, it's beautiful . . . just beautiful. Mam would have loved this. How *ever* did you construct it?"

Ralph watched his daughter, still stroking the body of the stones as if they were that of her mother. "My only regret is that I didn't think of doing it when she was alive – not interring her, of course – she was never *that* cooperative, but making this stone circle. I've been sitting, watching that urn of ashes on the mantelpiece and wondering what to do with it. She left no instructions – other than joking about Stonehenge, and it just came to me that it couldn't be impossible – after all, our ancestors did it – with ropes, levers and rolling logs. I thought, surely we can do it with back hoes and cranes."

"And you did it? Unbelievable! How long did it take?"

The old man smiled a devious smile. "The wizard Merlyn did it. I'm that old, he was a school chum of mine."

Ceri nodded, holding her hands out and looking askance at her brother-in-law. "It's the truth, albeit a convoluted truth. You probably don't remember Merddyn Meredith, Anthea. He was an old friend of ours from school. He's a retired architect and damn it, if he doesn't know someone who had done this before. He rekons he's going to start a business constructing stone circles now. There's apparently quite a market for it. He's a complete nut – into all kinds of voodoo and shit. We had to hear all about it when he was, 'finding the energy centre' of the earth and burying the crystals and all that shit but I must say, he's still quite a goodlooking man underneath the beard and the hippie beads. Gryff's kids call him 'Merlyn' – remember, the name Merddyn is the Welsh for Merlyn. They really think he's a wizard and of course, we haven't told them any different, and in fact, neither has he. Do you know, it only took a week to actually erect the circle, once all the stones were picked?"

"Unbelievable," repeated Anthea, still mesmerized by her surroundings. "Well, now we *are* certified eccentrics. Mam would be proud of us."

"Gryff and the kids wanted to be here when you saw it," Ralph said. "They were all so excited about it, but they couldn't get down here in time. We wanted to show you it before you stumbled upon it."

"Don't worry," Ceri said, "They'll be here for the interment ceremony. We have a Pagan Priestess coming to do the honours."

Anthea turned to Ceri, trying not to be anymore nonplussed than she had been already. "Of course, we've got a wizard and a Pagan Priestess. Do we have Druids coming as well?"

Ceri shook her head. "Mmmm, I don't know. What religion is Ian?"
Anthea looked puzzled. "Ian, my ex? Why?"
"Well he's coming too – Surprise!"

Ceri poured a large scotch and handed it to Anthea, who gave her a withering look in return. Ceri shrugged and took a swig. "Hair of the dog . . . I don't know why you're so upset, Anth, I thought you two parted on good terms, didn't you?"

"Oh my God, Auntie Ceri, yes – technically, but that doesn't mean that I wanted you to invite him here for my Mam's . . .eh . . . *interment* or whatever we're going to call it, without even discussing it with me. What were you thinking?"

"Well, perhaps I didn't think it through, but I can explain."

Anthea took the glass of scotch out of her Aunt's hand, hesitated a moment and then swallowed a healthy gulp. She sat down on the fireside chair and said, "Start."

Ceri searched her agile mind for the best possible way to frame what was an admittedly impulsive gesture of commiseration when she had encountered Ian in a London bookshop a couple of weeks before. He had come up behind her and swept her up in his arms in the most endearing fashion. He looked genuinely glad to see her and begged her to have a drink with him to, 'catch up'.

When Anthea and he had announced the separation, both Ceri and Sian had collapsed into despair. They had both forged a deep and genuine love for the bright, entertaining young man Anthea had brought into the family. They could not fathom releasing him into the wild again, wanting to keep him close and involved in their life like a treasured pet. The fact that there were no children from the union left little reason to maintain an awkward connection and when he remarried, rather quickly, the final ties were broken.

Ceri believed that Sian wept more tears than anyone for the devastating loss of someone she had a true kinship with. Anthea distanced herself both physically and emotionally from the situation giving the family a very unsatisfactory explanation that, 'they wanted different things'. Eager not to cause any further pain or difficulty, they accepted it as something she did not want to discuss in any detail.

Shortly after, Anthea took the job in Canada. Sian had confided in Ceri that she thought the break up was mostly over the fact that Anthea had been quite adamant before they married, that she did not want children. It had been something she'd stated firmly since she was a teenager, though no one really took it seriously. Ian had accepted this unconditionally, at first, saying that he did not feel an overwhelming need to have them himself, but, with age and time, Sian suspected that he had tried to coax Anthea into changing her mind. She believed that Anthea had initiated the divorce with the thought that he would be able to find someone who could fulfill that need for him. Respectful of their privacy, the family watched the painful desolation of two people who clearly loved each other but could not provide the future they saw for themselves, with each other.

"He looked so sad for so many reasons," Ceri said. "Did you know that he's separated again?"

"No, I didn't," Anthea admitted, shocked that the news had not reached her, but then realizing she had no reason to be informed.

"He simply said, 'It was me,' and he didn't say anything more than that about it, but if you could have seen his face. He looked bleak and desolate, fraught with misery – though still absolutely gorgeous! He said he was hurt that he wasn't invited to the cremation . . ."

"Well, it was a . . . a private affair," Anthea said, squirming in her chair, as she recalled his hands squeezing her buttocks while he shuddered inside her in the back room of the cremation centre.

Ceri warmed to the subject. "That's why I mentioned the interment ceremony – they were very close, you know. I thought he might feel better if he could come."

Anthea bit her lip, "but really Auntie Ceri, didn't you think that I might not want to see him there? He's not part of this family anymore. I don't know what to call him . . . he's not even a friend anymore – he's just my ex-husband, I guess."

Ceri could see the agitation overtake her niece but she sensed that there was an undercurrent of grief for the loss of something more intangible than an ex-husband. She felt angry at herself for not being more thoughtful. She should have had Anthea's feelings uppermost in her mind, not Ian's. The ceremony was meant to be a tender moment for Anthea with her family and her actions had diminished its sanctity.

Ceri reached for Anthea's hand and reassured her. "I'm sorry love, I should have kept my big mouth shut. Don't worry, I have his number. I'll call him and tell him not to come."

Anthea reached for the glass of scotch and looked at the mantelpiece clock. It was 7:05am. "Yes – no – You have his number? I'll call him. That might be better. You can finish my scotch."

Ceri and Ralph were busy in the kitchen, their congenial squabbling filtering, in lyrical notes, throughout the cottage. Gryff, Hilary and the kids were due around noon or so and the two were debating over which of them burned the gravy at the last family dinner. Both had a high opinion of their culinary skills, with very little evidence to support it. But, having shared so many family gatherings over so many years, they managed to bicker their way through to a good result, one scoffing at the other for any less than perfect offering. Anthea's offer of help was given no consideration and seeing the ponies outside the garden wall, she reached for a few apples and a knife.

The ponies were skittish and even the boldest of them backed away at first. She raised the apples as she cut them into pieces and soon, they caught the scent and decided it might be worth investigating. A pale dapple grey stretched her neck out over the wall enticing Anthea nearer with her twitching muzzle, and soon, her soft lips took the apple from Anthea's palm. She had forgotten how big and soulful their eyes were, their sturdy bodies a contrast to their gentle character.

A grunt from the left captured her attention. An almost white colt dared to come a little closer, curious as to what this new friend was offering. Borrowing her mother's courage, the little one trotted up for a share, allowing Anthea to stroke the velvet of its nose. She couldn't wait to see how excited the kids would be to do the same.

Hmmm, the kids, she thought. *What kind of mother would I make when I have such an aversion to being one? Any kid of mine would probably be over-indulged in all things. I would be a textbook example of an overbearing parent. They'd sense my disappointment in them if they were not what I wanted them to be, if they became something or someone that I couldn't hide my intolerance of.* The most remarkable thing she had ever observed in parents was how many of them loved and accepted their awful children. She couldn't help being suspicious of "unconditional love" – *those people are probably just good actors.* Her own parents were the real thing. She saw it in, not only the way they had raised their children, but in their acceptance of everybody in their circle of friends. People gravitated towards their warmth and openness in all things. Their social circle was made up of an eclectic collection of huge successes and abject failures, intellects and idiots, religious rights and liberal lefts and libertines of all races; all enjoyed, respected, and yes, *welcomed* for their diversity.

Anthea felt that her work provided her with more than enough satisfaction, plenty of opportunity to be helpful and nurturing, and its demands were limited by her ability to distance herself from it. It was probably the same selfishness that made her shudder at the thought of being responsible for how a human being turned out – after she pulled them out of a vagina – which was the easy part. *The hard part was, truly loving someone more than you loved yourself. . . or your facials.*

She walked on beyond the garden wall toward the pasture. The mist was crawling away and the sun played in the sky, darting in and out of the clouds in a staccato display of light and dark.

The stone circle straddled the meadow beckoning her into its embrace. She walked through it, touching each stone again as she passed in greeting and upon reaching the lintel stones, she sat on the stone bench beneath them. She tucked her knees up and let her chin rest on her knees, opening her mind to reflection. *What will I say to Ian?*

Ian was someone who had been willing to sublimate his most passionate need for children to be with her. *Was I selfish to marry him and believe that he could do that and not resent me for it later?* There were those small, treacherous ways, she would see and feel his longing for a child of his own. Sometimes, in a spontaneous moment, when holding someone else's child, in conversation or in his arms, he'd breathe them in; delight in their honesty, their shyness, or bravado. *He was particularly interested in the ugly ones; the ones whose features or personality were unattractive and got the least attention, the ones who pleased themselves more than they pleased the adults. In that way, he's more akin to my family than I am.*

If Mam were here, and perhaps she is, she would scold me for not having the grace to include him in the ceremony. Now that he's separated, maybe it wouldn't be as awkward. Then again, I'd have to see him, and that would be awkward – awkward for me, a kindness for him? Damn, this self-reflection isn't going my way! I'm really not suited to martyrdom. The most unselfish thing I've ever done was leave him so that he could find someone who could give the world a great father . . . and the irony is that now, I could make him one . . . if I weren't so selfish. Fuuuck! Letting him attend the interment would be – what? Agony? No, maybe just a simple kindness and nothing more . . . nothing more.

She went over the phone conversation in her mind. *First the pleasantries.*

Hi Ian, how are you? It's Anthea.

I'm fine Anthea, how was your flight?

Good, good, thanks. How's the job?

Great, thanks. How's Canada?

Great, thanks.

. . . Great.

Ian, you can't come to my mother's ceremony because I don't want to see your beautiful face and have to stop myself from kissing you so hard, I'd suck it off the bones it drapes over like some gorgeous, craggy mountain range of masculine perfection, damn it! Oh, and in a coupla days, I'm going to get rid of your baby.

Great, no problem, I won't come then.

Yep, no problem at all, she thought as she walked toward the house.

The rumbling of a car motor coming up the driveway made Anthea pause and hold her hand up to shelter her eyes from the sun's rays. They were early. Gryff's green van growled its way around the corner and pulled up in front of the house. The van doors opened immediately and seven-year-old Lewis tumbled out of the car, several bags dropping to the ground behind him. Four-year-old Cordy shrieked loudly and prepared to jump out and over the bags. "Catch me, Lewis," she demanded.

Lewis turned and put his arms out for her, but only until he was distracted by the sight of his grandfather running out of the house, frilly apron flapping in the wind. "Watch!" Ralph said, pointing a wooden spoon at Lewis. But Lewis had missed his sister, who landed half atop the larger bag. Her hands accepted the meeting with the ground first, followed by her backside, which went up and over them.

"Weally nice tumbow toss!" Lewis said, without the benefit of the letter 'r' but with sincere admiration. Cordy lay flat, arms and legs stretched out, happy to receive a compliment from her big brother and watching the adults from the ground viewpoint.

"Jesus Christ," said his father, Gryff, almost tumbling out of the van himself. "You didn't catch her you bloody nitwit."

Hilary came running around the van to check the damage, while carrying a dangling eight-month-old Edwyn under her arm. "Don't you bloody swear at him, Gryff, it wasn't his fault,"

Lewis looked at his grandfather who was lifting Cordy from the ground. "Mummy says Daddy swears like a pown stow, Gwampa."

"Did you know a porn star is a fish, Grampa?" Cordy informed him.

Anthea hugged her brother and she whispered in his ear, "Aren't you glad I talked Hilary out of naming Lewis after you Gwyff?"

Gryff squeezed her and answered, "Yes – and remember her second choice for his name was Wobin? Hopefully he'll grow out of it like I did - without as much 'twama as I suffod'. We've got a good speech therapist."

Ralph waved his wooden spoon at the children, scolding them for not waiting until the car stopped completely. Lewis was already clutching at Ralph's waist. "We couldn't wait that long to see you, Gwampa."

Ralph melted with joy, coaxing Cordy around to look at Anthea. "Look Cordy, Lewis, it's your Auntie Anthea from Canada."

Anthea leaned in toward the children. Cordy turned her head shyly, snuggling into Ralph's shoulder. Lewis, screwed up his face as he took the measure of Anthea. "I wemembow you bwought me some Indian moccasins last time, when Gwanny died. I gwew and they aw too small for me now."

"That's nice of you to remember, Lewis. I'm glad you liked them."

"I weally wanted a tomahowk."

His mother clipped the back of his head. "Manners."

Anthea ruffled his russet hair. "I knew I should have brought that Bowie knife I had in mind for you. Sorry kid."

Gryff rolled his eyes as he embraced his sister again. "There are days I would have let him have it. Nice to see you, Anteater," he said, resurrecting her childhood nickname.

This wasn't lost on Lewis who asked, "Why did you call her Anteater, Daddy?"

Anthea stared Gryff down.

"Cuz it sounds like Anthea – Anteater – see?"

"And because she has a big nose?" Lewis asked.

Gryff turned away so as not to show his response to his son. Hilary gave Lewis another cuff and followed up with one for Gryff when he began to snicker.

Anthea gave Hilary a hug for two reasons, one to greet her and another to thank her for taking her side against the two of them. "I feel sorry for you, Hilary. He's spawned a Mini Me. If it wasn't for you, the authorities would have taken your children away from him a long time ago. "

"And there are days I'd gladly give them – but they won't take adults," Hilary said looking down and seeing that Edwyn was still dangling from the crook of her left arm, fast asleep.

Auntie Ceri stood at the door holding Cordy who was ringing the dinner bell with gusto. "Grubs up!"

Gryff walked into the cottage, his lanky arm around Anthea's shoulder. "I didn't tell Lewis that you had a big nose, Anthea,"

"Good," she said. "You know I have a complex about my nose."

Gryff let her go into the door way first, giving her an extravagant bow as she went ahead. I "told him you had a big ass."

Anthea slammed the door behind her, just short of smashing Gryff's own nose.

The Cwtch seemed much smaller with three children and their accoutrements filling up every corner. The main house had five bedrooms and the annex, a renovated stone out-building had three more. Still, the booster seats, high chair, play pen, Barbie toys and Lego stations were like flags stabbed gleefully into the ground to claim every spot for Kid Nation. Hilary tirelessly tried to have the kids tidy up, and in fairness they often did, but even so, Anthea noticed that it was almost impossible to negotiate your way from one room to another without stepping on a stray, painful, piece of Lego.

Ralph and Ceri seemed blissfully unaware of this assault on their tranquil retreat, but Anthea could not help but set off a mental timer ticking down to the day they would leave. *How did they become so irritating, so fast?* Mercifully, Gryff's boisterous family was banished to sleep in the annex and so, at least they would be spared the night time ritual of whining, sudden onsets of thirst followed by multiple pee alerts, ghost inquiries, and tummy aches.

The study was a small but bright room with large windows showcasing the distant seascape. The land dropped off a perilous two hundred feet at parts of the beachhead and since their younger days, a large patch of the paddock wall had been built up to keep children within it.

In a high wind, even an adult could be blown off the bluffs onto the rocky crags below. Hilary had resorted, without apology to strapping a leash system onto the kids for any walks that might find them near the sea coast.

Anthea reviewed all this in her mind as she sequestered herself in the study, the ears of the wing chair curling around her as she watched the sea submit to the sunshine. It stretched like a blue ribbon across the horizon, untroubled and cordial to the sailboats that slid across its silky surface.

There were two phone calls she had to make. The most important one was to tell Ian that it might be better if he didn't come to the interment. *So, I'll call Carolina first. She should be up by now.*

"Heeelloo," came the gravelly response.

"Carolina? It's Anthea. Did I wake you?"

"Oh no, I was up at six taking the dogs for a three-mile walk."

"Really?"

"No. You woke me."

"Sorry – er, what about the dogs? They probably have to go out by now."

"I let them out when I went to bed at about five, but I'll let them out again. They don't seem concerned, they're right here beside me. Spock stole all the blankets and is laying sunny-side up." She put on a convincing Southern drawl, "Kina looks lak a real uuugly Baiby Jee-sus in a mainger."

Anthea paused, suppressing the urge to warn Carolina not to share that accent or image with Glynda, knowing it would only provoke her to make a point of it. Instead, she allowed herself a warm wave of relief and appreciation for Carolina's affection for Twiggy and Spock. She pictured the three of them sprawled out on the bed, each of them feeling they were in good company. She missed all three of them, already. "Well, don't let me keep you up. I just wanted to tell you that I'm at that number I gave you and to be sure you had no questions for me."

A loud yawn came over the receiver, and Anthea recognized it as Spock's. Carolina took it up and answered through one of her own. "Noooo problem here. We're all happy as pigs in shit – or should I say pigs in a blanket – no dogs in a blanket – you're making me think too much!"

"Alright, I'll go. But I wanted to tell you that I'm about to call Ian."

There was another long pause in the conversation, Anthea waited. The penny dropped.

"Ian? Your ex? Are you fucking kidding me? Why? Why now? You know, even though I've never met him, from what I've heard, I always thought you two were right for each other, except that you have this thing up your ass about no kids and all, but let me tell you, you must have been on crack when you let a guy like that go over such a wacko shit-thing like 'we wanted different things' – fuck that – *wanting different things* is about him wanting a mistress or necrophilia or some sick shit like that – wanting kids is something you can come to some agreement on – like having one kid and fewer dogs or something. Plus, there are Nannies for that sort of thing too . . ."

"Carolina . . . Carolina," Anthea said. "I'm calling him to tell him not to see me."

Another long silence followed by a loud sigh of frustration. "You're an idiot. Just sayin'."

Hearing the details of the situation did not change Carolina's critical evaluation of Anthea's intentions and she left her with no doubt as to what a slightly unbalanced, mildly alcoholic desparate, single woman would do, should Anthea want her advice.

A gentle tap on the door, and an opportune, "Come in," gave Anthea a discrete reason to extract herself from the conversation. It was Gryff. He peeked around the door and wiggled his eyebrows then began an elaborate pantomime of gestures that were meant ask who she was talking to. Anthea put the phone down and waved him in. He made a big show of tiptoeing into the room and sat in the chair across from her staring intently into her eyes.

"What?" she said, breaking the silence. This released him from the freeze frame he had placed himself into, and he clasped his hands as if he were about to lead her in a confession.

"What?" she said impatiently. "You wanted me for something?"

He bit his lower lip, and looked upward at her, announcing the delicate moment to come. "A little bird, Auntie Ceri, told me that you were going to tell Ian not to come this weekend."

Anthea felt her hackles rise. "Well, you can tell that little bird, to get her great big, yappy beak out of my feeder. This bird is quite capable of making her own decisions where her ex-mate is concerned."

"Well," Gryff ventured, "what if that bird's older brother thinks that she's cukoo if she does that?"

"Can we dispense with the avian references and speak like Homo Sapiens? It's none of your beeswax – or Auntie Ceri's in fact."

"Clever," he said, "so, what's the buzz?"

Anthea picked up a cushion and hit him with it. "Why does everyone think they have anything to say about this?"

Gryff looked at his sister, a serious tone overtaking his voice. "Because I kind of invited him too. I thought he might like to come – thought *you* might like him to come – he's separated, you know."

Anthea spun her head around to fix a fierce look on Gryff. "What? You too? Shit! You're all conspiring against me! Don't you think that if I'd wanted him here, I would have invited him myself? There's a reason he's my EX-husband and not my husband, you know."

"He said he was grateful to be invited – to say a proper goodbye to Mam and to say hello to you. The guy's still shattered. He's always loved you - never got over you. You left him. He would never have left you. You said so yourself, remember?

Gryff's confidence in his words stirred up even more uncertainty in Anthea's mind. He had unearthed old sentiments that she had studiously buried beneath layers of logic, handfuls of regret and acres of distraction. She held on to her emotions.

"But Gryff, what's changed? Ha! What hasn't changed? It's all a fucking shitstorm. Why put either of us through the wringer again? Besides, you don't know how he feels. You don't know how *I* feel." She gathered momentum, "Hell, *I* don't know how I feel."

Gryff took her shoulders and squeezed them. "You don't have to. That's what research is. Do your research, Doctor. Prove our hypothesiseseses . . . hypotheseees wrong."

Carolina had trouble getting back to sleep after Anthea's call. She could not stop thinking about the prospect of Anthea getting back with Ian. She remembered being hired when Anthea had just arrived in Canada. After the initial interview, she had thought there was no hope of getting the job because Anthea had seemed so aloof, humourless and judgemental; a minion of the upper middle class, unlikely to appreciate or even stand for what Carolina called 'my natural exuberance'.

At the time, Carolina was desperate to change her job as a hospital clerk, owing to the fact that the people she worked for then, didn't have any appreciation for that same 'natural exuberance' and she knew her days were numbered there. Dr. Gentile had given Carolina a flourishing recommendation, highlighting her excellent organizational abilities, billing knowledge and work ethic with the proviso that she came with a, 'natural exuberance' that not everybody appreciated but sensed that Anthea would. Neither saw themselves as "breeders" and thus, a match was made that stood the test of time.

Carolina was grateful for the position and for the several bonuses Anthea gave her for working long hours to set the office up so quickly. At the time, Lucia, was failing fast and Carolina knew that soon she would have to admit her mother to care. Anthea had offered a loan when on onc occasion money was needed to make ends meet, and Carolina had never forgotten that kindness.

Anthea had since relaxed her initial frosty demeanor and shown Carolina her delight in harmless mischief. Still, Carolina sensed that there was a certain sadness that swept over Anthea's face when she spoke of Ian. Perhaps regret still haunted her and stopped any investment in future romance. As a chronically single woman herself, Carolina sympathized. *Shit, finding a man was difficult enough, finding one who didn't have or didn't need children was even more difficult, finding one that appreciated 'natural exuberance'? Well, you were fucked.*

Carolina's cell phone rang and after finding it under Spock's rear end, she answered it.

"Hi Carolina, don't hang up. It's Melinda Thackery."

Flimsy cunt, thought Carolina, *she hasn't called me since the Fairmont fundraiser.* But curiosity subdued her impulse to hang up. Her sense of fair play made her balance that verdict with the fact that she acknowledged the starring role her own lady bits played in the drama. So, she took on a light-hearted, nonchalance that suited her purpose.

"Why would I hang up on you, Melinda?"

"Because I know you think I'm a flimsy cunt – sorry. I was trying to save my marriage and I thought Daniel wouldn't want me to see you again."

"Did he think I was a bad influence on you?"

"No, it was more because you smashed him in the face – remember?"

"Oh yes, how is his nose?"

"Crooked."

"Sorry. Does he want to see me to knock it to the other side?"

Melinda laughed a hearty, genuine laugh remembering the two of them dancing naked in the cold, night air. She had missed her and hoped that Carolina would come to a dinner party at her house the next weekend. Carolina turned that unlikely invitation over in her mind.

Melinda continued, "It's Daniel's artsy types. I actually like these people, though half the time I don't know what they're talking about. But they put up with me and I thought you might like to come too – you read books and shit and besides you'd liven the thing up a bit. Are you free?"

"Hmmm, probably. What should I wear?"

Melinda didn't miss a beat, "Something elegant – like panties."

Roger had it all planned out. He had invited Molly to his house for dinner on Saturday night and he thought he'd see where things led after that. He knew how to prepare precisely three fancy dinners, salmon, chicken parmigian, and vegetable stir fry.

Everything needed could be purchased at Seto's Little Market at the corner. He'd thought of flowers and a large bouquet of carnations adorned the table, though they did look a little spindly in the vase he'd put them in. He used real cloth serviettes and the good set of dishes without any chips in them. The cupboard was full of red and white wine in case she asked for either. Tom Jones was taking care of the mood music and all that was left, was for him to shave and shower.

A quick glance at the time made him pick up his pace. He put his nice black pants out on the bed and was looking for his nice black sweater with a collar. *It's slimming and not as tight.* After a good rummage around the bedroom, leaving drawers open and several bits and pieces strewn on the floor, he couldn't lay his hands on it and so grabbed the yellow and brown turtleneck that he felt a little self conscious in since he'd put the weight back on. In his haste, he cut himself shaving and had to spend far too long trying to stem the bleeding. That's when the doorbell rang. He was wrestling with the turtleneck, when he saw the black sweater in the clean laundry basket that had been beside the dresser for a couple of weeks. He picked Blizzard the cat out of the basket and placed her gently down beside it. She was eighteen, very frail and loved beyond measure.

When he opened the door, and saw Molly's wide, enchanting smile, he was filled with gratitude that this stunning young woman was interested in him. His arms went out instinctively and brought her to his chest in a splendid crush. He lifted her coat off her shoulders and he noticed that she wore a fresh green, floral dress with an astonishingly low neckline which she was more than capable of embellishing. His knees felt weak.

Molly liked the sedate black outfit Roger was wearing. It made him look sophisticated. As he turned to put her coat on the rack, the sweater took on an unexpected feature. The back of it was white with a thick layer of cat hair almost matching Roger's own head of white hair. She thought of brushing it off with her hand but decided better of it.

Roger grabbed her hand excitedly and led her into the dining room. Upset that he'd not had time to light the candles, he set about doing that and Molly had time to take in the scene. The first thing she noticed was an eight-by-ten wedding photograph of Roger and his late wife, Sheila, on the bookcase. Molly thought that Sheila had a face reminiscent of Greta Garbo, the high arch to the brows, the fine bones shadowed in the pale skin; a true beauty. She decided to pretend she hadn't seen it, so as not to distract from the obvious attention Roger had put into the present moment.

He raced from the kitchen and pulled out the chair for her, begging her to sit. He poured the red wine she had chosen, and triumphantly brought out some shrimp hanging precariously from two ice cream glasses. Roger sat down quickly and lifted his glass, "To living again."

Molly was touched by his summation of their courtship. It was as if she was suddenly aware that she was a woman and not only a mother. Her breasts had become ornaments again instead of vestigial appendages that had to be wrestled into restraints so that they wouldn't dangle uselessly and land in the butter dish. Now, they were to be attended to, holstered in pretty, lacy cups that showed them off like peaches in a crystal bowl. Once they were hoisted into place, she was able to find her waist again, strapping it with belts and chains Houdini would have had difficulty escaping from. And shoes. Shopping for senseless, strappy little numbers that were worthy of that rare indulgence, a professional pedicure. She was consumed by such frivolous pursuits after years of apathy and despondence; the small murmur of guilt when spending money on herself was quelled by the excitement of being attractive to someone again. Her body was shaking off the final pinch of a dull slumber and 'living again'.

Molly picked up a shrimp and cast a glance around the table. "Do you have any shrimp sauce, Roger?"

Roger jumped from his seat and excusing himself, ran into the kitchen. Molly heard the fridge open and then some cupboards banging. She waited patiently for his return, seeing another photograph of Sheila and Roger dressed up as Anthony and Cleopatra. Handsome graduation photos of his son and daughter were beside it. She sipped her wine and folded and unfolded the napkin, noticing that they were cloth and not paper – *classy*, she thought.

Roger came back, slightly out of breath, with a new jar of shrimp sauce. He twisted off the top and then realized he should get a container to put it in. Molly stopped him from getting up again saying, "Don't worry about that, I'll use my bread plate." She reached for a knife and then paused. "So, sorry to be a nuisance, but do you have any butter, perhaps?"

"Oh, of course, I should have thought. I'll just go and get it," Roger said.

"No, no, no, don't bother. It's fine!" Molly protested, feeling that she was being too demanding.

"It's no bother, I have to check the chicken anyway," and off Roger went into the kitchen.

Molly broke her bread with her hands and ate a shrimp slowly. Roger came back to the table with a brick of butter and two bowls of green salad. The butter was a little hard but she managed to put some on her bread which was very satisfying.

They chatted about his children, Ryan and Bethany briefly and Molly learned that they were both married with a young baby each. Molly wondered how he felt about being involved with her own, very much younger family.

"Keeps you young to be around kids," he said. "I loved every minute of raising my own and wish my grandchildren were nearer so that I could be more involved with them. I miss going to their games and competitions.

Nothing's worse than having nothing to do at nights and weekends other than watching TV."

Molly moved on to her salad and rather than ask for salad dressing began to eat it as it was. Roger reacted quickly. "Oh, I forgot the salad dressing. What kind do you like?"

"It's fine. I don't need the calories. Relax."

"Oh no, I can't eat it like this either. I'll get some – which kind?"

"Really, it doesn't matter."

"But, I've got all kinds – just say which one."

"Alright then, Balsamic please, or Italian, or anything, really."

Roger bounced back into the kitchen and Molly waited once more. The oven timer went off and continued to sound its alarm for some time. Molly thought she could smell something burning and worried that Roger was preoccupied. She'd go and help out.

When she entered the kitchen, Roger was nowhere to be seen. Molly looked around and saw no other exit other than the one leading to the outside of the house. Puzzled, she turned off the timer and pulled the chicken out of the oven. Roger came bounding up the back steps and into the kitchen, his face red from exertion.

"Where have you been?" asked Molly, stunned by his entrance.

Roger raised his hands and displayed two bottles of salad dressing, Balsamic and Italian, both unopened.

"I had to get these," he said nonchalantly.

"From where?" Molly asked. "Do you have a pantry in your garage or something?"

"No, of course not - from Seto's Market at the corner."

Molly burst into a fit of laughter, realizing that this man had been running back and forth to the corner store for all the items she had asked for.

"What?" he asked, confused by her reaction.

She fell into his arms and kissed his mouth passionately. He closed his arms around her, still holding the Balsamic and Italian dressing.

It was not long after that that they decided to delay the next course to fulfill a more satisfying hierarchy of needs. Roger was thrilled and if the truth be told, somewhat relieved that he found himself quite able to satisfy Molly's youthful vigour, and Molly was thrilled that she could do so under a massive 25th Anniversary photograph of Roger and Sheila that hung above the bed.

The parlour was bathed in a halo of late afternoon sunshine, the yellows glowing like amber, making it an inviting setting for Glynda to read her book, now that she was feeling well enough to enjoy it. Edna bumped around the kitchen trying to find something for their supper. The doorbell ringing was less surprising these days, as people dropped by to wish Glynda well. Molly and Orlagh had come over faithfully to do the cleaning in the last few weeks, although Edna was trying very hard, these days to keep things up, so as to lessen their load. She had difficulty fathoming why someone Glynda rarely spoke of would commit to do such a generous devotion of her very limited time to help them and she felt herself soften to these two hard workers in a way she had never expected. *After all, the woman was a widow with three children a Mongoloid brother and a full-time job to look after.* They rarely even accepted a soft drink or a cookie for their efforts, but arrived, scoured the house meticulously and then left after the most minimal of pleasantries, always rushing to another obligation. Edna had overheard that Molly had taken a few extra shifts at the hospital, and so assumed that money must be very tight. That she found the impetus to help in such a significant way touched the cynical old woman.

This time the doorbell was rung by Carolina whom Edna barely remembered from the night at the church concert. *It was probably her who gave me the flu I came down with the next morning.* Edna looked up one side of Carolina and down the other. *This one was a rather tarty sort,* she surmised, evaluating what looked like feathers on her coat and ridiculously high purple shoes. Her hair was teased in an untidy pile on top of her head, *like the floozies used to do in the sixties,* and was dyed a severe gypsy black. The red wrap dress she wore underneath showed her black bra and Edna sniffed as Carolina reluctantly bent over to take her shoes off, coming down to a more sensible height. Her bosoms were barely under restraint and might easily have oozed out like hemorrhoid ointment from a tube. Edna held her hands at her chest, waiting for the girl to struggle out of her foolish shoes. She took her into the parlour announcing her as, "Carol Anne."

Glynda put her book aside and gave Carolina a genuine smile. "Carolina, what are you doing here? You're all dressed up too."

"Yes, I'm going to a dinner party at a friend's house tonight. I thought I'd drop in and see how you're doing."

Carolina reached into her tote bag and brought out a large packet of Chinese food.

Glynda put her hand to her chest and thanked Carolina for her thoughtfulness. She knew money was tight for Carolina, and this generosity was not a small thing. "Will you have some with us? Edna, would you mind getting some plates?"

Edna shuffled as quickly as she could to the kitchen, impressed, excited, and relieved that the problem of supper was eliminated. Perhaps she liked, *this exotic dancer girl,* a little better for this very useful gesture.

"Oh no," Carolina protested, "like I said, I'm on my way to a dinner party, but I'm glad to see you looking so well. Is there anything else you need . . ." she looked at Edna as she picked up her tote bag, ". . . some punch or more magazines perhaps?"

Edna straightened her back and her face remained expressionless.

"Right," Carolina said with a grin on her face. "Well, let me know when you do. I have a lot of magazines with very interesting articles in them. Don't worry, I'll let myself out."

Carolina pulled up to Melinda's home, noting the high calibre of the cars squatting in the driveway. It occurred to her that she had no business cavorting with these people and she entertained driving away. She reached into her purse and took a couple of shots from the mickey she carried in there for circumstances such as this. *Tequila – nice surprise!*

She checked the car mirror and resisted the urge to put more make-up on. She'd tried to remember what Melinda had told her before – to apply it more subtly, emphasize either the eyes, the mouth; not both. She opened the car door and then shut it again and re-applied the purple eyeshadow. She opened the car door again and leaned into the side mirror of the car to apply the ruby lipstick.

It was an immense room, with towering ceilings. Exquisite art work hung at various levels made glorious by the deep blue of the walls. Five or six people were chatting, murmuring undertones and glanced up for a cursory smile at Carolina. She could not see Melinda there, but Daniel caught her eye and excused himself from his conversation, gliding over to greet her. He was a graceful man, catalogue handsome, but all she could look at as he approached was his crushed nose, which definitely drifted over to the left side of his face.

"Carolina," he said reaching his hand for hers, "you look . . . astonishing."

Carolina squinted, already feeling her hand itch. "What does that mean?"

He caught himself and clasped his other hand around hers, bringing her hand to his mouth for a chaste kiss. "No, really, I'm sincere. You are eye-catching. Not every woman can carry off flamboyant like you can."

Carolina still couldn't let down her guard. "Listen, you better not be fucking with me or I'll straighten that nose out for you."

Daniel looked into her eyes, squeezed her hand and let his voice become more strident.

"My God woman, you know, you are like a wild thing. Can't you just relax a bit and believe that I want to get along with you? I'm trying to save my marriage and I need you to help me. Melinda really likes you. She says, and I quote, 'the only angles on you are on the exterior not the interior – and that's a compliment, if you want it, OK?'"

"OK," she agreed, prepared to accept his entreaty. "Where's Melinda?"

Melinda was speaking with the caterer but Daniel didn't leave her hand go as he led her around the room. For some strange reason, that small gesture made her feel good, gave her the courage to engage these fine beings. She began feeling her confidence return. They came up to a man who was helping himself to the caviar and a touch on the shoulder from Daniel had him swing around, his face exploding with pleasure at seeing Carolina. It was Gerald Walker.

"Oh my dear, I was hoping to see more of you."

Carolina winced. "I would have thought everyone had seen far too much of me last time, honey."

Gerald laughed a hearty laugh. Daniel looked down at his drink and flushed.

"I don't see your lovely wife, Gerald – *Terror,* is it?" Carolina said.

Gerald laughed again, perhaps a little too loudly. "*Terra*," he emphasized, "well, she's gone. She left me for a masseuse, goddamn it."

Daniel excused himself, uncomfortable with the topic of masseuses.

"A masseuse?" Carolina repeated, a recollection coming to the fore of her mind.

Gerald reading her thoughts, whispered in her ear, "Yes, the very same one who gave Melinda the clap."

Melinda entered from the kitchen, directing everyone to the dining room. She was wearing a blue satin cocktail dress that Carolina figured to be vintage 1950's. Her hair was arranged in a charming updo which complimented the sculptured perfection of her porcelain face. She even had false eyelashes which Carolina initially resented because of Melinda's lecture about how cheap they can look. Though she had to admit, somehow Melinda could pull them off.

Melinda's face lit up when she saw Carolina and she hugged her with resolution, then spun her around to admire what she knew was an effort at restraint on Carolina's part. She led her to the table and sat her next to her own chair and across from Gerald. He sat beside an older woman who introduced herself as Eleanor. Carolina guessed her to be in her early seventies though time had etched its handwriting very lightly on her face.

Her hair was completely white and fell around her shoulders here and there from an untidy bun. She had extraordinary hooded eyes and a smile that completely transformed her visage from austere to remarkably beautiful. She had been talking to Gerald about the book Wolf Hall and how he should really make time to read both it and the sequel. "You love history, Gerald and you will enjoy the refreshing perspective she gives of Cromwell. He had been so vilified by history and certainly by Hollywood. History really is written by the victors, isn't it?"

Gerald swept his wine glass up to his mouth, swallowed and then added, "Unfortunately, that's where the majority of people learn their history, or indeed their opinions these days – from the twisted interpretations of a movie script. Are we talking Oliver Cromwell, the Roundhead? -executed Charles the 1st?

Carolina spoke up. "The book Wolf Hall was about Thomas Cromwell in Henry the Eighth's court. Oliver Cromwell was his great, great, great uncle, I believe - both extraordinary men."

"You've read it, my dear?" Elcanor asked, "Have you read the second one yet?"

Carolina admitted that she had not but that she was looking forward to doing so.

"It is equally as enthralling. What are you reading currently?"

Carolina hesitated. "I'm actually re-reading one of my favourite works in an effort to understand it better than the first two times I tried to read it."

Gerald looked up. "Is it the Bible? I've never even read it once, but I feel that I can't call myself well-read until I do."

"Well, what I'm reading might be a good companion piece to that. I'm reading Paradise Lost."

"Milton?" Eleanor said. "I don't remember that being a page turner. I'm impressed. Tell me what it is that you wish to understand more clearly about that work."

Carolina probed the expression on the faces of Gerald and Eleanor. Both leaned into her and seemed truly interested in what she had to say.

She hoped that she could put her quest succinctly; her desire to understand the nature of good and evil. What makes a good man do something evil and evil man do something good? She liked Milton's sympathetic view of Satan's fall from grace; Satan's courage to rebel against an omnipotent being. She asked them, "Isn't there something noble in that? Isn't that what a hero does?"

"My goodness, Carolina," Melinda said, "I had no idea that such grand ideas lurked under that hair of yours . . . I can see that it's my duty as hostess to lower the calibre of this conversation. My biggest concern is whether the print on the scarf I'm wearing is too small to match the one on my dress." Carolina searched Melinda's face for any sign of ridicule and relaxed into a laugh when she felt that that was not her intention.

"You know, Melinda," Carolina said, "Einstein did say that, 'Once you can accept the universe as being something expanding into an infinite nothing - which is something, wearing stripes with plaid is easy."

Eleanor pointed to an elderly gentleman with white hair almost as long as her own. "Which is exactly what my husband, Stuart, over there is wearing. Only Einstein could wear that outfit better. Bravo Carolina, bravo! Melinda, where have you been hiding this enchanting woman?"

Carolina looked around the table, at the kindly disposed faces who were smiling back at her, and she felt an inexplicable urge to say what she was thinking. She wanted to confess to them that she had no authority behind her opinions, that she had no post-secondary education as did noone in her family for as far back as you want to go. She was simply a receptionist in a medical office, but this was the first gathering of people she had ever been in where they did not ask what she did for a living; they asked about who she was. She heard her voice waver, perhaps it was the drink, but she placed her hand on Eleanor's and said only, "Thank you."

The evening seemed effortless. Carolina spoke with each of the guests, enjoying their knowledge, their talents, their wit. Gerald did not let his eyes stray far from Carolina, despite what seemed an honest effort not to leer at her as he had before. He drank only sparkling water which might have accounted for his measured dignity and Carolina followed suit.

Towards the end of the night, Carolina declined Melinda's offer of staying the night. She also declined Gerald's offer to meet him for a drink, saying, quite truthfully, that she was going to the dogs instead.

Carolina left work early that day, grateful for the reprieve that working with Dr. Gentile afforded her. In deference to his age, Anthea had ensured that the clinic days were kept short. Carolina found Georgia much more capable than she would have thought possible. She did not cater to her as Glynda tended to do. She was a demanding mentor and Georgia was probably too scared of her not to recruit all her latent abilities for any task. Things were good.

The late spring offered several hours of daylight ahead and she relished the idea of a brisk walk in the countryside, at Ty Bleu, with the dogs. No sooner had she opened the front door of the farmhouse, than Spock sprang toward her, anxious to cover her face with his wet kisses.

"Oh honey, if only you were a man," Carolina said aloud, rubbing his chops and kissing the top of his football face. Twiggy patiently waited her turn, sidling up and leaning against her leg, face lifted upward in a quiet plea for attention.

Carolina squatted down and caressed Twiggy's velvet head allowing Spock to jump over her into the yard. He took a few gratifying pees followed by a multitude of spritzers on anything remotely vertical to claim them for himself; *mine, mine, mine too, mine, there you go - mine as well, oops! Can't forget you guys, mine.* She watched him sniff the bushes and begin to assess his need to poop. This took time, unlike peeing, there seemed to be very specific criteria as to where this ritual would take place. Just when he seemed to have found the perfect spot, there was yet another to investigate. When he was satisfied with his selection, he would waddle forward on his haunches as a necklace of poop was deposited behind him. Twiggy, on the other hand, went discretely into the bushes and kept her business private.

In a matter of minutes, Twiggy was by Carolina's side, ready to accompany her anywhere she wished to go. Spock had just begun his return too, when he was suddenly distracted by some unseen calling. He lifted his nose into the air and then bolted up and over the rise beside the house.

"Shit," Carolina said, realizing that she must actively pursue him and make sure he returned. As she reached the top of the hill, she was relieved to see that he had settled to stare into the walkout window of the neighbour's house.

Carolina took off her belt so that she could use it to lead the dog back to his own home, hopefully without disturbing the people living there. No sooner had she strung the belt through Spock's collar than a voice came from behind.

"Spock and I are old friends, but I don't believe we've met."

Carolina turned to look into the face of a very attractive man who hopefully didn't have a wife.

"Well, hello. I'm sure I would have remembered if we had met. I'm Carolina. I'm dog sitting for Anthea while she's away. Nice to meet you . . .?"

"Jack, Jack Flynte. Where's Anthea gone?"

Carolina swept her windblown hair from her face and peeked through the dark strands that wouldn't be controlled. She let her lips part in the suggestion of a smile as she spoke. "Anthea's gone back to Britain for a few weeks – family stuff. I love to come to here and look after the dogs and the house for her. I live on my own in the city so it's like a holiday in the country for me."

Jack kept his eyes on hers as he knelt to pet Twiggy. "I'd ask you in for a coffee like a good neighbour should, only Spock and my dog, Scarlet, don't get along too well. Actually, the problem is that they get along too well. Every time she's in heat, Spock tries to get a date, if you know what I mean. I'm trying to breed her but it's not going too well. She won't let the sire near her."

"Come to think about it, I think I heard about this soap opera. Spock's a fine-looking boy, hard to forget a face like that. Who are you to interfere with true love?"

Jack Flynte laughed and revealed an interestingly cooked smile that she thought reminded her of someone.

"Believe me, I'm all for love of any kind, but I'd really like to get a good puppy out of her. She's got a hell of a blood line."

"I'm more of a mutt fan myself. Purity was never something I was very good at."

"I'm not a fan of it either – purity I mean."

Carolina licked her lips. "Are we talking dogs or people now?"

He kept his gaze on her. "I'm far too well-bred to answer that."

She gave him a look that showed her appreciation for his wit.

Jack looked at his watch. "Why don't you come over later tonight for a drink, if you're not busy."

After walking the dogs, Carolina had worked up a bit of a sweat and took a quick shower. She reapplied her make-up, put on fresh undies, and let her hair down. *It's not like I'm going to jump into bed with him or anything,* she thought to herself, *although he is, 'a fine-looking male'.* "Right Spock?" Spock looked up from the bed and stared at her, as if waiting for an explanation. Anthea had never said a good word about Jack as far as Carolina could remember. There seemed to be nothing but strained relations between them. She hoped that her seeing him would not be awkward in any way – besides, she was just being neighbourly – that's all.

Seven came soon enough and Carolina was knocking at Jack's door with a bottle of wine in her hand.

"Good thinking," Jack said when he saw the bottle. He showed her to the kitchen and lifted up another bottle he'd just opened. "Let's start with this one."

The wine went down smoothly and the second bottle was soon on the table. She was struck with how familiar he seemed to her as she watched his face while he spoke of his childhood, a seemingly privileged existence full of tony streets, divorced parents and country clubs. When he asked about hers, she kept the mob affiliations to herself, as she had learned that it either fostered what she labelled the 'Godfather complex' where people acted like they heard the movie score in the background of every conversation or it scared people away.

Nevertheless, Carolina could see that Jack was only a few sips away from kissing her. She watched him pull the drapes to the walkout window, claiming the sun's rays were too strong at this time of the day. She liked the way his buttocks rounded out the pockets of his well-fitting jeans and she imagined them contracted if for some reason needed to press his pelvis forward. The possibility of any awkwardness between her and Anthea or Anthea and Jack or indeed herself and Jack, should this happen, seemed to evaporate with the wine, and on cue, the two were in a lip lock; tongues rooting like a lizard species.

Tired of waiting the several seconds it took for him to engage her breasts; Carolina clutched at her left one and saved him the bother of trying to release it from its caged enclosure. He lapped at it, both hands necessary to hold the luxury of it. Just as she began to caress the promising collection of lumps in his crotch, the dog ran to the door barking. The music had drowned out the sound of several loud knocks. Jack jumped up and adjusted his erection as well as possible, confounded as to who could be at his door.

"Just a second!" he yelled out, as he grabbed a newspaper to cover any swelling that might remain by the time he got to the door. Carolina placed her breast back in its dwelling place and smoothed her hair. She rose from the couch and stood near the hallway, interested in who might be calling all the way out here. Jack walked slowly to the door to open it.

"Dad!" he said, with real surprise in his voice.

"Carolina?' said his father looking down the hall.

"Gerald Walker?" Carolina said.

The population of The Cwtch woke early that morning. There was a feeling of celebration in the household, despite the fact that they were making the final preparations for a funeral. Time had blunted the sharp edges of grief and while every space in the house or any space in a conversation was marked by Sian's absence, the fulfillment of her bizarre wish seemed to return her to them for the moment. Her name floated through the house again, carrying with it the excitement you'd expect, were she a bride.

Ceri's boys, Alyn and Huw and Huw's boyfriend, James had arrived and set to work in the kitchen preparing the last-minute details. Delivery vans arrived and Lewis and Cordy carried the smaller pots of colourful flowers into the pasture, placing them in front of each standing stone. Gryff and his father had dug a hole beneath the altar stone ready for Sian's urn which had a Faerie door pasted onto it – in case she wanted to get out. Cordy carefully inspected the spot, "where we were going to plant Granny," picking out the worms and grubs in case Granny didn't like them. She was relieved when Anthea assured her that Granny loved worms and spiders and all creepy crawlies. Lewis provided further reassurance by telling Cordy that Granny had told him that Faeries often disguised themselves as bugs. All you had to do was look at their faces and you could see how pretty some of them were. Cordy therefore, spent some time lying flat on the ground, hoping for a face-to-face.

Despite the forecast for showers, the morning was kind and the sun slowly warmed the afternoon so that coats were unnecessary. Hilary had dressed the children in white and crafted a wreath of flowers for their heads. Lewis would not consent to wearing one, but plucked a large daisy for his lapel. Spontaneously, the adults all wore their brightest clothing as they had guessed that Sian wouldn't have approved of anything dour.

A yellow TR 6 pulled up in front of the house and a large man unfolded himself from it. How he had ever collapsed himself into it, passed though everyone's mind when they saw him stand beside it. It looked as if he could have picked it up and put it aside in order to reach the pathway to the house. He wore a loose chambray shirt with no collar and well worn, knee length boots. His thick, grey streaked beard and long hair lifted with a stray wind and if he'd had a17th century hat with a feather, he would have looked like a very large Puss in Boots.

"Merddyn!" Auntie Ceri rushed into his arms.

"Ceredwyn Gryffydd, my darling, smother me in kisses, please!"

"Uncle Merlyn!" Cordy shrieked, as she pushed her Auntie Ceri away from Merddyn's embrace.

"Well, if it isn't my little pixie child. I have something for you in my boot. Just wait a minute."

Cordy looked with interest down into Merddyn's boot.

"Oh no, lovely girl, I meant the other boot," and he began to walk to the back of his car.

Cordy took pains to follow him and peer, expectantly at the boot on his other foot.

Merddyn chuckled to himself while he reached into the boot of the car and pulled out a pair of exquisitely crafted Faerie wings. The fabric caught the sunlight and sent prisms of rainbows to meet the eye.

"I love them!" Cordy screamed, jumping up and down, making his clumsy attempt to attach them to her even more difficult. "Where did you get them, Uncle Merlyn?"

He leaned into her ear and whispered. "I got them off a dragonfly."

Her hand flew to her mouth and she whispered back. "You didn't kill the dragonfly, did you?"

Merddyn thought quickly. "Of course, not, he wanted to trade them in for a new pair. These were too big for him."

The child nodded her acceptance of this and let a small laugh slip out. "Yea, these are way too big for a dragonfly!"

Merddyn was escorted into the house and had a drink in his hand within minutes. Shortly after, his friend arrived. Anthea watched her float toward the house and thought her well suited for the part of the White Witch/Priestess/ Faerie Thingy who would conduct the ceremony. Her tall, angular frame garbed in a lustrous purple gown evoked a Vanessa Redgrave type of authority and this no doubt, made her such a popular resource for any Neopagan's in the area.

Anthea stood half way down the staircase with Gryff behind her and took in the scene. "All we need is a band of dwarfs," she said to him.

Anthea went forward to greet Alisadon the Pagan Priestess.

The woman shook her head and introduced herself as Deadrie. She pointed behind her.

Anthea looked further down the driveway to see a very small scooter with a very large woman perched atop it. She dismounted and waddled breathlessly, carrying a wicker basket in each hand. She had an extravagant overbite and noticeable food stains on her short, violet robe. During the struggle to take off her helmet, she had knocked her glasses askew and agitated her frizzy hair to such an extent that it looked as if it was exploding off her head.

When she reached Anthea she looked less like a mystical priestess and more like a survivor of a feeding frenzy. She let the baskets drop heavily to the ground and wheezed a chirpy greeting to Anthea. "Hello, I'm Alisadon, the priestess for today's ceremony. Where can I deposit my candles and crystals?"

Anthea regained control of her chin and placed her arm on Alisadon's round shoulder. As she guided her to the stone circle, she noted that the woman was remarkably short and barely came up to her chest.

"And now the cast is complete!" Gryff said mischievioursly.

Alisadon looked up sweetly and thanked him.

More old and dear friends arrived, all of them dressed in the spirit of the occasion. Colourful, flowing skirts and shirts, many resurrected from the back of their closets; touchstones of hippy days, barely remembered without such proof as these ill-fitting, moth-eaten relics.

Anthea felt gratitude well up inside her upon seeing her father's joy in the company of deeply loved, lifelong friends who had shared Sian with him and yearned, like him, to feel her uncommon presence once again.

Despite this distraction, Anthea's anxious eyes kept watch for a car that might carry Ian back into her life, but none came. She had not phoned him and left the chance of a reunion to him.

When the time came for her to retreat to the pasture for the service, she stopped frequently to cast several backward glances in the hope that he would fulfill his promise. The depth of her disappointment surprised her and any attempts to discipline herself with a stern, pragmatic lecture on how much better it was that he did not attend was overwhelmed by a fresh wave of regret. She longed to see him again. Perhaps being back in what amounted to the epicentre of their love, had weakened her resolve to cast it away . . . to cast their child away. She had not contacted the abortion centre to book an appointment, though she had told her father she would be leaving for a couple of days the following week to see an old friend in London. She had to face the fact that she had never really been able to mine Ian out of her heart. No matter what purging system she employed, bits of him remained tucked in the unexplored corners, roiling under the dusty sediments of other, uninspiring lovers. Ian was deeply embedded in the blood and tissue which animated her – how could she kill it?

It was he who changed the rules of the game, she rationalized; *his insincerity had beguiled me into believing that children were not a priority for him.* Then, when his yearning for them began to seep from the small cracks in their relationship, her guilt for not being willing to set aside her own desire for freedom wedged itself into those cracks and exposed them as the sinkholes they were. *I had told him, upfront, that I didn't want dogs or even plants to worry about – nothing that would whine or die as a result of my neglect – not even perennials!*

When she came to Canada, perhaps because she found herself so lonely, she jumped at the chance to take Spock from a friend who was leaving the country. Not long after she adopted Twiggy from an animal rescue sanctuary – Spock needed company when she was at work. *Maybe I got the dogs to test my capacity for loving something difficult? Or was I simply so selfish that they were a way of filling a cold and empty space in my life with something living? Maybe I should have just grown cabbages.*

The light waned as the early evening beckoned. The candles and lanterns, all subjects of much testing in the previous weeks were lit, imposing a suitably metaphysical aura over the stone circle. The shadows cast by the flames seemed to animate the stone giants, coaxing subtle movement from them when your eye was focussed elsewhere.

Lewis and a couple of the older boys had retreated into a shed at the corner of the pasture. They had swiped a couple of candles and a lighter and were immersed in the schoolboy pleasure of producing what they called, 'Blue Angels'.

One of the boys had perfected the art of flatulence to such a degree that he was able to produce an impressive methane flame if he did so into an ignited lighter. Lewis was captivated by such magic and vowed to the other boys that he would not tell the adults about this, "Fwigging cwazy" ritual.

Alisadon The Priestess called the service to order and in doing so, beseeched the "Four Corners and Watchtowers to assist in guarding the spirit and soul of the departed." She lit a branch of sage grass with a lighter and a cherubic Lewis stood, fascinated, beside her. He politely raised his hand several times, into the air, begging a question. Bestowing a serenely indulgent smile on this little enthusiast, Alisadon reached a hand out to stroke his chubby, pink cheek, "Yes, my angel, what is it?" she cooed.

Lewis, eyes rapt on the flame coming from her lighter asked in a clear, loud voice,

"Can I fawt on yow lightow?"

A murmur went through the crowd as they tried to acertain what he'd said. The older boys fell over laughing, holding their stomachs while Alisadon earnestly asked him to repeat the question. Before he was able, the ever-watchful Hilary grabbed him by the arm and pulled him to her, her hand clasped firmly over his mouth as he struggled to repeat his request. Hilary, shook her head vigorously saying, "It's nothing, please go on."

Satisfied, Alisadon continued her solemn task and bowed deeply, waving the sage grass theatrically, as she beseeched The East, to invoke the element of air, then The South, for the element of fire, The West, for water, and in the final, unfortunate appeal to the North, she turned her back to the audience, bent over and flashed her stark, white panties and equally doughy thighs, due to the fact that her mini-smock failed to cover what it was supposed to. The boys shrieked with wicked delight again but the adults were too busy trying to restrain themselves from doing the same to chastise them.

Undaunted, Alisadon continued her evocations and poems that thankfully did not involve any further calisthenics. When she stepped aside to allow Ralph his eulogy, Ceri discretely whispered an alert in her ear to avoid any future gynecological spectacles.

Anthea watched her father, who held Sian's urn as if he were holding her waist. She had never seen him look so alone; so rarely had she seen him standing without her mother beside him, and the grief of the early days of January threatened to intrude again. She scanned the faces before her, hoping that Ian's would be there to take the sting out of her eyes, but Ian had decided not to come. *That was surely for the best.* She let her expectation go and gave her full attention to the proceedings.

Ralph came forward to speak. He cleared his throat and took a deep breath, willing himself to smile. He let his gaze rest on each person present, sending with it implicit thanks for their support and then began.

"You all know that Sian was the speaker of the house, not me. She was able to show you the universe in a grain of sand with a few well-chosen words. She had strong opinions, and death would be the only thing that could stop her from telling you what your opinion was. So, she asked me to apologize on her behalf for leaving you all without one. She didn't like death anymore than she liked sleep because it took her away from whatever she was interfering with at the time. And looking around this circle, I know that everyone here was the better for her interference in their lives.

She was a fearless woman, whose only fear was being dull or worse being trapped with someone dull. No chance of that in this company. That is why she surrounded herself by you when she was alive and why you were all invited here to this unapologetically eccentric service at her death; to celebrate a force of nature through the only ruling body or higher power she ever acknowledged, the Force of Nature.

She loved nothing more than her family, friends and pets. Let's face it, what else is there? And, when she loved you, as I can attest, you felt like the chosen one. And she chose each and every one of us.

Since Sian always had to have the last word, I will leave it to her once again. I vaguely remembered something she'd said years ago, in jest and finally found it written down in her book of quotes. And to prove that I did listen to her when she rambled on, I have placed these words on her tombstone. It reads:

Sian Myfanwy Gryffydd,
Born March 1st 1946 – Stopped talking: March 1st 2013
A woman of profound intelligence and staggering beauty:
Forced to write her own epitaph for fear of understatement."

Ralph held up the plaque, his eyes shining, a smile ordered on his face. Anthea draped her arms around his shoulders and felt Gryff hold hers. Ralph gave the plaque to them and lowered the urn into the earth.

Alisadon began throwing petals onto the urn and then cast them up to the sky. Everyone followed suit finding the baskets of petals she had dispersed amongst them. The song, 'Jade Is The Girl of The Hour' rose from the speakers in the shed, its joyful tune willing the crowd to rock back and forth and soon break into a circle of dance led by Alisadon and Merddyn. The sky, like an old lady tired of waiting in line for a toilet, let it be damned and finally released her beleaguered sphincter. A torrent of rain fell down on the dancing procession.

"Perfect . . . perfect!" Ralph said, raising his head to the bruised sky. Cordy lifted up her skirts and kicked off her shoes. "It's one of Granny's rain dances!" she yodelled to her grandfather who leapt forward like the athlete he used to be, to join her in the rain dance.

Anthea danced too; glad that the wetness on her face could have been raindrops. Soon, she tore herself away from the giddy mob and walked back to house. She felt her body shiver, but she was not cold and a low moan came from deep within her chest.

The darkness swept over her quickly as she made her way further from the pasture but the glow of the large flood lights on the driveway were a dependable beacon. Her eyes strained, blinking away the raindrops spilling onto her lashes, as she looked ahead and saw the hazy outline of a figure walking toward her. It loped side to side, shoulders swaying, head crouched into a coat collar. She quickened her pace, allowing herself, against her own better judgement to think, *I think that's his walk . . . it's him.*

She stopped, wanting to be sure before getting any closer. *Anthea, if it is him, don't make a fool of yourself. It's dark; he won't have seen me yet. Get control . . . be casual.* Despite her caution, her breath quickened and her stomach clenched with excitement as each step made her more certain it was Ian. His head was down, his face buried from sight. She made herself take a deep breath before she stepped into the light.

"Anthea?" came the familiar base tone of his voice, splitting the sound of the rain tapping the driveway. She swept her hair back from her face, and wiped beneath her eyes, aware of how frightening she must look with makeup splattered under them. All that extra time she had taken with her appearance today, just in case he turned up, was drooling down her face with the snot from her red snout. She sniffed heartily and answered, "Ian? You came."

He jogged toward her pulling his hands out of his coat pockets in a plea.

"Your Dad invited me. I hope it's ok with you . . . after . . . after last time - I'm so sorry I'm late," he said.

"My Dad invited you? I thought . . . never mind."

"Anyway, my car packed in on me half way between here and the village and I waited for some help but then decided to leg it here. Do you believe not *one,* not *one* fucking car came past for me to hitch a ride?"

"You should have called here. Someone could have picked you up, after all, seems everyone wanted you here."

He looked helpless. "Except you? No cell service anyway."

She decided to ignore that question. It came out more like a challenge. "Come, they're all in the stone circle." She saw this puzzled him and jumped at the chance to change the subject. "Yes, the stone circle in the pasture. My mother never wanted a big fuss - just a pagan ceremony at Stonehenge." She waved him forward, "I'll show you. It defies description."

He grabbed her hand and she felt a shiver run through her spine. She wasn't cold this time either. For a moment, she imagined that he was about to lean in to kiss her

"Anthea, can we talk soon? You know I've left Dana – I know what we said, but everything's changed . . . I still love you."

"No," she said firmly, breaking his grip and striding toward the pasture, "nothing's changed." *And you wouldn't love me if you knew what I'm about to do.*

The next morning, Anthea woke early, rifling through her broken suitcase for a dress she hoped she had remembered to pack. She had left it all until the last minute and the one new thing she had indulged herself with was a sky-blue summer dress that she felt played to her eyes and covered her pot. She remembered taking it out of the shopping bag and setting it aside but could not find it in the scrimmage with the suitcase. She didn't want to take the time to unpack everything methodically now, because, if she were honest, she wanted to get downstairs before Ian was awake. He had gone to the annex last night to sleep on the pull-out couch. If the kids were consistent, they'd be up and sticking pillow feathers up his nose by now.

Last night had been awkward. After she had shown Ian the stone circle and introduced him to the few people who didn't know him, they all came back into the house for a feast. He fell willingly into the familiar pattern imprinted on him by many other years of blissful moments in the old house. Still familiar with the kitchen, he helped with the serving and clearing up as if the years he had spent away from The Cwtch mattered little. Often, during the clatter and chatter, she could feel his eyes rest on her as if to ask, "why not?".

Auntie Ceri, less than skilfully, and certainly less than sober, manipulated every conversation with Ian to ascertain his current status – dating? Casual dating? Serious contenders? Chances of reconciliation with previous love interests? She was shameless. Anthea finally pulled her into the study and spat a warning to back off with the interrogation. They were not getting back together. Nothing had changed between them other than he had left his second wife. The last thing Ian needed was to be reminded of his track record and the last thing Anthea needed was for him to think that they would ever get back together. She would never raise his hopes like that because she had nothing to offer him. They had both moved on and the only thing they could hope for is a long-distance friendship and only that, because he's such a great guy who deserves to remain on good terms with a family he was so devoted to. That's what we all hope to gain from this. That's why she didn't stop him from coming to the celebration. "Do you understand, Auntie Ceri?"

Auntie Ceri lifted her chin, looked down her short nose at Anthea, a slight sway to her stance and replied, "Bollocks" and left the room.

Just as she pulled a yellow dress over her head, Anthea remembered where she'd put the blue one. She'd grabbed it and tucked it into the outer pocket of the suitcase. Her relief at finding it was far more than it should have been, but having that little blue dress was strangely reassuring, because when she had put it on in the store, an older woman, who had reminded her of her mother came over and said, "Oh my dear, that's such a romantic little number and what that does for your eyes!" Nothing is more sincere than an unsolicited compliment from someone who has no motive to do so. At the time, Anthea did something she herself had not expected. She reached over and gave the woman a powerful hug finding herself unable to say anything more for fear of blubbering all over her. The poor, mystified woman smiled a gentle smile and went on with her business. Today, she would wear it with the little blue and white cardi she had had for years.

Anthea came down the stairs to find Huw, Ceri's younger son, pouring a cup of tea from the old brown bottomless teapot that had been his grandmother's. He was as roughly hewn as the Rhossili rocks. His broad shoulders sloping away from cauliflower ears that had blossomed from years of holding up a scrum long enough to pass the ball to the faster, more agile Alyn.

"I came over here because I didn't want to wake Ian who's sleeping like a baby on the couch," Huw said, his hair flopping over his scarred forehead like straw.

Huw poured the tea. "Want a pastie, Anthea?"

She groaned at the thought, "No thanks, just tea."

"Not hungover, are you? Didn't see you drink!" Anthea didn't respond. "Well, your fancy blue dress sets off the green around your gills lovely. Any occasion I'm not aware of?"

Anthea frowned. "No, I just felt like wearing something summery. It's still freezing in Canada."

Huw sat across from her, unconvinced, and took a loud sip of the scalding tea. "I don't mean to pry, but what's the situation with you and Ian? Mam said you two are getting back together."

Anthea let her head drop, then lifted her eyes to Huw. "Your mother is causing me nothing but grief. Why doesn't she interfere in your life instead of mine?"

"You think she doesn't? She's already bought a mother of the groom's dress for whichever one of us gets married first. And, she said she's even had custom jewelry made – out of our baby teeth which she's kept in box under the bed all these years"

Anthea's jaw dropped.

"I think she's kidding, but I wouldn't put it past her. She's even researched the protocols for gay weddings and considers herself an expert already. I told her that she's nothing but an old embarrassment," Huw added.

"What did she say when you told her that?"

"She said it was her greatest ambition."

Anthea chuckled and gulped her last sip of tea. "Well, at least we outnumber her. We just have to stick together on this. Oh, and Ian and I? Just trying to be old friends – how about you and James?"

Huw smiled shyly. "It's going well – we've talked about it. Maybe someday. I want a family, kids and all – it won't be easy - it takes courage, you know."

Anthea looked into the green of Huw's wideset eyes. "Yep . . . courage."

"Oh, and a uterus," Huw said deviously.

"More tea? Nice walk along the beach?" Anthea asked quickly, diverting an awkward insinuation.

"No thanks, but, I'll take a cup over to James and see you later."

A light breeze lifted her dress as she walked down the path to the shoreline. Trying not to let her torment steal this moment from her, she took her sandals off when she felt the sand fill them and swinging them by the heel strap to the happy cadence of 'Jade is The Girl of The Hour'. Even the tide seemed to lift its fine white petticoats to the lyrical beat of the song. She walked past the wreck of the Hellvetia, the rotting ribs of the misbegotten ship clawing its way out of the sand; a grim warning of the treachery lurking in this idyllic scene.

She reached the spiky tail of rocks that harnessed "The Worm's Head" peninsula to the shoreline, visible and accessible for only a few hours of the day, at low tide. Hardly dressed to take on the challenge of what the Vikings had imaginatively named "Wurm" or Dragon, she perched herself atop one of the smoothest rocks she could find, letting a wet finger of seawater surround her feet, then retreat. She made a promise to herself to venture out to the farthest reaches of the Worm before she left. For now, sitting beside it, stroking its moist scaly back was enough.

This will all be over by next week – the good and the bad of it. I'll be back in Canada, alone, my little ghost gone, missing this place, these people. That thought brought Canadian faces to her mind; Molly, Carolina, Glynda, Clive and Audrey, Spock and Twiggy – even sweet Gavin. Not such a long list of friends, but people who she'd grown attached to over the last few years and who had earned her affections by their sincere offer of trust and support, along with many shared moments of laughter. They were a good lot. She wished they were here with her, that her family could meet and enjoy them, know them like she did, love them, yes *love them* like she did. She would call Carolina later today.

She closed her eyes and lifted her face to the weak sun, pushing its way up into the sky. The gulls sang their raspy plea as if hoarse from keening lost loves. She felt the breeze cool her face and then, a warm pair of lips grasp her own. This startled her so much that she swung her shoes upward and heard a cry of painful contact with one the oversized buckles that had appealed to her so much when she bought them. "Ian! What the hell are you doing? I almost impaled myself on this rock, for God's sake," she cried.

Ian's hand covered his eye as he said, "Jesus, I'm sorry – for impaling you – but, it must be said - not for the kiss. I recognize those looks you gave me last night."

Anthea was panting, partly trying to recover from the shock; partly savouring the kiss and the humour. "You were drunk . . . and you're bleeding."

Ian pulled a wad of tissues out of his pocket and applied pressure to the wound. Anthea lifted it away and pried the wound apart. "It's not gaping, no stitches needed, you idiot."

Ian was looking straight into her eyes. "I am an idiot - for letting you leave me."

Anthea dug her finger into his wound and as he drew back with a yelp said, "Don't you ever take no for an answer?"

"The one time I did, I've regretted to this day. Anthea, let's just give it a try. We don't need kids – we have – what . . . four dogs between us?"

Anthea stopped herself from smiling. "You see? This is what you do. That cute fucking schoolboy act."

"OK, I'll try not to be cute – not easy for me, but look, Auntie Ceri says you're coming to London for a couple of days next week. Why don't you stay with me and we can see how it goes? That's all. Nothing complicated."

Anthea felt the flutter of panic in her stomach. "Nothing complicated? Fuck you and the horse you road in on! Let's not rehash this again. It's not fair to either of us. Let's just get along, shall we?"

"That's a cute Canadian expression you used there – not the fuck off thing – the horse thing."

Anthea held her head and let out a long shriek. She walked away and he caught up with her, bending his bleeding head toward her.

"Not fair? Not fair?" he repeated, and began to unleash a torrent of long suppressed frustration. "What's not 'fair', is that we didn't really try hard enough to keep our marriage together. I can't leave you again without trying to convince you give us another chance. I still *love* you. I'll *always* still love you! Hell, I've tried to love women much nicer than you, prettier than you, but I can't because I've never *stopped* loving you."

Anthea turned to him dropping her shoes in the sand. "I have no words for whatever that was - a compliment or an insult? It doesn't matter. We know that we loved each other – that wasn't ever the issue, was it?"

"The *issue* Anthea, was that you didn't love me enough – *you* gave up on *me* – remember? And what about what happened at the . . . the crematorium?"

Anthea felt an angry tide rising in her. She felt cornered and unready to go back over this well-travelled territory. She wished at that moment that he had not come. "Ian, enough, please . . . that was a terrible mistake. Do we really need to quarrel now? I let you come to pay your final respects to my mother, not to lecture me on our past."

Ian sighed and pursed his lips as if trying to hold back words that were in danger of spilling out. "Right, you're right. I'll go. But I want you to know, now I understand how someone could not want children with someone they don't love enough - because that's why I left my second marriage."

He paced back and forth, arms punching the air for emphasis, delivering his soliloquy like a Shakespearian protagonist, shaking with the effort of crumbling restraint. "I'm sure that I married Dana because I thought she'd be a great mother – and she will be, but with someone who loves her more than I did. She tried to convince me that having a child would fill the space between us, but I knew it wouldn't because *you* were in that space. You were always in that space. The only 'terrible mistake' we made was divorcing. And this is what I know now: better not to have children at all than to expect their little lives to support ours, instead of us supporting theirs. Not having children was always your hang up – not mine – you just pinned it on me."

Anthea stood up, feeling a new wave of rage sweep through her. "You're blaming me for your second divorce? You can blame me for the first – OK, I'll accept that, but whatever happened between you and Dana is not my fault."

Ian looked defeated. "But it is your fault. I'm trapped. The only way I can go forward is to go back, and you won't come with me. You wouldn't come with me then, and you won't come with me now."

She looked straight into his eyes and willed herself to speak calmly. "Ian, I don't want to be responsible for anything - especially your happiness or lack of it."

Blood ran freely down the side of his face and she reached a hand forward to stem the flow. He pushed it away. "Don't worry, that wound will heal."

She watched him walk down the sand too stunned and helpless to do anything to stop him. The wind, angrier than before, seemed to take his name from her mouth and cast it out to sea. She looked down and saw that her shoes were soaked, the tide claiming her, and the sky-blue dress, blood stained.

The tide had turned. Anthea knew she must have been out at least an hour and a half and that she should go back to the house. As she walked the foot path toward the cottage, her sandals emitting small squeaking sounds as if she were squashing a colony of rodents underfoot, she could see the floral-patterned figure of Auntie Ceri, approaching, all straw hat and billowing scarves.

Fuck! thought Anthea. *Here we go.* Anthea looked around helplessly, realizing that there was no escape route.

"Yoohoo!" came the greeting from Auntie Ceri. "That was a long walk. We've got brunch ready to go. We're waiting for you and Ian." Auntie Ceri nudged her conspiratorially. "Did you two have a nice, romantic liaison on the beach?"

Anthea made a furtive glance at her Aunt. "I haven't seen him in a while. Didn't he come back to the cottage?"

"No," Ceri said. "We thought he was with you. Didn't you see him on the beach?"

Disturbed that he had not returned, Anthea said, "Well, yes. He was with me for a while, but then he . . . left."

Antie Ceri's eyes narrowed. "Things did not go well, I take it?"

Anthea was defensive. "Why would you say that?"

"Well, there's blood on your dress."

Anthea had forgotten. "I hit him with my shoe buckle – by mistake!"

"That's what they all say in my line of work. But, I don't want to pry. You're not on trial here. I just hope his body doesn't wash up on the beach, that's all."

"Now, Auntie Ceri, just because he's not with mc, doesn't mean that he's dead," Anthea said, in a patronizing tone.

"No, but it means that you two had a fight or he'd be walking back with you now."

"How do you know that we had a fight?"

"Deductive logic, my dear. Huw told me Ian had gone to find you on the beach. He obviously found you because you cracked him on the head – blood on your dress being the evidence of that and if you hadn't had a fight, why wouldn't he be with you now? No further questions, Your Honour."

Anthea rolled her eyes and let them rest on Ceri's own curious gaze. "Hc wants to get back together."

"And you hit him with your shoe?'

"He snuck up and kissed me and I had my shoes in my hand – then I hit him with my shoe buckle – opened up a one-inch lesion."

"And, I gather, he didn't open anything up in you. You know, he did confide his situation to me when I met him at the cafe. I knew you had noone special in your life - haven't had as far as your dad could tell me and I thought, we all thought . . . and he thought, perhaps it would at least be worth talking again. Were we so wrong?"

Anthea sat down on the side of the pathway, drained of all energy and close to tears.

"How would it even work, Auntie Ceri? I live on the other side of the world. I went as far away as I could, thinking that I might have the chance to start a new life. What I knew I couldn't bear, was the chance I'd run into him in London with his lovely new wife and six gorgeous children . . . three dogs, a horse maybe . . . several cats, gerbils - goddamn cabbages in his garden! He says he doesn't want all that, but really, can you ask anyone to give that up? Worse, can you ask anyone to have all that if they don't want it?"

Auntie Ceri grasped Anthea's hand and held it in both of hers. "You make it sound like a biological imperative that cannot be superseded? You should have talked to me before you broke up the first time, *cariad.* Do you know, I didn't want children either? I was quite happy to have my husband and my career. But I will say, the boys have turned out to be one of my better bad decisions. They grow on you, like a kind of mildew, children - hard to scrape off once they're there. There's really no good practical reason to have them anymore, it's not like you need them to till the fields – hell, they won't even cut the grass. But, when they're there, real and infuriatingly alive, you can't imagine being without them. On the other hand – they're expensive, revolting little shits. Take your pick – but I'll tell you this, good kids are much easier to find than a good man."

"But even if we did try again, there's no guarantee it would work."

"You want a guarantee? Buy a dishwasher. There are no guarantees in life, *cariad.* If there were, your Uncle Bryn wouldn't have died of an aneurism at fifty-nine when he had two parents who lived into their nineties. Your mother wouldn't have died, as fit as she was. I can't say it better than Samuel Beckett, 'Ever tried? Ever failed? No matter, try again, fail again better.'"

Anthea wiped her wet nose with her dress. She lifted her chin to look into Auntie Ceri's concerned face. "If I did have kids, do you think they'd have the Gryffydd nose or the Brock Beak?"

Auntie Ceri patted her arm. "Good question, and can you live without ever knowing the answer to that? Mind you, you might not have to make any decisions if Ian's concussed and has been blown off the cliffs. Let's go find his body."

"What the hell happened to you?" Huw shouted playfully from the porch when he saw Anthea step through the garden wall. "You look like you've been in a fight. I'm bloody starving, waiting for you, girl."

Auntie Ceri sent him a venomous look and the timbre of his voice changed to that of a pleasant inquiry. "Are you hungry? We've got a full-English waiting for you."

"Is Ian back?" Anthea asked hopefully.

"Alyn gave him a lift into town to get his car fixed. He took his bag. I think he's going back to London as soon as it's done – something about riding a horse out of town."

Anthea's shoulders caved in a little and she glanced back at Auntie Ceri with a look of defeat.

"Ahh, and here's us hoping he'd been blown over the cliffs." Ceri said turning to Anthea. You go wash your face and put another little outfit on, my girl," Ceri said. "Brunch can be held off a little longer for you."

A loud groan came from the rest of the group. Ralph watched Anthea go by him and sensing her distress, turned to Ceri for guidance. An almost imperceptible shake of her head stopped him from following her.

"Well, as glad as I am that Ian isn't scrambled on the rocks, I'm still bloody 'ungry, so how 'bout I scramble the damn eggs, instead?" Huw pleaded.

"Look what I've got!" came a shrill entreaty. Lewis held up a cell phone. "Thaw's someone speaking weally funny on it." Huw took the cell phone from him and listened, his eyebrows colliding and then springing apart. "They're speaking Chinese or something. Lewis, did you dial numbers on this phone?"

"Just to see if it was woking, Uncle Huw."

"Whose cell is this? Anyone recognize it? Where did you find it, Lewis?"

"On the couch in the Annex."

Huw laughed. "It must be Ian's. I wonder what his charges are going to be."

Auntie Ceri told Huw to call Alyn's cell to tell Ian to come back for his phone. "He can eat brunch with us."

Another chorus of moaning erupted and Huw went to the kitchen counter and made himself a bacon butty.

The alarm clock screeched its annoying wakeup call and Carolina thumped the 'off' button. She dialed the number she'd been given for the cottage and after a few rings a cheery voice answered the phone.

"The Cwtch," sang Ceri.

"Oh," Carolina said, unsure if she'd made the right connection, "Is this where Anthea Brock is staying?"

"Oh, you sound Canadian. Yes, yes, you have the right number. Who's calling then, love?"

"It's Carolina, her secretary. I hope I'm not disturbing her, but there's something I thought she should know."

"Not at all, *bach. I*'ve heard a lot about you. I think we'd get along famously. We were just going to have breakfast, which turned into brunch which is now officially afternoon tea, but she's finished her food. I'll get her for you."

Anthea had heard Ceri shouting into the phone as if she were calling across the ocean without one. She came to the phone and took it from her Auntie, before Ceri could engage in a long-distance gossip session with Carolina.

Edna had died the night before. They were trying to track down her son, Art before they scheduled the funeral. Carolina confided that

Glynda was worried that Art would be found and would take the house from under her as well as any money Edna had left. Glynda had been uncharacteristically open about this fear, since he might try to take everything.

Regret clutched at Anthea's chest. *Poor Glynda, one fucking thing after another.* She told Carolina to give Glynda the name and number of Anthea's estate lawyer. Glynda would be in good hands and Anthea would call in a favour her lawyer would be glad to return.

"Oh," Carolina said, as an afterthought, "Saxon keeps asking about the fund raiser. I told him you've got him pegged to do a ballroom dance with his niece just to shut him up."

"Ha! What did he say?"

"Something rude about a part of your body that I've never heard of."

"Always creative," Anthea said, "Yeh, I hadn't thought that idea through, yet. But, Georgia said she would do it in a minute and Saxon would do it in three if his granddaughter begged him to. She'll work on him. You'll see. It'll happen. And who wouldn't pay to see that?"

"Any other news?" Carolina asked.

"Not really, the interment went well, a wonderful collection of weirdoes, just as my mother would have wanted. We'll see how the rest of my holiday goes. Who knows I might meet the man of my dreams here."

"Bring one for me too. I can do weird; it's the socially upstanding ones I can't tolerate."

"Hmmm, sounds like there's a story there."

"Isn't there always?"

"Once, just once, I'd like to have a better story than you do, Carolina."

"You've got a couple of weeks to work on one. Catch ya later."

Anthea returned to the table to see no one there except Ian. He was pushing the scrambled eggs around his plate. He raised his red, swollen eye to her and small shiver of guilt crept up her spine, more for her reaction on the beach than for the clubbing of his eye. She should have given him the dignity of listening to him. He deserved that. She was well aware that he deserved more than that, but still could not see how they could put Humpty Dumpty together again, *considering what I'm going to do to Humpty Dumpty.*

"My cars fixed, so I'll be heading off soon. The bacon's good," he said into his plate.

She sat at the table and touched his hand, surprised at how familiar it still felt. His short, well shaped finger nails, the agile fingers that knew their way around a body whether on the operating table or in a bed. There had been no better lover. No puerile fumbling or idiotic mumbling. No meandering the meadows sniffing for hidden truffles. He knew exactly where the truffles were! She sighed, letting the memory hold her there for too long.

"What are you thinking about?" he asked.

She pulled herself back into the room, "Truffles."

The deep creases she'd named 'The Tree' appeared in the middle of his brow, "Truffles. Truffles?"

"Forget the truffles. It's a terrible metaphor I thought of when I was thinking about you and me."

His face remained still. "How much distance do you envision between the 'you' and the 'me' . . . and the damn truffles?"

She chewed on her lip. "Well, there is the whole of the Atlantic Ocean for one thing. Forget about the truffles."

"The Atlantic Ocean – a minor gulf compared to some distances."

That comment took her breath away, its authenticity hitting a soft spot she could no longer guard. "I know."

"I would have come back anyway. You mean too much to me to have you so far away that we'll never talk again. Can we not let that happen?" he said, his hand forming a peace sign, the fingertips reached down the contours of her face to catch a stray tear.

Anthea felt an impulse to tell him about the pregnancy. *Maybe he had the right to know? It was an IUD pregnancy and so terminating had good medical logic. Perhaps he'd understand.* But she shut it down with the mantra she had been chanting all her life. What she had always believed, *my body, my choice.*

They locked into a fierce embrace, as if trying to stop the tide from dragging the other away. Ian looked, beyond Anthea's arching neck, with his one good eye, to see two perfectly round eyes peering through the window. Lewis had discovered that if he stretched himself up onto the tips of his toes, he could just see into the cottage kitchen. He was very interested to see what Auntie Anthea was up to, as was the rest of the family, standing just out of sight. He ran immediately, to tell them what he had seen.

Anthea left The Cwtch in the middle of the night, thinking she would have plenty of time to sleep after the procedure. Just outside London, she felt a sticky wetness between her thighs which validated the severity of the cramps that had started a half hour before. She pulled into a rest stop, grabbed a dress from her suitcase and tied a sweatshirt around her waist. Scanning the shop, she navigated her way to the diaper section, stiffling her shock at the price of them. In the restroom stall she wiped the blood off with baby wipes and pushed one of the diapers between her legs, dutifully handing toilet paper through the gap to the elderly lady who cried out for it in the stall next to her. Noticing that there was no sign of a yolk sac in the bloody debris on her clothing she stuffed them into the plastic bag and threw the loose dress on to disguise the bulk of the diaper. The cramping was bearable with the help of a few pain capsules and she set the GPS to the nearest hospital, not allowing herself to examine anything but her physical state of being, for fear of surprising herself.

A rowdy group of revelers stormed down the hotel corridor and woke Anthea from the deep sleep she welcomed after her release from the hospital. She trotted to the bathroom and saw only a faint, pinky discharge on her pad. The cramping had eased to a dull discomfort. She placed a cold hand on her belly, closed her eyes, and allowed a long sigh to bend her head. *So, that's it. Time to move forward.* She reached for the shower handle and let the warm water wash away the fatigue.

That phrase about God laughing when you make plans filtered through her thoughts. She had always found making plans a comforting ritual; listing your intent like beads on a rosary, fondling them into existence. Not allowing distractions to that sacred order had been the key to achieving her most prized accomplishments. It was like applying a clinical incision to matter, distinguishing what nourishes or negates. Establishing order from chaos was what she was good at. People like Carolina, Molly, Gryff and Hilary seemed to embrace it, as if it had its own mysterious beauty, hidden from Anthea's appreciation. She had seen them cajole it, thumb their nose at it, never fearing its ability to topple them. With this in mind, she felt clear-minded and at peace with her decision.

As she gathered her toiletries she noticed multiple messages from Ian. He had called The Cwtch and they told him that she was in London visiting friends. Why didn't she tell him she was coming to London? Could he be added to that list of friends she intended to see, as he'd taken a few days off work and would like to start their new found 'friendship' with a dinner on him? She returned his call, glad for the opportunity to retrieve something that was lost.

He stood at the door of her room, his wide smile opening up to release a giggle, as he pressed a bottle of Barolo into her hands like a child with buttercups. "Your favourite – and there's more at the restaurant I booked." He noticed her jeans and lifted his coat to reveal a suit. "Hey, we're not going to a dive, I booked a good restaurant – don't worry, not 'our old favourite'- another one almost as good but without the memories. But, if you want to slum it, I'll cancel and take you to the one Auntie Ceri took me to."

She let herself stare at him: examining his features, lifting the smell of him, the sound of him into her senses.

"Anth, are you going to let me in or what. You've got that look on your face. You know, the one that . . . no sorry, not that one - I swore I'd behave myself - the other one. You know, the one where I never know what your thinking? That one . . . ok, what are you thinking?"

She reached out and took his face in her hands and planted a kiss on the middle of his forehead – right where the tree was sprouting, it's roots now blurring as he raised his eyebrows. She let her lips drift downward to rest just beyond his open mouth. He stared back at her, "What? What have I missed here? This is a very poor beginning to our platonic friendship. Pretty sure, Plato, himself would already have a hard on. What's happening?" He began to pull away, but she held him there, and whispered, "Chaos."

"What? Did you say chaos? Anthea, what does that mean? I don't know what to do. Are you ovulating?" he said, squirming to put the bottle down on the near-by console.

"No, not at all. I'm pregnant," she said as she stifled his response with a deep kiss.

"Umm, I have a few follow-up questions, if I may," he said, liberating a corner of his mouth.

"It's yours, in case your wondering, but I have an IUD and Late Maternal Age so at the very least, there's a fifty per cent risk of miscarriage."

A stern looking, older woman in the room across the hall opened her door and began to shush the other noisy patrons, now collecting farther down the corridor. But, her interest was deflected by the drama unfolding between Anthea and Ian and she made a weak effort to look like she was closing her door. They both sent a challenging stare to the half of her face still visible. Her face soured even more and as she shut her door they heard her say to her husband, "That woman across the hall is pregnant with a sexual disease – slut."

"She has a point," said Ian.

SECTION THREE

ADVANCED HOMECARE STUDIES

THE WINDING DRIVEWAY OF TY Bleu swallowed the car into its interior. Even in the dim light of the late evening, Anthea could see that the trees had finally released their leaves, trusting that there was a promise of summer ahead. Three weeks had changed so much. Her head spun with prospects plucked from the future. She turned them over and over, examining each for its integrity like a squirrel with a nut. Her hand pumped the horn as she anticipated the circus of acrobatics and yelps of glee that would be unleashed when Carolina let the dogs out.

She had hardly opened the car door when two bobbing heads scrambled to get at her, tongues and ears flapping like flags in a windstorm. She fell to her knees and let them envelop her, Spock's hard head hitting her chin as he threw himself into her body. Twiggy, shivered with excitement trying to find any space close to Anthea inbetween Spock's frantic spasm of motion.

Carolina laughed heartily, enjoying the spectacle. "Welcome home boss! I'd give you a hug too but I don't think there's room for three of us."

"That's OK, I'm a walking wad of dog spit anyway - nice to know that you're missed."

When Anthea came downstairs, a hot bowl of pasta and two large glasses of wine were on the table, the fireplace was lit and Mozart was floating through the room. She felt such gratitude towards Carolina for taking the worry out of leaving the dogs, Ty Bleu and her office. If Carolina could only run her own life as well as she ran Anthea's.

Anthea eagerly asked for any news. Carolina balked. "Wait a minute, Missy. You're the one who went on holiday. You're gonna have the most interesting stories – except maybe for what happened to Glynda . . . and Molly. Oh . . . and me of course."

Anthea pointed a finger. "Tell me, tell me NOW!"

Carolina sat up in her chair and leaned in toward Anthea, eyes wide, relishing the thought of her reaction to all the news. "Good, I can't wait to tell you anyway – I'll give the short version and let them fill in the details but, Gynda's ex-husband, Art The Bastard, showed up at the funeral. He expected to inherit the house and whatever money Edna had left. Well, it turns out the old dragon had just made a new will – cut him right out of it and left everything to Glynda – and Edna, that canny bitch, had a lot more than she let on. She was loaded! He gets nothing, the rotten fuck," she spat theatrically to the side, "may he rot in Milton's hell." I told him, right to his face that when he made Jesus Glynda's personal saviour, JEE-SUS took up the slack and made sure he got nothing! Oh - also, Glynda told me - but it's a surprise, Edna had left instructions that ten thousand dollars was to be given to Molly and her daughter to thank them for all the time they gave, cleaning and looking after the two of them. Isn't that wonderful? Who'd have thought that horrible old hag had it in her. I mean, I brought her porn and I got nothing!"

Anthea's mouth hung open during this newsbreak. "Not such a horrible old hag, after all, eh?"

"Oh, yes she was, believe me, she was a chronic bag of bile and misery," Carolina corrected, "but, a rich one!"

"Wow, and Molly? What's happening there?"

"I'm betting she and Roger will shack up. I told her, don't let a good 'un go, like YOU did.

Anthea's hand flew to her mouth, bumping her wine glass and splattering some on the tablecloth. Carolina casually blotted it with water from the water glass, not letting the prospect of stains interrupt the flow of her news bulletins.

Anthea's mouth dropped open conveniently as Carolina guided the food on Anthea's fork towards it, without a break in the torrent of speech spilling from her own mouth.

"Then, Georgia said she and her grandfather would *absolutely* do a dance for the fundraiser, since she would sulk until he agreed to it . . . he caved in almost immediately. That girl has a bright future! There's a whole pile of people at the hospital willing to show their talent, though some, I'm sure have been sadly misled by their parents into thinking that they have any. But we do have dancers, musicians; Clive's doing a magic act with his wife, Audrey – who knew? – there are a couple of stand-up comics, and comedy sketches – get this one - Bob The Nurse is doing an Arkansas Hillbilly sketch with the Rita The O.R. Clerk's bluegrass band – and Glynda is determined to be well enough to sing opera with her boyfriend, Flavio."

A large piece of bread caught in Anthea's throat, causing her to cough it back up onto her ravioli. "Glynda and Flavio? The waiter from the restaurant who plays the violin? They're an item? Yes!"

"Well, she says, 'No!' but I see how he looks at her. She says he's a lapsed Catholic and they could never agree on religious doctrines. I think he can win her over if he brings a nice capicollo to the table. I mean, who can refuse a nice capicollo?"

By then, Anthea had another mouthful of ravioli and nodded her support to this theory. She coughed, asking for water as she struggled to clear her throat to speak. "So, that's everyone, but you. Anything happened in your life in the last three weeks?"

Carolina filled Anthea's glass. "Me?" Carolina said, shrugging her shoulders dramatically, "Not really, unless you count the fact that I almost fucked your neighbour Jack Flynte *and* his biological father, Gerald Walker – who's a Supreme Court judge by the way – different last names – apparently, the result of a seedy scandal at the time."

Anthea flung her hand out in a gesture of incredulity, knocking over the full glass of wine. Carolina folded the tablecloth in on itself so that the wine would not reach the floor and kept talking as Anthea dabbed at the floor with a dishcloth. “Yep, but don’t worry, I said *almost* but that’s not to say I won’t. Now, tell me about your holiday.”

ADVANCED CLINICAL STUDIES

ANTHEA AND THE STAFF BUCKLED down for a long clinic day, not only because it was the first week back from a holiday, but also, because an early morning delivery had delayed its start.

Anthea had missed the action and the overwhelming sense of purpose a satisfying work day provided. It was reassuring, comforting even, to realize that, as nice as a holiday was, nothing exhilarated her as much as helping the little ones into the world and solving those intimate worries for women, some of whom barely understood the beautiful mechanics of their femininity, others, who were determined to govern it with as much intelligence and integrity as possible. She was born to do this job, excited to get stuck into it again, and get some momentary relief from her increasingly complicated personal life, where solutions were often far messier than a surgical procedure. In a brief but uncomfortable moment of insight, she wondered if, by getting a divorce, she had tried to cut out the offending part and let a fine scar cover the assault.

With this disturbing thought boring its way to the forefront of her mind, she drove slowly around the blind corner of her office building into the parking lot. Her careful habit served her well, since today, as she did so, something unexpected greeted her.

"What the fu . . .?" she muttered. Her parking space was occupied by a large horse which was attached to a black Mennonite buggy which was attached to the large sign which said, "Dr. Anthea Brock", in three-inch, bold uppercase, Roman letters. There were no other parking spots available, and so Anthea realized that a call up to the office to have the owner remove it would have posed further complications – where do you park a horse and buggy these days? So, she parked her car in front of the entrance to the building until she could arrange to have the horse 'towed' away.

The smell of coffee wafted from the staff lounge and Anthea thought a smack of caffeine would do her good before broaching the issue of having had a renegade Mennonite steal a parking spot with your name on it. She curled a finger at Carolina from the office hallway, where her frustration wouldn't be seen by a full waiting room of patients. She sucked at her coffee and led Carolina to the lounge window, pointing at the four-legged interloper. Carolina resolved not to react.

"What? What's the problem, Doc?" she said blandly.

Anthea wouldn't rise to the bait. "Just deal with it now. Here are my car keys. I'm going to see my first patient." She turned and walked over to retrieve the patient's chart.

Carolina tossed the keys into the air. "Oh good, please tell Mrs. Martin to get off the table and move her horse."

Anthea dropped her head into her chest, grabbed the chart and opened the door to Exam Room One. "Hello, Mrs. Martin, kids, congratulations on Baby Number Eight!" she said perkily.

Carolina sat back at the front desk, taking advantage of a lull in the activities to review the log of phone messages Georgia had taken off the answering machine. Gavin had left a message to remind everyone that he was sitting an exam today and would not be in. Most of the others, were fairly routine queries which she could handle. But one, in particular, caught her eye before she put it on Molly's desk for a nursing response. It read, 'Mrs. Yazov wants you to call her about something – she says she smells like chickens. Please call. Carolina pointed this note out to Georgia, thinking that she must have misunderstood Mrs. Yazov's imperfect English.

Molly overheard the conversation and had difficulty speaking due to a fit of giggles seizing her. She held her stomach and crossed her legs trying to stem the threat of wetting herself.

Carolina folded her arms and waited for Molly to continue, her impatient expression only serving to send Molly into further paroxysms, necessitating an emergency run to the washroom.

The toilet flushed and Molly came out drying her hands. "OK, I was going to keep this story for lunch time but . . . since you asked. Mrs. Yazov was told by the hospital to call if she had any signs of fever or *foul* discharge after her surgery – so she did – she *smelled 'fowl' like rotting chicken*!"

Georgia folded her arms and turned to Carolina, feeling redeemed by Molly's input. "See, I did get it right!"

Carolina wouldn't concede this one and handed Georgia a dictionary. "Here, you are neither old nor foreign. English or something like it *is* your mother tongue. Check the spelling."

Another message was from a patient who had been given a bloodwork requisition to check her hormone levels for menopause. She wanted to know how long before the test she should stop drinking water so that her hormones were not diluted. Carolina called her to advise her that drinking water would not 'dilute her hormone levels' and that she could do so without worry. The patient politely thanked her for her time but wanted to hear that from someone with more medical knowledge than a secretary. Carolina held her tongue and put the message on Molly's desk.

Anthea came out of Room One with Mrs. Martin's post-partum pap smear and swabs.

Molly lifted her arms in a helpless gesture and passed the next chart to Anthea. "Welcome home, Doctor! Here's the path report for the next patient – Sylvie? The little girl with the foreign object embedded in the vagina? Remember – the Barbie brush? She's here for her post-op check."

Anthea looked puzzled.

"Everything's fine. No more discharge – foul or otherwise," Molly said, winking Georgia's way, "just one concern. She wants her Barbie brush back! Yes, ladies, it's a full moon."

Before Anthea had a chance to react, Molly held up a small, pink Barbie brush, an extra one she had brought from home.

"Spoke with the mother on the phone last week and she told me her daughter's been asking for it. You can tell her where NOT to put it this time."

Toward the end of the morning, Carolina decided to let Georgia try her hand at checking the patients in, while she did some overdue billing. Georgia's task was to ensure that the urine samples were collected properly, and to transfer the patient's chart to the doctor's retrieval pile.

Anthea trotted out of an exam room anxious to use the bathroom. She spied Georgia at the reception desk, poking at the urine sample bottles with a pencil, in an effort to get them aligned in sequence. She was leaning as far away from them as possible, a sour look of revulsion plastered on her face.

Anthea, unable to watch this scene with the resignation she usually reserved for Georgia's activities, momentarily delayed her quest for the toilet and said, "Here Georgia, use a glove."

Angus finished the last of his shredding and ventured to the back room to fill the ultrasound gel bottles, a task he kept as a reward for his diligent completion of other tasks.

Two smartly dressed men came to the desk and the younger one offered Georgia his card. "John Novack from Phillips Pharmaceuticles to see Dr. Brock at 12:00pm. This is my V.P., Ari Sharma. We're a little early."

Georgia took the card and censored her impulse to ask them for a urine sample, "Dr. Brock just ran into the washroom," she said, just as a symphony of loud, farting noises came from the nearby, but unseen back room where Angus was squeezing the plastic gel bottles with gusto. The two men guarded their straight faces and pretended not to hear the spectacular eruptions, accompanied by a series of high pitched giggles. They did however, race each other to find a distant seat in the waiting room.

Minutes later, Anthea emerged from the staff bathroom to find Georgia resuming her quest to align the urine sample bottles with the pencil inserted into one of the fingers of the latex glove.

Georgia turned to her and said enthusiastically, "Oh Dr. Brock, you're finally done in the bathroom; these two guys are here to see you."

~

Molly filled the rooms with the first of the afternoon patients and heard a familiar voice at the front desk. "No, no my dear, I'm here to see Dr. Brock for my cataracts. I went to my gynecology appointment last week, I remember that; such a pleasant fellow but not very thorough. I'm having trouble with my pessary and he didn't even check down there."

Georgia was holding the patient's health card and trying to find her name on the patient roster. She discovered that the patient had missed her appointment the week before with Dr. Gentile, and offered to rebook her for the upcoming week.

The old lady looked perplexed and riffled through her large purse for something. She brought out a crumpled card and handed it to Georgia, saying, "That is the right date isn't it, dear?"

As Molly passed the desk, Georgia looked to her for guidance. Molly took the card from Proud Mary's shaking hands and saw that it was for an opthalmologist, Dr. Burn. Molly winked at Georgia and guided Proud Mary, away from the waiting area. The faint smell of alcohol came from the old lady as she took her into an empty exam room. Molly squeezed her hand and said, "Mary, I think you're a little confused today. This is Dr. Brock's office – she's your gynecologist not Dr. Burn – he's your opthalmologist – the one you're to see for your eyes."

Mary looked around the room and then consulted the card again, running an arthritic finger under the day and time. "No, dear, I already saw the gynecologist last week. I need my eyes checked today."

"No Mary, you went to the Optometrist last week. Did he check your eyes then?"

Mary thought about this, her eyes looking up into the distance trying to will her mind to filter this new information. "Well, the young man did seem a little unprepared when I had my bottoms off. I thought perhaps he was a little shy, bless him."

Proud Mary prepared to leave but Molly rubbed her stooped back and told her that she was sure Dr. Brock would see her today to check her pessary. "Did you drive yourself, Mary?"

Mary smiled a wide, beautiful smile. "Oh yes, I just passed my test again."

Molly sighed, and handed her a drape. As Molly left the room, she heard a weak voice asking, "But will she check my eyes today?"

~

Gavin handed his exam into the proctor, feeling the familiar euphoria that accompanied a job well done. He only wished that he had someone to share it with. Just then, an email came from Anthea.

"How'd exam go? If you're not already celebrating, The Gynesaurs invite you to Ty Bleu tonight to either celebrate or lick your wounds. Most staying over so they can drink and contemplate life on the veranda at sundown: all indications point to a full moon. Just come - don't bring anything.

A smile crossed his face at the thoughtfulness of the invite. A dose of feminine counseling from The Gynesaurs might do him good. He noticed how much he laughed around these older women, closer to his mother's age than his own, yet with dispositions so different from his mother's caustic view of what life had to offer. Why not, he thought, and wrote back, *"Thanks for the offer – I'm in need of my personal I.C.U."*

~

As Gavin rocked the steering wheel gently back and forth to navigate the driveway of Ty Bleu, he enjoyed the playful dappling of light that sought its way through the canopy of maple trees bending over his car like a nosy cluster of busybodies. He relished the idea of being in the country; at looking at a sea of green other than that created by O.R. scrubs. And there she was: Ty Bleu, crouched amid the rolling landscape, her joyful red roof, peaked like steeples, bound between the fading blue of the sky and the blue exterior of the house.

He stopped and took in the sight, wondering if he'd ever be able to look at a scene like this and call it his own. It must be a fine feeling to come to a place and feel that it has been waiting for you; that you could paint yourself into the canvass and belong to it. The oblong container he was raised in never offered itself up to him in that way. As a child, each step closer to it stirred up regret at having to continue the approach; a persistent instinct to flee from it nagged him. He remembered steeling himself to confront the grim shroud of indifference that would greet him as he entered its spare frame. But this house had a name. Ty Bleu had a soul.

The front door opened and two creatures sprang from it as if electrified by the flick of an unseen switch. He pushed his way out of the car and allowed himself to be consumed by spongy, wet tongues eager to connect with his own.

"Twiggy! Spock!" he heard Anthea command. "Off! Damn you!"

"No, no," Gavin protested as he held one writhing head and then the other, "This is great!". He rolled with the dogs in the grass, wrestling each of them onto their backs, legs paddling the air like overturned June Bugs.

Carolina, Molly, Georgia, Clive and Audrey came to the door to watch the match, parting naturally to allow Glynda to step to the front. Glynda wore a snappy, purple fedora on her bald head, which had been given to her by Georgia. She wore it well, with the assurance from Georgia that it was "cool as shit".

They brought the hors d'ouvres out on the veranda to witness the last murmurs of the day submit to the hovering twilight. Anthea raised her glass and looked into the expectant faces, waiting for her words. She felt a little wave of emotion rise to constrict her throat as it crossed her mind, that the wild and restless Atlantic Ocean separated the loves of her life and these were the people who would balance that precarious bargain. She tried to summon a Shakespearian quote about friendship that she was made to memorize in school and began it, hoping she would do it justice.

"As my old friend, Shakespeare, would have said, 'Those friends thy hast, and their adoptions tested . . . tie them . . . to yourself . . . with bonds . . .?"

Carolina helped her out. "and their adoptions *tried*, grapple them to your soul with hoops of steel."

They all looked at Carolina.

"Hamlet," Clive said nodding.

"Polonius to Laertes," Carolina added, who upon seeing the shock on everyone's face, no matter how many times she imparted serious knowledge, felt that she probably had cause to be a little insulted. "What? I read, OK?"

"Indeed, you do!" Anthea said as she waved her glass in a circle in acknowledgement of everyone there, spilling a good bit onto the veranda. "To The Gynesaurs".

"To The Gynesaurs," came the united response and with that, Anthea reached into a bag she had placed beside her and brought out triangle patches constructed out of Poise pads; a pissed off dinosaur head was stamped onto them. She peeled off the backing and ceremoniously slapped one on each of her friends. Ever the gentleman, Clive Gentile gave a courteous bow and Audrey followed suit with a dainty curtsey. "I will wear it with pride," he said.

Inside at the dinner table, the conversation turned to what had transpired since they had last seen Anthea. No one was willing to contribute anything until Anthea gave a synopsis of her time away. It was here that she confided that she and Ian were considering giving their relationship a second chance.

"Oh, my God!" Molly squealed, "Are you going to move back to Britain?"

"Am I out of a job?" Georgia asked, worried about her tattoo budget.

Anthea quelled the impulse to scold them for being more concerned about their jobs than her happiness. She looked at Clive and gave her tacit approval for him to speak. He let a slow smile recruit each muscle of his face, letting his silence fill each crevasse of space between himself and the six pair of eyes focused upon him. "I have a friend in The Toronto Cancer

Centre who told me of a position that would be perfect for Ian. He's going to apply for it and he's got a damn good shot at it."

"That's worth toasting," Molly said with relief as she rose from her chair. "But, I'm not toasting anything without Anthea having wine in her glass. Perrier, indeed, it's not decent."

Carolina and Clive turned to Anthea as Gavin reached for the wine bottle. Anthea raised her hand against it shaking her head. "Not today, I'm afraid. Not for a long time – I'm pregnant – with twins!

The rest of the table were thunderstruck, only the chime of Carolina and Clive's glasses bumping Anthea's brought them back from their stupor. Then, a shriek erupted from them all, including Spock and Twiggy, who were always ready to celebrate with unreasonable gusto, any comings or goings.

SECTION FOUR

FINALS

LATE SEPTEMBER BLEW IN COLD, inhospitable winds that hinted at frost, but The Best of Medicine fundraiser attracted a large, generous and mainly curious crowd. Flavio took delight in organizing the food, while Molly organized the silent auction. Anthea had pulled every string, using shameless tactics to get four local 'celebrities' to be the judges of the talent show. One was the Mayor Harriot McCurtle, ancient, but as sly witted as any predator could be and more than able to insult the talent-less with gentle truths. The second one, Nat, was a sweet-looking boy-band member who had garnered some attention from the industry and had recently scored a solo recording contract. The third judge was ball-room dance instructor and part-time musical theatre performer, Elizabeth Belamy, and the fourth, a real Judge, a Supreme Court Judge, in fact, the august Gerald Walker.

Andy, a medical courier started the program off with an excellent Louis Armstrong impersonation. Mayor McCurdle said that she'd actually met Louis, back stage in Atlanta in 1965 and asked Andy, jokingly, if he re-membered the night they spent together – singing hymns. Nat thought Andy was 'awesome'. Elizabeth appreciated anyone who was multi-talent-ed, and Gerald said that the fact that he could really play the trumpet set the bar intimidatingly high.

Next, Clive and Audrey came on stage loudly, running behind a puff of smoke. Audrey was dressed in a black top hat and cape and Clive was her beautiful assistant. Every trick they did went alarmingly wrong, seem-ing to injure the beautiful assistant in the most horrifying ways. When she finally sawed him in half, a large amount of blood came dripping from the box and the curtain came down abruptly. The Announcer took control immediately and told them not to worry, that there were many competent surgeons in the house. The audience loved it and roared their approval. Nat noted that it too, was "awesome".

To give the audience some variety, the next competitors were Georgia and Rex Saxon. Georgia came on stage dragging her shy partner behind her. He loomed above her, his head cast down, looking awkward in a grey suit that was a little too short in the arms and a little too tight at the mid-drift. Georgia had cast off her sinister apparel and had her hair dyed orange, heavily backcombed, in a sixties flick up style. Her green mini-skirt was cut either side to allow for movement.

When the music began, a soft sigh swept through the audience. It was Lulu's, To Sir With Love. It had been the only one of exactly twelve different songs they had each suggested that they could agree upon, Georgia's offerings being "mumbling gibberish" or 'too goddamn suggestive' and her grandfather's being "old fart crap" or 'too lame".

When Saxon threw off the restriction of the jacket to dance in shirt-sleeves, his heft seemed to be absorbed into his body as he moved effortlessly from one step to the other on the balls of his feet, spinning and guiding his granddaughter from one extravagant lift into another. The elegance that must have dwelt there years before disciplined his massive frame and revealed the skill that he had once possessed. Georgia's supremely arched back, perfect splits and points created momentary sculptures as he held her delicate physique above and beside him. The two drifted through the song with the well-remembered words falling off the lips of those watching, rapt until the last, low chord strummed.

Saxon's peers were stunned to see this hidden creature crawl out of his rough-hewn casing, and it cast a spell upon them. The silence that followed gave way into spirited applause. Gerald Walker said that it made him wish he had a grand-daughter to dance with. Elizabeth Belamy praised the integrity of the dancing and the art of the story-telling. The Mayor said Dr. Saxon reminded her of her own grandfather, whom she said was a craggy Scot with a heart as warm as porridge and Nat said Georgia was "awesome".

Several other acts came on the stage and the most that could be said of them was that they were better than the Mime whose act was far too long and boring and who got so frustrated with the audience talking, he shouted a loud, "merde" and walked off.

The Mayor recommended another line of work - perhaps, telemarketing? Nat said it was awesome. Elizabeth sympathized, saying that Mime is not a well understood art form. Gerald said he didn't understand it.

When Glynda came on stage, looking small, thin and nervous, everyone waited patiently to hear her sing. An elaborate wig covered her bald head and a red satin dress draped off her white shoulders, shocking those who knew her best, at her willingness to show them. Flavio had convinced her that she deserved this kind of glamour. She looked at him, resplendent in his black tails and she nodded her consent for him to start. She watched him lift his violin and cradle it with the same tenderness he shared with her, agile fingers touching the neck of the violin as if it were her own. The first beautiful strains of Verdi's, Va Pensiero broke away from the instrument and filled the hall.

Glynda's small bosom rose and fell as she anticipated her start. Her head bowed and Flavio guessed that she was unable to begin. He skillfully manipulated the melody to come around to her entrance again and the audience did not seem to notice. He gave a nod of his head in an effort to engage her eyes and she looked back into his. She tried to siphon his confidence into herself. His body swayed like a parent lulling an anxious child and with the next almost imperceptible nod of his head Glynda let her voice out of its cage. It was filled with insecurity at first, but gradually rose from the ground and soared into the air.

Anthea, Carolina, Molly, Gavin and Georgia watched from the sidelines through a mist of emotion. She had done it. She was singing her solo. As Glynda prepared to build the power of her voice for the last chorus, her church choir, quietly walked on to the stage behind her. This was Molly's doing. She had contacted Lorna and asked if they would participate in this beautiful surprise. They formed a rich, black background against which, the crimson of Glynda's dress was inveigled like a cameo.

When Glynda heard her choir support her melody, she turned and cast her graceful arm to them. The audience clapped briefly, to acknowledge them and then listened for the finale. By the time it came, they were on their feet, not for the courage of a cancer survivor, but for the sheer recognition of something hauntingly beautiful.

Several minutes later, the judges all declared her performance "awesome" in the true sense of the word. They would have declared her the winner there and then, if there had not been one final act left. This was Bob The Nurse's "Blue Grass band".

Billy-Bob – aka Bob The Nurse, came on stage, backed by Rita The O.R. Clerk's bluegrass band in full Hillbilly regalia, beard and banjo in tow and announced that he was going to introduce everyone to some of his family from Arkansas who were part of his band called, "The Saggy Asses". The first was Cousin Jebediah, a large man in white linens, a white straw hat and a fiddle; by day, Orthopedic Surgeon, Dr. Charles Moody. Billy-Bob began his introduction speaking with the true Ozarks accent he was raised with, taking time to pick his teeth with a toothpick.

"Ladies and gentlemen, Jebediah is the lawyer of the family and the only one to graduate grade six. He knew the value of a good education because as he says, 'no one can ever take it away from you – they tried twice but they could never prove anything in a court of law.' Yep, Jebediah has studied crime so long, he's getting real good at it. If you want to engage his services, his office address is Dumpster #3."

Next Billy-Bob summoned Saxon's secretary, Bernice, dressed as "Granny" on stage. One side of her mouth was full of black gum that was supposed to be chewing tobacco. She carried a wash board and her "powerful electrolyte replacement drink labelled XXX and known as, 'Southern Cyanide".

Billy-Bob continued. "Granny is special to us all – not only did she win the Arkansas Women's League tobaccy spitting contest last year, she is also the epitome of good motherin'. Why, she breastfed all her fourteen children and several of her grandchildren – just this morning. Yep, Granny likes to brag that she has spectacular control over her bodily fluids – except one."

The audience groaned loudly at this one – more in discomfort than appreciation for the joke.

Billy-Bob, cleared his throat and moved on quickly.

Anthea stood in the wings waiting to be introduced. While Bob had had them all practice the song they were going to sing, he had not told them about these colourful introductions. Bob had cajoled her into being one of "The Twins", Ellie May. She was in Dixie Dee shorts with her heavily gravid belly exposed beneath a checked shirt tied under her greatly enhanced breasts. She had long, blonde braids, work boots and a straw hat with a sunflower on it. Next to her was her twin, Elli-Phant, a two-hundred-and-fifty-pound orderly from the hospital in an identical outfit. Billy-Bob called them on stage. They played the spoons.

"Feast your eyes on the twins, Ellie-May and Ellie-Phant - who is also Ellie May's paternal uncle. Now the genetics involved are both complex and disturbing, so we won't explain them in polite company. Rest assured, they are being studied by the genetics department of the University of Arkansas and in the twins issue of Penthouse magazine."

Anthea glared at Bob The Nurse, trying to get his attention and hoping to convey her opinion that he should be a little more discreet with the material he was delivering. She felt the mild discomfort of some of the crowd but there were many who laughed wildly and whooped encouragement. Billy-Bob kept going. "And now, one of the stars of our show, a suprememly talented musician," Billy-Bob pointed to a stick coming out of a wash tub. "Here is Cousin Beauregard." Daniel Thackery had joined the group to offer his services as an accomplished guitarist but was now handed the wash tub.

"Beauregard is a class act, which I might add has aroused suspicion in the close-knit Hillbilly community because he insists on closing the door to the outhouse when he relieves himself. As one local woman put it . . ."

Billy-Bob gestured to the side of the stage at which point Carolina came on wearing a sparkly, puffy square-dancing dress, with a hat that had a price tag hanging off it. She put her hands on her hips and looked Daniel up and down, stopping to focus on his crotch and said, "What the hell does he have down there that's so damn special?"

This got a good laugh and while Daniel looked a little aggrieved, it was not as bad as what was to come.

Saxon had heard about the Hillbilly skit and thought it might take the saccharine out of the dancing effort he'd done solely to please his granddaughter. He loved the idea of dressing up like a Hillbilly and singing a blue grass number. It was with relish that he wore red long johns, work boots, a long, grey beard and made himself toothless and clueless. He thought the stuffed chicken Bob The Nurse gave him at the last minute lent authenticity to the sketch and he waited eagerly to be introduced.

"And now, a man who can play an organ with his mouth better than anyone I've tried . . . here is Cousin Cletus on the harmonica. Now, Cousin Cletus has been a champion chicken choker for as long as anyone can remember. So long, in fact that he has developed a very, very personal relationship with his chickens and every now and then, a special chicken comes along and he has brought her along to share in his big moment tonight. He tells me she is a lot like a girlfriend to him. Ladies and Gentlemen, I give you Cletus and Britney.

If Saxon could have swallowed Bob The Nurse whole, he would have done so then. Bob the Nurse moved over to the other side of the stage and talked faster. "Now bear with me, I have a treat for the ladies cuz here is. . . Cousin Billy-Ray!"

Gavin nonchalantly walked on stage with his hands in his overall pockets, bare-chested, blonde hair flopping over his forehead, chewing a straw.

The women in the audience shrieked and whistled like sailors outside a brothel. Billy-Bob lapped it up and signalled his encouragement to continue, which they did.

"Now . . . now Billy Ray has always been a bit of a Ladies' Man, what with the hair and all, and he wants me to let you know that he likes his women to be women and NOT chickens – *mostly,* though he does confess that he's a breast man - but emphasizes, for you feminists out there, that he primarily admires chickens for their intelligence."

Saxon glowered with disapproval which could still be seen despite the beard and hat. He chewed savagely on his corn cob pipe and Bob, sensing he had crossed the Rubicon, quickly began to play the introduction to the song to fill the awkward moment.

Saxon's reaction was not missed by the audience and a roar of approval came from them when the contagious rhythm of the folksy music took over. The song parodied the plight of hospital funding and was entertaining without being as risqué as the introduction. By the end of the song, the audience and entertainers all danced like wild Hillbillies to the talented accompaniment of The Saggy Asses.

Billy-Bob The Nurse was forgiven, but the judges recommended that he disqualified from ever entering again unless he submitted to pre-screening.

Anthea woke the next morning, having slept a deep and satisfying sleep, knowing that, "The Best of Medicine" had been an unparalleled success. She had many sponsors come forward after the performance, saying that they had rarely laughed as much for even a professional comic production. The good humour had worked its magic and those with deep pockets, dug into them gleefully.

She made an observation that what she feeling was euphoria. It seemed to lift both her body and her spirits into that rare state of blissful contentment. Part of this was due to the relief of having accomplished a task that was beyond expectation, and part of this was due to having had great sex. Mostly, it was the sex. She rubbed her belly and rolled to the other side of the bed and spooned with Ian, who was spooning with Spock, who was spooning with Twiggy.

Before she let herself sink back into the folds of sleep, her father's parting words came to her. He had just lifted her bags into the car and he held her face between his hands. He said, “You know, lovely girl, sometimes happiness is as simple as finding something that you thought you’d lost.”

Molly stirred to the smell of coffee and a tickle under her nose. Angus held his new rat, Sheila, in his hands and wanted to wake his sister with a whiskery kiss. Orlagh and Callum had brought her a coffee and scone for breakfast in bed and Fiona clutched a bouquet of rapidly wilting marigolds. Angus was anxious for Molly to hear his proposal that they should invite Roger to live with them, so that he could be close to Sheila. The kids had talked amongst themselves and decided that it would be great if they would get married first, mainly because Fiona wanted to be a flower girl, but if not, living together would be cool too. Molly responded that Roger may not want that sort of commitment. They assured her that they had already discussed it with him and he had said they should try to convince Molly that it was a very good idea. He would be very lonely for Sheila otherwise.

Glynda came from her Oncologist’s office with good evidence of remission. God had heard her prayers and guided the doctors to do their good work. She decided to phone a decorator to come and help her “put some lipstick” on the old house, and then booked a spa holiday for herself and Flavio for much the same reason.

Georgia decided that her future lay in dance and not academics. So, she began to research how much an exotic dancer makes an hour and was quite impressed by the internet testimonials.

Carolina poured a glass of excellent Shiraz and sank into her armchair to finish what she had started. She opened her copy of Paradise Lost mid-way and began to read aloud to herself. After a couple of pages, she stopped to try to analyse the content, re-reading some of the foot notes, in a disciplined attempt to understand the depths of Milton's teaching. She had always aspired to be the kind of person who would read this revered tome but she had come to confess that Paradise Lost was becoming a 'lost' cause to her. However, she wanted to be able to read the staggering beauty of the last two lines of Paradise Lost, "*They hand in hand with wand'ring steps and slow, Through Eden took their solitary way.*" knowing that she had journeyed with Adam and Eve to the book's end and their new beginning. *Maybe someday I could put enough money aside to take a literature course and have a knowledgeable lecturer guide me through it.*

She glanced at another book on the side table, Hilary Mantel's "Bringing up the Bones," and thought that it might satisfy her vow that she follow Mark Twain's mantra, 'A man who does not read good books has no advantage over the man who can't read them.'

She opened a window, hoping the night air would bring her fresh resolve. But Milton's powerful words began to blur again, into a black smudge on the page, so she put the book down, for good. She let her head find the softness of the chair's headrest and closed her eyes.

A delinquent breeze played with the pages of the book, leafing through them like a busy librarian. The tortured spine of the old book gave in and book rested open on page 264, where a hurried message had been hand written in Italian over the text of the page.

"Carolina, it is in the cantina
5 cinder blocks down - 7 across.
I love you
Papa"

The End

AUTHOR'S BIOGRAPHY

PATRICIA H. OLIVER WAS BORN in Abercraf, Wales, to a rowdy family of storytellers who believed laughter was the best medicine for any ailment. She earned a master's degree in health from the University of Western Ontario. Her love of classic tales by Charles Dickens, Stephen Leacock, and Oscar Wilde, often found lying next to her science textbooks, motivated her to pursue a minor in English literature.

Oliver spent most of her life working with body parts as a gymnastics coach/administrator and a Physician's Assistant in an obstetrics and gynecology office and is especially thrilled to now write tales focusing on the naughty bits. *The Gynesaurs* was inspired by her time observing the intriguing and often hilarious encounters between professionals and patients. She's currently retired and lives in Hespeler, Ontario, with her husband, Joe. She is also the proud mother of three grown children: Jessica, Erica, and Evan. This is her first novel.

Made in the USA
Columbia, SC
28 September 2017